NO TIME FOR LOVE

A Novel

by

J.B. MILLER

No Time For

Love

A Novel

by JB Miller

TABLE OF CONTENTS

COPYRIGHT.. 6

ABOUT THIS NOVEL................................. 7

DEDICATION 8

CHAPTER I -*TIME*....................................... 10

CHAPTER II - *JUDGMENT*.................................. 21

CHAPTER III - *BLESSING*.............................. 28

CHAPTER IV - *PETER* 33

CHAPTER V - *EMBARRASSMENT*....................... 41

CHAPTER VII – *PALIO* 47

CHAPTER VIII - *INTERRUPTION*...................... 52

CHAPTER XI 78

PALIO & GEORGINA 78

CHAPTER XII – *FRUSTRATION* 82

CHAPTER XIII – *PALIO'S FAMILY* 98

CHAPTER XIV – *CHATHAM & TRIP* 108

CHAPTER XV – *PALIO & MARIA*...................... 126

CHAPTER XVI - *BEST FRIENDS*.................... 132

CHAPTER XVII - *COINCIDENCE* 137

CHAPTER XVIII - *SPYING*............................ 147

CHAPTER XIX - *CAUGHT*............................ 154

CHAPTER XX – *THE MEETING* 172

CHAPTER XXI – *POSSIBILITIES* 190

CHAPTER XXII – *EXTENDED FAMILY* 195

CHAPTER XXIII – *SCHOOL TIME*.................... 199

CHAPTER XXIV – *PLANE FLIGHT*.................... 205

CHAPTER XXV – *BI-COASTAL* 219

CHAPTER XXVI – *CHLOE*................................... 229

CHAPTER XXVII – *PLANE FLIGHT CONT.* ... 235

CHAPTER XXVIII – *THE CHASE*...................... 247

CHAPTER XXIX – *DISCOVERY*.......................... 255

CHAPTER XXX –*THE THREAT*.......................... 267

CHAPTER XXXI – *CONFUSION*......................... 274

CHAPTER XXXII – *INTERSECTION* 281

CHAPTER XXXIII – *THE SPY*.............................. 301

CHAPTER XXXIV –*SURPRISES* 311

CHAPTER XXXV –*MAD DASH* 317

CHAPTER XXXVI – *MORNING AFTER*........... 328

CHAPTER XXXVII – *DIVERSION*...................... 346

CHAPTER XXXVIII – *THE ZOO*....................... 354

CHAPTER XXXVIX – *INFORMATION*............. 360

CHAPTER XL – *DEFLATED* 367

CHAPTER XLI – *LOST & FOUND* 372

CHAPTER XLII –*PROGRESS*.............................. 384

CHAPTER XLIII – *ON THE WAY*....................... 394

CHAPTER XLIV – *HOPE*...................................... 427

CHAPTER XLV – *EXPOSED*................................ 437

CHAPTER XLVI – *RESOLUTION*...................... 456

EPILOGUE 461

ABOUT THE AUTHOR.. 464

COPYRIGHT

ABOUT THIS NOVEL

This novel is for every mother on the planet who does her best to keep it together, when in reality she simply can't do it all, especially when it comes to love. And that's OK, because sometimes love finds us in the most unusual places. Here is to having love find you at every turn.

DEDICATION

To my children who love me despite my flaws

"We always believe our first love is our last and our last love our first."
-Anonymous

≈

CHAPTER I -*TIME*

≈

It seemed that everything in Chatham's life revolved around time – or lack thereof. There just didn't seem to be enough of it, especially for what she loved most, sleeping. Who had time for that?

Chatham dragged herself through the double doors of her master bedroom, trying hard not to notice the basket of unfolded clothes by the doorway. She stumbled down the hall and into the entry, tilting her head back in order to aim her voice upward. Chatham knew if she yelled loud enough it would reach beyond the second-story balcony and into the closed bedroom doors of her childrens' rooms. Definite time saver.

"Everybody up and at 'em!" she cried out. "In the car in fifteen minutes, and breakfast is ready!" The promise of food was a sure-fire motivator.

Chatham staggered into the kitchen and poured herself a cup of lukewarm coffee. Had she been on time this morning, the pre-programmed, freshly brewed coffee would have been just that – fresh. Now it tasted like warm cardboard. She grabbed the frozen breakfast from the freezer. Thank goodness for Eggo waffles, nutrition on the run; they shaved minutes off the morning routine and left her with little guilt, knowing that her children were getting twelve essential vitamins. It's nice to know that food manufacturers understand the modern family, Chatham thought as she lathered a waffle with syrup for her oldest son, P.J. The remaining frozen treats were left in the toaster for easy access while she organized lunch boxes in assembly-line fashion.

Peanut butter and jelly, an all-American favorite she thought, as she pried the pantry door with her foot, nudging the peanut butter toward the front of the cabinet, while stretching her entire body toward the refrigerator to obtain the jelly. But wasn't there a kid in one of her children's classes who was allergic to peanuts, meaning, no one in the entire school could ever eat peanut butter again until adulthood, for fear of exposing that one child to even a scent of peanuts? She tried to remember. On second thought, she shoved the newly made PB&J into the fridge and made a quick turkey on wheat. She didn't want to buck the system. It wasn't that kind of school.

Next. Peter Junior. Her mentally delayed eleven-year-old ate fruit roll-ups, Kraft Swiss cheese (individually wrapped slices), apples, and wheat thins. Chatham knew her son's picky diet by heart. She grabbed a knife, sliced up the Fuji apple, and stuffed it into a Ziploc baggie before adding an ice pack to keep the contents cool. If the cheese texture did not remain identical to its *fresh out of the refrigerator* state, Chatham knew that her son would not eat it. Tactile Integration issues. She shifted the cold pack directly over the cheese slices and zipped the lunchbox shut.

Her twelve-year-old daughter, Madison, was allowed to use the bank of microwaves reserved specifically for "upper division," consisting of the seventh and eighth graders in the school. Noodles in a cup could work. Just zap some water and pour. Chatham stuffed the

Styrofoam cup container, a plastic spoon, a prepackaged serving of baby carrots, and a chocolate pudding into the purple lunch pack.

"Good morning," P.J. announced as he bounced down the berber-clad stairs on his bottom.

"Good morning, honey. Please walk down the stairs. The carpet is starting to break, OK?"

"Oh no, it's broken?" P.J. asked, concerned that one of his favorite activities might be coming to an end.

"Yes honey, it's almost broken. You can skip instead, OK?"

"OK, I will." He skipped over to the kitchen counter, climbed up onto his stool and inspected his breakfast.

"I need a fork."

"Open the drawer and get one."

"I can't reach it," he said, straining to reach the drawer directly next to him. "It's so far."

Chatham knew it was easier to simply get the utensil than wait for P.J. to complete the task. She reached in, withdrew his favorite giraffe fork and went back to gathering up the lunch boxes for transport.

"I need a napkin," P.J. whimpered. He liked his breakfast set just so. At least the waffle passed inspection, Chatham thought thankfully.

Chatham watched her quirky son inspect the syrup container.

"It's empty."

"What's empty?"

"The syrup. You need to buy some at the store. Mom? You drive in your car to Safeway, you get the syrup and you pay the money."

"Ok, honey, I will. It's time to eat your breakfast now."

P.J. returned to the task at hand, downing his waffle in less than five bites.

"I'm done." "I will put my plate in the sink," he announced as he gingerly picked up the plate and placed it in the sink to be cleaned. "May I watch a movie?"

"No, honey. Go in my bathroom and brush your teeth."

"Ok, Mom. I will use my big bird toothpaste." P.J. disappeared down the hallway.

Time was ticking. Chatham grabbed all three containers in one hand while clearing the preparation with the other and wiping some syrup off the counter with her elbow. Ants had been a problem lately and she didn't want to offer an open invitation for another visit. Chatham hesitated. Something was missing. She just knew it.

"Drinks! Don't we have some of those big gulp, artificially colored, cool-aid bags that come in a handy ten-pack box?" she muttered, dropping everything back on the counter and plunging her body deep into the back of the pantry, her slightly out-of-shape fanny protruding out from the cabinet doors. "I know they're here somewhere."

"Hey mom, whatcha mumblin' about?" Madison asked as she sauntered into the kitchen.

"Bingo! Done," Chatham said to no one in particular as she grabbed the box of mega gulp drinks and shimmied her way back out of the abyss.

Madison was at the front of the pantry grabbing the blue jar of marshmallow puff.

"And no pure sugar before school," Chatham instructed, pawing the melted marshmallow offering from her daughter's hands.

"But don't you think *confection of the gods* will really help me in school?" Madison coyly pleaded.

Chatham chuckled. "As much as I love that you are so interested in my advertising work, I don't believe indulging in this creamy confection will help you with math." She put the jar back on the shelf, making a mental note to hide the jar from the kids later. Chatham tended to shove things to the back, sometimes forgetting about them completely. Maybe that strategy had something to do with the ants.

"Aw Mom, come on," Madison petitioned. "I need a boost to start the day."

"Well boost your way to a nutritional Eggo waffle. It's in the toaster, ready to go," Chatham smiled, trying her best to appear cheerful.

As she grabbed the drinks from the pantry, she fondly remembered how her husband Peter had inspired her with the slogan for that campaign. Madison couldn't have been more than three. She had somehow opened a jar of marshmallow puff and had gotten it all over her fingers and face. Some things never change.

"You should go after that one, Chat," Peter had chuckled. "Tell the marshmallow fluff guys that eating it is like heaven. Look how happy she is. Where's your camera?"

"She's on a sugar high Peter, that's why she's so giddy."

"It's the confection of the gods, Chat." He had

snapped a picture just as Madison smeared the gooey mess all over her eyes and cheeks.

"Mommy make-up," the baby had giggled.

Chatham did end up going after that campaign. Now, almost every family in America had a jar of Marshmallow Puff in their pantry.

"Mom? Mom! Didn't you hear anything I said?"

Chatham jumped, hitting her head as she yanked her body out of the darkened food closet. Madison shifted her weight, jetted out her hip and folded her hands in front of her chest.

"Mom, we had waffles yesterday morning *and* the day before." She rolled her eyes to complete the objection. The full-fledged teen years were fast approaching.

"Ok, then boost yourself over to a bowl of 19. 100 percent."

"Yeah, yeah. 100 percent of all essential vitamins," Madison mimicked as she grudgingly opted for the bright red box of vitamin-based cereal.

Camp, the six year old and youngest of the Ross brood, wandered into the kitchen, a bit disoriented from exiting a room other than his own.

"Mom, did I sleep in your bed last night?"

"Yes, honey, you did. I think you were achy. Are you feeling better?" Chatham felt his forehead, hoping that he would not need to stay home from school today. She had a conference call of the *do not cancel* variety.

"I'm hungry," he answered grabbing a banana from the delicate glass bowl on the kitchen table. Chatham liked the Orefor's bowl; its intricate etchings sparkled in the morning sun. It was a wedding present. Chatham liked to look at it; it reminded her of happy times. Besides, most of her wedding gifts were crammed into a buffet cabinet somewhere in her dining room and hadn't been used – well, ever.

Chatham ran up the stairs two at a time to get school clothes for the boys. They had maybe five minutes. She grabbed a pair of jeans and a t-shirt for Camp and leaned over the railing.

"Coming down," she projected in sync with the falling debris. Chatham was glad that, for the most part, her children were self-sufficient. Other than needing her to choose their morning outfits, which was something she enjoyed doing. When Camp's pair of jeans that were two sizes too big turned into high waters practically overnight, Chatham knew that she might be doing something right. After all, if they continued to grow, she wasn't a total failure.

She still had to cut the tags out of P.J.'s clothes the moment they were purchased so that they didn't itch him. When he took that task on himself, the brand new shirt or sweats ended up in a pile of shreds on the floor. Maybe he'll be a surgeon, Chatham thought as she grabbed P.J.'s favorite flag shirt and soft fleece sweatpants. She wadded the outfit into a ball and launched it over the banister.

"OK everyone, I'm getting in the car NOW," she called out on autopilot while jogging down the stairs.. "Don't forget your homework and make sure you take a sweatshirt with you!"

Chatham's voice trailed off as she grabbed the lunches, headed down to the garage and loaded the forty-pound roller backpacks (what the heck was in there?) into the family car, a tawny colored SUV Sequoia that fit eight; mandatory for carpooling.

"Mom! Mom!" She heard her daughter screaming. It wasn't a hurt scream; rather, a pissed-off kind of scream. Amazing how a mother could tell the difference with only a slight change in the shrill. She chose to ignore it. Teenagers.

Chatham opened the door from the garage just as P.J. and Camp barreled down the stairs two at a time with sweatshirts in hand. She noticed that Camp had pawned his Game Boy Advance from the toy bin on the way. You could say he had an addiction. She decided to let it slide this time. P.J. had a bright purple plastic container under his arm, which contained his favorite Barney movie. Holding something precious helped P.J. feel secure during transitional moments like getting in the car. He climbed into the front seat, next to Chatham and Camp climbed into his self-assigned spot in the back.

Madison came tearing down the stairs and barreled through the garage door with ballet bag on one shoulder, point shoes on the other, and an open cosmetics pouch in her hands, which she thrust at Chatham as evidence.

"What is it, Maddy? Come on, we have to go."

"Look, empty."

"I can see that, honey.

"Where are my hair nets? I had ten in here, and they're gone. They're all gone, see?"

"Are you sure that you kept them in that particular pouch? You have other pouches on your dresser."

"Mom, they are all see through so that I can see what I have put in them. All the other ones have pins or ribbons or stitch kits in them." Madison looked in the car and pointed accusingly. "He stole them, I just know it."

Camp was too engrossed in his backyard basketball game to pay any attention.

"Maddy, it's not nice to accuse your brother. Why would Camp take your hair nets? He doesn't take ballet, and he has short hair."

"Mom, he stuffs them in his spider man wrist sprayer. I've seen him do it. I know that's where they are."

Well, he is creative, Chatham thought. "Camp, is that true?"

"Huh? What? Oh, hey Maddy." Camp went back to pressing the hand held buttons at rapid-fire speed.

"Camp! Answer my question. Did you borrow Madison's hair nets for your spiderman toy?"

"He stole them, Mom."

"Who me? Uh, I ran out of the spiderman web spray, Mom, and silly string doesn't make good ones. I invented a new kind of web," he smiled, obviously proud of his ingenuity.

"Camp, go upstairs and get your sister's hair nets. Now, please."

"OK." He bounded out of the car and up the stairs. Chatham opened the garage door and started the engine. She was already seven minutes late for pick up.

"Here, psycho," Camp said as he tossed the hair nets toward Madison.

"Pipsqueak," she said under her breath, proceeding to pull the hair nets out of the device one by one.

Chatham backed the car out of the garage. Just as

she reached the end of the driveway she stopped suddenly. She had a feeling that all of the morning tasks had not been completed.

"PJ, did you brush your teeth?"

She recalled hearing the sound of *The Lion King* movie coming from her room as she headed down to the garage this morning. And she hadn't turned it on.

"I can't," PJ replied, a pained look on his face. Chatham always had to double-check her cognitively delayed son. Too many directions on his plate, and he surely missed something. He was put together differently than other kids, or that was how the neurologist chose to explain it. No syndrome, no disease, just delayed to the tune of half his life behind.

"What do we say in our house, PJ?"

"I-can-do-it!" he spat out in a frustrated, syncopated tone.

"So go upstairs and brush your teeth. Right now."

"I can't. I'm not going!" PJ crossed his arms defiantly across his chest with a huff.

Great, Chatham thought. Here we go with the transition issue. No time for this. Must resort to bribery.

"PJ, do you want to go to Chucky Cheese?" Chatham inquired.

"Yes," he answered, his arms falling to his sides, a look of hope on his face.

"OK. First teeth, then Chucky Cheese. We will wait right here for you."

"OK, Mommy. I will," he said. He slipped out of the car, ran upstairs, hopefully brushed his teeth, and returned in less than a minute.

Is eleven too old for Chucky Cheese? Chatham wondered as she backed the car into the street, closed the garage door with the automatic clicker, and proceeded to pick up her carpool.

CHAPTER II - *JUDGMENT*

≈

"Running late today, Chatham dear?" Annette, one of the mothers in the carpool asked in a strained voice. "You do know that my Herby needs to get to school at least ten minutes early in order to get settled before class begins," she reprimanded with a fake, forced smile.

Chatham ignored the comment and loaded the backpacks into the rear of the car.

"Now Sarah has a piece of paper in her backpack that needs to be given to Olivia in her class. I need for you to walk her in and make sure the transfer happens. You are walking the children in today, aren't you?"

Chatham bit her lip. This woman was too much. "Actually, I think it's great how independent they are all getting, don't you? I was planning to take them to the carpool drop off today. I hope that's OK." She shut the trunk of her SUV.

"I'm so proud of them, aren't you?" Chatham added, doing her best to plaster the perfect smile on her own tired face. She climbed back into the driver's seat before Annette had a chance to object.

"OK Annette, we need to be off. Have a nice day." Chatham quickly pulled out of the driveway, glad to be far away from the Stepford wife mother in her matching white with green piping tennis outfit and lime green Adidas sneakers.

Chatham looked in her rearview mirror. There was Annette, cell phone plastered to her ear while blowing kisses to her flawless little darlings as they cruised away.

"Never Neverland," Chatham mumbled under her breath as she coasted down the street.

"Guess what?" Herby, the oldest of Annette's children, asked innocently.

"What?" the rest of the kids answered in chorus.

"Babies come from a vagina."

From that point on it was pure damage control.

"Now Herby, is that really appropriate to discuss this early in the morning? Why don't we talk about what fun things you are doing at school?" Chatham suggested.

"Gee, Mrs. Ross," Herby said sheepishly. "We're studying family life at school and babies come from vaginas. But the dad has to put his penis in the mom's vagina first. Well, it takes nine months, I think. Not to put it in the vagina or anything."

"Ooooh. Gross!" the other kids yelled.

"You're such a freak," came a voice from way in the back.

"What's a freak?" the youngest, Sarah, inquired.

Great. Now ten-year-old Herby, obsessed with the word for the female genitalia, has given the entire carpool a graphic depiction of baby making. Is five too young to know about the birds and the bees? Have to call Herby's perfect mother and give her a heads up.

"OK, who'd like to listen to Radio Disney?" Chatham quickly suggested, hoping to divert attention from the sex education lesson.

"Me, me, me!" the car patrons chimed.

"He was a skater boy, she said see you later boy," the song spewed.

Avril Lavigne. Chatham knew that one by heart due

to Madison's recent attendance at the popular singer's concert and her relentless recitation of every lyric this famous artist had ever uttered. Chatham wondered whether or not the teenage ex-girlfriend actually got back together with the now famous rock star boyfriend she had dumped when he was only a skateboard slacker. Or was someone else singing the song, telling the girl that she blew it and now skater boy is another girl's golden ticket?

"Life's just not fair," Chatham concluded out loud.

≈

Chatham pulled into the private school roundabout, diligently following the orange cones. Her husband Peter had felt strongly about private school education. After all, he had gone to the Country Day School in Marin before heading to private college at USC. When Chatham tried to explain that she ended up at USC, the same place, minus the social standing and private school route, Peter wouldn't hear of it.

"You're from out of state. Of course you got into SC Chat," he had said as though location was her golden ticket. "How many Jersey girls go to school in LA anyway?" She had accepted his explanation. She had accepted most everything about Peter.

Chatham pulled around the coned lane, the carpool monitors immediately detectable in their neon vests emblazoned with The Park School's signature emblem, a regal lion sitting atop a castle.

"Hurry now! Hurry up!" the head monitor signaled, hands flailing wildly as Chatham coasted into line. The ultimate school goal was to reduce carpooling time by at least fifteen minutes in the morning and afternoon in order to remain the perfect elementary school good neighbor. There had been some complaints lately that parents were loitering in the parking lot; a definite disturbance.

"My god, they must have had five cups of coffee already," Chatham exclaimed as an attendant practically assaulted her vehicle. Before she could come to a full stop, the passenger doors flew open and the children were shooed out.

"Must hurry, yes, must make good time today," the brilliantly clad parent monitor recited. "That's right. Have everything? Very good. On we go. Bye, Mrs. Ross!" The doors slammed before she could even say goodbye.

Oh no, Sarah, the five-year-old, forgot her backpack. Chatham rolled down the window.

"Sarah!" she yelled, holding up the bright pink Barbie backpack. "Sarah!"

"Just throw it to me, Mrs. Ross. I'll see that the little tike gets it," the head monitor promised, his reflective gear popping up without warning.

"Oh, thanks Mark," Chatham effused as she tossed the pack through the passenger window. Chatham put the gear in drive, exactly as she saw Victoria, the volunteer coordinator, out of the corner of her eye. She released the break, floating the car forward through the cones toward the exit, desperately trying to avoid contact.

"Chatham, oh Chatham! Yoo-hoo," a determined voice said. Victoria's heels tapped their way along the pavement at lightning speed. There was no ignoring her. Damn, thought Chatham as she slowed the car to a stop once again and rolled down the passenger window. PJ was in the front seat, which helped block the view. Victoria's size zero body, fake eyelashes, and poofy black hair approached the car. The prominent magenta folder she carried matched her shoes perfectly.

"Oh Chatham, I'm so glad I caught you. I haven't seen you at school the past couple of days, and I've been meaning to talk with you."

Talk with me? How about talk *at* me? You're gonna suck me of all my extra time, of which there is absolutely zero, so that you can look good by obtaining 100 percent volunteer efficiency on your little attendance sheet tucked somewhere inside that obnoxious neon pink folder you probably sleep with, Chatham thought. She plastered on a bright smile masking her disdain. "Oh, Vicky, hi. I didn't see you."

"It's Victoria," she corrected.

Chatham tended to call people by their shorthand names; it saved time. "Sorry I haven't been around lately," Chatham offered, purposefully avoiding being cornered by Tricky Vicky as best she could.

"Oh, well, no matter. We're here now." She opened the dreaded folder. "As you know we are aiming for 100 percent volunteer commitment to the tune of fifty hours per volunteer, per year." Victoria looked up at Chatham for emphasis. "And under Ross, I see…" She scanned the list, every name with a row of checkmarks next to it for various volunteer assignments – lunch duty, library helper, field trip driver – except for Chatham's. "Well, actually, I don't see anything. How can that be?" Her confused state presented the perfect opening for PJ.

"Hi, I'm PJ. This is my Barney movie. *Barney's Magical Movie Surprise*, produced by Disney Studios.

Rated G."

Victoria looked at PJ quizzically.

Chatham put the car in gear and released the break.

"OK then Vicky, I'll talk with you soon. Good to see you. Have a nice day."

Victoria was still studying her spreadsheet when Chatham glided out of earshot. Thank goodness she got out of that one. Before she knew it, she'd be color coordinating the paints in the art room, cleaning up the hot lunch serving dishes, and lining up the carpool cones at 5:00 a.m., just so everything was in order for the day. Not that these jobs weren't necessary. Chatham was willing to help. But she preferred tasks that did not involve actually having to be there. The jobs themselves weren't the problem, but she had no time to listen to private school mom gossip and politics. She'd learned her lesson before with the talent assembly. "Did you hear that Willard is trying out for the lead in the play – again?" one of the over-involved parents had commented.

"You're kidding! Your Billy is one hundred times better, and I'm sick of seeing Willard in the plays. I mean, who has a name like Willard anyway?"

"He's only doing it to beef up his high school resume. I heard him tell his mother that he didn't even like doing plays. And do you know what she said?"

"Tell me." The woman had leaned over to whisper, but actually raised her voice.

"She told him, and I heard it clearly: "If you want to go to Harvard, you have to try out for the school play. But, if you don't get the lead, then quit. It's not worth it."

Chatham cringed at the memory of those petty

mothers. Never again, she thought.

She inched the car forward. The exit monitor had his stopwatch in hand and looked disapprovingly at Chatham for her less-than-proficient exodus.

CHAPTER III - *BLESSING*

≈

Within a few minutes, Chatham was back on the highway headed to PJ's school. PJ went to the neighborhood public school. It was that or special education. Chatham could not imagine putting PJ in a classroom of kids who couldn't communicate in some other town where he would not know anyone. There were only a few schools that hosted pure special-ed classes. She figured it was much better to have him at his neighborhood school with millions of "normal" kids as role models.

Chatham and Peter didn't know that PJ was "special" until he was about ten months old when he crawled by dragging a leg behind him. He took a long time to reach every milestone, but he was high functioning. "Communicatively Handicapped" was the official educational label, but really, he was mentally retarded.

Chatham felt comfortable at the local neighborhood school. Everyone seemed to be from a similar socio-economic background, and it wasn't as competitive. Kind of like how she grew up. She also loved her son's many teachers. P.J. spent P.E. and reading in the regular classroom and the remaining part of the day in the learning center with three teachers and only six kids. That was where he received intense one-on-one training in subjects that were particularly difficult for him. All in all, the boy functioned at about a kindergartener level.

P.J. also worked with several therapists. The Occupational Therapist focused on fine motor skills like handwriting and cutting with scissors. The Physical

Therapist emphasized gross motor skills such as climbing and running, and the Speech Therapist helped him form correct sounds to understand proper grammar. It was the perfect set-up for her son, and Chatham was grateful that the school designed the program with him in mind.

Chatham signaled to exit the highway.

"Mommy, I want to go to Chucky Cheese. When are we going?" PJ asked enthusiastically.

"How about Saturday?" Chatham answered with a forced smile, her underlying depression not supporting it.

"How do we get there?" he asked, not waiting for a response. "I know," he continued. "First we go left, and then we go right, and then we stop the car, and then we get a ticket, and then we see Chucky Cheese."

"Very good, PJ. That's right," Chatham responded absentmindedly. She had heard his perseverating behavior before.

"I want to go to Chucky Cheese. Mommy, how do we get there?" he repeated.

"PJ, you just told me how we get there, first we go…"

"Left, then we go right."

"That's right, honey. So first you go to school and do your work, and then we will go to Chucky Cheese, OK?"

"OK, Mommy," he answered with a satisfied smile. "I will do my work, and then we go to Chucky Cheese."

"That's right PJ, perfect."

"Yeah. Perfect. Mommy?"

"Yes, honey," Chatham answered blandly. She knew what was coming.

"How do we get there?"

OK. Time to drop PJ off.

The carpool line to the school was too long which meant they would be late. Chatham opted for the "tricky way" around the side street. It would bring her right to the front of the line.

"Oh no!" PJ shrieked. "Where are you going?" Her delayed son only felt in control when he knew the routine. Any changes and chaos could ensue.

"It's OK, honey. I'm going the tricky way today."

"No, no. We go that way!" He pointed to the passing car line; his anxiety was clearly building fast.

"PJ, remember the fun tricky way where we go around the long car line and we get to be first?" she said hopefully.

"Oh, OK Mommy. I know." Although he still looked anxious, Chatham knew she had a few minutes to show him that they really were going to his school. She whipped around the shortcut street into the school driveway and right up to the school roundabout. There were no car monitors at PJ's school. It was a looser process where you coasted in when it was your turn. Pretty simple.

"Get your backpack and lunch box, honey. Have a great day. I love you." Chatham gave him a kiss on the cheek.

"OK, Mommy, I will. I will meet you right here after school at the pick-up spot," PJ instructed as he exited the car, gear in hand.

Chatham blew him a kiss and watched in her rearview mirror as PJ continued waving until she was out of site. He had no idea that he was delayed and simply lived in the moment. In many ways, PJ was the most well adjusted kid she knew.

≈

Chatham exited the school and changed the channel to her favorite easy- listening station. She let out a deep sigh and scooted her seat up. Hunched against the steering wheel, Chatham looked just like those old ladies who really couldn't see, but somehow faked their way through yet another driver's license renewal. A remix of a Cat Stevens song played in the background.

"I'll try to love again, but I know...the first cut is the deepest, baby I know." Chatham thought about her Peter. She missed him so. No one could ever replace him, she thought as she wiped her eyes with the edge of her sleeve.

"Snap out of it, Chatham. You're a hazard waiting to happen," she commanded. Chatham sat up straight, changed the station to *Alice,* and rolled down the window to get some air. It was all she could do to hold herself together.

"I must be depressed," she concluded. "Why else would I be crying on a perfectly beautiful day? And talking to myself." She gazed out at the surrounding landscape. "I mean for god's sake, look where I live!" She watched the kite-borders navigate across the San Francisco Bay. One boarder jumped at least six feet over a crashing wave with the aid of his multicolored parachute. A giant peace sign in the middle of the chute revealed itself as he readied his board for the next white water challenge.

"Amazing," Chatham said absently, as she turned to scan the lush green, rolling hills thanks to the fanatic environmentalists in Marin. "God's natural air conditioner," she whispered wistfully, watching the fingers of fog cascade down the crevasses of Mount Tamalpais.

"So it can't be where I live. I love it here," she flubbed between tears.

CHAPTER IV - *PETER*

≈

It was her junior year at USC, the year she met Peter. They were both taking "The Art of Persuasion," a highly sought after course on campus, especially among frat boys. And Peter was a natural persuader; he hardly needed any lessons. He was never at a loss for words.

"Hey Chat," he said to her about a week into the course. "Want to join forces this quarter?"

Chatham was caught off guard. "You know, work together on projects and stuff? We're supposed to go co-ed and all."

"Oh, yeah," Chatham responded, quite flustered at being faced with this benign proposition from the best-looking guy on campus. He was so confident with his sporty navy polo sweater and white collared shirt peeking out from under the overlay. Peter had wavy blond hair that hosted natural highlights and a chiseled chin that said strong sense of self, comfortable in his own skin. He definitely had a charm about him.

Although Chatham was excited to be noticed by the most popular guy at USC, she was a bit preoccupied at the time. Freaked out was more like it. She was studying every free second she had in order to get an "A+" in persuasion. It would bring her GPA up to that coveted gold ring, the 4.2 she desperately needed. When the big ad firms like Saatchi or Ogilvy came to interview, she wanted to make sure she was first in line for the offer. Chatham recalled that first interview too well.

"Mr. Saatchi, I love advertising," she said, as

smoothly and confidently as possible. "I actually had an idea for the Cheerios cereal brand you represent. Oh, sure, I'd be happy to share it with you. You see, I want to specialize in slogan and jingle writing. I've been doing it ad hoc since I was four. It's what I was born for. Well, here goes. *Cheerios are good, Cheerios are fine. Let's all share our Cheerios, no way they're all mine!*" Her 'diddy' was met with a blank expression. "It's from a child's perspective," she quickly added.

"Hmm," the interviewer grunted. "We'll be in touch."

OK, so she didn't get a job with one of the biggest companies, but she did land a great gig with the hottest boutique agency in San Francisco, Gorman and Strausberg. It kept her on the West Coast and, more importantly, in Peter's backyard.

Peter was from Marin County, just minutes over the Golden Gate Bridge. He lived a fine upper crust life in Belvedere, a small town of multi-million dollar mansions surrounded by water. The family house was at the crest of the island, showcasing the most breathtaking view of San Francisco and the Golden Gate Bridge Chatham had ever seen. Not exactly the maple tree-lined streets of her one horse hometown. His was more like Paradise.

Peter and his sister, Chloe, had all the comforts that money could buy. Yet they were grounded. Chloe was a bit organic, but that was cool in Marin anyway. They were a wholesome family, not at all affected by their silver-spoon upbringing.

Chatham often wondered what he saw in her when he could have any girl he wanted.

"Every girl I've ever known is too plastic, too perfect, or too petty," he had said to her one night over a cup of fresh clam chowder at Fisherman's Wharf. "Chat, you're the real thing."

He had reached across the table to squeeze her hand. "You're what I want, Chat. You're it. I don't care about anyone else, because no one makes me laugh like you do. No one makes me think like you. I'm crazy about you, Chat." He had flashed his perfect smile before adding, "Growin' old together will be one hell of a ride."

It was his way of proposing.

Sometimes Chatham thought he was like an old soul who had to make the most of his short time on earth.

Peter ended up running a portion of a mutual fund for Morgan Stanley Partners, a large Investment firm. They were married right after college and started a family within a year. "A real team," Peter said.

He was a great dad, too. Always taking the kids to Giants games, the batting cages, a round of golf. Chatham had no complaints. They were still in love after thirteen years of marriage.

And then it all came to a halt. Just like that. No warning whatsoever. Total devastation.

Peter died in a terrible car accident while out of the country on business. It happened in Sweden, by that Igloo hotel where you sleep on blocks of ice. He was coming home late from a business dinner and, just as he turned the corner, another car came screeching out of the hotel parking lot, losing control of its brakes on the ice. Chatham's husband was definitely in the wrong place at the wrong time.

Chatham flew over to Sweden after the accident with Peter's best friend Trip. Trip was basically a Peter double with brown hair. They were best friends who grew up next door to each other. Trip studied to be a Veterinarian at UCLA so Chatham saw him often while dating Peter. And, of course, Trip was best man in their wedding.

After the funeral, Trip became part of the Ross household. Kind of like a brotherly replacement for Peter. Sunday dinners became a pattern that no one wanted to break. Trip even had his own key now. Chatham didn't know how she would have survived without Trip by her side; he brought so much life back into their lives.

She remembered when Trip was doing his residency at an animal hospital in San Rafael when a client brought in a pet to be examined. Trip had never seen a lemur before. He was fascinated. He came over to the Ross house for dinner that night and declared that he had found his purpose.

"I'm going to import exotic pets to America. And I'll be their vet, too. It's a perfect combination. I'll call it Pets Around the World."

"Isn't that just a fancy way to say that you want to travel for a living?" Chatham asked, chuckling at her friend's creative occupational aspirations.

"Yeah, there'll be some of that for sure. But these animals are totally cool. I've been studying up on one-of-a-kind creatures from the rain forest and the Australian Outback. It's my calling."

Chatham and her kids had met more exotic animals than most people would see in their entire lifetime. Camp's favorite was the purple polka-dotted frog lizard – a small frog with a lizard tail that was literally purple with white dots. It only ate flies, which Camp spent many hours capturing with his Venus flytrap plant.

Madison kept a Parachirp from Brazil for a few months. It was a cross between a parakeet and a pelican. And it talked. Go figure.

Chatham had to admit that having Trip as part of their lives helped lessen the sadness. But she still had her periods of fogginess that she couldn't shake.

≈

Chatham wiped her tears and decided she really didn't have time to go down memory lane today. Too much to do, not enough time. The story of her life. She pulled back onto the road. Glancing over at the woman in the next lane, she saw the petite woman behind the steering wheel of a shiny black BMW Convertible. She wore a soft cream-colored scarf around her jet-black hair. She sported Jackie "O" sunglasses and a big grin.

"Nice car, nice glasses, nice life," Chatham sighed, wondering if she'd ever have that kind of carefree existence. Life was so hard now, being a mother, father and bread-winner for her children. She never had time for herself, and it was beginning to take its toll.

It took the jingle she had programmed into her cell phone to shake Chatham out of her forlorn state.

"Whatcha gonna do? Whatcha gonna do? Whatcha gonna do when they call for you?" Chatham kept one hand on the wheel while digging deep into her miniature leather backpack for her link to the outside world.

"Hello?"

"Hey sis, it's me."

"Hi Chloe!" Chatham loved it when she called her sis, even though they weren't anymore – technically."

"Guess where I am?" Chloe said, playing the "I can top that one*"* game.

"Hmm. On a submarine in Russia with the head of the KGB?"

"Close."

"What? Chloe are you in trouble?" Chatham heard a champagne cork popping in the background, a slight giggle through the phone.

"Chat, relax. I'm with Gabrielle."

"What happened to Adam the Art Officiondo?"

"Yeah, well I officiated him out of my life. He was way too involved in making paintings out of duct tape and nails. Cool, but not too much range."

"OK, so now it's Gabrielle?"

"I'm not sure if that's his real name or not, but that's what he likes me to call him."

"Mysterious. Let's see, tall dark and handsome?"

"How about short, bald, and cute as a billiard ball?"

Chatham could almost see her rubbing his head, a soft purr eeking out over the wire.

"And, you're in a private jet on your way to – Bimini?"

"Wrong again, but closer." Chloe lowered her voice to barely a whisper. "We're in his eighty-five-foot yacht, full staff and all, on our way to his private island off the coast of Maine."

"What the hell does this guy do? Chloe, how did you meet him?"

"Kind of funny really. I was in that cool store in

SoHo where they serve you champagne as you try on clothes. You know, the one where they have cats, dogs, birds and that pet lion cub wandering around? Well, they had just put me in this flowing scarf outfit with a studded Boustead and my hair was wrapped up in a bunch of twisted scarves when he walked in. I think he liked the outfit. I've been seeing him for three weeks already. Oh! And his family runs some candy empire or something. What can I say? He's adorable!"

"That's great, Chloe. I'm sure –j"

"Chatham? I gotta go. The natives are getting restless, if you know what I mean. Kiss the little monkeys for me. Love ya!"

Chatham snapped her cell phone shut. To be in love again, she dreamed.

"Who has time for that anyway?" she mumbled, resigning herself to the fact that her life had no room for love, at all.

She wiped her nose on her sleeve. Chatham's nose was running like a sieve. "Damn! I don't have time for a cold. Not now."

She fiddled around the car for a Kleenex. "Probably picked it up from one of the kids," she garbled. "And they picked it up from one of the gremlins at school, whose mother sent him with a green gooey nose so that she wouldn't miss her social tennis match or standing nail appointment. Like I have time for any of that!" she yelled to no one in particular.

Chatham was beginning to sound like the woman who stood at the corner of Sir Francis Drake Boulevard and the Bon Air Shopping Center, ranting and raving at every car that passed by. At least that lady was on drugs. What's my excuse? she wondered.

Chatham swore there was a napkin in the car somewhere. She plunged her hand into the abyss of the glove compartment and withdrew a fist full of Happy Meal toys, first aid supplies, and melted jolly ranchers. No napkin. Oh, what the hell, she thought. She wiped her nose on her sleeve again and took a deep breath to calm her nerves.

I'm thirty-five years old, for god's sake, she reasoned. Isn't that supposed to be the perfect age? Slightly more wise, settled, yet still attractive?

She pulled the driver side visor down and flipped open the mirror to get a closer look. Chatham pulled the rubber band out of her lifeless, mousy blond hair and let it hang loosely at her shoulders. She absently wound the rubber band around the gearshift, joining tens of others. She hadn't even brushed her hair this morning. Who has time for that? Besides, it's only carpool, she concluded. And it's not like anyone important was going to see her. Her only date was with some kids and their annoying mothers. In fact, she couldn't remember ever really dating, other than her beloved Peter. And she had married him.

CHAPTER V - *EMBARRASSMENT*

≈

Chatham's signature Caribbean blue eyes looked tired, exhausted even. Her fair skin was pretty uniform other than the splash of freckles around the T-zone due to teenage sun damage. It's true that her lips could use some plumping and her crows feet were beginning to show, but all in all, she was not unfortunate looking.

She glanced down at her fingernails. What was once a crisp French manicure had turned into a discolored display of muted pink and beige. She precariously peeled off the rest of the chipped ends so that the muffled color at least blended in until she had time to do her nails again. Maybe tonight after the kids went to bed. She shut the mirror and tucked the visor away absently.

Chatham drove along the frontage road, glancing at the shop signs as she passed. Furniture Store.

"I'd love a new dining room set," she longed. "But I'm too tired to entertain."

Beauty Spa. "Pure pampering. But I have no time to go."

BMW Car Dealership. "Maybe next year." She patted the dashboard of her very practical Toyota.

"Oh!" Chatham shouted out, sitting up at attention. "Now that would be good. I can fit *that* in."

With focus saved for claiming a winning lottery ticket, Chatham swerved into the strip mall and barreled into the parking space in front of the 24-hour exercise outlet. It was a sudden decision. She burst into the front door, not really noticing the posters of world champion body builders lining the walls. Offerings of Pump Iron powders and Body Sculpting Vitamins were encased in the glass welcome counter.

"Hi there, welcome to Exercise Anytime. It's our spec-i-a-li-ty, day or night," the desk clerk recited with a casual smile.

Chatham unconsciously winced at the weak slogan, but she was on a mission. She braced her hands on the counter and leaned forward, almost frothing with determination.

"Look. I *need* to try this place. If I don't come in right now I probably won't ever come in because I don't have time to even think about coming in other than when I just did, which is right now… which is why I am here." She paused. "Did you get that?"

"Uh yeah, I think so," the nice-looking attendant responded.

Chatham watched as his eyes quickly scanned her physique.

"Did you want to work out in your pajamas then?" he said as gently as possible.

Chatham looked down at her tattered Lands End shirt, which covered a pair of faded purple long johns she'd had since college. A tan windbreaker completed the ensemble.

"Oh my god," she whispered under her breath in sheer panic. She looked up, trying her best to deliver a convincing explanation. "I mean, uh no. These aren't really pajamas. I would have curlers in my hair if I had pajamas on, right?"

The attendant raised his eyebrows, clearly confused.

She straightened up to appear more confident. "These are the new fashion... Loungewear, I believe is what they call it. Yeah. I got them at Nordstrom's. Work-out section?"

"Nice, very nice," the attendant responded kindly. "How about the flip-flops then? Or would you care to demo the new air-cushion, water-pump shoes that we offer?" he suggested. "Of course you can probably get these at Nordstrom's, too, but since you're here and you're ready... why not give them a try?"

Chatham suddenly noticed how charming he was. Clearly he didn't buy her Nordstrom bologna for a second, but he was sweet enough to go along with the crazy lady's claim. Total embarrassment.

"Maybe I should just come back later. Because, I just thought . . ."

"No, please. Look, we're empty right now," he said. "All the diehards leave by 8:00 a.m. This is the *come as you are* hour. And, you are as you are and, I mean, you should come in, just as you are. Well, you know what I mean."

Chatham couldn't help let slip a tiny smile at the floundering attendant. She knew he was making it up.

"In fact," he said scanning the room as though ensuring no one was listening. "We have a special today. First visit gets you a free T-shirt and shorts. And, you can still demo the workout sneakers. What do you say?"

Even Chatham could tell he was hoping she would accept, although she wondered why. She couldn't help but feel her spirits lifted slightly. She noticed a jar of jellybeans on the counter with a *guess how many and win a free membership* sign propped up against it. Why jellybeans were even in a gym designed to shape up the people that indulged too much of those kinds of things was beyond her.

"Well, I guess that could work. I do have thirty four," she looked at her watch, "thirty-three minutes. And I could use the escape – I mean the workout."

"Great. Settled. Here's your bonus outfit." He handed her a neon green tank top that said *E. Anytime* on it. Lovely. And a pair of green shorts with the backside promptly displaying the name *Exercise Anytime*. Just what I need, she thought. Something to draw attention to my ass.

"You look like a seven," he said, handing her the demo sneakers.

Chatham felt him brush against her wrist as he passed the sneakers over the counter. She wondered if it was intentional and then quickly dismissed the thought.

"Yes, I am. How did you – Oh, do you have a hair tie?" she blurted out, suddenly needing to dig through her purse to hide the adrenaline surge that completely overtook her.

He passed her the neon green band, designed to match the outfit. "Will a green rubber band do?"

Feeling the heat rise in her face, Chatham quickly looked down at the ground only to see her chipped red toenail polish. It practically screamed at her from her open-toed thongs.

"Now that's attractive," she mused.

"I'm sorry, did you say something?"

"Uh, no. Thanks. Gee, I should change right?"

"Good idea. Here's a locker key. Over there across the gym is the women's locker room." He pointed to the door that said *Chicks Only*. "If you change real fast you'll have a solid (he consulted his watch) thirty minutes to work out. The first rotation starts at the butt-buster machine, which you could skip."

She could tell he was being serious. Chatham's stomach flip-flopped. Was it that obvious she hadn't been to a gym in ages? She hoped her cheeks weren't the color of her nail polish.

"The sequence should take you about twenty-five minutes, which gives you a few minutes to change back into your, um, very fashionable lounge ensemble," he said with a warm smile. "Sound good?"

"Sounds great. Thank you for everything!" She was beginning to relax a little, but she was desperate to get out of her ridiculous clothes.

"Oh, and I guess 3,000," Chatham said off handedly as she left the desk with a little bounce in her step. She might as well try to win a free membership. After all, the staff sure seemed friendly. And ridiculously handsome. She wondered if maybe he was Italian.

As Chatham opened the locker room door, a poster of a woman whose biceps were larger than most women's thighs confronted her. In my dreams, she shrugged. Now do I pump or squirt these shoes to make them work she pondered

The locker room door closed gently behind her as if ushering her into a new place, a new possibility.

≈

"See you later, Brett," Palio called out to his club manager as he gathered his things. "Got to get back to New York."

"Dinner with your dad?"

"Yeah, and meetings."

"Do you ever stay in one time zone for more than a day?"

"I wish. I'll be back tomorrow night."

"Hey, tell your father I've got five bucks on him this weekend."

"You're on. See you."

Palio quickly grabbed his backpack of reading material, taking one last look over his shoulder to see if he could spot the interesting woman who burst in this morning. It wasn't every day that one of the gym's clients caught his eye, especially one wearing specialty loungewear. He smiled to himself. She was quite the character... I didn't even ask her name, he regretted as he blasted out the front door and into his Mercedes SL convertible rental.

CHAPTER VII – *PALIO*

≈

Palio cruised down the highway. He had to hurry if he was going to make his flight. That beautiful, but strange woman had totally distracted him. He could hardly blame himself though. She was definitely not your average patron at E. Anytime. And Palio had seen just about everything at his gym.

Running a hard-core health club chain was not exactly what Palio had in mind, but, then again, his father's extensive portfolio included lots of wacky investments. A jelly-bean manufacturing plant, which Palio had been running for the past several years, a miniature sailboat company, and the health club chain were among his dad's favorites. The family moved to the states from Florence, Italy when Palio started high school. They settled in lower Manhattan, in Little Italy of course, where Palio attended P.S. 234, the local public school on Chambers Street. The family moved to New York City, the land of opportunity, with little money. It was the candy company that really put them on the map.

Palio's father was looking at the want ads over coffee one morning when he saw a confection factory for sale.

"What do you think?" he had said to Palio's mother. "We have a chance to buy a whole factory full of your favorite confections. It must be an omen." Mrs. Capriatti had felt the same, and so they were determined to make the purchase. But where to find the money?

Mr. Capriatti had made a good friend named Monte

who ran a small Italian restaurant in Greenwich Village. They played chess together in Washington Square Park after mass on Sundays. Monte was more than happy to invest in his friend's dreams. His restaurant was doing well, and he had the extra cash. Besides, what better way to advance the presence of Italians in America than to invest in one of his own? Little did Monte know, but he would be paid back ten fold his investment.

The Capriatti family was now the number one manufacturer of gourmet jellybeans worldwide. Palio couldn't help but feel he had a little something to do with its success, having run the factory for the past seven years. But it was his mother who chose the new colors and flavors. It was her favorite thing to do, and jellybeans were her favorite sweet. She would dream up new flavors, and Mr. Capriatti would find a way to make them.

"Roberto," she would say. "I had a dream about cheesecake last night. Blueberry cheesecake with a hint of meringue."

"Oh Lucia," he'd exclaim. "You are a genius. What should we call it?"

"How about blueberry meringue cheesecake?" She would give him that knowing smile, that beam of success.

"Pure brilliance! And so it is."

Now, blueberry meringue cheesecake was the number one flavor they sold. She had been a natural.

As Palio pulled onto the main road near the airport, he thought of the strange woman once again. He wondered what his father would think of her. Probably just be thankful some woman has been able to intrigue me, he thought to himself. His father was always trying to set him up. God bless him, he just wanted his son to be happy.

"Palio, my boy, my only son, you are my pride and joy. But you're thirty-six-years old," his papa had said over breakfast one morning.

"Uh, thanks?"

"Isn't it time you thought about settling down? Meeting a nice girl? Like Maria, the Porticello's daughter? You've known her since high school, practically your whole life. What a lovely girl she is. And she likes you, my boy! I heard it from a very reliable source."

His father had meant well. Palio's mother died two years ago from a sudden aneurism that started in her foot and traveled to her brain in less than twenty-four hours. It was a pure tragedy of which the entire family still had not recovered. As a collateral result, Palio's father focused almost exclusively on Palio's well-being and happiness.

"Pop? Maria? I don't think so." Marrying Maria would be like marrying a direct relative of Don Corlioni. She was a wannabe mafia princess, who wasted no time letting you know it. She'd be a better match for his best friend, almost brother, Gino who was obsessed with the mafia.

Palio remembered his one and only "arranged" date with Maria all too well. It was soon after mama died. He was running the candy business when he agreed, after much harping from his father, to take her on a date.

"Palio," Maria had said as she scooted past him, claiming the seat that allowed her a clear view of the entire restaurant. "I do know people. I have connections. So if you need the competition to drop a color or flavor from their jellybean line, it can be arranged. Maybe you want them to stop selling peanut butter fluffernutter or coconut surprise or something? Yes?" She looked at him with a wink.

"Gee, Maria. Nice of you to offer. But the jellybean business is good as far as I can tell. No problems to speak of."

"Well, think about it. It can be arranged. We'll make them an offer they will have to accept" she whispered, leaning closer to reveal her plunging cleavage.

Maria wasn't unattractive; dark bushy hair, deep brown eyes, medium height. She was only slightly overweight but with an unusually large chest. Palio was sure he couldn't tell where her breasts ended and her stomach began. Years from now – well, he was afraid to think about it.

Maria ran the family confection business now. She was the natural choice according to Palio's father. Maria Porticello had come up in the world and was known as an astute businesswoman. Besides, Mr. Capriatti thought of her like a daughter, and he was still pushing for some sort of union between the two families. What better way than to have her manage a part of the family portfolio? "Palio, our candy company is solid. Let Maria do the babysitting now. I need you to turn my newest gem around," his father had proposed during one of their recent weekly dinners.

"Sure, Pop. I can part from the candy world. I think I've had enough sugar to last me a lifetime. What kind of job did you say it was?"

"It's an exercise club. I need you to make it rock solid. Expand it as you see fit. And you can spend some time on yourself too for once. What do you say?" Palio's father had spread his arms wide, ready to seal the deal with a hug.

"Papa, you know me. I'd do anything for you. It sounds interesting," Palio had concluded, returning his father's embrace. He had only been to San Francisco once and actually looked forward to the idea of spending some time away from Manhattan.

Palio never did meet up with Maria during the transition. In fact, other than that first date, they never seemed to be in the same place at the same time. The last he heard, the competition had dropped all blue jellybeans from their line.

Palio's mother always told him that *love conquered all* and that he shouldn't stop until he found it, like she and Papa. But Palio's father was convinced that Maria would love Palio more than he could ever dream. Why was he pushing for Palio to get married anyway? Who wants to deal with having to commit to someone, start to grow old together, and then watch them die before their time? It was not for him. Not now. Not ever.

CHAPTER VIII - *INTERRUPTION*

≈

E. Anytime was a 15,000-square-foot facility spanning two stories. The downstairs consisted of wall-to-wall metal machines painted white for a cleaner, crisper look. Each of the machines was edged with bright green trim to match the outfits they offered. The upstairs housed the hardcore cardio equipment, which included stair masters, step cycles, and treadmills.

Chatham walked around. She was a little nervous, especially now that she knew she was on her own. She had seen the cute counter boy leave in a very sleek convertible just a few minutes ago. Her disappointment came as a shock. Why did she want to see that guy again? Sure, he was gorgeous. Sure, he was sweet. But she barely had time to think about working out, let alone dating. Besides, he probably thought she was a colossal freak show.

Wandering around the giant gym, she noticed that there seemed to be a contraption for every muscle group in the human body. Some Chatham had never heard of. The Humerus Strengthener promised to firm up the bone between the tricep and bicep. Chatham had no idea that bones could be firmed up with machines. Wasn't that what calcium was for?

The Amazon Axon machine professed to tune up the micro fibers in the muscle tissue that sent electro currents to each muscle group. Chatham wasn't sure about that one either. Sounded a little too sci-fi. In fact, being in a room filled with steel and chrome contraptions was a little more than intimidating. It was downright terrifying.

Luckily there were only a few people in the gym so Chatham wasn't risking total and complete humiliation. A large black man with bulging lycra-clad thighs and forearms like Popeye was perched on a bench hoisting a solid steel bar above him. A woman with cropped spiked hair sported a ripped tank shirt that said, *Don't even fuckin' look at me.* She was doing squats with free weights that had to be at least 100 pounds-each. Chatham couldn't help but stare; she was sure the woman's face would burst like a balloon from the pressure. The female Amazon must have felt Chatham's eyes on her. She set down the large barbells and walked directly over to Chatham.

"Can I help you with something?" She thrust her face a solid three inches from Chatham's nose. "Is there a problem?"

Chatham was mortified. "Uh, problem? No, no problem. I was just. Well, I'm not sure what I'm doing really."

The beefy gal just laughed and walked away.

"Ditz," Chatham heard her say under her breath as she jumped up to reach the chin-up bar and proceed to do one-handed lifts. Chatham decided not to pick a fight.

The other patron was lean and sinewy, like a marathon runner. He was oblivious to the sweat he was spraying over the railing as he sprinted on the treadmill set at an incline of 10. Chatham shielded her head as she stepped under the railing on her way to the arm section of the machines. She scanned the choices for every muscle in the arm known to man. The first machine said *Triceps* with an arrow pointing to the underneath portion of the arm. She looked at the extra skin hanging down from the underside of her arm. Definitely a machine she could benefit from. She was thankful that some of the machines had pictures on them to show the beginner what to do, kind of like a workout for dummies.

Chatham was able to figure out how to change the weights and adjust the levers on most of the machines. Although on the hydraulic pull-up contraption she didn't quite get the concept. She set the machine at 120 pounds and was flying up and down on that piece of equipment like a high-speed elevator.

Chatham felt a little better after her condensed workout. Her cheeks had a rosy tone, and the endorphins helped her feel less depressed. She even broke a slight sweat. As though it was a natural output of her elevated state, Chatham actually found herself thinking about the handsome man who had helped her earlier. She wondered if there was a way she could inquire about his work schedule without appearing interested.

She shook her head from side to side. What's wrong with me? she thought. It must be the effect of the exercise. Why else would I be preoccupied with a loser counter boy who probably borrowed his father's fancy car to impress some girls? She reminded herself of that Avril Lavigne song about the loser boyfriend. Definitely not for her.

≈

Palio made it to the airport in record time. He took his Mercedes to the valet and sprinted to catch the flight to JFK. He tended to cut things a little short, a strategy for managing time. No sooner had he stepped onto the craft then the 777 airplane door closed firmly behind him. It was scheduled for a 5:40 p.m. arrival, plenty of time to make his weekly dinner with his father.

Palio liked to sit next to the window, but there was only an aisle seat left on this flight. He took his First Class seat of 2B without complaint, stored the carry-on bag in front of him, and grabbed the SkyMall catalog out of the seat pocket. Palio stopped at the ad for the Sharper Image nose hair clipper. The advertisement said it was their biggest seller. Maybe I should break down and get one of those soon, he thought, absently checking to see if any hairs were protruding. He didn't notice the attractive woman seated next to him.

Palio turned the page. Loungewear.

"I can't believe it," he said out loud to no one in particular, an instant smile on his face. There in full frontal was an ad for Lands End loungewear. I guess they weren't pajamas after all, he thought, amused at his interaction with the mysterious suburban woman this morning. He couldn't stop smiling.

"Can't believe how cute they are? Or can't believe someone would actually wear them out in public?" the voice next to him responded, a sensual laugh completing the comment. Palio turned to behold one of the most beautiful women he had ever seen. He had been too rushed to notice. Her thick, shiny black hair was pulled back tight in a bun that rested at the nape of her neck. Palio found himself wondering what it would look like hanging loosely at her shoulders. Her soft olive skin was perfect, not a wrinkle or blemish anywhere. She wore no make-up, except for a hint of mascara that accented her long dark lashes and a subtle pink lip-gloss that drew attention to her soft, full lips. Her brown eyes were sharp and attentive, a woman who knew how to compete in a man's world.

The attendant handed a glass of champagne to Palio and his seatmate.

"Here's to flannel," the sexy woman toasted as she crossed her long legs in Palio's direction.

Palio smiled, nodding in her direction. Suddenly his phone rang. He could tell from the caller ID that it was Gino.

"Gino! What's up?" Palio answered. "I'm on the plane now."

"Hey, Palio, Ya know what I saw last night? Huh?"

"Gino, you've got to stop watching that TV show; it's not real life."

"Oh no? Ya wanna bet? I saw big Al reach into washing machine numba four in da laundramat, and do ya know what he pulled out? Well, do ya?"

"What, a gun?" Palio asked, eyes rolling.

"Yeah. That's right. It was an oozie, swear to gawd."

"Gino, you're killing me. You've got to get a life."

"Yeah, that's just what I thought. He's out to kill some-body. Fuckin' wacko. I shoulda tailed 'em."

"No Gino, you should not have. And I'm glad you didn't. Look, you have a family now. Me and Pop. And as a brother I'm asking you, don't get caught up with your imagination, OK? I love ya, man. Let's go get a beer when I'm home."

"I'm still comin' to get ya, right?"

Palio nodded his head. "Yep. I'll call when I land!" He hung up and smiled to himself. Gino was part of the Capriatti family now, like a brother really. He was in charge of security at the miniature sailboat operation. Mr. Capriatti knew that Gino could protect the plant single-handedly from any burglar who might want to steal the newest prototype before it came to market. Palio's dad was a little paranoid. This sailboat thing was his latest obsession.

Gino resembled your typical Italian gangster. The opposite of Palio. He wore a black leather jacket to cover his white tank t-shirt, which showcased his bulging muscles. A regular at the local body builder gym, he looked like a white Barry Bonds with a greasy hair do. According to Gino, there was always some unsavory character lurking around, and he was sure something big was going on at all times. At least he was on top of things, Palio thought.

Palio stretched out in his comfy chair, bracing himself for the long flight.

CHAPTER IX - *WORK*

≈

"Oh my god, I am certifiably late!" Chatham shouted as she screeched into the garage, slammed the car door and ran up the stairs three at a time. She threw her pajamas on the floor and burst into her office.

Chatham's office was a converted bedroom closet. Luckily it had a window so it didn't feel like a total cave. The put-it-together maple laminated desk unit filled an entire two walls, as though it was custom made for the space. Soft sea foam green paint colored the walls. She had read somewhere that green meant peacefulness, something she could use more of, so she and the kids had painted it one Sunday. Chatham thought it would be a good bonding experience. They dropped more paint on the floor and on themselves than on the wall, but she used a small burgundy throw rug to cover up the stains. All in all it was a fine job. And, they had fun doing it.

Chatham also had an office in the city. But lately, that was mostly used for client meetings. She preferred the zero commute to her little office nook at home.

The back of her office door hosted many of Chatham's successful campaigns. The ones that paid the bills got top door space, and she often looked at them when she was stuck for a fresh approach.

Poppy's Preserves: preciously prepared generation after generation. The campaign was designed to tug at the consumer's heart. A picture of the grandkids making grandpa's famous jelly recipe inspired mothers everywhere to contribute to tradition, like buying a jar or three of

Poppy's Preserves. After all, wasn't upholding tradition a part of every mother's job? Chatham briefly wondered what traditions she was passing on to her family. She couldn't think of any. Not one. I'm a total failure, she thought as her eyes moved down the door to the next prized catchphrase.

The Idle Spur was a chain of family restaurants, serving Texas-style barbecue food. It was a sensation. The owner of the restaurant chain, a true Texan with his dirty boots and spurs, really wanted the tag line, *Shit kickin' good*. It wasn't until Chatham convinced him that a swear word couldn't be used on television ads, featuring him, of course, that he reluctantly agreed to the new slogan: *All Beef-No Bull*.

"Hell, that's sayin' the same damn thing. Bull shit, right? Isn't that what people will think?" a sly smile spreading across his face.

"Well yes, Hank. Essentially, you're correct. However, the networks will likely take it. I think we're safe using it."

The *All Beef-No Bull* campaign became so popular that the franchise went from opening one new restaurant every six months, to one a month. She just hoped they could keep up with the growth. The next phase of the campaign was to bring in a younger spokesman. Someone that could be groomed to take the place of Hank, whose health was rapidly declining due to his smoking four packs a day of filter-less Marlboros, a true cowboy's cigarette. She scribbled on a yellow sticky note pad and affixed it to the winning poster. GET YOUNG GUY WITH HEAVY TWANG!

One of her favorite campaigns was *Vatican Air: get there on angel's wings*. She knew she was stretching it a bit with the angel metaphor, but word had it that the Pope himself was fine with it. It was a start-up, no frills air carrier that was overbooked as soon as it launched. The public thought that god personally had his hand in that venture.

Chatham was amazed at the success of the Catholic church. It was a non-profit powerhouse. Not only did they control more than half the religious affiliation in America, but they had holdings in banks, real estate, healthcare, and now airlines. They even had their own line of organic food. Horganic they called it. Holy Organic. They figured if the Jewish religion could have kosher, they could have Holy.

All profits for each of the Catholic-church ventures went to the Catholic Charitable Trust, which created more revenues than any business in the United States. Non-taxable, of course.

The edges of Chatham's desk unit were lined with snapshots of the children, like Christmas cards around a doorway. Kids artwork filled the walls and various pottery creations lined each available nook and cranny. "Mommy, I love you," was completed with a drawing of her and PJ, *Happy Mother's Day* on a brass paperweight, a picture of Camp as the theme. *Mom and Me*, a mother/daughter portrait by Madison. Her children were her inspiration.

And then there were the lists – on sticky backed paper – everywhere.

STORE: vitamins, toilet paper, dishwashing liquid, lunchmeat, pancake batter, apples, tampons, wheat thins.

TO DO: orthodontist appointments for Madison and

PJ, doctor appointment for Camp, MAMMOGRAM (don't make it three years)!

MEETINGS: back-to-school night, PA meeting, Bunko (don't miss it this month...it's been six already), Book Club (cancel again, no time to read).

Chatham sat at her desk, her dog Fluff, the family golden retriever named after one of Chatham's campaigns, plopped down at her feet. She heard the front doorbell ring, but chose to ignore it. Chatham needed to focus on an excuse for her tardiness to the conference call that was already in session. It was a major client. This one account alone paid for the monthly mortgage and braces on her two older children's teeth.

Chatham fiddled with the "see all" video camera atop her computer screen so that it would only see her, and not the entire family wall of fame. She dialed into the conference.

"Welcome to your conference. If you are the host..." Chatham cut off the standard recording and punched in her participation code, joining the conversation..

"Well sir, I think Chatham would be best equipped to address that request," her artistic partner, Tom, countered as Chatham beeped into the group. "Chatham, is that you?"

"Yes, I'm here Tom. Sorry I'm late." She did her best to look out of breath for the camera. She knew her partner wasn't going to be too happy with her. "Traffic was hideous getting into the office today. Entire bridge was closed down, some terror scare or something. Lots of guys in green army clothes with guns. Kind of wild, really. Thank goodness it was a false alarm."

"Is that so?" was all the client had to say. His big nose looked three times its normal size. Was his camera on close-up mode?

"Yes, Harlan. A bit of a scare really. I'm glad everything is OK. Aren't you?" She tried to deflect the attention.

"Of course, of course," he growled. "And how are you, my dear?" he leered into the camera. He was squinting. "E. Anytime? New slogan?" he inquired.

Oh shit. Chatham had accidentally moved the camera to focus on her colorful new shirt instead of her face. She quickly redirected the camera and did her best to smooth it over.

"Oh, the slogan. Actually, a new client we're considering." A quick "see only" camera view of Tom revealed his shocked expression. "Yes, chain of health clubs, very upscale. They're going national."

"Sounds like a strip club more than a health club," he said licking his magnified lips. Disgusting.

"OK," Chatham quickly added. "So what do you think about the television jingle, Harlan?"

"I need to hear it again, will you sing it for me Chatham, my dear?" A look of salivating anticipation was displayed on his enlarged face. He fiddled with his red tie and then ran his fingers through the extra layer of gel that slicked his salt and pepper hair into place. Her client was clearly waiting for her to burst into song.

Harlan was her biggest client, so she put up with a lot. A wealthy, larger than life Jewish New Yorker who owned a tiny candy company that cornered the market on lemon drops and a successful yacht company. He built yachts for just about everyone on the Forbes list of wealthiest people in America. And with yachts came crews. Harlan was always surrounded by the most gorgeous playboy type women and most stunning men Chatham had ever seen. Kind of like the Hugh Hefner of the seas, minus the silk robe.

"Well, if you'll excuse my off-key range, I'd be happy to." She covered the microphone with her hand and cleared her throat so that she could quickly kick Fluff out of the office. The dog liked to howl along whenever Chatham sang. It must be in his key or something. The doorbell rang again. Chatham wasn't expecting anyone and her account with UPS instructed them to leave any packages on the porch. No time to answer the door. She hoped they would go away.

Chatham closed the office door and positioned her face within the camera's vision.

"As you know, it goes to the tune of Marilyn Monroe's *Happy Birthday Mr. President*. We checked; it's in the public domain, so we can use it."

"Yes, very good. Sing away." Chatham could see Harlan lean back and put his feet up, a smug look of satisfaction spreading across his face as though he were remembering some less than lucid moment. He popped a lemon drop into his mouth and sucked loudly.

Chatham launched her power point presentation, coordinating the edited yacht footage with the Marilyn Monroe look alike aboard.

"OK, here goes." She clicked the presentation launch button. Crystal blue waters, sandy beaches, and bathing beauties. The yacht coasted into the frame, resting a pool's length from shore. Marilyn appeared, and Chatham prepared to sing. And Fluff began to howl. Chatham adjusted her range to dovetail nicely with the dog. She leaned in close to the telephone speaker, doing her best to imitate Marilyn's soft, sexy voice.

"A special boat for your day, a day of all days. A special boat for your birthday, so come sail me away." The camera zoomed in on the Marilyn double as her skirt blew up, producing a sensuous giggle of which Chatham provided the audio. They hadn't yet hired a famous recording artist to do the voice-over. Once Harlan and his board signed off on the idea, they would move into casting mode. The campaign was set to launch on the fourth of July, right before the fireworks display on all the major television networks.

"Chatham, my dear. How lovely. Lovely indeed. And wonderful acoustics I might add. Do you have back-up?"

"Actually, it's a sample undercut of the tune, but that will be cleaned up when we hire the artist. We were thinking maybe Shania Twain? And Pamela Anderson as Marilyn?" Chatham could tell he was imagining Pamela in that outfit by the creepy gaze in his eyes.

"Interesting thought. I'll need you to come to New York this weekend, of course, and present the jingle in person to the board. You've got my vote. And if you get theirs, we're a go. Shall we say Saturday? 9:00 a.m. sharp at my offices on Park."

Chatham cringed. Camp had a soccer game, PJ had Special Olympics swimming, and Madison had ballet. She did her best to travel as little as possible, especially after the nanny fiasco, but this was her biggest client and the campaign would help pay for next year's tuition and PJ's speech therapy bills.

"Sure, I can make it. I'll be there," she said with a forced smile.

"Wonderful. It's settled. See you then. And Chatham, my dear?"

"Yes, Harlan."

"Wear the dress. Goodbye, Tom." Click. He was gone.

She shuddered. Harlan could be such a creep sometimes.

"Chat! What the hell are you thinking?" Tom demanded.

Chatham opened her office door to quiet her operatic dog. "You can't go to New York. Hell, you can't go anywhere without a nanny for those kids. And what's with the health club gimmick?" Tom asked. "Are you keeping something from me?"

"Of course not. This is my shirt from the gym."

"You at the gym? That's hard to picture."

Chatham feigned her surprise. "Hey now, mister…"

Tom was her partner, but he was also her friend. He was an artistic genius in all media forms. He was the one who put together the entire presentation, minus the jingle. That was Chatham's arena. They made the perfect team. They had worked together at Gorman and Strausberg in San Francisco. When she went off on her own, he had desperately wanted to come with her. It was the best decision she ever made professionally. And she adored him.

Tom lived in San Francisco with his partner Theo. Theo was a body builder, and Tom was a slight artistic nerd. They completed each other's sentences.

"So what are we gonna do?" Tom asked. "You know you're not a fan of the nanny thing."

"Yeah, I don't want to do that again," Chatham winced. She did not have fond memories of nannies, au pairs, or babysitters. And yes, there was a difference. Besides, the kids needed her around, especially now.

"Trust me. I'm aware."

A light bulb suddenly went off in Chatham's head.

"I know! You and Theo can watch the kids! Tom, I'd be forever in your debt, and you know how much the kids love you and Theo. I'll stay with dad and be back Sunday night. We need this one, Tom."

"My god, the things I do for you. What do you take me for?" There was a hesitation in his voice.

"Tom, what is it?" She could see him pouting through their electronic connection.

"It's nothing really. Never mind."

"Come on Tom, what is it?" Chatham didn't need any more surprises. She had enough on her plate.

"Well, alright. Can we sleep in your big fluffy bed? With the giant down comforter covered in those soft yellows and oranges, you know like you'd find in Tuscany or something? It's so much more my style. I mean, please, Theo likes all that metal and chrome... yuck."

Chatham laughed as she watched Tom stick out his tongue and open his eyes wide. The camera was definitely in zoom mode today.

"Sure, whatever makes you happy. Thanks Tom,

you're the best!"

"Tell me something I don't know."

"OK, gotta go to the store because we are basically out of everything and then I have to pick up the kids. I'll send you my comments for the final presentation tonight after the kids go to bed, OK? Oh, and I should leave Friday morning. Ugh, I need to book a flight now."

"You're lucky I'm a night owl. Theo will be fast asleep while I slave away at creating the perfect Caribbean water tone for your presentation." He pretended to file his nails, a false look of exasperation as he rolled his eyes in defeat.

"Sorry, Tom. I will try to do it earlier if I can." Chatham always had guilt associated with her day in some form or another. She could never please everyone, least of all herself.

"Don't worry, it's not really a problem. Besides, I like to look at his muscles when he sleeps. They are so defined, it makes me shiver."

"Tom, too much information."

"Sorry. I can't help it. So anyway, I'll e-mail with you tonight and see you Friday morning for sure. Kisses." He leaned into the camera with his gigantic lips and let out a giant puckered smooch. "Over and out."

The more Chatham thought about it, the more she decided that the trip to New York might be just what she needed after all. Minus the Marilyn Monroe dress, of course. But, if it meant getting the client to sign off on a major campaign, she could handle it. Yes, she concluded. This could work.

Chatham always booked her own flights. With the ability to reserve online, who needed a travel agent? She inspected Vatican Air's schedule. As an executive member, all flights meant triple miles and she could sure use them. Maybe she would have enough miles to take the kids to Hawaii one day, for free, she thought as she perused the departure times. Within two minutes she had booked and paid for her flight to New York. The Internet saved Chatham time, which was at the top of her priority list.

She opened her email in a smaller window on her desktop. Chatham was a long time subscriber to *CheapHotels.com*, which sent her daily offerings of the best hotel deals around the country. She opted for three to five stars so that the online service didn't send her to the total dumps. Up popped the options: The Plaza, Hyatt Regency, Marriott, and The Pierre. Chatham had always wanted to stay at the Pierre, and they were offering a half-price discount for the weekend since it was off-season. Chatham clicked yes, entered her credit card information, and the confirmation number was sent to her almost immediately.

The next call was to her father. He was at home as usual, tinkering in his workshop, creating the next woodworking piece of art for one of his grandchildren.

"Hi Dad, it's me," Chat bellowed into the phone. Her dad's hearing wasn't what it used to be.

"Chatham, that you? You sound kind of distant."

"Yes, it's me. Turn up the volume on your phone," she shouted into the headpiece.

"Ahh, that's better. Hi, honey. I'm just whittling a little horse drawn carriage for PJ. His birthday's coming up, right?"

"Oh Dad, he'll love it. Just like the ones in Central Park?"

"Well, as close as I can make it."

"You're the best. Hey listen, I have a surprise for you."

"A pie? You know how I love pie."

"No Dad, a surprise," Chatham said slowly and succinctly.

"Oh, a surprise. Now who wouldn't love a surprise, especially from his favorite daughter?"

"Only daughter, Dad," Chatham retorted automatically. It was a little joke between them.

"Only daughter? How do you know I haven't had an alleged affair and sired a child in the last few months?"

"Dad, your siring days were left with the renaissance. Besides, I know it's been four months since you've seen any of your grandchildren."

"And three days. When are you bringing those precious little angels out here again?" Chatham's father lived for her kids.

"As a matter of fact, how would you like a little company this weekend?"

"A little fun money? Now what would I use fun money for?"

"Dad, I said company. Not fun money."

"Oh, let me turn this damn volume up. OK, there we go. Now what did you say, Chat honey?"

"Company. Would you like some company this weekend?" Chatham wondered if her father really was hard of hearing of if he simply used an imaginary disability to make a point.

"Why for heaven's sake need you ask? And which one are you bringing with you?"

"According to the fairness quotient, it's Camp's turn. But I was thinking of maybe going solo on this one."

"Oh bring him along. I'll keep him busy. Besides, I think it's great how you bring each of the kids on a trip with you each year. I mean why not, especially if I'm here. I'll take any or all of 'em." He loved all his grandchildren the same. "So what's the occasion?"

"I have to come to New York on business, actually. Saturday meeting."

"A weekend meeting? Who would ask such a thing? Asking you to take the weekend away from your family? Well, almost your entire family. What is this world coming to? When I was working in Manhattan, at the leading Direct Mail company, I might add, I never had a –"

"Dad, listen. It's my biggest client. And I could really use the money. Camp is next in line for braces."

"Well, that will cost a fortune. So, who is this schmuck who's making you fly to New York on a weekend?" he asked. Chatham's father was a family man through and through.

"You remember the yacht company?"

"Oh, the big boat builders. I know those boats. I once made a replica of their Sorbonne model. Nine inches long with perfect features. Discovered that they needed to add to the hull to make sure it weathered the storms through the Bermuda triangle. Do you remember how I tried to tell that company about the hull problem?" Her father was still reeling from the rebuke.

"Yes Dad, I remember. They thought you were a

little off your rocker."

"They should have listened to me. I know my carvings, and I create the dimensions with perfection. When my little horse-drawn carriage is perfect, you will think you are in a miniature version of Central Park waiting for your chariot to take you for a ride. You'll even feel like you have a warm blanket wrapped around your legs to shield you from the chill. I have a demo out with a friend of mine who drives one of the park carriages. A little test marketing on this model you could say."

Chatham's father was well known for his wooden replicas. His hobby had turned into a booming business. New York developers, sculptors, machinists, you name it. When they wanted to show what their next contraption or project was going to look like they had Chatham's father create an exact depiction out of his little pieces of wood. It was uncanny how exact he was. He said it helped pass the time now that mama was gone and in between Chatham and the grandkids' visits. Chatham knew he loved his work and although he missed her mother, he liked that his opinion mattered every now and again. It gave him a sense of purpose.

"Who is watching PJ and Madison while you are away? Do not tell me you are hiring another live-in. Please tell me you are not hiring another au pair."

"No Dad, never again. I promise. We are all allowed a mistake in our lives."

"You are just lucky you have that good friend to help you out. He's a keeper that one."

"Dad, Trip is family. But he can't watch the kids. You know he runs his pet store on the weekends. He's way too busy."

"What's he selling now? Iguanas from Paraguay or something? Love those wild creatures."

"Actually, he said he was coming over with some new breed of beaver or something to show the kids this week."

"How the hell does he find those things?"

"No clue. He has relationships all over the world. You know, Trip. He's always in some exotic country trying to import weird three-headed snakes or purple turtles. I don't know how he does it." Chatham chuckled to herself, recalling the many bizarre animals Trip had brought over for her kids to enjoy.

"Well, if you ask me, he should travel less and spend more time with a family, like yours."

"Dad, don't start with that. Trip and I are friends; that's all. He was Peter's best friend for god's sake. Me and Trip would be weird."

"Weird, shmeered. He's family. Might as well make it official."

"Dad, stop it." Chatham had been listening to her father encourage a union between she and Trip for two years now. Trip was a great guy, but they really were just good pals. Besides, she wasn't even close to being over Peter. How could she ever love again? Not ever, she concluded. It's just how it had to be.

"Tom and Theo are coming over to watch the kids. It's one big happy family," Chatham said, attempting to put a positive bounce in her voice.

"Peanut butter and jelly? Good thing I am so modern now. Your mother would roll over in her grave if she knew her grandchildren were being exposed to two puffers like that."

"Mama would have approved, Dad. You know she was a liberal at heart. Besides, not only is Tom an integral part of my business, he's a great friend. And you know the kids love watching Theo lift weights. He's going to be in some championship exhibition next month, and he promised to show the kids how he could lift them all with one hand."

He chuckled. "Just tell him to be careful. He better not drop my precious little angels."

Chatham sighed. She was ready to wrap up this call. "So, maybe Trip needs to go on a pet shopping spree in New York?"

Her father just had to give it one last try. She knew he desperately wanted to see his daughter move on, but she wasn't ready. At least, she didn't think she was.

"Papa, this is business. I told you. I'm only bringing Camp so that you can see one of your grandkids at least every few months."

"OK, OK. I was just asking. I just want to see you have a little fun, that's all. You know, maybe go on a date once in a while. But your love life is none of my business, so I will drop it." And he did.

"We'll see you this weekend, Dad. I love you." Chatham hung up the phone. "A date? Yeah, right."

CHAPTER X – *TRIP*

≈

Chatham ran upstairs to throw in a load of laundry and make the kids' beds. She quickly put away a stack of videos, gathered her backpack, and headed back to the car. She knew that she barely had time to make it through the aisles at the Safeway before it was time to pick up the kids.

Just as she opened the car door, she heard it again. The doorbell. Who could that be? she thought. Who in their right mind would wait all that time, or even think someone was home to answer the door? It had been at least twenty minutes!

Chatham bounded back up the stairs and opened the front door.

"Hey, Chat. I figured you were on a conference call so I'd wait." Trip stood there with a creature on his shoulder. Some sort of cross between a baby leopard and a skunk.

"What is that?" Chatham asked. "Does it spray?"

"Oh, the stripe on the tail? No, it's harmless. Doesn't even have his teeth yet. Isn't he cute?"

"I guess. What the hell is it?" she asked again, moving way aside for him to enter.

"It's a skoonard, a cross between a skunk and a leopard."

"How is that even possible?"

Trip shrugged and held up the small animal. "Like the spots?"

The creature was light brown with white spots,

small, pointy ears, and a bushy tail. It was about nine inches long, a baby. The white stripe along the tail was the part that Chatham wasn't sure about.

"Are you sure that thing won't spray?"

"Nah, he's cool. I got him in Russia last week. Already have a buyer," Trip explained as he fed the animal a large pellet. "Loves dog food. Not sure why, but that's all he eats."

"Trip, you are a piece of work," Chatham chuckled. "I didn't even know you were out of town." She went back into her office to grab the cell phone she had forgotten. Chatham wondered why he hadn't told her. He seemed more aloof lately. Trip followed Chatham into her office.

Chatham made a mental note to print the web page she had up on the screen; Vatican Air. The flight schedule to New York was displayed.

"Yeah, it was a 48-hour turnaround. I'm a bit beat." He looked at her computer. "Heading east?" he asked nonchalantly.

"Oh, yeah. I have to go to New York this weekend to do a final sign off on a new campaign. Kind of a bummer, but I'm taking Camp with me on this one."

"Sounds good. Who's watching Maddy and PJ?" he asked, as though it was his business as part of the family.

"Tom and Theo, actually. I would have asked you, but you have the shop on the weekends." She didn't want to hurt his feelings. He was part of the family, and she wanted to keep it that way.

"Puff and Fluff? Are you sure?" Trip was fine with Theo, but Chatham knew Tom's persnickety attitude bugged him.

"Trip, you know they love the kids. And Tom is my business partner. He has a vested interest in this account, too."

"Well, maybe I could have gotten someone else to watch the shop this weekend. You could have asked." He looked slightly hurt.

"Oh Trip, I'm sorry. I'll ask next time. Definitely. You're still coming over for dinner Sunday, right?"

"Will you be back in time?" he asked.

"Scheduled to, barring any delays." She looked up and smiled. "I have to go. Stay as long as you want." She gave him a quick kiss on the cheek and headed back to the garage. "Don't forget Special Friend's day at Maddy's school on Friday," Chatham called out as she launched her way toward the garage. It was time for the afternoon mommy shift.

"Nice outfit," Trip called after her as she bounded down the stairs. Chatham had already forgotten about her neon shorts. Her personal attire always seemed to be the last thing on her mind. At least she understood why Trip was smiling so much when he first came in. He had never seen her in such short shorts before and certainly not in the obnoxious green she was sporting. She must be a shocking sight.

≈

After she left, Trip slumped down in the soft leather chair in Chatham's office. He wasn't sure what he should do. He had hoped that he would have gotten to spend a little more time with her, especially since the kids were at school. She'd be less distracted.

He stared at her computer screen, feeling dejected.

How am I ever going to make her see? he wondered.

Without really thinking, Trip pressed the print button on the computer toolbar and stuffed the flight schedule into his pocket. He read the email that confirmed her reservation at The Pierre. He printed that page, too, although he wasn't exactly sure why. He then headed into the family room to deposit the creature in the cage he had built. He always showed the Ross kids his imports before they were delivered to their new owners.

CHAPTER XI
PALIO & GEORGINA

≈

Palio was about to hail a cab at the airport curb for his ride into New York City when Georgina gave him a gentle tap on his shoulder.

"Can a poor girl offer a fellow a ride?" she asked. She hoped her short, fur-lined brown leather jacket and deep brown virgin wool skirt, cut well above the knee, would get his attention more so than it had on the plane.

"You don't even know where I'm going yet, Georgina," Palio objected lightly.

"I took a chance that you were heading into Manhattan like the other 99 percent of the people here." She smiled innocently.

"Well, yes, as a matter of fact I am. And, yes, thank you. I will join you." He held open the door of the town car that had silently glided to a stop directly in front of them. The driver jumped out to escort the couple into the back seat. Georgina waved him away without a glance.

"Sorry I fell asleep during the flight," Palio apologized as he climbed into the back seat after Georgina. "I've been doing a lot of back and forth lately and sleep seems to be the one item that's been left off the agenda."

"Oh, please, do not worry. I completely understand. I had so much reading to do, I didn't even notice." Truth be told, Georgina enjoyed watching the rise and fall of Palio's strong chest as he slept. His black cashmere mock turtleneck sweater looked so soft and inviting that it took all she had not to lean over and nuzzle into him.

Palio was more than she had bargained for. She knew that she had a mission that needed to be accomplished to further her empire. What she didn't know was that she thoroughly enjoyed it. No time for daydreaming, she scolded herself.

"Thanks for understanding. So, tell me about you," Palio said.

"Oh, me? Not much to say really. I'm in New York on business. You know, typical meetings and too much eating." She didn't want Palio to know who she was quite yet. She wanted their official meeting to be a surprise. It would give her the advantage.

Little did he know, she had arranged to be seated next to Palio on the aircraft. She wanted him to want her, without knowing much about her at all. It was going exactly according to plan.

"Tell me about it," Palio patted his stomach. "I haven't had time to work out in ages. I'm starting to look like a canola."

Georgina flashed her sexiest smile. "Oh, I don't think so."

Palio fidgeted in his seat.

"So why are you in town?" she asked after a moment.

"I live here," Palio said without thinking. "Although, I'm spending a lot of time in San Francisco, too. So, I sort of reside in both places right now. Like you, business."

"Sounds exciting," Georgina followed, making a conscious attempt to steer the conversation.

"I guess so. It seems all I think about lately is when

I'm going to sleep or what airplane meal I'll get on the next flight: the rubber chicken or the Salisbury steak surprise?"

They both laughed knowingly.

"It isn't very appetizing, is it?" Georgina agreed. She never touched airplane food. The only reason she sipped the cheap champagne that they served on the plane was to bond with Palio. She never drank anything other than Dom Perigno. Veuve Cliquot if she was absolutely desperate and nothing else was available. But she couldn't let Palio know that her tastes were above the stratosphere. And she could afford them.

Georgina's little trip to New York was designed to increase her fortune to surpass that of Donald Trump, the real estate maven, and Michael Bloomberg, the new rich mayor who sponsored his own election. It was the Capriatti fortune that would get her there, and she wanted it. They were the golden family of New York City. With them in her pocket, she would be dining with the likes of the Tisch and Rockefeller families on a regular basis. She would own New York.

Palio and Georgina made idle chit chat as they crossed over the Triborough Bridge and into the city of bright lights.

"So where can I drop you?" Georgina asked nonchalantly. She wanted to know where he was staying so that she could have him watched.

"You can drop me at the park, if that's OK."

Georgina was surprised at the request. "You live in Central Park?"

Palio chuckled. "I'm meeting my father there."

The driver made a right turn off Fifth Avenue and

onto 59th street.

"I can get out here, thanks. I like the walk." He turned to face Georgina. "Thanks very much for the ride and good luck in New York."

Georgina was caught off guard. "Oh, yes, thank you. You too." He closed the door and waved before she had a chance to object.

Georgina was disappointed, the only consolation being that they never exchanged their full names. At least their official meeting would still be a surprise.

She settled back into her seat and closed her eyes. All she could see was Palio in his dreamy sweater.

CHAPTER XII – *FRUSTRATION*

≈

Chatham looked at the digital clock on the dashboard. She had twenty-five minutes to get groceries and be at the head of the carpool line at PJ's school. PJ got out at 2:52 p.m. Chatham never did understand the unusual quitting time; it had something to do with funding cutbacks, which meant that being on time for Madison and Camp's 3:00 p.m. departure was basically impossible. Chatham was always late to The Park School in the afternoons, but it wasn't so bad. She was sure to miss Tricky Vicky, which actually gave her more time in a roundabout way.

"Thank goodness for a spot," Chatham thought as she saw the back-up lights of a seventies pinto in the parking space directly in front of the grocery store. The old couple took their time backing up to the tune of one mile per hour, which gave a little white Honda time to zip into stand still directly opposite of Chatham. Apparently, he too was waiting for the spot. Chatham tried to catch the eye of the twenty-something driver to let him know that she had been waiting first. He was too busy rocking his head up and down to drug-induced music to notice her.

Chatham prepared for the showdown. Just as the old people pulled away, Chatham honked and turned in an attempt to beat the zipper car into her spot. But the kid was faster. He swerved around the old couple's car, which still had not completely left the scene, and snuck right into Chatham's space.

She rolled down the driver side window to object.

"Hey, that was my space, and you know it."

The headband clad hippy just looked at her. "Was."

"No, IS. Is my parking spot," Chatham corrected herself. The Gen X-er just laughed and headed off into the shopping market. Chatham leaned out of her window and yelled.

"Would you steal from your own mother?" She just said the first thing that came into her head.

He stopped, looked back and answered firmly. "She's the one that taught me." With a quick smile he turned on his heels and walked away proudly.

Chatham wanted to cry. What was this world coming to? Parents should have to apply to have children. But what could she do? Continue yelling at someone who was no longer there? Run after him and demand he move his car? Hit his car? Several unsavory options ran through her head, fantasies where she came out the winner for once. Instead, however, she decided to simply drive around until she found another spot. And she did. Chatham found a nice wide parking spot, unlike the compact-only spots that blanketed the parking lot closer to the store. She found a full-sized parking spot that fit her car perfectly, a whole quarter mile away.

"Well, at least I'll get some more exercise," she thought as she headed for the trek to the store.

She had fifteen minutes. She could do it. Chatham grabbed a shopping cart and made her way into the store at a clipped pace.

"If I do one quick sweep down each aisle, I won't forget anything," she told herself as she headed to the deli section first. There were only three people in line for fresh deli cold cuts. Chatham couldn't help but overhear two of the women talking. She recognized them as mothers of younger children at Madison and Camp's school.

"Did you hear that they're raising tuition another 15 percent this year?"

"What? You have got to be kidding. This is the fifth year running. It was supposed to end three years ago."

"I know; that's what I thought. But from what I hear it has to do with building an endowment. They want a big fat bank account to show the independent school circuit that they're a contender."

"So, when they say that they need the increase for supplies and salaries, that's just not true?"

"Exactly. It's all image. I know someone on the board."

Chatham let out a huge sigh. Tuition was about to hit $20,000 per child. She knew that her kids were happy at the school so she didn't want to take them out, but when Peter insisted on private school, he was supposed to stay alive to pay for it.

"What can I get for you, ma'am?" the deli counter person asked.

Chatham snapped back to the here and now. "Um, what do you have on sale?" she said almost automatically, wondering how she would keep up with the family expenses.

"Well, we have pimento loaf on sale today, $3.99 a pound."

What was pimento loaf anyway? Chatham wondered. Was that the stuff that looked like baloney with olives and dots of gooey red mush interspersed throughout? Well, her kids sort of liked baloney, and they might not notice the green and red gummy stuff. She could cover that with mayonnaise.

"Three pounds, please." I can freeze some, she reasoned as she accepted her wrapped package of lunchmeat and exited the deli.

The next stop was the peanut butter and jelly section. Her kids liked Jiff, the creamy kind. One of the grocery workers was organizing a shelf of Smuckers with stacks of boxes surrounding him, blocking her purchase.

"Excuse me," Chatham said as kindly as she could. "I just need to get a jar of peanut butter."

"You'll have to come back ma'am. The dolly is being used down in meatpacking and these boxes are too heavy to move. I strained my back and worker's comp tells me I can't lift anything." He looked to be about three hundred pounds.

Maybe if he exercised a little, Chatham thought. "Oh, that's OK, I can move them. I carry my children. It shouldn't be a problem."

"Well, ma'am, I have to tell you that I cannot be responsible for your actions, and I will not be held liable."

Since when did can stackers become legal experts? "I understand. I'm just in a hurry and don't have time to come back later."

Chatham reached for the first box. How hard could it be? She put both arms around the middle of the large cardboard container, spread her legs hip distance for support and lifted. It was heavier than she thought.

"Maybe I should put my back into it," she contemplated.

"I wouldn't recommend it." He pointed to the full

back brace that was part of his skeletal structure. Regardless, she was in a hurry and she needed to get some peanut butter. It was a staple in her house. And she didn't have time to come back.

Chatham wrapped her arms around the base, spread her legs like a body builder while imagining she was lifting the can stacker and relied on her back as much as possible. She felt something tweak. Put it down, she told herself, and lowered it as quickly as possible. Chatham leaned on the box, heaving with exhaustion.

"You were right," she said to the employee.

"People never listen," the worker commented and went back to placing the strawberry preserves in their coded space.

Chatham was about to leave when she noticed that the box she had been struggling with said Jiff on top. Duh. Chatham ripped open the container and lifted out a brand new jar of creamy Jiff peanut butter.

"Hey lady, you can't do that," the staff employee protested. "That's my box and it hasn't been labeled yet."

Chatham just looked at him. She wasn't about to give it back. "Was," she said with a smile. Chatham placed the plastic jar into her shopping cart and moved on.

"Chatham, yoo-hoo," came a voice out of nowhere. An instant surge of adrenaline, the stressful kind, shot through her, letting her know that this was a voice she wanted to avoid. Tricky Vicky, the vampire of time, was skittering toward her in bright orange sandals and matching skin-tight stretch Capri pants. "I can't believe I'm seeing you again. What a coincidence."

Chatham wondered whether she had planned it. And

how many times did she change outfits in a day? "Oh Vicky, twice in one day. How are you?"

"It's Victoria," she corrected, clearly annoyed. Just as quickly, she recovered. "I'm just dandy. Thank you for asking. But what I want to know is how are you?" She looked at Chatham with that false-concern-for-others look.

"Me? Oh, I'm fine. Thanks for asking." Chatham attempted a fake-private-school-mom smile.

Victoria made no apology for staring at Chatham's day glo outfit. She even seemed to approve.

"Why Chatham, you look so – trendy," Vicky said favorably. Standing together, the two of them looked like an ad for psychedelic cotton candy.

"Oh, this," Chatham said, again forgetting that she had it on. "New client." She couldn't think of any other excuse to explain why she would wear such a thing. If she told Victoria that she was exercising, it would immediately turn into a rumor that she was on the prowl for a new husband. That's how rumors worked when Victoria had anything to do with them. She operated by free association.

"So, are you exercising again? Trying to get in shape?" Victoria asked with a knowing smile.

"Me? No, who has time for that? I'm swamped with kids and work. That's all I have time for. But thanks for asking." She inserted a fake smile to convince the nosy rumor starter.

"It must be so hard for you, not having a husband anymore and all." Victoria subtly angled her left hand to remind Chatham of her five carat Tiffany diamond with matching one-carat diamonds on the sides.

Was she really going to tell Tricky Vicky that she

still cried at night? And that she worried about absolutely everything from money to her kids' emotional well-beings? That she is getting older every day and will probably never meet another man? Or that no man could ever replace her wonderful husband? Should she tell her all that?

"Oh, it's getting better, thanks. Kids seem settled again."

"Well, you're so strong, that's all. Me? I need my Herby to do absolutely everything for me. I am so helpless. Why I can't even re-arrange my Saran Wrap drawer." She fluttered her eyes with forced humility.

Chatham doubted that very much. Victoria was the volunteer vampire who's mission in life was to make sure she sucked the time out of every living creature; all in the interest of meeting her quotas and filling out her detailed spreadsheet that was practically tattooed to her body.

"I know how valuable your time is, Chatham, which is why I wouldn't ask you to do anything for the school that would be too consuming."

Leave it to Victoria to weave the conversation to her agenda. "What did you have in mind?" Chatham asked weakly, knowing that avoidance wouldn't work forever.

"Oh, it's tiny really. I was just hoping, because I have saved this special job for you, specially, that you would come up with the theme for this year's auction? You are so clever with those little diddy's you do. Why, isn't this one of yours?" Victoria lifted a box of Cheerios with a very irate looking psychotic child on the cover with a bubbled phrase coming out of his mouth: "They're mine," the child was telling the purchaser of the box. "And look, how lucky, it's the only one on sale in the entire aisle; ten boxes for a dollar. Well, I would buy it, of course, but I'm afraid it just might scare my little Gordo." She gently replaced the box.

Chatham loved that campaign, but how could she explain to Vicky that she recommended against the blood-sucking kids on the box? She wanted a table filled with brothers and sisters playfully wanting the cereal for themselves, even though most families did act closer to the current depiction. Oh well, she might have to stay away from cereal ads for a while.

"So," Vicky continued, "I was hoping that you could fulfill your volunteer obligation to the school by entertaining this teeny, tiny request just this once. OK, Chatham, my dear?"

It sounded easy enough. Come up with a theme and slogan. She could do that in about a minute. "Well Victoria. You know how much I do love helping. It's just that it's only me now. I don't have a Herby to help me. But I do want to contribute. So, sure, I can do that."

"You are such a doll. Thank you so much. OK, so you have a meeting tomorrow morning in the after-care room after drop-off. See you then." Tricky Vicky waved and was off in a flash, her neon orange sandals clicking their way to the exit.

"She didn't even have any groceries," Chatham said to the box of Cheerios. "I think she followed me." Chatham grabbed ten boxes of the cereal and continued on her way. The next aisle contained PJ's favorite food – crackers. Chatham proceeded to fill her cart with every box of wheat thins left on the shelf. Because she limited her grocery shopping to once every two weeks, other than milk and meat, Chatham knew she needed at least fourteen boxes of crackers for PJ. He ate a minimum of one box a day. She stepped up on the aluminum edging to obtain the last box of crackers from the very back of the shelf. When she climbed down she glanced over to see a woman gaping in horror at the overflowing cracker cart.

"How in god's name can you eat that stuff? Do you have any idea how many saturated fats are in a single serving of wheat thins? Not to mention the trans fats that they don't even tell you about? They actually build up the plaque in your heart and eventually kill you at a young age." This woman was raging. Typical Mill Valley organic. Purple flowing gauze skirt, braids, gunnysack slung over her shoulder and across her chest, wool socks, and classic Birkenstocks. Birkenstocks were so popular in Marin that the company was headquartered there.

She let out a defeated sigh. Chatham was getting tired of the interruptions. She was now going to be late to PJ's school which categorically meant chaos. "They're for my son."

"What are you trying to do, kill him?" she accused.

"They're low sodium," Chatham retorted as she turned her cart around and quickly exited the aisle. It wasn't any of that woman's business that wheat thins were one of the five foods that PJ actually ate. What did she want her to do, feed him wheat grass through an IV?

Chatham put the woman out of her mind and made her way to the cheese aisle. She went right to the spot where the fat-free Swiss was kept. Empty. It didn't even say fat free any more. The brand new sticky label said 2 percent.

Chatham began to panic. This was the only store in Marin that sold PJ's cheese. How else would he get his protein? She frantically looked at every label of Kraft single-sliced processed cheese and couldn't find one that said fat-free

Swiss.

"Looking for the fat free?" the store clerk asked as he loaded the lunchables onto the shelf next to her.

"Yes, it's been right here at the edge of the row for years. Are you out of it?"

"Discontinued."

"Discontinued? Why?"

"Didn't sell enough." He continued stacking.

"But I buy it every two weeks. In fact, I buy all of it every two weeks."

"I don't know what to tell you. Maybe if you had bought all of it every week they would have kept it." Now she was feeling guilty for not stuffing her refrigerator with more cheese than PJ could eat.

"Can I speak to the manager?" Chatham asked, almost desperate.

"Wouldn't do you any good. He has nothing to do with it. It's the numbers. You know, the bar codes tell all."

Chatham's shoulders sunk. Where would she find the cheese?

"You could write a letter to corporate. They're in the Midwest somewhere. Might take a while, and there are no guarantees they'll answer you, but it's worth a try."

"Thanks," Chatham said, totally defeated as she wandered aimlessly toward the check-out counter.

"Maybe I can approach Kraft with a new ad slogan

and get a year's worth of PJ's cheese in exchange," she said to herself as she moved her cart down the aisle. "In fact, they don't even have a tag line. All they have is a logo."

Chatham's mind started to turn with variations on a new slogan. Kraft: where health and food combine. Kraft: food creations for your health. Kraft: krappy food for everyone. Totally preoccupied, she stepped into the ten-items-or-less line and began unpacking her load.

"I'm sorry, ma'am. You can't put your items here," the snippy rule-following clerk insisted. "This is only for ten items or less, see?" He pointed to the sign directly above him. "See the sign? It says ten or less, not ten or more." He was not about to let her through.

Chatham loaded her cart back up without speaking and moved toward the one line that was open without an express sign of some sort looming overhead. Just as she was about to enter the aisle, Gen-X knocked the edge of her cart with his hip and slipped in right in front of her with his three cases of beer and barrel of twisted red licorice.

He looked back and smiled. Chatham was too tired to object.

"I can't believe what he did to you," a soft, scratchy voice said as Chatham stepped up in line to pay for her groceries. Chatham looked up to see the check-out attendant batting his eyes demurely. "What is this world coming to?"

Chatham looked a little more closely. Was it a he? Or a she? It sounded like a cross between a woman and a man. He had big, rough hands, hairy arms, an auburn wig, and perfectly shaped breasts. Lots of make-up and overly feminine behavior. Chatham looked closer to see if she could see an Adam's apple bobbing up and down in his throat while he spoke.

"Well, never you mind." He looked up out of the corner of his eyes. "I single bagged him. They'll probably break." He leaned forward to make sure no one heard.

"Uh, gee, thanks. That was nice of you." Chatham swiped her ATM card and pressed in her secret code. Cash back? She pressed no. She knew the account was low.

"You have a buy one, get one free on the wheat thins today. And you earned 500 airline miles. Not such a bad day after all."

She noticed his perfectly manicured pink fingernails as he handed Chatham her receipt. "Thank you for shopping Safeway and have a nice day." He gave her a genuine smile.

Chatham was sure it was a man acting as a woman, but she didn't want to continue to stare.

"Thanks, you too." She looked at his nametag. Tina.

Chatham exited the store parking lot and shifted into Mario Andredi mode as she drove to PJ's school. As she expected, PJ was the last one waiting. He was distraught.

"Mommy, I not can find you," he said, tears forming in his very emotional eyes.

"Oh, honey. I'm so sorry. Mommy was late. But here I am, and I am so happy to see you."

"I am happy to see you, Mommy," PJ responded with an instant smile. "Why did you pick me up?"

"PJ, I always pick you up. You know that."

"I waited for you."

"I know. I'm very sorry PJ. I will try not to do that

again."

"You don't do that ever again, Mommy." He shook his finger at Chatham with mock scolding. Her son liked to control the situation.

"OK, honey"

"Mommy? No speech today." PJ was taking his authority in his own preferred direction. She could almost see the wheels turning in his brain. If Mommy owes me for being late, then I can get out of going to speech lessons where I have to work hard. "I will go home and watch a movie." He was very sure about his decision.

"No speech today. You're right. But first homework, then reading, then a movie, OK?"

"OK, Mommy, I will." He seemed satisfied with the plan. P.J. settled back in his seat and turned to look out of the window. Chatham was sure he was trying to memorize every landmark in his little world.

Chatham arrived at The Park School several minutes after carpool was over.. Now that Madison was in seventh grade, she tended to walk to the front of the school and hang out with the kids whose parents were late. That was exactly where she was waiting when Chatham arrived. Chatham glided to a stop in front of the school and rolled down the passenger window.

"Hi Maddy," she called. Her daughter and a friend were deep into flirting with a group of boys that were awaiting their chauffeurs.

Maddy turned toward the car and popped her eyes open wide. "Go away," she mouthed and turned back to her friends.

"Maddy, honey. It's time to go," Chatham urged in

as gentle a tone as possible. She put the car in park and turned off the engine. "Could you go get Camp out of aftercare?"

Maddy just ignored her mother. Was this a mother's reward once her children reached pre-puberty?

"See you tomorrow," Madison said to the group, a miss popular smile accompanying her exit. She loaded her backpack into the car and slipped in to the front passenger seat.

"Drive please," she said urgently under her breath to her mother.

"Drive? We have to get Camp."

"Mom, please! I am just going to die," she said sinking out of sight of passersby.

Chatham shifted the car into drive, made a circle around the parking lot, and stopped in front of the gym where aftercare was housed. She turned to face her daughter.

"Madison, I have had a tough day. And you were disrespectful when I pulled up in front of the school."

"I think he's going to ask me," Madison squealed, unable to contain her excitement.

"Ask you? Where? Who? What are you talking about?"

"I think Dane is going to ask me to the upper-division dance."

"Oh, is that all," Chatham said. "I thought you were in trouble or something. You sounded terrified."

"Oh Mom, you know I get A's. Can you believe it? Dane. I can't wait to tell Julia. She's just going to die."

"Well, before you do that, could you use a different

word and can you please run in and get Camp?"

"Oh, sorry Mom. I miss dad, too. But Dane. Oh my god!" Madison exited the car on a cloud and headed to aftercare to retrieve her brother.

Chatham remembered that feeling. That all-consuming emotion when you know someone likes you. It reminded her of the time she first saw Peter on campus at USC. He didn't even know she existed. Well, he did, but she didn't know he did. It was like it was yesterday. She was leaning against a large boulder on the student lawn, eating a deli sandwich when she accidentally knocked over her soda. She had looked up to search for a garbage can just as he walked across the lawn in perfect view. He looked like a GQ model gliding across the grass in his SC sweats and Rugby shirt. She had thought he looked in her direction. She had just about died right then and there.

"Hi Mom," Camp said as he threw his backpack into the car and climbed in. Chatham looked at Madison; she was still beaming.

"Here." Camp handed her an envelope with Mrs. Ross written on the front in calligraphy.

"Who's this from? Your teacher?"

"No. The neon lady gave it to me."

Chatham opened the envelope.

Dear Chatham, Thank you so much for agreeing to Chair this year's auction. We can't wait to hear your theme. The aftercare room has been reserved for you and your committee for tomorrow morning after drop-off. Please stop by the market and pick up donuts, coffee, and muffins so that you can kick off your first meeting in the right direction. OK, that's it for now. Thanks again.

Victoria.

"Chair? I never said I'd chair anything! I just agreed that I'd come up with the theme. I have no time for this. I should have known. Tricky Vicky is at it again."

"Mom, calm down. What are you talking about, and who is Tricky Vicky?"

Chatham would have to do something about this, but not now. She filed the problem away in her mental to-do list and attempted to put on a positive front.

"Never mind, honey. It's nothing. So Camp, how was school?"

"It was cool."

Cool? Was this a new word for Camp? "Oh, so – what made it so cool today?" She was curious where the new attitude came from.

"Well, Alex brought a snake to class. A giant albino python. Ten-feet long. We watched it squeeze a mouse to death. Cool. Totally."

Do all well-adjusted six-year-old boys talk like this? Chatham couldn't remember.

Camp reached for his Game Boy, which he had stored in the seat pocket in front of him. Thank goodness, Chatham thought. Back to his normal self.

Madison leaned over to turn on *Alice* radio as Chatham exited the school grounds. At least she had a handle on her children. She hoped.

CHAPTER XIII – *PALIO'S FAMILY*

≈

Palio was meeting his father at the little pond in Central Park where people sailed remote control boats. He walked along the path that led to the pond, reflecting on his new acquaintance. She was gorgeous; there was no doubt about that. But there was something about her, something hazardous. He couldn't quite put his finger on it. In fact, he couldn't even put his finger on her name. Georgina, wasn't it? Or maybe it was Grace?

"There I go again, not getting names," Palio said out loud to himself as he quickened his pace.

A homeless man sitting on a bench and sipping beer out of a paper bag heard him.

"I know whatcha mean, pal. I can't remember much of anything no more. Makes life kind of easy when you think about it."

Palio pulled a ten-dollar bill out of his wallet and handed it to the bum.

"Tell me about it. I can't even remember the time zones."

They both smiled knowingly, and Palio hurried on his way.

"There you are, son!" his father greeted him with a warm smile and a hug. "I've got so much to tell you."

"Hi, Papa. It's good to see you."

Palio knew his father was eager to show him the newest designs. It will be our biggest seller," he had told Palio last week over dinner.

Mr. Capriatti liked to take part in every new design

that the family miniature-boat company produced. It was his hobby, his passion, his love. It was a tiny operation that Mr. Capriatti ran personally. Small but mighty. The Capriatti Sailing Company created the coolest, sleekest, fastest miniature sailboats ever made. Mr. Capriatti was most excited about his new aerodynamic treasure.

Palio watched his father as he breathed on the shellacked teak siding, buffing it with a special rabbit hair cloth he created, a strong revenue producer already. He carefully unrolled the new miniature spinnaker sail, a giant blue jellybean prominently displayed. Palio noticed the name "Lucia" painted on the stern. Mother would be pleased.

"Hey Papa, looks like another winner," Palio said, his hand resting affectionately on his father's shoulder. Mr. Capriatti smiled as he gingerly set his pride and joy into the edge of the pond.

"Here, hold the remote, but don't turn it on yet. I just want to look at her." The soft pink and orange sunset created a picture perfect postcard of the sleek craft. His dad was in his glory.

But Palio was sure his dad didn't just want to show him his newest creation. No, Mr. Capriatti definitely had something on his mind. He had told Palio over the phone that he had just finished reading the *Da Vinci Code*, a novel about a secret religious society whose mission in life was to protect the Holy Grail. Leonardo Da Vinci was a purported member and, because the Capriatti family was also Italian and Catholic, Palio's dad was obsessed with the work of the artist. He was currently in negotiation with the Louvre to purchase the *Madonna on The Rocks* painting, a key focus in the book.

"So Dad, what's up?" Palio asked hoping to get to the point of the visit. He was starving and wanted to head to Monte's down in Greenwich Village. Best Italian food in New York City, and the restaurant of his father's best friend. It was in a basement near NYU. The food surpassed anything found in Little Italy.

"Do you remember the painting? The Holy Madonna that I am talking to the Louvre about?" He switched on the remote control and watched with satisfaction as his Lucia glided gracefully across the pond, gathering speed as the spinnaker filled with wind. She looked almost regal.

"Dad, you can't be serious."

"It would mean so much to your mother, god rest her soul," his father said, making the sign of the cross.

Palio bowed his head out of respect.

"Palio my boy, I am so pleased with how you have agreed to help me with the health club chain. You did so much good with the jellybean operation, and I know you will turn our little line of clubs into something fabulous. I have faith in you!"

"Thanks, Pop. The new business is different, but interesting to say the least." The intriguing girl from earlier that afternoon popped into his head.

"All those beautiful bodies everywhere. Maybe one will catch your eye, eh?" his father added subtly while pretending to fix a glitch in the remote.

Palio finally tuned in. "Pop, please. I am not interested in dating a greased-up, buffed-up, pumped-up Amazon woman. Nothing personal. Just not my type."

"Palio, Palio. You never know. You never know, my boy."

Palio had to agree, albeit reluctantly. That scattered woman did walk in off the street. Stranger things have happened. But that was the San Francisco location. He was headquartered in New York. I mean really, how often would he get out there anyway? And once she realized that she had walked into a place filled with steroid pumping purists, she'd probably never come back again. He didn't even ask her name. . .

"Palio, didn't you hear a word I said?"

"Huh, what? Oh, sorry Pop, my mind was somewhere else."

"Somewhere worth telling me about?" he asked with a wink.

"No, just thinking about business – how to grow the club line."

"Oh, good. Always planning you are. I love your competitive spirit. Speaking of which…"

"Huh? Wait. Pop, what are you up to?"

"Well, my boy. Seeing as you are such an able-bodied young man and have such a knack for growth and persuasion, I had a little favor to ask you."

Palio wasn't sure he liked the sound of that. "Look Pop, I'm on the red-eye back to the West coast tonight. I've got to visit the San Francisco location one more time before I sign off on management, and I'm starving. Can't it wait?"

"Of course, of course. Let's go to dinner. It's settled then," Mr. Capriatti concluded as he scooped his treasure out of the pond and kissed it lovingly. "My Lucia, you will win the trophy for me this weekend. You are a lucky girl you are." He gently placed her inside the custom teak box lined with sleek black velvet.

Palio watched him close the lid with care and lock it. "Dad, why do you lock the box? I mean who's going to take it?"

"You never know, my boy. They're animals these mini-sailboat racers. The kids are the worst. See that little freckled faced brat over there?" he motioned with his chin.

"Looks harmless," Palio responded.

"Harmless, my ass. Stole the rudder off the number one seeded boat at the championship last year and put it on his own boat . . . *The Dinker*. He thinks I don't know how he watches me. He is worried about my Lucia. That he is."

Palio noticed that the kid kept looking at his father out of the corner of his eye. He did seem a bit intense. Sure enough, the kid was making his way over to the bench where Palio and his dad were packing up.

"Catch ya Saturday, *Pop*," the little monster squawked as he walked by, his eyes zeroing in on the lock. "Yeah, you wish," Mr. Capriatti sniffed back.

Palio couldn't believe what he was hearing. "For god's sake, Pop, he can't be more than ten."

"Don't let 'em fool you. He's a wolf in a boy's body jacket. He'll do anything to win; just you wait and see. I call 'em as I see 'em."

The Capriatti men finished gathering their things.

"So make yourself useful." Mr. Capriatti elbowed his son in a playful manner. "Hail us a taxi already."

They walked toward the road that ran through the park, Palio holding his hand up for a taxi with its rooftop light still on. A cabbie came out of nowhere and screeched to a halt in front of the duo.

"Where ya goin', pal?" the Brooklyn driver asked, leaning out of the window. The smell of cigarettes was heavy on his breath.

"Monte's. Bleeker and Third," Palio replied as they climbed into the back of the cab and settled in for the ride to the Village. There was a sign on the back of the driver's seat that stated in bold red letters: IF YOU ARE A CASTING AGENT, PRODUCER OR DIRECTOR, PLEASE TAKE ONE. Palio lifted the black and white sheet of paper out of the plastic holder. It was a full headshot of the driver, Brad Waynewright. His acting resume was attached. He'd been an extra in an Indie flick and had made an appearance in a shampoo commercial. No lines. Palio noticed that the guy was from Texas. Another wannabe New York actor.

"Heck, why not," Palio said under his breath as he replaced the picture in its bin. "And driver?" Palio directed up front. "I'm starving. My bet is that you can get us there in a New York minute."

"Not a problem, pal," the driver committed in a perfect Brooklyn accent, slamming his foot on the gas pedal and screeching his way toward the park exit. "Getcha there in no time. No time at all."

Palio thought he sounded authentic. Like a true actor.

"So what exactly is settled Pop?" Palio asked. He wanted to get back to this so-called favor his father needed. "You haven't even told me what the favor is," he said, looking for a seat belt that didn't exist.

The driver alternated between flooring the gas and

jamming the breaks as he navigated his way down congested Fifth Avenue. It was enough to make anyone but a real New Yorker sick in ten seconds.

"Not to worry. It's just a little negotiation on my behalf. For the dear sweet Madonna painting your mother would want me to have."

"Dad, you've got to be kidding. The Louvre will never give that up."

"They won't, but the owner may," he said with a sly smile.

"And who might this owner be?" Palio was afraid to know.

"From what I have been told. She's a nice young woman about your age. Heir to an olive oil empire. Pure Italian. She sounds lovely," he said with a quick wink. Mr. Capriatti was lost in his memories.

"Pop. Pop! Listen. You have got to stop trying to get me married. I am not interested. Not now. Not ever. OK?"

"Palio, Palio, my boy. Look at all the great years your mother and I had together, god rest her soul." The sign of the cross again. "I loved her as god loves his church. I did, and I still do." Mr. Capriatti looked off in the distance, a tear welling. "But she is with Jesus now, and I am still here. So I will do good things for her, for her memory.

"Look, if I ever meet someone as wonderful as Mama I would jump at the chance, OK? But understand. She doesn't exist." Palio turned away, resigning himself to the fact that no woman would ever be as wonderful as his own mother. Not that he would want to marry his mother or anything, but he knew in his heart that the woman for him would have to have some of the same qualities.

Palio's mother was funny, innocent, happy, always singing-a true lover of life. To her, the bottle was not just half full, it was overflowing. She found joy in living, every step of the way. Palio remembered how she would be in the kitchen for hours, the whiff of cookies or cakes sailing up to his room making it hard to study. She would knock on his door and offer him a slice of warm blueberry bread or an apple popover, fresh out of the oven. And always with a cup of warm milk.

Mrs. Capriatti also loved to make up fun little rhymes and verses, keeping the men of the household on their toes. If Palio forgot to clean up his room he would find a note on his pillow that night: *When life is cluttered, it's hard to find, where on earth to keep your mind.* Palio would laugh at the thought of losing his mind in one of his many piles. He would stay up until his room was spic and span.

"OK, so it's settled then. I will not push you to marry, and you will do me this small favor. I have invited her to meet with you and she has agreed to consider my love for the Madonna." He gave Palio an innocent smile.

"How did you manage that? She lives in Italy."

"I can be very convincing when I want to. Besides, she said she was coming to town for a meeting with the MET, and I simply invited her to squeeze you in. And, if you like her and all goes well, you can invite her to my little boat race this weekend. If all goes well."

"Dad, you're impossible," Palio sighed, leaning over to kiss his father on the forehead.

"Oh, and I asked Maria if she would help you

should you need it. It's up to you, of course." His father fiddled with something in his coat pocket that wasn't there.

"Maria? I haven't seen her in years. I don't know why you think I might need her help anyway."

"She's a loyal girl, Palio. Word has it, she still has a thing for you. Not that it's any of my business, not at all. Your love life is your own concern." He leaned in close to Palio and lowered his voice. "She's moved up in the world, you know." Palio's father shifted back in his seat, raising his voice to its normal decibel. "She only wants to help, what can I say?" he shrugged.

Palio wasn't sure what to make of his father's last comment, but before he could ask for an explanation, the driver pulled up to the curb in front of Monte's.

"Nice accent," Palio complimented as he handed the driver an extra twenty.

"Hell, I gotta do whatever the hell I can in this god-forsaken place." The authentic Texan in him was so strong that Palio thought he might find a gun rack somewhere in the vehicle. "Thanks for the tip, pal," he said, turning his Brooklyn accent back on. He handed Palio a resume. "Keep it, ya neva know."

Palio watched the cabbie screech away to the next fare, a cowboy hat finding its way firmly onto his head.

≈

Father and son were greeted by Monte himself with hugs and kisses. Entering the threshold of the classic Italian eatery was like going back to Italy at its finest. Real pictures of Florence, Rome, and Venice filled the walls. Waiters shouted Italian across the restaurant at the cook, the bus boys, and each other. The tables were crammed together family style, which no one seemed to mind. It was like coming home.

"Roberto, Palio. Buena Sera. It's been too long," Monte effused with true loyalty and admiration.

"My friend," Roberto said kissing Monte on both cheeks. "It's only been a week, but I agree, it seems like a long time."

"And Palio my boy, what a lady killer you are now. When are you getting married, eh?" he asked as though programmed by Palio's father.

"It's not on the forefront of my mind, but I'm sure you'll know as soon as I do. Right, Pop?" Palio gave his dad the eye. What is it with Italian men? All they talk about is having a good woman around.

"Nothing like a good woman to keep you honest, eh Palio my boy?" Monte winked. "I have a great table for you this evening." He looked up and snapped his fingers twice. "Leo, get my friends a bottle of Val Pollicelli."

To an outsider, it looked as though Italy had come to Greenwich Village.

CHAPTER XIV – *CHATHAM & TRIP*

≈

Chatham needed to unwind. It had been an eventful day. Thank goodness this was the one day of the week when her children did not have an activity. The normal routine was to arrive home after 7:00 p.m. Camp was training to receive his black belt in Tae Kwon Do, which meant three-hour sessions four days a week. Madison's marathon ballet classes never ended before the dinner hour and PJ's speech lessons were recently increased to one and one half hours, four days a week due to the Fast Forward program that promised to help him process information more efficiently. Chatham spent most afternoons driving and waiting. She had her cell phone, a digital tape recorder, and a stack of advertising books by her side to keep her company during the waiting time. But today it was home directly after school.

As soon as they arrived, the children played with Trip's new creature, the skoonard thing that he caged in the family room. He left a note that said he promised to pick it up tonight after the kids had seen it. They loved it. Chatham let them play with it for an hour and then moved into Ross-routine mode.

The children had just finished dinner; they'd each taken a shower and were in their pajamas. Madison was in her room doing homework to the music of Pink. Camp was at the kitchen counter eating a bowl of mint chip ice cream and finishing his homework challenge pack and PJ was in the old au pair room, watching a Barney video. She decided it was OK to take a bath. If they needed anything, they could come in and ask her.

"I'll be in my bathroom if anyone needs me," Chatham announced. A round of OKs followed her as she entered her room and closed the bathroom door. She turned on the hot water, added a packet of de-stress bath salts, and settled in. Simple contact with warmth did wonders for her mood. There was some truth to the Calgon, "take me away" slogan. She would have to find a bath company to pitch. She could use more of this kind of life. Chatham settled into the tub, the treated water melting her cares away.

How nice it was to have no foreigners living with them in their home anymore, Chatham reflected. She could run around naked if she wanted to like she used to do when it was just her and Peter and the babies. No risk of running into some nineteen-year-old whack job about to get off work. Or the ones who sit in their room and never leave. She wasn't sure which was worse.

Chatham was convinced she was a failure at hired help. After Peter died, she had to hire someone to help with the kids since she was working full-time and all. She remembered the disaster all too well.

"So, Mrs. Ross," the agency interviewer had said peeking over her glasses at Chatham and her three children. A look of disapproval plastered on her judgmental face. "You are a single mother then?"

"Why yes, I am. My husband died suddenly."

"I see," the woman commented as though they just would not live up to her expectations. "Do you own your home Mrs. Ross?"

"Yes, yes I do. Is that a problem?" Chatham wasn't sure what this woman wanted to hear.

"That's fine," she sniffed as though there was an offensive smell in the air. "We are an upscale agency, Mrs. Ross, and we are quite careful as to whom we send our lovely au pairs. You see they come from stellar families in Europe, and we want them to have a similar experience while they are in the United States for their year abroad. The host family is essentially their family away from home."

"Oh yes, we are a very close family," Chatham found herself explaining. "We will most assuredly make her feel right at home with us." She forced a smile.

"And where will the au pair sleep?" the woman requested, wiping what appeared to be a dog hair from the bottom of her long skirt. She took some notes on her clipboard.

Chatham took the agency representative up to the extra bedroom they had set up. It had a double bed with a Laura Ashley comforter. There was a television set that had cable with 110 channels. The only one in the house, actually. The Ross family only watched videos. Chatham had decorated the room with posters of the United States and the San Francisco bay area in particular. She even put together a basket with maps, guidebooks, personal sundries, and snacks to make the au pair feel welcome.

"Mmm, hmm," the rigid representative mumbled as she scanned the room and fiddled with the basket. "I see there is no attached bathroom. Will she be sharing one with the children then?" a look of disapproval prevalent.

"Oh no, of course not," Chatham quickly recovered. "She can have the bathroom across the hall. The children still use ours, I mean mine, for the most part." Chatham couldn't get used to the singular. "They may go in to get a drink of water now and then, but she'll have complete privacy. I guarantee it."

"See that a lock is put on the door. We don't want the little ones bothering her when she is off duty."

"Absolutely. I'll see to it right away." Chatham wondered whether she was the one working for the agency.

By the grace of god, the Ross family was accepted and entered into the system. That is after Chatham paid a deposit of $4,000, only partially refundable if things didn't work out in the first thirty days.

The process provided two applications at a time. The agency had pre-selected the au pairs based on *matching* criteria.

The first application was from a Swedish girl who lived outside Stockholm. Her application said that she wanted to become a teacher and that a year living abroad with a host family would help immerse her in the world of children. Cultural cross over was an excellent experience for future teachers of Sweden. She also had a younger sister and several cousins who she babysat on a regular basis.

The many pictures she sent were very cute, and she looked happy. Chatham took the next step in the process and called to have the mandatory phone interview. As soon as Chatham introduced herself, the ax fell. The girl had already matched. Well that was fast, Chatham thought. Less than twenty-four hours.

It didn't take long for Chatham to learn that the same applications were given to East Coast families as well. So if the girls were called by a New York family and a California family, they could have their choice.

The second application was a girl from France. That could be good since Madison and Camp were taking French at their school, she had thought. Maybe she could teach them something. Chatham had called right away.

"Bonjour," came the voice from the other end of the international line.

"Bonjour, je ne parle pas bien votre langue." That was about all Chatham knew in French, and she wasn't sure she even said it correctly. "Parlez vous Englais?"

"Yes, I speak a little English," said the female voice.

" Hello, my name is Chatham Ross, and I am a host mother from the United States. We live in California. Is Amalie there?"

"Ahh, Amalie. No, she is not here. She is on holiday."

"Oh, that's nice. When will she be back?" Chatham asked, expecting it to be any time.

"In a month, yes?"

"A month?" Chatham was quite surprised. She looked again at the application. It said that the girl could start anytime. "Do you have a telephone number where I can call her?"

"Yes, she is in the Reunion Islands. I will give it to you."

Chatham thanked the woman and proceeded to dial international once again. It was next to impossible to get through, with so many international codes and all. She enlisted the assistance of the overseas operator and after about ten minutes, she heard the phone ring.

"Bonjour," came a young voice from very far away.

"Bonjour, is this Amalie?"

"Yes, it is. Hello."

"Hello, Amalie. My name is Chatham Ross, and I am a host mother from California."

"Yes, hello. Nice to meet you. What part of California are you from?"

"San Francisco. Marin County, actually. It's over the Golden Gate Bridge and only a few minutes from the city."

"Oh, I like San Francisco," she said, a bit more enthused.

"How many children do you have?" she asked next, not wasting any time.

"I have three children, and I am a single mom." Chatham thought she would spring the single parent thing on her as quickly as possible.

"Oh," Amalie said, with less enthusiasm this time. "You are alone and have three children. That's a lot, oui?"

"Well actually, it's kind of like a team. At least that's how we like to think of it." Chatham spent the next twenty minutes selling the au pair on the pluses of being part of the Ross family, how she wouldn't have to work the entire 45 hours a week and that she would almost always have weekends off.

"And where will I sleep?" the girl asked. That was critical. Chatham described the layout of the entire home, room by room.

"And your room has a lovely bed and chair and television. There's a bathroom across the hall. You're across the hall from the boy's room."

"The guest room sounds nicer with the sleigh bed

and the attached bathroom. I would rather have that room." Chatham was beginning to think she was interviewing for a job and not the other way around. They talked about the car that Chatham would provide for Amalie for work and personal excursions, and Amalie's inability to cook and clean. Vacation time was a focal point of the conversation.

"I will need to have two weeks off for Christmas because I want to travel with my boyfriend. And I will have to leave three weeks early, before the year is up because I want to start at the University. Maybe I can also have another week in March so that we can all have a break from each other." The agency guidelines were pretty clear. Two weeks off, paid, at a mutually convenient time and preferably in pieces. A full year commitment was part of the agreement.

"Oh, that would be fine," Chatham found herself saying, not really thinking about the inconvenience.

Kids laundry was OK with Frenchie, if she had to, but she was hoping that Chatham had a housekeeper to do that.

"And when can you start Amalie?" Chatham asked, her heart not quite in it. In fact, Chatham realized that the girl hadn't asked anything about the children, not even their names.

"In two months, I think. I want to finish my holiday, and then I want to go back to France for a month to say goodbye to all of my friends that I will not see for a whole year. And my boyfriend, too, who will come to visit. He can visit, oui?"

Once Chatham heard the start date she finally had an excuse to get off the telephone. It just wouldn't work.

Chatham needed someone yesterday.

A month later after they hired a girl from Australia, Chatham got the phone bill. Seven-hundred dollars for the call with the French princess. She went to the large map in her son's room. Where the heck was Reunion Island? She looked for twenty minutes before she found it off the coast of Madagascar near Africa! And she didn't even hire her. This au pair stuff was expensive.

The girl from Australia was a disaster from the start. Her application listed all the right things: loves kids, enjoys cooking, has a big extended family. The pictures were a bit hazy though, and the phone interview was a bit odd.

"Allo?"

"Hello, is this Marcia?"

"Yeah, it's Marcia. Who's asking?"

"Oh hi. This is Chatham Ross from the United States. I'm a host mom from San Francisco." Chatham heard yelling in the background.

"Put a sock in it!" The voice on the other end had screamed at some savory character in the background. "OK, I'm back. So tell me about your three little koalas." Well that sounded promising. Chatham decided that the third time had to be a charm, and so she hired her.

It had started out OK. A family trip to the library on day one. Marcia opened up a library card and checked out forty books. A little excessive, but she professed to be a voracious reader. The next day Chatham had suggested that Marcia and Madison walk to the mall together; it was only twenty minutes from the house. They were back in less than an hour, and Madison was crying hysterically.

"What happened, honey?" Chatham had asked,

concerned with her daughter's distraught state.

"Marcia bought me a CD, but she said I didn't say thank you. So she took it back and told the counter girl what a disrespectful child I was and gave it back to her. Mommy, I did say thank you." Oh boy, a severe disciplinarian. Chatham was having doubts.

Less than a week later Chatham had come home from work one evening to find her neighbor sitting at the kitchen table.

"Tanya, what are you doing here?" Chatham asked, surprised at the unannounced visit.

"Well, your nanny, au pair, whatever she is, asked me if I could watch the children for a few minutes and that she'd be right back. I said sure, for a few minutes. I looked out of your window and saw her running out of the garage with a suitcase and into a taxi. I opened the door in time to hear her say, San Francisco Airport please."

The agency claimed that single parents were always high risk.

That was two years ago, after which Chatham decided she had to make a change before her children were emotionally scarred for life. Chatham left her successful position at Gorman and Strausberg to form her own small advertising business, allowing for total and complete flexibility and total and complete stress.

Her husband's life insurance policy combined with her earnings enabled the family to stay in their home and keep the children in their schools and activities, but not for long. Peter did come from a well-to-do family, but she was told that his money was tied up in the family estate. Chatham had to work furiously to keep their life at status quo.

On the emotional side, she was grateful for Peter's best friend Trip. Chatham felt so safe with him around, and the kids adored him. He was always bringing over some bizarre creature from another time zone to entertain the family. And he was so dependable, always showing up just when she needed him. Chatham had no idea how Trip felt about her. He was simply her husband's best friend and when Trip died, that friendship rolled right over to the family.

"Mom! Mom! Come quick!" Camp was screaming at the top of his lungs.

Chatham sprung up out of the tub, still covered in suds, and grabbed her robe that was draped over the edge. She raced out of the bathroom at superhero speed.

"Camp? What is it? Camp, where are you?"

"Mom, in here. Hurry!"

Chatham ran into the family room. The half-skunk, half-leopard creature had gotten out of its cage and into Fluff's dog food. It was shoveling the food in like a glutton from the renaissance. Fluff barked at the animal, who just looked up at the Ross family dog and returned to its feast.

Chatham approached the creature gingerly. "Shoo," she said, swooshing her hand through the air to emphasize the command. "Go away, you... you... what are you anyway?"

The amalgamation looked up at her and bared its long yellow fanged teeth. It was not about to comply when it had a ten-course meal to indulge in. Chatham told herself to stay calm. Didn't Trip say it didn't have its teeth yet? She motioned to Camp.

"Get a paper bag, one of the big grocery ones."

Camp climbed up on the kitchen stool and opened the long narrow cabinet above the sub zero refrigerator where they kept paper grocery bags.

"I'll just put the bag over it and put it back in its cage, OK?" She was talking more to herself as a calming measure. She took the bag from Camp and slowly approached the gorging monster. She looked around slowly. Madison and PJ had joined the commotion, albeit from high up on the kitchen counter.

"What are you doing, Mommy?" PJ asked, apparently fascinated at his mom's tip toeing dance. "I want to dance." He jumped off of the counter and started dancing around like a ballerina. "Madison, you do it," he called to his sister who taught him all he knew about dancing.

The skoonard caught site of the bag and the pair of twinkle toes and freaked out. It lifted its tail to reveal its rear end and sent a loud baffooning gaseous noise into the room.

"Oh my god!" Madison squealed. "It's a skunk!"

Fluff rolled around on the floor trying to paw the scent out of his nose. He was almost convulsing. All three children ran upstairs and locked themselves into the bathroom. That left Chatham to corner and capture the beast. She grabbed a giant plastic chip bag clip from the snack drawer and put it on her nose to reduce the intoxicating smell. She also reached into the kitchen closet for the broom to use as a weapon if necessary. That animal had long teeth.

"Trip, where the hell are you?" she asked in a

pinched, nasal voice as she crept around the corner looking for the AWOL creature. "You said it wasn't a skunk." Just then she heard a key turning in the front door and in walked Trip.

"Woah, what did you guys do in here?" he exclaimed, holding his nose as tightly as possible. He took one look at Chatham and started to laugh. Her robe was half open; she had suds all over her hair and a giant potato chip clip on her nose.

"Is the broom a prop?" he asked.

"Trip, what the hell did you bring over here? I told you it sprayed. Now we can't even find it."

"Did it eat the dog food?" he asked suddenly alarmed.

"Yes, it did. You told me it ate dog food."

"*All* of it?" he asked, beginning to look pale.

"I don't know. It got out and was eating the dog food. I was taking a bath as you can probably tell." She walked over to Fluff's bowl and looked down. "Yep, he ate all of it."

"That's just great," Trip said, with a worried expression.

"Trip, what the hell are you talking about? What is it, a Gremlin or something? Next thing you're going to tell me its name is Mogwey, and I shouldn't feed it after midnight. Trip, the smell is unbearable!"

"OK, Chat. Calm down. There is a solution. Look, it does eat dog food, but it's not supposed to eat more than about five pieces a day. If it overeats, it builds up toxins in its system and has to release it. Any act of stress will do that and, well, you get a foul smell."

"Oh well, you didn't tell me all that when you abandoned him."

"Chat, come on. As I said, there is a solution. If you feed him a pill that the vet gives cats for bad breath, then it negates the toxins, and it emits kind of like a deodorizer spray from its mouth. I know, it sounds totally bizarre."

Chatham was not sympathetic.

"So, do you have any cat breath pills?" he asked sheepishly.

"No, Trip. I don't have cat breath pills. Probably because I don't have a cat. You, on the other hand, have had several cats. Weird cats, cats with polkadots, cats with wings, cats with beaks. Where the hell do you find these bizarre monsters?" Her patience was basically gone.

"OK, I think I might have some in the van. I'll be right back." Trip ran out the front door and left it open.

Exhausted, Chatham plopped down on the family room couch. Out of the corner of her eye, she saw the skoonard leap out from inside the piano, run down the entry steps, and dash out the front door. She heard Trip in the distance.

"There you are silly boy. Here, have a breath mint."

Within five minutes, Trip was walking back into the house with the creature in his arms.

"Oh my god, Trip. No. Not again."

The animal couldn't wait. He let out a very loud burp that she could almost see. Chatham wanted to cry. They would have to stay in a hotel.

"You can take the nose ring off now," Trip said as he walked out to put the animal back in the van.

Chatham gingerly removed the giant plastic clamp

from her nose and, with hesitation, breathed in a short bit of air. It was basically clear. Only a trace from the original tar based toxic blast remained. Amazing.

Chatham re-tied her robe, pushed her hair back with her hands, and headed upstairs to free her children from their self-inflicted cage.

"It's OK, come on out. You can breathe now."

Each of her children had a wet towel around their head to mask the smell as completely as possible. Chatham's look of confidence was all they needed to remove their filters.

"Wow," Madison said. "No smell."

"Cool," Camp added. "Totally."

"I can smell, Mommy," PJ declared. "Can we dance now?"

"No, PJ. No more dancing tonight." She picked up the towels from the floor and tossed them in the sink. "OK troops, it's time to brush your teeth and get in bed." Chatham didn't know how much more she could take.

The children scattered to their bureaus and quickly donned their pajamas. The bathroom was soon abuzz with activity and then, finally, they were in bed.

Chatham kissed each of her children and wished them goodnight.

"I love you, sweet dreams," she said to each of them in turn. It was a Ross-family ritual. She had to wait for their same response before she closed the door.

"Mommy?" PJ asked.

Chatham hoped his request wouldn't last long. He tended to have particular needs, even at bedtime. "My friends need some water."

"PJ, they're fine. I love you, sweet dreams."

"No!" he protested. "They need water."

Chatham decided to comply, just to move the process forward. She went into the bathroom, filled a plastic cup part way with water and brought it to PJ.

"First Barney, gulp, gulp, gulp."

Chatham was glad to see that PJ was finally engaging in imaginary play. It was a definite three-year-old milestone that he had not completed as early as last year. The latest neurological therapy trend was to get a delayed child to live each stage of their life over again. If they filled in a missing gap, like crawling before walking or interactive play, then they would fill in the missing piece of the puzzle that they needed and would grow up to reach their greatest potential, at least that's what the theory claimed. Chatham had heard of and researched so many theories; she didn't know what to believe. But she was open to most things. After all, she did live in Marin, the land of anything goes.

"Then Big Bird, gulp, gulp, gulp. And now Mickey Mouse, gulp, gulp, gulp. OK, Mommy, I'm done." PJ rolled right over, closed his eyes and was asleep before she completely closed the bedroom door.

Chatham took a quick pit stop in the kids' bathroom to look in the mirror. She had forgotten that she had put bleach cream on her upper lip while she was taking a bath.

"Oh my god, Trip!" she thought. "Maybe with all the commotion he didn't even see it." She wiped off the white cream and tried to convince herself that he didn't notice as she cinched her robe and headed back downstairs.

Trip was waiting with two glasses of Chianti by a

newly lit fire.

"Thank god for good friends," she said as she gladly accepted the spirit. "But I'm still mad at you, Trip. I can't believe you brought that thing over here!" she exclaimed. She could feel her blood pressure starting to rise again.

"Look, Chat, I really am sorry. I didn't think he'd get out of his cage. Besides, you know how the kids want to see all of these wacky creatures before they go to the new owners."

"Yeah, I know. At least it neutralized itself, you're lucky for that," she said as she sat down next to Trip on the couch and put her feet up.

Almost automatically, he reached for her clean feet and began to rub. Chatham almost purred with pleasure. Peter used to do the same thing.

"So, who's getting this little beast?" Chatham asked as she closed her eyes , beginning to feel the tension release from her body.

"Do you know that guy who runs the dry cleaners by the gourmet market?" Trip asked as he gazed at Chatham's gorgeous reflection in the firelight.

"Oh great. I'm not going there again. What if he doesn't figure out how to neutralize? All my clothes will smell like tar."

"Don't worry, he knows. He still wanted it though. Guess how much he paid?" Chatham pulled a figure out of thin air.

"A dollar."

"Try fifty."

"Fifty dollars?"

Trip sported a large grin.

"Fifty thousand dollars," he said slowly, making sure she heard the number. What Chatham could do with that kind of cash!

"My costs added up to about three grand, including a few bottles of very good Russian vodka, and a bottle of rare Russian red wine, which you are drinking right now."

"How much did this cost?" Chatham asked.

"About as much as your monthly mortgage," he answered nonchalantly.

Chatham almost choked. "Trip, you shouldn't waste your money like that!" she reprimanded. She knew that every penny counted for her family, and she considered Trip like family.

"You're worth it," he said casually.

Chatham settled back enjoying the rub, oblivious to Trip's last words.

"You are too much, Trip," she said in a drowsy tone. Some business you have there."

Chatham closed her eyes again and unintentionally fell asleep, her foot still on Trip's lap. They sat in silence like a couple who had been married for years.

≈

"Do you miss him?" Trip asked softly as he watched Chatham's robe rise and fall peacefully. He had been waiting so long to tell her how he felt. Maybe this would be the time.

"Peter?" she replied. Chatham wasn't asleep after all.

"No, the skunk," he answered, doing his best to sound jovial again. It was quiet for a full minute.

"Yes, I miss him. It's tough sometimes. Other

times, we're doing OK. I think it's me. The kids bounce back so much easier."

"They are resilient, I know. Do you think you'll ever move on? You know, try again?"

"I don't know, Trip. I just can't imagine."

They drifted off into a comfortable silence as the fire's flames danced to classical music somewhere in the background.

CHAPTER XV – *PALIO & MARIA*

≈

Palio and his father sat at their favorite table at Monte's, near the back with a view of the entire restaurant. Monte's was a classic. The ceiling was lined with fake bunches of grapes hanging down from a wooden trellis. Straw covered bottles of red table wine were interspersed throughout the grapes, along with Italian cake boxes. One wall was covered with a mural of Venice with its many winding canals and gondolas. A small balcony where guest singers came on Friday nights to croon in Italian was set in the opposite corner.

Palio learned his Italian geography as a kid sitting at one of Monte's tables. Each glass-covered tabletop had maps of Italy inserted between the top and the white linen. The entire country could be examined town by town if one cared to learn. Palio spent many an afternoon learning stories about a little village on the border of Italy and Spain where Monte met his wife. Or a tiny canal that Monte used to visit as a young boy. The restaurant was really more like a second home.

Mr. Capriatti was somewhat of a revered legend at Monte's. Everyone knew how he made Monte himself over two million dollars from his investment in the jellybean factory. The Capriatti men were somewhat like royalty when they stepped over the threshold.

"Mr. Capriatti, sir, on the house." The chef himself clad in his classic white coat and puff pastry hat placed a plate of bruschetta in front of father and son. "In honor of your visit, enjoy." And he was gone. Just the right touch of good service, never failed.

"Don't look now Palio, but an old friend is coming over."

Palio wondered who it could be. He was too busy to catch up with old friends. Why, he barely had time for his best pal Gino.

"Good evening, Mr. Capriatti," the woman effused, leaning over to kiss Palio's father on both cheeks. "It's so nice to see you."

Palio had no idea who this dark haired beauty was. She had a figure to stop a mac truck and curly chestnut hair that looked like an Arabian stallion. She moved with grace and poise, a woman who definitely came from somewhere important.

"Ah, my dear, won't you join Palio and me for dinner?" Mr. Capriatti offered. Palio stood up to pull out a chair for the mystery woman.

"Yes, please, join us," Palio followed, not knowing who he was talking to.

"Why thank you, so nice to see you again Palio. How are you?" The soft-spoken woman was sensual in every way.

"I'm sorry, do I know you?" Palio asked, still baffled. Mr. Capriatti laughed a hearty, friendly laugh.

"Do you know her? Palio, you must have jet lag. This is our Maria. I know you haven't seen her in a while, or I'm sure you would have remembered." Mr. Capriatti looked affectionately at Maria, like he would a daughter.

Maria's eyes twinkled with amusement. Palio was clearly in shock. "Wow, Maria. You've, um, you've changed."

"It's been a while hasn't it? You look well," she answered gently.

"Thank you. And you, you look, amazing really."

Maria smiled demurely.

"So tell me, Maria," Palio's father said leaning back comfortably in his chair. "How is our little factory doing?"

"Oh Roberto, things are going so very well. Thanks to the notes you found in one of Lucia's memoires, we have created lemon blackberry and creamy confection. They are our number one flavors behind the infamous blueberry meringue cheesecake, of course. I ran some numbers. Thanks to Palio," she said, nodding her head in his direction, "we are running lean and mean as they say. We're poised to grow at 50 percent this year. I hope you are pleased."

"I am indeed, Maria. You've done an excellent job."

Palio listened in amazement. She was smart, too. How long had it been since he had seen Maria? Years at least. What a difference time can make. He was glued to her.

"Well, I really must be going Roberto."

"So soon?" he asked.

"I have another appointment," she said, glancing at Palio. "Thank you for the visit, and I will hopefully see you this week at the factory?"

Palio jumped up to help her out of her chair.

"Thank you, Palio," she beamed, giving him a light kiss on the cheek. "Maybe we will see each other again soon."

Palio was at a loss for words. He watched Maria

make her way across the restaurant, as though she were floating on air. He found it funny that two men in dark suits were waiting to escort her out of the restaurant. They both opened the restaurant door for her, looking left and then right before she departed. As the door was closing she tossed her long mane over her shoulder and gave Palio the most genuine smile. How did she know he would be watching?

"Good car service," Palio observed as he turned back to his father.

"I told you, didn't I?" Mr. Capriatti said with smug satisfaction.

"Told me? Told me what? That she's transformed into a dark-haired goddess?"

"That she has always had something for you, remember?"

"Papa, please. That is not the girl you made me take to dinner a few years ago. I am telling you right now, I would have remembered, believe me."

"Palio, Palio, you need to see the world around you more clearly. She was right in front of you all the time. She just hadn't gotten out of bed yet, if you know what I mean."

"Gotten out of bed? Who would want to with her in it?" he muttered under his breath. Maybe his Papa knew him better than he thought. "What's with the double escort? Can I get that car service?"

"If you go out with Maria, you too will have a personal valet," his father explained. "I told you she's come up in the world. When will you believe me?" Palio's father leaned in close. "When will you realize how Maria feels about you? Has always felt about you?"

Monte came over to the table, two plates of Fettuccini Alfredo in hand. It was a signature favorite.

"How is my beloved father-and-son team? After all, I owe this all to you," he said as he gave a sweeping gesture. "For taking my little candy investment and turning it into Willy Wonka's empire. And now the beautiful Maria will take it to new levels. Tell me you need more money for something. Anything."

Mr. Capriatti winked at his close friend.

"Maybe Palio here will need your help. He has taken over our little health club and is trying to make more links in the chain. He's bi-coastal now," Mr. Capriatti effused, as proud as a father could be.

"A man of the world you are, Palio. But any good man needs a good woman, right?" Monte and Roberto nodded in unison.

"And if I am not mistaken, a good woman just walked out of my restaurant, no?"

"OK, OK. The two of you are like gossipy old ladies. I saw her, OK? And yes, she's changed. For the better." Palio said with a playful exasperated expression.

"Roberto," Monte shouted. "A cause for celebration. Palio will be getting married soon, and I will be an uncle. Leo, bring over another bottle of Val Pollicelli for my friends," Monte commanded, arms waving with delight.

"Yes, let's celebrate. I am going to be a grandfather before too long, eh Monte my friend?" Palio's father was ecstatic.

"I said I liked what I saw, not that I'd father her children." Palio shook his head. "You two are impossible."

As the best friends celebrated, Palio couldn't help but feel apprehensive. He had just been re-introduced to a woman he thought would end up like a shriveled prune, but had turned into a goddess. And yet, as stunning and sexy as she was, something was not quite right. He couldn't put his finger on it.

Palio looked at the couple two tables over. Her mousy blond hair was absently tied back in a rubber band, a barrette slightly askew. She was dressed in a sweater with a big Turkey on it, no doubt to celebrate the coming holiday. He was in a black leather coat straight from SoHo. His dark hair was slicked back like the Fonz from Happy Days. They were giggling, holding hands and gazing into each other's eyes with genuine affection. They couldn't have been more different. Yet, they looked so at ease with each other, like the good Lord had planned their union from the beginning.

CHAPTER XVI - *BEST FRIENDS*

≈

Trip left around ten after which Chatham closed the fireplace grate, put the wine glasses in the sink and climbed into bed. She felt so lucky to have Trip in her life. He took the place of Peter as naturally as if he'd always been there. Chatham cared for him deeply, but she had never thought of anything beyond platonic. Still, she wondered. What would it be like to have Trip in her life and that of her children's forever?

The phone rang almost on cue. Chatham picked it up, knowing who it was.

"He is such an asshole. I mean who the fuck cares if the dinner dishes aren't done? I have to transcribe this entire fucking deposition by tomorrow morning and all he cares about is whether or not I did the fucking dishes."

"Henrietta. Are you sleeping on the couch again tonight?"

"Wouldn't you? You've got to be kidding if you think I'm going to sleep next to that log-sawing oaf, especially after that comment. I don't know why I stay with him, I really don't."

Henrietta, the court reporter, was Chatham's best friend. They were both in the maternity ward at the same time, first child for each. Chatham a girl, Henrietta a boy. Chatham was taking her first walk around the floor after the delivery when she saw this exotic looking half-French, half-Mexican woman sitting in the main lounge watching QVC. Her robe wasn't the designated white with blue dots, open flap and all, that the hospital provided to patrons like

Chatham. Hers was a Victoria Secret number; black velvet with red silk lining. She wore high-heeled slippers with a cute puff of red feathers on top. And she had a cell phone in her hand, which was not allowed in the hospital.

"Um, excuse me," Chatham said to her that fateful day. "I'm not sure you're supposed to be using cell phones in the hospital. Something about disrupting pace makers or something."

"Aw, fuck the lot of 'em. If they're ready to die, they will anyway. Besides, I'm going to die if I don't get that gorgeous diamond and sapphire ring. Now that's to die for, wouldn't you agree?" And she was serious. Chatham sat down next to her, the two of them watching QVC in their bathrobes, eight hours after giving birth. They had been best friends ever since.

Chatham turned the television on and punched in the channel for QVC. It was part of their conversation.

"So I went to the gym today," Chatham confessed, slightly proud of her completely irrational adventure.

"You? Exercise? When the hell do you find the time? In between work and driving to fricking kingdom come every day of your life?"

"Actually, right after drop off. That Herby in my carpool is going in the wrong direction. He was rambling about baby making today. Last week it was about how long a man's penis grows on a yearly basis. I can't have the younger kids hearing that."

"Aw, fuck 'em. He's just like the rest of them. Probably being taught by his dad that the size of the male genital is directly proportionate to success. They're all bastards, this one is just starting younger."

Chatham laughed. Henrietta basically hated all men, starting with her own husband. Although, deep down, Chatham knew that she actually loved him. She just blew a lot of smoke. From Henrietta's perspective, men were happiest when the house was clean, dinner was on the table, their boxers were neatly put away, and they were getting sex on demand. They could give a shit about the rest.

"They all just want another mommy to take care of them. Except in the bedroom. Then they want a porn star. You can have the whole fuckin' lot of 'em."

"But what about last weekend? How was the Pebble Beach Lodge?" Chatham asked with interest. Henrietta let out a soft satisfied purr.

"The spa was great. Sex wasn't bad either. Otherwise, he just fucked himself by playing golf both days. Improved his score by four strokes, he said. He thought he was a fucking god or something. But hey, enough about me. Tell me about this brush with physical exertion."

"Well, like I said, I went to this new gym. You know the one on the frontage road near my house?"

"The steroid outlet?"

"What?" Chatham had no idea what her friend was referring to.

"E. Anytime? It's where all the Schwarzenegger wannabes go, darling. Most of them work for Jiffy Lube or the loading dock at Home Depot."

"Oh my gosh, really?" Chatham changed to a more playful tone. "The counter guy was cute though."

"Honey, forget it. Loser, OK? Don't even think about it."

"I'm not, give me some credit. No one could match Peter anyway." Chatham sighed, thinking it likely that she'd never love again.

"Chat, come on, you have to move on sweetheart. It's been five years already. No more depression. I mean, they are all dick-wads, I know. But hell, who knows, you might meet someone who'll pay for dinner once in a while."

"Would be nice, wouldn't it?"

"Oh my god!" Henrietta's outburst jolted Chatham out of bed.

"Henrietta, what is it? What happened?"

"I found a fucking gray hair. Can you believe it? I'm going to buy that *never get gray again* solution they had on last night. It's guaranteed. I fuckin' hate getting old."

It was just like Henrietta to get so worked up over a tiny gray hair. She loved her for it. Henrietta confronted life head on. "Would you look at that?" Henrietta exclaimed, referring to their favorite television program. "Now how about that for a night on the town?"

Chatham listened to the television pitch.

"Not only will you feel wonderfully sexy in this cheetah bra and thong set, but the adjustable, natural-contouring-lift device allows you to be any size you want for the occasion. Sporting event? You may wanna be a little rounder, softer. That special night out? Pump it up, darling, and you will shine."

"My goodness, Kathy!" the assistant cried out. *"You look like you have implants. And it's so natural. Absolutely fabulous!"*

"That's right, ladies! You will look amazing for any occasion. Just a little pump on the hidden underside and off you go."

"Oh my gosh, Kathy, the phones are lighting up on every line. I hope our viewers can get through to get the benefits of this amazing sexy undergarment set. A woman's special secret."

"OK my friends, we are only offering this exciting ensemble for two more minutes. And it's yours for only $69.95 for the set. Hurry and call now. If you can't get through just keep trying, and we'll get you looking like a goddess in no time."

"I'm definitely in," Henrietta said.

Chatham was already fumbling through her purse for her credit card.

CHAPTER XVII - *COINCIDENCE*

≈

Mr. Capriatti arranged for Palio to meet the owner of the Da Vinci painting at 6:30 for coffee the next morning. Palio had to catch a nine o'clock flight back to San Francisco, so he only had about an hour before Gino picked him up.

Palio loved early morning in New York City. He bought a copy of the *New York Times* and a coffee from the vendor stationed at the foot of the massive steps of the Metropolitan Museum of Art. Fifth Avenue was already abuzz with activity. The dog walkers were setting out with their brood of afghans, toy poodles, and pugs. Nannies were hurrying up the stairs of brownstone's dotting Fifth, pressed and ready to attend to the many youths inhabiting the homes of wealthy non-working socialites. The cabbies, horns blowing, were in full gear. It was commute hour down to Wall Street. Most people took the subway, but not on the Upper East Side. You could almost bet if the executive didn't have a private car service, he'd be taking a taxi. It was easy to spot them. They were the ones resting comfortably under the heated awnings of their residences while the doormen braved the volatile weather to hail them their morning ride. Palio had the same set-up, but usually walked out to the corner and flagged a taxi himself. He thought it a bit arrogant to expect the doorman to act as a servant. After all, the title was self explanatory, wasn't it?

Palio sat on the cool steps, opened the paper and quickly became absorbed in a story about a Mafioso who had been caught in Little Italy. Drugs were the trade of this particular crime family, and the Laundromat was their meeting place.

"I can't believe it!" Palio exhaled. Gino had been right. He had suspected something was going on at that Laundromat in the old neighborhood. Palio would never doubt Gino's instinct again. He was born for surveillance.

Palio glanced up to see a stretch black limousine approach and park directly in front of him. A larger-than-life, godfather-bodyguard type darted out of the front passenger seat, did a quick scan of the block, and gracefully opened the door for some sort of VIP. Palio went back to reading his paper. It wasn't as though he hadn't ever seen a celebrity in his life. Besides, locals didn't stare.

"Hello Palio," came a soft voice, like a whisper on the wind.

Palio lowered his paper to meet a black leather miniskirt and knee-high boots that begged for attention. He continued his scan up the body, which revealed a black wool turtleneck with RL embossed ever so subtly on the edge of the sleeve. Further up, he met the face of Maria, the dark-haired goddess.

Palio stood up quickly, spilling his coffee on his pants.

"Damn," he exclaimed, more embarrassed than anything.

"Here let me help you," Maria offered, taking the napkin out of his hand and dabbing the spill close to his lap.

"Maria, wow. What a surprise. What are you doing here?"

"Oh, didn't your father tell you? He asked me to

come along, in case you needed some support with where the jellybean factory was at financially. You know, in case the painting owner needed additional verification?" She smiled softly in his direction.

"Actually, he mentioned something about you helping. And here you are." He was at a loss for words.

"Can I, um, buy you a cup of coffee?" Palio still couldn't believe how she'd changed.

"That would be wonderful, thank you," Maria responded.

Palio gently put his hand at her elbow, guiding her toward the street vendor. Before he knew it, two of the chaperones were standing on either side of them, escorting them the twenty feet they needed to travel. Palio was taken back.

"Oh, don't mind them. They are my escorts. I'll have a decaf if that's alright with you." She waved the protectors away.

Palio was more than curious. "What are you, some kind of VIP or something? Body guards?"

"Actually, I do some international work, in addition to running your father's confection factory. Thanks to you, the factory is running very smoothly and does not require all of my attention." She batted her eyes modestly.

"International? What kind of international, may I ask?"

"Oh, sure. It's world wide-security, actually. Lot of work in Europe lately with all the French disdain for Americans. I think the change of name from French fry to Freedom fry has upset the Parisians just a bit. We make sure our executives abroad are safe and comfortable."

Maria quickly changed the subject. "So, have you met the esteemed owner yet? Your father is set on that painting for his collection."

"Oh, the olive princess. At least that's what Pop calls her. We haven't met. Although I don't think I'll be too hard to spot. I mean who reads the paper on the steps of the MET in the middle of morning rush hour?"

They both chuckled. Palio thought Maria had a wonderful laugh.

≈

After a few minutes of sipping their coffee in silence, Maria brought up the olive oil princess again. It was the only thing she could think of to talk about, and she longed to keep the conversation with Palio going.

"So do you know anything about this woman?" she asked. She had an idea what to expect from the Italian woman. She was probably a rich heiress that spent all of her time being waited on. That usually meant lots of jewels, and she was likely going to be very skinny and beautiful. Just my luck, Maria thought.

Maria remembered her own round physique all too well. The night she had her one and only date with Palio, she could tell that he would want someone more exciting. Someone who was good to look at any hour of the night or day. She made the necessary changes over the past several years. Liposuction, Botox, cheek implants, hair styling, diets, and a personal trainer had done her well. Maria was pleased when she looked in the mirror, and she could tell that Palio was too.

"Nothing really," Palio said. "I know more about this painting that we're supposed to get."

Maria glanced over Palio's shoulder to see a woman gliding toward them. She was instantly deflated. Long, sleek legs clad in charcoal brown silk pants led the woman's graceful approach. The matching bolero jacket barely covered the cream-colored silk blouse with one too many buttons undone. She walked with poised confidence, like a runway model who owned the runway. Yet there was something dangerous about her, Maria thought. Or was that simply jealousy speaking?

"Hello again," the elegant woman said as though they had been friends for years. She noticed Maria, looked her over as though she thought she wasn't worth the time.

"The woman from the plane flight. First class," Palio said. The woman practically beamed. "I never did get your full name."

Maria had no idea they were already friendly. Didn't he say he had never met her before?

"I guess it never came up. I'm Georgina, Georgina Bollietteri." She offered her hand. Palio took it, clearly already under her spell.

"And I'm Maria." Maria thrust her stubby hand out. She preferred to be on the offensive.

Georgina looked at Maria's hand and coiled. "Oh, nice to meet you." She did an about face to Maria and turned her attention to Palio. "So your father tells me that you want to talk with me about my precious painting. Might want to persuade me somehow was how he put it."

"Can I buy you a cup of coffee?" Palio inquired.

Georgina was gorgeous; there was no double about that. But surely Palio was here for business only, Maria thought.

"Actually, I've reserved a private booth at The Plaza Grill. I thought coffee there might be nice," Georgina offered.

Palio consulted his watch. "My friend Gino is picking me up to head back to the airport soon... how about –"

"We can take my car," Maria blurted out, secretly wishing she could drop the foreigner off at the nearest puddle.

"Oh, how very kind of you. Yes, that would be lovely," Georgina replied, sounding grateful. The bodyguard held the door for the threesome, encouraging Palio to enter first. Maria was about to enter next when Georgina slipped in front of her and in next to Palio.

"You'll probably want to sit in front with your friends; it is so very cramped back here," she directed to Maria as though it were the only option.

Palio was already on the phone with Gino, giving him the new location. No support from that front.

Maria climbed into the front seat, sandwiched between her trusty guardians. This was not what she had in mind.

≈

The car let them out in front of the New York Landmark on 59th and Central Park South. It was one of the centers of the city. They could see the *Good Morning America* window across the street in the GM building, ritzy Bergdorf's at the corner of the plaza, and Central Park directly across the street, which afforded guests views other than cement skyscrapers. A horse-drawn carriage was letting its passengers off in front at the time of their arrival.

Palio knew the driver.

"Hey Marco, how's business?" Palio inquired as he escorted his two female companions toward The Plaza entrance.

"Oh, you know, Palio. It's seasonal. But I am going to make extra money selling these replicas." He showed Palio a miniature wooden twin of his horse- drawn chariot. "My friend makes them, and I will sell them for twenty-five bucks a piece. I have orders like hotcakes. Here, a gift." He handed a replica to Palio. It was a horse-drawn carriage with two people in it. It even had a miniature blanket to keep them warm on those cool New York nights.

"But don't you need this one to get more orders?"

"No, he gave me an extra, just in case."

"Ingenious," Palio exclaimed. "Thanks Marco."

"Tell your Papa hello for me. I'll see him at the boat race this weekend. He's going to win. I just know it. I've got ten dollars on him."

"You and the rest of the world."

Palio waved to Marco, slipped the toy into his pocket and headed up the stairs to attend to business.

≈

Palio, Georgina, and Maria entered the mahogany-coated, clubby restaurant, which was furnished with burgundy leather booths and tables with brown-leather easy chairs. The walls were covered with framed pictures of famous people that had dined there, interspersed with classic paintings of various hunting scenes. The restaurant's windows framed the greenery of Central Park. Palio half expected to see a man with a polo mallet come leaping out of the bushes on a thoroughbred and through the window at any time.

The waiter showed them to a booth in the far corner of the room. It was where important people like Mayor Bloomberg and Donald Trump did business. There wasn't room for three in the tiny booth so Georgina suggested that Maria seek refreshment at the long mahogany bar. This was a private negotiation.

Palio felt bad for Maria, she so much wanted to be of assistance. That part of her had not changed. But this was business, and he could tell that the olive princess was used to being in control.

Georgina wasted no time. She leaned forward as far as the table allowed, her blouse plunging open to reveal a hint of natural perfection.

"Look, I don't really care about the painting. It was something my family lent to The Louvre way back at the beginning of time. Something about it being safe there. I think I'm somehow related to Da Vinci via a thrice-removed lineage."

"Sounds interesting." Palio wondered where she was going. "So, if you don't care about the painting, why didn't you simply agree to sell it to my father? You would earn a fair price, and my father would have the painting that my mother adored."

"Because there is something else I want." She smiled at Palio.

"Can we help you, Maria? Georgina suddenly declared, clearly repulsed at the intrusion.

"Actually, it's what I can do to help you," she said brusquely. "Palio, your ride is here. It's time to go."

Palio consulted his watch.

"You're right. Look Georgina, I have to go or I'll miss my flight. I'm so sorry this was so short. Can we continue our discussion when I return? I'll be back for my father's boat race on Saturday." He looked at Maria for support.

"Why don't you join me, us, and we can see where we go from there?" Palio didn't want to exclude Maria; after all, his father had always thought they belonged together. And he liked Georgina too. Palio owed him the possibility, and the way he saw it, he could visit with both women, fulfill his fatherly duties and see where it all led.

A vision of the woman in a Land's End nightgown and chipped nail polish on her toes jumped into his head. He couldn't help but smile. What was it about that woman that continued to distract him? Here he was with two of the most beautiful women in Manhattan, and all he could think about was someone from suburbia living on the opposite side of the country. Palio shook off the thought and addressed his guest.

"That is, if you are still in town and don't have other plans."

"Well, yes. I will be here over the weekend," Georgina replied coyly. "I'm staying at the Pierre, Suite 200. Shall I expect you at noon then?"

Palio stood up, put down a twenty-dollar bill for the coffee and gathered his soft brown leather jacket. He reached for Georgina's hand.

"Until then." And he was gone.

≈

Maria attempted to give her goodbye, but Georgina

already had her cell phone glued to her ear, too busy to be bothered.

"Bitch," Maria whispered as she made her way out the front door of The Plaza and toward her personal chauffeur.

Maria watched Palio step into the black BMW M5 driven by his friend. Maria couldn't believe she had still never met Gino, what with both of them being pseudo family members and all. Then again, she was hardly paying attention to the back of the driver's head. She only cared for his passenger.

Her heart leapt when Palio turned her direction to wave goodbye.

"See you Saturday," Palio called out as he and his friend sped away from the famed hotel.

"Until next time," she replied, her hand held up in a gesture of farewell. "Until next time."

CHAPTER XVIII - *SPYING*

≈

"So, do you own a Da Vinci?" Gino asked nonchalantly.

"Well, not exactly. I mean, maybe. I think we will. I'm not exactly sure."

"What the hell is that supposed to mean? You either do or you don't."

"I don't exactly know what she meant. She said there was something else that she wanted. Hell if I know."

"Did it happen to come in a brown leather jacket, wool slacks and Gucci loafers?" Gino described Palio's outfit perfectly.

"Huh? What? You've got to be kidding. I have no idea what she wants."

"Well, I'm sure she'll tell you by the sound of it."

"Yeah. I'm taking her to the boat race on Saturday."

"I thought you were going to be in San Fran."

"I'll be there today and back tomorrow. The next day is Saturday and, since I don't have to get her until noon, I can sleep for once." He opened the paper to the metro section. He didn't really have a chance to read it earlier.

"You can have that fuckin' jet-set life, ya know? I like my little world of solid ground, right here. Ya know what I'm sayin'?" Gino was really a small town kind of guy.

"Here it is! Gino, did you see the article about the Mafioso that they caught? It says, 'Tony Bambini, Mafia Boss, was arrested late last night while doing his laundry at.

. .'"

"At the fuckin' Laundromat. Was I right or was I right?"

"Suspected leader of the Italian mafia, Bambini is being charged with drug trafficking, money laundering, and false tax returns. Isn't that how they got Capone?"

Gino shook his head. "The question is: who's gonna take over now that Bambini might be out? That's what I want to know."

The friends were deep in thought as they made their way to JFK.

≈

Maria descended into the back seat of her personal limousine and settled back for the ride to the factory. Her driver rolled past the entrance of The Plaza when something caught her eye.

"Stop! Wait right here." Maria crouched down low in her seat so that she wouldn't be seen.

Georgina looked up and down the block before clambering into the back of a Rolls Royce, which would escort her to her next meeting.

Maria happened to know that the car belonged to none other than Italian Mafioso, Johnny Bambini. Bambini was a larger than life Italian with slicked black hair, tailored pin striped suits and a fleet of Rolls Royce's with giant B's on the license plates. To get a meeting with Johnny Bambini meant that you had something he definitely wanted. Otherwise, he'd send his gumbas to make the deal.

"Follow that car," she commanded to her driver. "And don't, I repeat, don't lose them." This will be very interesting, Maria thought as she kept her eyes glued to the woman in the fancy car ahead.

The Rolls Royce made its way down Fifth Avenue, around Washington Square Park, took a left on Bleeker and a right on Broadway.

"Don't lose them," Maria insisted when the upscale automobile was temporarily out of their vision.

"Not a problem, Miss Porticello. You can count on me," the driver stated, confidently.

Maria kept a keen eye ahead of her. She didn't want to miss a thing. Within three blocks, they were directly behind the Rolls as it pulled up to the infamous Laundromat. Maria watched as Georgina sauntered into the Laundromat, disappearing into the unknown.

"Give me some audio," Maria commanded.

"Sure. No problem." The driver pressed the audio surveillance button on the dashboard. A spiral antenna rose discreetly from the rear of the limo to zero in on the conversation.

"Such a proposition is very tempting. I will need to give it some thought." Maria knew it was Bambini talking.

"Twenty percent is more than fair, and you know it," Georgina responded. "Soon you will be the leading olive oil importer in America, making more money than you do from any of your other operations. Now what could make a better combination?"

"And you will expand your olive oil empire to have more money than you need in a lifetime. You drive a hard bargain."

Maris saw a WNYW news truck pass in front of the sleek vehicle, its microwave dish all, but obliterating the surveillance mechanism's signal.

"Bruno, what's wrong?" Maria insisted.

"Sorry, Miss Porticello. Interference. Let me try another frequency." He fiddled with the knob until he found the correct megahertz. "OK, here we go," Bruno said, once again tuning in to a clear channel.

"Are you in town for a few days?" Bambini said.

"Just a few. I will be attending the race this weekend with Palio Capriatti." Maria pictured the olive princess tilting her head coyly.

"Ahhh, the big little boat race. I have a lot of money riding on that race. My bet is on the secret weapon from Roberto Capriatti. It's such a coincidence that you are attending it with his son, the most desirable bachelor in the city. You should move quickly."

Georgina lowered her voice. "Actually... I'm planning on –"

All of the sudden, the receiver dropped again. It was the part of the conversation that held the most interest for Maria, and she couldn't hear a thing.

"Get me a signal!" Maria demanded. "Of all the wrong times!"

The driver nervously flipped the channel until they were tuned in again.

"I wouldn't discount the yachtsmanship of that little red-headed boy," Georgina assessed. "I hear he knows how to traffic parts."

"It's his grandfather. He takes his larger-than-life yachts and shrinks them down to size. I don't trust him; he doesn't have instinct. Robert Capriatti, on the other hand... Now there's a man who gets rich by natural knowing. He smells an opportunity, and he turns it into a gold mine."

"Soon you shall have your gold mine," Georgina promised.

Maria heard Bambini pour two glasses. Champagne, probably. Typical Bambini, she thought.

"A little Dom Perignon to seal our deal, my dear?"

"To a very successful enterprise," Georgina toasted.

"Yes, my dear. And may you find success with your little plan."

"Damn," Maria exclaimed. What little plan was he referring to? She listened as they clinked their glasses together. Maria thought it was over until she heard some rustling of bodies.

"For luck," Georgina whispered as she planted a loud kiss.

"I do feel lucky, my dear," Bambini responded, returning the kiss with longer, more passionate sound effects.

"Get me out of here," Maria commanded, slumping into the soft leather seat. What was really going on?

Maria didn't know what to make of this interlude, but she knew that whatever accord they had reached, it wasn't good for the Capriatti men. She had done business with Bambini in the past, and he wasn't known to be a fair man. He would have to be watched.

Furthermore, Maria wasn't going to let this steely woman, this snake lying in the grass, interfere with her own personal plan of marrying Palio. This woman was trouble; she could feel it.

"Take me to the factory," she ordered her driver.

As they pulled away from their impromptu stake

out, Maria noticed a car similar to Palio's friend Gino's parked at the opposite corner. He was watching the whole scene unfold. She hadn't had the wherewithal to take down Gino's license plate number when they left The Plaza. She was too concerned at the time whether Palio would turn around and acknowledge her as he departed; and he had.

"Pull over," she commanded. "Who do you think that is?"

The driver put on his Maui Jim's and glanced in the direction of the Beemer.

"Looks like a cop," he concluded. "Special Services, I think. They're usually built, ya know what I'm saying?"

Maria looked ahead at Bruno's reflection in the rearview mirror. She was agitated by the whole situation.

"What exactly does that mean, Bruno?" Maria demanded. "Do I know what you're saying? Of course, I do. You said it, didn't you? And I heard it, didn't I? So, I know damn well what you're saying."

Bruno seemed to ignore the outburst. "It's a cop, for sure," he said simply.

They sat in silence as they watched the muscle man crouch down low in the front seat of his M5, peering above the steering wheel through a pair of binoculars. Maria could tell that he was holding them the wrong way. Special Service guys never used binoculars, and they never crouched. They blended in, like one of the locals, all the while tapping conversations with their radio-controlled earpieces and lapel pins. This guy had on a Guinea T and was smoking a filter-less cigarette.

"Should I say something to him?" Bruno asked his

boss.

"He looks like a kid on mischief night or something," Maria concluded as she watched him fumble with an instamatic camera. There's no way that would reach the necessary distance. She found him endearing in a childlike sort of way. "He sure looks familiar, but if there's a cop on this, then we shouldn't be here. So let's go."

Bruno pulled ahead of the other stakeout car and stepped on it. Maria glanced out of the window at the car just as the driver turned his head in her direction.

As their eyes met, lightning seemed to strike. Maria could feel her face flush. She had never seen a more beautiful man in all her life, not even Palio.

CHAPTER XIX - *CAUGHT*

≈

Chatham woke up early to get her workout outfit in order. The sticky note on the bedside lamp contained the slogan she intended to use. It came to her in the middle of the night. Thank goodness she kept sticky notes and a pen on her nightstand. Many of her good ideas came to her at the oddest times. She rummaged through the sewing kit that her mother-in-law gave her when the kids were born to find iron on lettering that would create the effect. The box was a hodgepodge of pins, colored thread, material scraps, and whatever else mothers had on hand to fix lost buttons, rips, and hemlines.

Chatham remembered a Barney the Dinosaur Halloween costume she had made for PJ one year. She had used iron on appliqués to spell BARNEY in glow-in-the-dark purple. The letters, combined with the black-light necklace she had PJ wear, let her keep a close eye on him as he ran at lightning speed from house to house. Halloween was his favorite holiday.

Chatham drank her morning coffee and ironed while watching *The Morning Show*. Multitasking gave her comfort.

"Sexy or Spinster, which one are you? Take our quiz and determine where you fall on the attractive meter. Are you emitting sensuality in your relationships, or are you truly a hands-off kind of gal?" Chatham turned the volume up.

"Question number one: Do you wear pajamas or nighties?"

Chatham looked down at her LL Bean flannel nightgown.

"I stay warm to ward off colds," she said defensively to the television segment host.

"If you answered flannel pajamas, leading psychologist Dr. Mary Meyers says, get out of bed and run to Victoria Secret fast! You are a spinster."

Oh great, Chatham thought.

"What if you don't look like a Victoria Secret model? No one looks like a Victoria Secret model," she barked at the television. "Unless, of course, you *are* a Victoria Secret model." Chatham was ready to turn the channel, barely noticing how determined her ironing had become.

"Now, not everyone *is* a Victoria Secret model," the perfect television hostess admitted.

Chatham smiled knowingly. This interviewer had some common sense after all.

"However, if you feel beautiful, you will look beautiful. That's also what Dr. Meyers says. So all of you women out there who may think you are spinsters, get out of bed, run to the nearest lingerie shop, and buy something that makes you feel beautiful. OK, that's all the time we have. Tune in tomorrow morning for *muscle or muck, what kind of shape are you in?*"

Chatham pressed the power off button on the remote. "I'm already doing something about that," she said to the black screen, holding up her new creation. "Much better, now you have meaning." She returned the sewing kit to its resting place, packed the new and improved work-out outfit into her stylish new gym bag and got the morning in gear. Chatham decided that she was going to give this exercise thing a real effort.

Chatham had been thinking about the health club quite a bit, especially as it related to a particular employee. She couldn't help wondering if he would be there today. It was foolish, probably, but she couldn't help it. He'd been so nice to her.

"Mom? Madison isn't being nice," Camp yelled from the upstairs bathroom. They were behind closed doors.

"Camp?" Chatham called up the two-story foyer. "What are you monkeys doing?"

"Mom!" Camp yelled again from somewhere inside the bathroom. "Madison, stop it! I look like a dork."

Chatham made her way up the stairs and into the kids' bathroom.

"Come on Camp, it's crazy hair day. You look great," Madison encouraged.

Chatham did her best not to burst out laughing. She subtly covered her mouth with her hand and pretended to cough.

"Why Camp, it looks – well, it looks cool. Totally," Chatham said. She was making an effort to relate on his level. Madison had done up Camp's hair in tiny colored rubber bands, about fifty in all. His hair looked a bit like a rainbow. On the ends she had clipped tiny barrettes that she had found in the back of the linen cabinet, where Chatham stashed a bunch of baby clothes and old memoirs.

"I forgot that I kept those," Chatham whispered as she picked up one of the cute butterfly clips and examined the blend of colors. Sadness suddenly overcame her as she remembered how she and Peter had gone shopping one Saturday afternoon when Madison was a tiny baby. They had found the cute hand-painted accessories at The Pink Rabbit in San Anselmo, a store filled with pink and blue monogrammed blankets, silver rattles, and picture frames – all available for engraving. So many things still reminded her of Peter. She did her best to appear cheerful.

"OK, you two. Breakfast is ready, and –"

"In the car in fifteen minutes." They answered in unison. Madison and Camp pointed to each other. "Jinx, owe me a soda."

"Am I that bad?" she asked.

"Like a broken record, Mom," Madison said, in mock exasperation.

Chatham smiled and closed the door behind her.

"Mommy, may I wear my bathing suit?" PJ asked as he zipped up his navy blue farmer John wet suit by reaching behind for the long back zipper string. PJ liked to wear things that clung to his body, sort of like a second skin. It helped him feel more in control in relation to his position in space.

"PJ, bathing suits are for swimming, honey. You can wear it after school."

"Please, Mommy. I will wear my bathing suit and then I will wear my clothes over my bathing suit. Deal?" He held out his pinky to seal the agreement.

Chatham wasn't in the mood to argue today, she wanted to keep the positive momentum going.

"Mommy? Mommy, please? I will wear my bathing suit. It's OK."

"Oh, alright, PJ. Just make sure you wear something

over it, OK?"

"OK, I will." PJ's day was off to a perfect start.

A quick glance at the digital timer on the thermostat in the hallway reminded Chatham that twelve minutes were left before they absolutely had to leave. Don't stress, she told herself. It will all come together.

"OK, everyone. I'm packing breakfast, and we're taking it with us. I'll meet you in the car in ten minutes." She was proud of herself at how calm she was appearing – on the outside.

Chatham threw on some designer sweats that she had bought years ago after Camp was born and she had planned to lose her baby-bearing weight; she had never worn them, but they were still in style. It was a definite improvement over yesterday's outfit, and she wanted to be presentable should a certain someone be on duty at the gym.

She gathered the toasted cinnamon bread from the kitchen counter and placed the slices on napkins to catch any crumbs that might drop in the car. She segmented a few granny smith apples and tossed them into individual baggies for the kids to munch on and proceeded to haul the backpacks down the stairs and into the car. Her strategy must have worked. Everyone came bouncing down exactly as she opened the garage door and turned the key to start the engine. Maybe this was going to be a good day after all, Chatham thought as she handed the morning sustenance over her head to awaiting hands in the back seat.

Chatham looked in her rearview mirror to make sure that she wasn't about to collide with any passing cars. That's when she saw her daughter.

"Madison! Oh my god. What did you do to your hair?" Madison had spray painted her hair bright orange, completely.

"Mom, it's crazy hair day? Duh?" Chatham didn't even recognize her daughter. "Isn't it just perfect?" Madison was admiring her creation.

"Perfectly, uh, interesting, honey. A little bold, but interesting nonetheless. Does it come out?" Chatham wanted to remain upbeat.

"I think so. The can said it did after a few washings. Besides, orange is one of the school colors. I'm being patriotic, full of school spirit."

Chatham reminded herself to get a bottle of hydrogen peroxide from the drug store.

Carpool actually went smoothly. Herby's mother was standing at the curb as usual, in a crisp white tennis dress adorned with periwinkle piping, telling her lovely prodigy that next time he shaved his head for crazy hair day, he should think about going to a barber. Her gentle suggestion was followed by the perfect suburban-mom smile. Chatham swore she practiced that precise face in front of the mirror every night before going to bed. In reality, she was probably doing her best to cloak her hysteria at her son's non-reversible patchwork.

Chatham was ready to head off any unnecessary discussions this morning by having the movie Freaky Friday up and running on the in-flight DVD player that hung down from the center ceiling of the SUV. She even had five sets of headphones so that she could listen to her soothing Hari Krishna music while the kids laughed out loud when Jamie Lee Curtis woke up in her daughter's body.

Chatham opted to drop PJ off first due to her impending meeting at The Park School. Since she was actually on time today, the change in schedule could work. She pulled right into the roundabout, waved goodbye to PJ, and blew him at least ten kisses as she made her way back through the neighborhood and onto the highway.

As she merged into highway traffic, Chatham thought she heard a cellphone buzzing. Her phone was of course deep inside her purse, which, unfortunately, currently lived under five library books, a jacket, and a bag of Cheez-its on the front passenger's seat. She quickly dug through the heap until she reached the persistent vibration, which she reached just as it was about to catapult to voicemail.

"Hello?"

"Well?"

"Well what?" Henrietta never introduced herself.

"Are you pumping iron today?" Chatham could hear the kids in Henrietta's carpool. They were arguing over which DVD to watch on the short ride to school. Henrietta's two children attended the Park School as well. Chatham and Henrietta often spoke on their carpool mornings. You could call it moral support.

"Yes, as a matter of fact, I am. I have a quick meeting and then I'll be there."

"What's the meeting?"

"I don't know. Tricky Vicky cornered me at Safeway yesterday and asked me to come up with the theme for the auction."

"Are you sure that's all she asked you to do?"

"That's what she said. But Camp gave me a note from her yesterday afternoon. There might be a bit of a miscommunication, but it's nothing I can't straighten out. I agreed to come up with the theme, and I have a good one in mind. Should be a piece of cake."

"She's got me doing decorations. I don't know how the hell she did it, but here I am, heading up something I know absolutely nothing about."

"Tell me about it, like I have any time for this. Try minus zero."

"Maybe we can make it a factory kind of theme. You know "We Can Make it Together," through this god-forsaken private school bullshit. What do you think?"

Chatham laughed. "Yeah, and we can line the walls with all of your shoes. Every factory makes something right?"

"Absolutely. My red-pointed, heart-covered shoes can be for love and my green neon shoes can be for peace. I think you should suggest it."

Chatham had come up with the theme for the auction in the middle of night. She was ready for the meeting. This will be easy, she thought. Just reveal it to the crowd and be done with it. I'll be able to get to the gym by 9:15 if all goes according to plan, she decided.

"OK, see you there."

"Did she ask you to bring anything?"

"Oh my gosh, thanks for reminding me. I have to get coffee, donuts, orange juice, and muffins."

"I've got the quiche and fruit. Do you want me to get the juice for you? I'm stopping at Safeway."

"Oh, would you? I have to go to Sweet Things for

the other stuff. Vicky is pretty picky when it comes to food."

"Why are we such suckers?" Henrietta questioned.

"I have got to learn to say no," Chatham agreed. "See you there."

"Yeah, bye."

Chatham heard Henrietta yelling at one of her kids for spilling chocolate milk on the seat as she hung up. We're all the same really, Chatham thought as she made her way into the bakery strip mall entrance a block away from school.

"OK, everybody, I need to run into the bakery for a minute. You all stay here. Madison is in charge. Maddy, lock the door behind me, OK?"

Madison just nodded. The carload was completely silent thanks to 100 percent preoccupation with Jamie Lee Curtis playing the electric guitar during the wango tango audition in the movie, while inside her daughter's body.

Chatham walked briskly across the parking lot and into the specialty bakery.

"What can I get you?" the male voice asked, with a bothered tone.

Chatham was too busy scouring the glass display case to look up. "I'll take six bran muffins, six blueberry muffins, two dozen glazed donuts, and enough coffee, for, I don't know, twenty-five people?"

"Yeah, well, that's gonna take a while lady," the voice responded abruptly.

Chatham looked up to see none other than the parking-lot thief. He wasn't too happy to see her either.

"Oh, it's you. How nice to see that you are applying

yourself to something other than thievery." Chatham gave him the biggest smile she could muster.

"I can't help it if you're too slow, man. So, what was it you wanted again?"

"You heard her, buddy. And throw in an extra dozen donuts if you know what's good for you."

Chatham turned around. In line behind her was a scary looking homeless character. He looked a bit like a bug or frog or something slimy.

"Oh, hi, um. Thank you."

He leered at her approvingly. "Working out today?" he asked.

"Well, uh, yes, I am. How did you know?"

"The bag."

Chatham looked at the bag over her shoulder. She had grabbed it when she got out of the car so that she had something to help her carry the breakfast feast.

"So, lady. Here's everything and, uh, the coffee's on the house, OK?" The bakery worker glanced at the scary looking gentleman almost as though he was hoping for some approval. He was zeroed in on his reaction.

The homeless man just nodded his head slightly.

"See you at the gym, sweetheart," the scaly looking man promised as he opened the bakery door and departed.

"It's sixty-four dollars," the boy said, his head hanging low.

"Wow, that's pretty expensive for some muffins and donuts, don't you think?"

"Oh, well OK. How about fifteen dollars then? Would that be about right?"

"Sure, thanks." Chatham paid the boy. "By the way,

who was that character and how do you know him?" she asked, now that the young man was actually being civil.

"He owns the place," the boy answered. "Owns this whole Shopping Center. Hope I don't get fired," he reflected under his breath.

"I'll tell you what. If you promise to stop stealing people's parking spots and places in line, I'll put in a good word for you. Deal?" She reached out with her pinky, just like her kids taught her to.

The boy looked at her like she was a bit wacky, but offered his pinky just the same.

"Yeah, deal. Thanks."

Chatham gathered her items and exited the store, jogging across the lot to her parked car. Now she was late, her normal mode of operation. She could feel the stress building as she predicted what type of animated discussion Herby was initiating inside her car. Drugs, sex, violence? He didn't tend to bring up the more mundane subjects like sports or movies. He liked to stir things up, a true sniglefritz.

Chatham zapped her car beeper to unlock the car. She loaded her spread into the back storage area. No one looked up; no one moved. It was a car full of video zombies. Chatham just smiled as she climbed into the driver's seat, put the car in drive and headed to The Park School.

"Good morning, Miss Ross," the purple reflective monitor attendant greeted. "And how is our Ross carpool today?"

"Hi, Mark. We're fine thanks."

He opened the doors so that the brood could unload.

Again, no one moved. The monitor stuck his head inside the car to see five heads with earphones looking in an upward direction as though they were following their cult leader.

"Tsk, tsk, Mrs. Ross. I thought you signed the Car School Agreement." Chatham had forgotten that she had signed the volunteer car school contract in which she agreed to introduce challenging and interesting facts or problems during the drive to school. If the children turned in the facts or solved the problems, they would get extra credit toward their year-end grades. They even received a Certificate of Accomplishment during a special assembly at the close of the school year. Chatham scrambled for an explanation that would be acceptable to the inquisitioner.

"Well, you see, we were actually *doing* our car school. I told the children that I needed a theme for the auction this year, since I'm in charge of coming up with one. I volunteered with Victoria." Chatham smiled and the monitor nodded approvingly. "And, I thought that if I inspired them with laughter, it would spark their internal creative process so that they could help me come up with an interesting, money-making theme for all to enjoy. The movie is designed to illicit laughter. See?"

The monitor watched the kids, all of whom were smiling.

"And, um, if they turn that idea in, then the teacher would gladly credit them with participating in the creation of the school's most important event of the year. Now wouldn't that be just so very interesting and contributory?"

"Well, Mrs. Ross. I must say, it's quite inventive. Original, creative, thought provoking." He leaned in and whispered. "I won't say a thing. Forget I ever witnessed the infraction."

Chatham turned off the AUX on the car dashboard unit, which zapped off the movie immediately. "OK kids, thanks so much for your ideas. Now don't forget to contribute them in class today."

Everyone grabbed their backpacks, scrambled out and ran off to class.

"Mrs. Ross?" the monitor asked, as she was about to drive off. "What's the theme?"

"Now, Mark. If I told you, it wouldn't be a surprise, now would it?" She smiled coyly and released the brake. A parking spot had opened up and this time, she was going to claim it.

"Yoo-hoo," came a familiar voice like fingernails on a chalkboard. "Oh Chatham dear." The tap of wild purple heels could be seen and heard far across the school parking lot.

Chatham was just getting out of her car. "I'm so glad you didn't forget the refreshments. You know how these volunteers are; they simply flock to food. Pulls them in every time. Can I help you carry something?"

"Sure, thanks Vicky... I mean Victoria. Could you grab the –"

"I'll just take this bag of sugars and meet you inside, OK? Alright then, see you in there."

Chatham watched Victoria as she held the tiny bag at arms length. She wasn't used to hard labor. Balancing the oversized box of donuts and the bags of muffins with one hand, Chatham grabbed the twenty-pound vat of coffee and accompanying bag filled with cream and stirrers with

166

the other. She closed the hatch with one hand and used her hip to snap it shut. With great finesse, she waddled over to the extended care room to deposit the buffet.

"Chatham dear, did you remember napkins?" Victoria asked, as soon as Chatham walked in the door.

"They're in the bag with the cream, I'm pretty sure."

Victoria pulled out a wad of white diner-style napkins, the paper-thin kind.

"Oh, how original. Maybe we'll just give everyone two."

Chatham decided to ignore the comment and turned her attention to digging for her sticky notes somewhere inside her purse. She tended to put important things in "special spots," to be remembered. Unfortunately, the opposite tended to occur, and she would go months before discovering that she had placed the only flashlight in the house inside the empty cereal box or her daughter's script for the play behind the stereo. The logic behind her hiding place choices was somewhat convoluted, but it made perfect sense to Chatham. Why wouldn't she put the flashlight inside the Captain Crunch cereal box? If there was a power outage and everyone got hungry, they would likely eat cereal. When they reached in, they would find the flashlight and be able to find the bowls and spoons. The stereo was a perfect place for her daughter's important document. Chatham knew that her daughter had to practice singing to a CD that the drama teacher had provided; she would see the script when she practiced.

Chatham finally found the auction information stuck to the inside of the zipper pocket of her purse where she kept change. Of course, she said to herself. When I reach in to get change to pay for a cup of coffee, I'll find my important note.

After a few moments, Victoria took to the podium she had erected at the front of the daycare room. She enjoyed an audience.

"Good morning and welcome everyone. Thank you all for being here this morning. I can see that several of you have already discovered the continental breakfast we have set out for you. Please, enjoy." She motioned to the spread as though she was hosting an elaborate party in her own home. "As you know, I'm Victoria, the head of parent volunteers at our school. You've probably seen me around campus recruiting you to head up committees or work in your child's classroom."

The crowd all seemed to nod in unison. Tricky Vicky had cornered them all at one point or another.

"So, today we are here to start the ball rolling with our annual school auction fundraiser." She motioned for Chatham to approach the podium. "And with us today is our new Auction Chair, Chatham Ross. Let's all give her a hand for stepping up to the plate." Everyone applauded with sincere gratitude. It was the one job that no one wanted to take on. The Auction Chair was directly responsible for raising over $200,000 for the school's budget. Word had it that two years ago when the auction came in $50,000 shy of goal, the chair herself had made up the difference.

Chatham was completely caught off guard. She looked over at Henrietta who was raising her eyebrows in a "*see?*" gesture. Chatham would have words with Tricky

Vicky later.

"Hi everyone. I'm Chatham. Um, well, I had an idea for the theme for this year's auction." She looked over at Victoria to emphasize the word idea as the extent of her involvement. Just then Victoria needed to fiddle with the buckle on the side of her lime green clutch purse. "So, um, yeah. Last year we did a night in Tuscany, which was really neat. I was thinking that this year since we're so focused on more diversity in our school, that we could go with a universal theme. My idea is *Passport Around The World*. We could embark on a trip to each continent with our passports. Each dining table would be a different country and the silent auction area could have planes and old ships that would be our transportation. Color wise I had the old world browns and tans in mind, with a hint of shimmery copper or something along those lines. Turquoise sheer could offset the earth tones and bring in the water aspect of the theme."

The room was silent.

"Well, that's it." Chatham sat down and breathed a deep sigh of relief. She always got nervous at presentations. Waiting for the group's reaction seemed like an eternity.

Chatham thought she heard clapping from someone in the back. She looked over. Thank goodness for best friends. The entire room, followed by spontaneous conversations consisting of decorating ideas, seating plans, and entertainment, quickly joined the applause.

"Oh my gosh," one woman blurted out. "Maybe we can get a trip around the world on a private yacht donated. Chatham, isn't one of your clients some big boat builder person?" Chatham was wondering how this stranger would know such a thing. "I read about it in Ad Week, and I could have sworn the article mentioned your name."

"I didn't know there was a spread on that campaign."

"It was on the cover. Something about the richest boat maker in the world and awaiting a new campaign to bring his more modest boats to the masses? Are you working on that one?"

Chatham never gave away trade secrets before their time. "Um, not exactly sure which issue that was in, but I'll be sure to pick it up. Thanks for the heads up."

For the next two hours, she met with every committee head and sub-committee head. She listened to ideas about which shade of blue the overlays should be: sky blue, aqua blue, sea blue, royal blue, navy blue. Chatham never knew there were so many blues. One woman spent a full twenty minutes explaining how her décor sub committee was in charge of planning the color of the water in the dining centerpiece vases.

"Should we make it the color of the ocean? Here's the problem. Which ocean? Or which sea for that matter? When I went swimming in the ocean off Maui over Easter break, it was actually kind of murky. That would make it a gray blue color. On the other hand, I went to Israel several years ago, before all the violence erupted, of course, and I swam in the Dead Sea. It was the first time I ever floated without having to scull. Do you have to scull when you float?"

Chatham looked at her blankly.

"Well, anyway, there are parts of the Mediterranean that are almost see-through green blue, which would mean we would have to make the water sort of greenish bluish. What do you think?"

Chatham looked over at Henrietta who looked just as exhausted from the onslaught of minutia. "Get me out of here," she mouthed as subtly as possible. She emphasized her plea by bending down to pick up something imaginary and showing Henrietta her hands in prayer position.

Henrietta responded with the OK finger and thumb circle sign. Just as Victoria walked by, Henrietta raised her voice to a "hear all" level. "Why Chatham, it's almost noon. You're going to miss your doctor's appointment. You have to go!"

"Yes, Henrietta. Thank you so much for reminding me." She stood up to address the crowd. "Well, thank you for coming everyone. I actually have to go because, well, I have an appointment. You understand."

"But Chatham," Victoria objected. "The captain can't leave her ship. You haven't met with all the sub-sub committee heads yet."

"Well this ship needs to leave port. But Victoria, why don't you cover for me as first mate." Chatham knew that Victoria loved to tell people what to do. She just didn't want to get her hands dirty.

"Oh, sure, I can do that." She stood up and clapped her hands. "OK then everyone, let's focus."

Chatham looked over at Henrietta who was pretending to lift weights while displaying a very elaborate stretch. Chatham quickly slipped out the door before anyone had a chance to stop her.

CHAPTER XX – *THE MEETING*

≈

It was 12:30 p.m. by the time Chatham arrived at E. Anytime. She put herself under a time crunch once again. Pick up time was fast approaching and she hadn't even made the call to Hank from The Idle Spur regarding the need for a new voice on his commercials. Who knew how long that call would take. His mood depended entirely upon whether or not he had gone hunting yet. And she really wanted to work out today. It was her new promise to herself to do something on a regular basis that not only helped her feel better physically, but mentally as well. The counter attendant was an added bonus that gave her that extra reason to show up....not in pajamas.

Chatham attempted to release her stress by breathing in deeply and imagining a running brook and butterflies. It wasn't working. Her mind drifted back to her current frustration. How could she not have known that Vicky would want more than a simple theme? She wanted blood. Chatham was convinced that Victoria truly was a vampire, sucking every free moment of Chatham's time from now through her entire existence at that school if Victoria had her way.

I'll just have to delegate, she concluded to herself as she applied a soft shade of pink lipstick to soften her lips and dabbed on a hint of light brown eyeliner to brighten up her tired blue eyes. She forced herself to smile.

Chatham exited the car and headed across the parking lot toward the gym. As she opened the club's glass and chrome door, she noticed the sporty Mercedes SL parked in the owner's space. Must be a coincidence, she convinced herself. It couldn't possibly be.

"Welcome to E. Anytime. It's our Spec-i-a-li-ty day or night. What can I do you for?"

Chatham was slightly deflated. Yesterday's counter clerk wasn't working. Even so, she wanted to exercise. Isn't that what she was there for?

"Hi, I tried the gym out yesterday, and thought I'd give it a try again. You know, join. I was thinking of the special plan you offered on your sign in the front." The neon green sign in the front window said: THREE MONTHS FOR THE PRICE OF ONE. NEW MEMBERS ONLY.

"Uh, sign? What sign?" Chatham turned around and pointed.

"That one, the bright green one. In the window." The attendant looked in the direction of her pointing finger.

"Oh, the green one. Yeah, I see it." He tried to read it backwards. "Huh. What did you say the offer was?"

"It says three months for the price of one. That is if you go outside and look at it. It's a little easier to read that way." She smiled. Chatham had patience for slow people. After all, she had to deal with people having patience with her son PJ on a regular basis. She wasn't convinced, however, that the employee was affected by sheer genetics. His delay seemed to be more self induced.

"Wow, good offer. OK, so now I'll need to get you registered and everything. What's your name?"

"Chatham. Chatham Ross."

"How do you spell Chatham?"

"C-H-A-T-H-A-M."

He typed it in. "Cool. And, uh, how do you spell Ross? Oh, duh." The attendant smacked himself in the head. Maybe he is shaking out the cobwebs, Chatham thought. "R-O-S, uh, S. Yeah, that's it."

Chatham counted as she waited for the employee to enter the correct spelling of her name into his computer. She couldn't help but noticing that the club employee had more facial piercings than Chatham thought physically possible. It wasn't a shock to see a stud in the soft skin of his nose and through his tongue, or just below his bottom lip and along the edge of his right eyebrow. But the hanging hoop inserted in his nostril bone and the diamond stud protruding out of his cheekbone were a bit much.

"How did you get the one in your chin?"

"Oh, yeah, that one really hurt. They went in under my tongue. Had to snip the little thingy and now I have a real long tongue, see?" He proceeded to stick out his tongue. It was horrifyingly long. Like a giraffe.

"Wow, neat," Chatham said. She quickly looked down, afraid she was going to upchuck right there on the counter.

"Yeah, thanks. So, do you have a phone number?"

She swallowed, took a deep breath and lifted her head with a smile. "Sure. 888-2001."

"Got it. I just need to do some input stuff. It'll take a minute or two."

"No problem." Chatham let her eyes drift to the counter. The jar of jellybeans was still there. The attendant noticed her field of vision.

"So, hey, did you want to enter the contest or anything while I'm getting you registered?"

"Contest?" Chatham responded.

"The jellybean one, man. I've been counting them all day. Problem is, I can't win cause I work here. But if I quit, I can win and then workout for free."

"Wow, great plan."

"Yeah, I thought so."

"Well, I guessed 3,000 yesterday, but I never filled anything out," Chatham offered.

"OK, I'll put you down for three big ones. Want to know what I guessed?"

Chatham indulged him. She didn't have a choice if she wanted to get in and work out. "Sure. What did you guess?"

"See, thing is, I can't decide. It's either just one big rainbow jellybean that they chopped up into lots of little ones. You know, to fake everybody out? Or, it's about ten trillion of them that they glued together."

"Gee, I never thought of that. Good perspective."

"Yeah, I thought so. Think I'll go with one. I'll probably win. No offense or anything."

"None taken, really." Chatham was ready to move on, the clock was ticking.

"So, uh, do you have a Visa or Mastercard or Discover Card or anything? We take those double ATM/credit card things, too."

Chatham reached into her purse and handed the attendant her American Express card.

"Gee, sorry. Don't take the green ones."

That's ironic, Chatham thought, since absolutely everything in this place is green. She pulled out her Visa.

"Will this work?"

"Yeah, that'll do it." He swiped the card and handed it back to her along with the receipt for her to sign. "Alrighty, you're all set. You get the three month trial that you can apply to a full membership if you like it and all."

"Great, thanks." Chatham waited until he pressed a button that turned the turnstile entrance from red to green. She entered the large metal filled room. First stop, locker room.

≈

Palio's flight arrived on time, and his car was waiting at the curbside valet as ordered. Even though he had had no seatmate during the cross-country excursion, he still was unable to rest. His mind was swimming with scenarios about business and family and love. Love had not been on his mind for years. He had always been too busy. Not that that had changed. He was ten times busier now with all of his father's projects. But it seemed to be on his mind lately, constantly really.

"I'm getting older, that's it," he said to himself as he tipped the valet attendant and pulled away from the curb for his ride to Marin. "I must be ready to settle down, that has to be it," he thought. "Why else would I even be considering my options?"

Palio couldn't help thinking about the couple in the restaurant. They seemed to be total opposites, yet completely compatible. He almost yearned for the soul mate that everyone dreamed of. That one person he could be totally and utterly at home with. He wanted someone who he could share his life and love forever with, just like his parents. "Maybe she is already in my life," Palio panicked. "She could be right in front of me. What if I miss her?" He began to analyze his relationships, searching for what was to come next in this area of his life that had never really been fulfilled.

What about the Italian olive oil princess with the Da Vinci painting? His father desperately wanted the painting, yet Palio felt that there was another motive on the beautiful owner's agenda. Somehow he knew there would be a price to pay, and it wouldn't necessarily have a dollar sign next to it. She was beautiful and smart and exciting. Palio admitted that adrenaline was high when it came to Georgina.

And Maria, what to do about her? She had been his father's favorite for years. Palio had to admit, she had really changed over the years. And loyal? No one could be more so. Maybe he was born to be with Maria. It wasn't such a terrible thought. Sometimes things that are meant to be are there all along.

"What's wrong with me?" Palio asked himself as he waited to order a breakfast biscuit at the McDonald's drive through.

"Nothing, absolutely nothing," the order taker said slowly over the speaker.

Was there a hidden camera in the menu board? Palio thought it was only a speaker. "Oh, sorry. I was daydreaming. I'll have an Egg McMuffin," Palio ordered.

"That will be $2.30 at the window," the cashier responded. Palio drove up to the window and paid for his breakfast. The McDonald's employee handed him his hot meal and her phone number. "Call me anytime," she smiled, a big gap between her teeth prominently displayed.

"Oh, thanks." Palio was caught off guard.

She looked around and leaned forward. "I get off at seven."

Palio smiled politely and departed as quickly as he could.

"Or maybe the McDonald's muffin maker," he thought.

A few minutes later he parked his custom rental in the owner's spot and made his way into the club that he was assigned to expand.

"Hey, dude, what's up?" the pierced counter boy said, addressing Palio as though he were a regular customer. "You wanna partake in the triple freebie offer, man? Or maybe guess if these little jelly dudes are maybe just one giant jelly dude? Then you can win free membership for a whole year. It's totally cool." The attendant was clearly proud of his sales ability.

Palio couldn't believe how many piercings that poor kid had gone through.

"How'd you get the one in the nose bone?" Palio asked.

"Oh, that one. Yeah. It hurt – totally. You're the second person who has asked me today. Some chick mom wanted to know about the chin one. I showed her my tongue and all 'cause they snipped my thingy."

"Your thingy," Palio repeated, not quite believing what he was hearing.

"Yeah, see." The boy stuck out his very long tongue for the second time in less than ten minutes. Palio was curious.

"Suburban mom?" Could it be?

"Yeah, she was cool and all."

"And where, pray tell, is this, what did you call her, chick mom, now?" The pierced one swung around until he pointed at Chatham's ass, which was sticking out over the edge of the chest lift machine. "Yeah, that's her butt. Over there."

Palio followed the tattooed-covered hand in the direction of where his intriguing woman was, ready to lift a bar of weights that appeared much too heavy.

"Hey, Palio!" Brett, the manager called out. "Welcome back, man." Brett slung his arm around Palio's shoulder and led him into the main office. "We've got the guy in here from Buff Body magazine. He wants to do a full-on feature about the expansion of the club for the cover."

Before Palio could even confirm if the woman was, in fact, the woman from yesterday, he was dragged into a meeting that was sure to last a long time, and was quite important for visibility.

"Well, hell, if it isn't the most eligible and richest bachelor in New York City! Right here, in this little sleepy town, tryin' to make himself a new empire." The man pumped Palio's hand as though he was pumping water from a well. "Now your name wouldn't be like Darth Vadar or nuthin'?" A fierce cackle emitted from somewhere deep within the throat of the visitor. His plaid short-sleeved shirt, thick-rimmed black glasses and high water polyester pants were a far cry from a body builder magazine image. His twangy accent didn't fit either. "Aww, sorry, I just love to joke."

"I'm sorry, aren't you here to talk about the club?" Palio shot a look at Brett who just shrugged.

"Well, hell, any publicity is good publicity, right?"

"It depends," Palio replied, "In where your interests lie."

"Aww, hell. Am I that obvious?" The man's demeanor suddenly changed. He took off his glasses, pushed back his oily locks in one slick motion and tore off his nerd top to reveal a tight black t-shirt with the letter B on the center. His voice fell a minimum of ten octaves. "I'm here with a message. From Mr. B."

"As in Bambini?" Palio answered.

"Yeah, that's him."

Palio was more curious than concerned. He knew that Mr. B had always admired his father for not becoming part of the mafia like so many other successful Italian immigrants.

"And what is this message you are here to deliver so far away from home?" Palio inquired.

"I actually like this place, ya know what I'm sayin'? Maybe I'll tell Mr. B to set up operation on the other coast, you know, enjoy a little sunshine and all."

"You were saying," Palio continued. His jaw was set in a firm, annoyed manner.

"Yeah, so, the message. Mr. B. says that he'll make you a deal. You seal the deal with the olive princess, I mean the entire deal, family and all, and he'll make sure you stay number one in jellybeans and little bitty boats for the duration."

Palio looked at the man with shock and disbelief.

"What exactly are you saying? Sell my family businesses to Georgina and marry her?"

"Yeah, somethin' like that."

Palio was not pleased. "Listen, pal, you need to leave now."

Brett got up to escort the visitor out, fast. The interloper shook him off.

"OK, I'm goin'. But what do I tell Mr. B.?"

Palio turned toward the man and said in a syllabic, syncopated tone, "You tell Mr. B that I don't sell, and I'm not the marrying kind. Period."

The message delivery man ran his fingers through his hair nervously. "Look, if I don't come back with a yes, then he'll chop my balls off, ya know what I'm sayin'?"

Palio thought for a moment. "Well, I wouldn't want you to be skewered, even if you do deserve it for disrupting my establishment. On second thought, tell him fine."

Brett jumped up in protest. "Tell him fine? What? Palio, what are you nuts?" Palio just smiled. "Tell him you talked to me, and I said fine."

The man nodded at Palio and pumped all the life out of Palio's hand once again. "Thanks Mr. Capriatti, sir. Really, thanks a million. You saved my balls and everything." The man ran out the door as fast as he could before Palio would have a chance to change his mind.

"Palio, my god, what the hell are you doing? That's like making a deal with the devil," Brett pleaded.

Palio got up to pour himself a cup of coffee to counteract his constant state of jet lag. He looked out of the office window into the gym, which was when he saw her.

"Wow, she came back," he said out loud without realizing it.

"What?" Brett replied. "Who came back? Palio, what's gotten into you?"

"I'll be right back," Palio said absently as he swung open the office door and headed into the main gym with one swift step.

"She actually came back," he said under his breath. "Amazing."

The gym outfit was a definite wardrobe improvement, although he thought she looked kind of cute in the disheveled morning attire she had on the other day. She had taken the neon gift clothes and added a bit of style with a cute white undershirt, neon blue socks, and a bright pink headband. She even reworked the lettering on the shorts from E. Anytime to: *I get mine at Exercise Anytime, where do you get yours?* Catchy, he thought. He made a mental note of it.

Palio chuckled to himself as he watched her simultaneously pump and squirt the demo sneaker. Too much pressure and the shoes would pop. He could tell she wasn't a regular workout kind of girl, but she was starting to look the part. Just then, she stopped at the thigh-thinner machine, examining the levers and weights, clearly confused.

"Hi there," Palio said. "You actually put the pads on the outside and push inward, like this." He moved the lever so that the padded bars were in place and showed her how she was supposed to sit, spread eagle.

The mysterious woman looked up at him, clearly frazzled. "Oh, duh," was all that came out of her mouth. "That's pretty obvious."

"What? You don't spend every waking moment at the gym trying to look like good 'ol Jenna over there?" Palio teased.

She scanned the walls. "Well, yeah. Thank god," she responded. "Is that what will happen if I do? Maybe I should quit while I'm ahead," she laughed.

"You're a natural," he smiled, encouraging her to give the machine a try. "I'm Palio by the way."

"Chatham," she said warmly. "Chatham Ross. I'd shake your hand, but I think mine are a little nasty right now."

Palio laughed. She had a great sense of humor. "That's OK, maybe next time."

Chatham got on the machine, her legs straddling the pads. "Well, I guess here goes."

Palio tried not to stare. She was definitely a beautiful woman, just a different kind of beautiful than he was used to.

"Just follow the numbered machines and let me know if you need any assistance. I'll be at the counter greeting our guests." He didn't want her to know that he owned the place, but he wasn't sure why.

"Thank you," she said and got back to her workout.

≈

Great, Chatham thought as Palio walked away. Just spread your legs as wide as you can Chatham in front of the gorgeous man... that'll make him attracted to you. Nothing says love like cellulite. Why did she always seem to find herself in humiliating situations with this very attractive stranger?

He was definitely helpful, maybe too helpful for just a clerk. Actually, she couldn't believe such a nice-looking man had the same job as the pierced freak with the horrifying tongue. Wasn't he a bit old for that? Wasn't he going to do anything meaningful with his life? she wondered. Well, it was none of her business. She was here to workout, not to eye the hired help.

She looked at her watch; only thirty-five minutes before she had to pick up the kids. Chatham waited until the nice man had departed and proceeded to push with all her might. I could get used to this, she thought. What a way to workout frustrations.

≈

Palio pretended to be busy with paperwork and welcoming club members, but he couldn't help glancing up at Chatham as she attempted the machines in ascending order.

He was also preoccupied with this sudden veiled threat. Palio had never had to deal with any mafia issues. His father had always made it known that he would not take part; yet Palio's father was the most generous man to everyone. He was universally loved by the good and the bad and that was how Palio expected it to stay. This odd visit today rattled him. And how did Georgina fit in? Palio was more than curious, which was why he superficially went along with the suggestion. He wanted to see where all of this was going.

≈

This was only Chatham's second time to the gym, but she already felt a little better. Maybe the depression was due to a lack of endorphins and not just her attempt at being super woman. Chatham couldn't help but notice that the counter man was glancing in her direction every so often.

No, Chatham, she scolded herself. You've got to be kidding. Hi dad, yeah I'm dating a health club counter clerk. Her dad would tell her that her mother was rolling over in her grave. Although, Chatham couldn't help but think that the gorgeous employee was also endearing. And she had to admit, she was more than happy that he might be curious about her as well.

Chatham finished up with the butt-buster machine and walked over to scan the class schedule list posted on the wall: Spin Class, Power Yoga, Pilates. There was a new class starting in two minutes, and it promised to be a power workout and only twenty minutes long. Must be intense, she thought. She could finish it and be done in time to pick her kids up from school. Body Boxing sounded interesting.

"Why not," she said aloud as she stepped into the room reserved especially
for the class. The walls were padded top to bottom. Chatham stood in the center of the room with the other patrons. It was then she noticed that her classmates were at least twice her size. In fact, their arms made her arms legs look like wet soggy noodles. What was this gym called again?

"OK people, listen up," the instructor blared from her headset, her muscles bursting from the tight black spandex outfit that looked as though it had been painted on. "This is how it's gonna work. We pair off in twos. Try to find someone your same size so you don't crush them – Lizard." She darted a look of warning at a young guy with Popeye biceps.

"Not a problem, Mirella baby," he said leering at her. "Why don't you be my partner?"

"Because I want to live, Lizard. Besides, I have a date tonight and I don't want to show up with bruises."

Chatham wondered what kind of guy would date a woman whose leg muscles were bigger than the average man's chest. And what did she say about bruises?

"Go with her," the instructor commanded, pointing a finger at Chatham.

Chatham turned around to see none other than the homeless man from the bakery. He had changed his outfit and she wasn't sure which was worse. Lizard's looks matched his name. He had greasy brown hair and some sort of slime that covered his exposed skin, which reminded her of swimmers before a big competition. His hands were clad with gloves that were missing the ends of the fingers and his spandex outfit literally had scales on it. But he was about the same height as Chatham, so she could understand why the instructor suggested the match.

"Yeah, alright," she said glancing over at Chatham. "You're new, right?" the instructor inquired, a sly grin across her mouth.

"Well, yes, you could say that," Chatham answered, a little unsure if she should have. "Second time actually," she lied weakly.

"Well alright! We've got a virgin everybody, don't do her in too hard, OK?" The instructor did a quick about face before Chatham had time to protest.

A heavy metal rap song blasted out of the speakers. The class members gritted their teeth and punched their fist into the palm of their hands, in unison.

"Are you angry?" the instructor demanded.

"Yeah," everyone growled.

"I said, are you angry?" she screamed at the top of her lungs.

"Yeeaaahhhhh!" the class roared even louder.

Chatham gulped. She wasn't quite sure she was prepared for this. Suddenly, she felt a strong pull on her arm.

"What are you doing?" Chatham exclaimed, dumbfounded. She glanced at Palio, wondering what he was thinking.

"Time to go," Palio said as he pulled her arm.

"But I –"

Before she could turn around completely, Lizard's wind up was on its way to her solar plexis.

"Contact," he exclaimed as he launched Chatham up in the air, off her feet and into the arms of Palio.

≈

Trip made a quick stop for his morning java at the Starbucks in the strip mall close to his house. It happened to be close to Chatham's house as well, which was why he wasn't surprised to see her SUV in the parking lot. Out of curiosity he peeked into the exercise outlet's window, not expecting to see anything familiar.

"Oh my god!" Trip exclaimed. He blinked several times to make sure that what he was witnessing was real. There was Chatham, lying comfortably in the arms of a tall, dark, and handsome foreigner. He put his face up to the window, cupped his hands around his eyes to shield out the sun. He could have sworn that she wasn't moving, at all. Panic mode set in.

Trip raced into the gym, hopped over the railing and burst into the office where Chatham lay. He had forgotten that his newest import, a neon orange pelakeet, was still on his shoulder.

"Get me some smelling salts," Palio barked at Brett the manager as he laid Chatham down on the office couch. Brett opened a cabinet on the wall that was filled with every kind of first aid ointment, bandage, brace and chemical resuscitation element made. It was a necessity in a hardcore facility like E. Anytime. Palio broke the capsule that was handed to him and waved it in front of Chatham's nose. The strong ammonia fragrance made Chatham wake with a start. It was enough to jolt someone out of a deep coma.

"Sorry to shock you," Palio apologized. His face was inches from Chatham's.

"Hi," was all she said.

Trip didn't know what had happened, but he wasn't going to let someone else move in on his territory. Who was this stranger anyway? And what the hell did Chatham think she was doing in her trendy short shorts and day glo gear? Was she finally ready for romance again?

"I'll take it from here," Trip said, not giving Palio a chance to offer an explanation.

"I'll take it from here," the bird said, mimicking his owner.

"I doubt she'll press charges," Trip continued.

"I doubt she'll press charges," the bird agreed. Trip just wanted to get Chatham out of the fitness factory and back to where she belonged, with him and her family.

Chatham, still dazed, weakly protested the exit. "Trip, what are you doing here? I'm fine, really."

Trip ignored her protests and lifted her up in his

arms. As he made their way out of the office, Chatham noticed a miniature carving of a horse drawn carriage on a desk.

"Trip, wait." Chatham shouted to the handsome man that had been so close to her face. "Where did you get that?"

But Trip was too quick. "Let's get out of here." He whisked her out of the gym and into his car for the ride home.

Chatham laid down on the back seat of Trip's store van and fell asleep.

CHAPTER XXI – *POSSIBILITIES*

≈

"Time to get up, time to get up," the orange glow bird recited, like a living alarm clock. "Rise and shine, rise and shine," the creature continued.

Chatham rolled over and squinted at the bedside clock. It was 8:30 in the evening. Had she been sleeping all afternoon? She lifted the covers and looked down. Someone had taken off all her clothes except her underwear. What was going on?

"Well, it's about time. I was beginning to worry about you," Trip said as he entered the room, tray in hand. He handed Chatham her robe and turned so that she could slip it on. It took her a good three minutes, what with the sharp pain she felt as she stretched her arms and inserted them into the armholes.

"Done," she said, wincing. She was still confused as to what she was doing in bed and how she got there.

Trip reached around her to stack two pillows for added lumbar support.

Chatham complied by leaning back against the pillows.

"Ow," she said as she felt a severe cramp in her stomach.

"Yeah, bit of a bruise I'm afraid."

Chatham opened up her robe slightly to discover a large purple fist mark in the middle of her stomach. That's going to turn purple, she thought as she retied her robe.

Trip placed the dining tray with chicken noodle soup, Ritz crackers, and seven-up on Chatham's lap.

"Here you go, my little patient. The doctor said you'd be OK; you just need rest. How do you feel?"

"Trip, what am I doing here? I have to pick up the kids." She was becoming more coherent, which meant the onset of worry.

"Not to worry, I took care of it." Just then her brood bounced in the room and launched themselves up onto her princess-and-the-pea height bed.

"Mommy, we missed you. It's OK, I will take care of you," PJ promised as he leaned over and gave her a big hug.

"Thank you, PJ. I love you, too. Did you do your homework?"

"I did it," PJ responded with confidence.

"Mom, what did you do to yourself?" Camp asked directly. "You look really bad." Thank goodness for honesty, Chatham chuckled to herself.

"Yeah, Mom. Did someone beat you up or something?" Madison asked, poised to hear all the dirty details. "Some guy called to see how you were doing, but Trip hung up on him." She looked at Trip as though she was waiting for an explanation for his irrational behavior.

"Maddy," Trip objected, "let your Mom get some rest. Come on, everyone out and on with your pajamas."

Maddy and Camp leaned over to give Chatham a kiss and scampered out of the room.

"Well, you seem better now at least. Can I get you anything else before I go?" Trip asked.

"Can I get you anything else before I go, before I go?" the animal copied.

"Trip, where did you get that dazzling creature?"

"Oh, the pelakeet? Kind of vivid, huh?"

"Like a lava lamp."

"Yeah. I looked to see if he had batteries when I got him. I've never seen anything so bright either. He's going to a ventriloquist magician who wanted something other than a dove to pull out of a hat. Go figure."

"Trip?" Chatham asked, as she watched him stroke the bird's wing. "Thanks."

"Thanks? For what?"

"I'm not exactly sure, but I think you saved me from something."

"You looked pretty cozy actually," he blurted.

Chatham just smiled. "Oh, the counter boy? If I remember correctly, I think he saved me, too. I think I went into a class for experts, not amateurs."

Trip stared at her, silent and frowning.

"Palio is such an interesting name," Chatham mumbled, holding her forearm over her forehead.

"Do you want me to stay?" Trip asked.

"No, you've done enough already. I'll be fine. Thank you again, Trip. You're the best friend a girl could hope for."

"Well, the kids are all set and I need to vamoose. Just go to bed early, and you'll be fine. Do you want me to leave the bird to keep you company?"

"No, thank you. I don't mind visits, but short ones when it comes to your precious imported animals if that's OK."

They both laughed, remembering the previous skoonard disaster.

"OK then, you stay in bed and I'll get the kids settled before I'm off." He leaned over and gave her a kiss on the forehead, as any caring friend would do.

≈

Trip closed the door to Chatham's room. Leaving her was the last thing he wanted to do. He longed to stay with her for the rest of the night, to sit on her bed and comfort her. Reminding himself that he needed to be aloof in order to make her come to him, he tried not to focus on the "friend" term she had so easily thrown out. That had hurt. She had meant it as a sweet gesture, a compliment really… it was anything but. Will she ever see me as anything, but Peter's best friend? he wondered.

The real problem that night was he couldn't get that moment out of his mind. She had been lying in the arms of some handsome stranger, looking at him as if suspended in time. Her beautiful blue eyes were staring at the stranger the way he longed for her to look at him. Part of him wished he hadn't seen any of it.

Trip quickly put the kids to bed and headed to his van. Tomorrow was a big day, and he had to be ready.

≈

Chatham heard the front door shut. She climbed out of bed and made her way up to her children's rooms to wish them sweet dreams.

"Thanks for covering for me," she said to Maddy. "I love you, sweet dreams."

"No problem, Mom. Do you feel better?" Maddy asked, worry etched across her face.

"Like a million dollars."

"What time do you leave tomorrow?"

"Crack of dawn. Don't worry, I'll get you up early." She leaned over to kiss her daughter, careful not to wince as she used her stomach muscles to stand up straight. She would have to have a talk with that slimy guy at the gym the next time she went. And, yes, she was going back again. Especially if the man who had saved her was there. Who was he anyway?

Chatham tiptoed into the boys' room and kissed each of them on the forehead. They were already fast asleep. She made her way down the stairs and back to bed for what she hoped would be a good night sleep filled with sweet dreams.

CHAPTER XXII – *EXTENDED FAMILY*

≈

"Mom, I can't find my Tae Kwon Do belt," Camp yelled from under the massive pile of clothes in the upstairs laundry room.

Washing and drying clothes was easy. Phase One: throw dirty clothes into washing machine, add pre-measured Tide tablet, and press "on" button. Chatham even bought a plastic basketball hoop and hooked it up so that each wad of clothes tossed from afar actually made it in and not somewhere else like behind the washing machine, never to be found again. The kids loved to play *clothes basket*.

Getting the clothes into the dryer took a little more effort, which meant more time, Usually they sat sometimes for a day – or more, but they eventually made it to phase two.

But folding them? You've got to be kidding. Who has time for that? The Ross family basically lived out of the wash-and-dry pile on the laundry room floor.

"I think it's still in the car, honey. But you don't need it in New York," Chatham called out in a garbled fashion, her mouth full of toothpaste.

Madison bounced into the bathroom and reached around her mother to grab a hairbrush and eyeliner.

Chatham spit out the toothpaste and rinsed her mouth.

"Are you supposed to be wearing make-up to school, Madison? I vaguely remember the school dress code saying something like, NOT ALLOWED. Does that ring a bell to you, honey?" Chatham absently applied the liner to her own eyes after confiscating it from her daughter's hand.

"Mom, please. I'm in Upper Division now. The rules get a little more relaxed. Kind of like, *don't ask don't tell.* Some girls even show their stomachs, Mom." Madison retrieved the liner as Chatham put it down, applying a very light shade right above her lash line. Chatham suddenly realized that her daughter was growing up before her very eyes. She would have to pick her battles.

"Well, it's really not that noticeable. Just use your good judgment, OK?"

Chatham made one last sweep through her closet, making sure she wasn't overlooking something she might need for her long weekend in New York. She was having dinner with her sister-in-law tonight and then the big pitch tomorrow. Finally, a relaxing time with Dad to complete what she hoped would be a productive trip. What was she forgetting?

"The dress!" Chatham exclaimed, grabbing the white billowy Marilyn Monroe outfit from the back of her closet door. She had rented a replica from the costume store in San Francisco in the heart of the Castro district. "Can't forget this, or I'll really blow it," she said to the racks of out-of-style suits and faded sweatpants she had interspersed throughout her closet. Her dirty laundry was piled neatly under the shoe shelf in a small built-in compartment. The stepping stool assisted her with those high-ceiling storage spots that contained – well, she hadn't looked in years. Must get an organizer for this disaster area, Chatham thought as she exited her room.

The doorbell rang right on time at 7:00 a.m. The kids were dressed and ready for school and Chatham's car service was set to arrive any minute. It was one morning that actually ran smoothly.

PJ leaned toward the door, scrunched up his nose and in his most commanding voice said, "Who is it?"

"Little pig, little pig, let me come in," the voice from behind the door responded.

PJ started to laugh. It was a personal joke between them. "Not by the hair of my chinny chin chin."

Chatham smiled. She loved watching her son have such a good time.

"First I'll huff and puff and blow your house down and then I'll squish you into a little bowl of smashed bananas," the deep voice promised, only a thin production door separating the predators.

"You can't blow my house down, it's made of bricks. And I'll eat you, banana man!" PJ was laughing so hard he wet his pants. The door flung open.

"You're here!" PJ exclaimed, hugging Tom and Theo. "I have to go to the bathroom."

"Good to see you too, pal," Theo laughed as PJ ran down the hallway, his pants already past his knees.

Tom looked at Theo disapprovingly.

"Grow up." He abruptly stepped pass his boyfriend and swooshed his way through the front door.

"Oh Tom, Theo." Chatham hugged them both. "Thank you for being on time." She looked beyond them to the black Lincoln pulling up in front of the house.

"OK, so we have to go now so that we don't miss our flight. I left a list of telephone numbers, doctors, schedules, and stuff like that. Madison can fill you in on everything. Theo could you maybe take PJ to school today and Tom can you take Madison? Oh, and it's special friend's day in Madison's class. Today, actually. Can you both go? Is that OK? OK, well, I think that's it. Backpacks are packed with lunches in them and oh, what else?" Chatham asked while giving each of her children a kiss and hug in turn. She had to find PJ in the bathroom to deliver his goodbye.

"Go, sweetheart. Have a great time and don't worry about a thing. Enjoy yourself; you need it. We'll be fine."

Chatham looked over Tom's shoulder to see Theo picking up Madison with one hand.

"Oh my god, can he really do that?"

Tom shooed Chatham and Camp out. "Have fun, goodbye, win this one. Loves and kisses."

The front door closed behind them as the driver opened a door to an awaiting adventure.

Chatham's stomach was still tender from yesterday's interlude, but she had taken two Advil to numb the pain. She climbed in and settled back next to Camp and closed her eyes for the drive to the airport.

CHAPTER XXIII – *SCHOOL TIME*

≈

PJ ran ahead of Theo. He wanted to show him his classroom. Having practically seen PJ grow up, Theo was proud of his independence.

"Hey, duh boy. Can you say heeeelllooo?" The two bullies appeared out of nowhere.

"Hi Petie. Hi Billy. I am going to my classroom." PJ was all smiles.

"Duh boy, where *is* your classroom?" Billy asked with a sarcastic tone.

"Number 28. My classroom is 28," PJ said confidently.

"No, it's not duh boy. It's 25, they changed it, right Petie?" Billy looked at his pal, a snicker in his eye.

"No, it's not," PJ said emphatically. "It's 28. My classroom is number 28." PJ was getting anxious. Potential change in routine.

"Yeah, that's right. Number 25," Petie said, snickering to Billy.

"You better hurry duh-boy. Mrs. Abartini is in 25."

Theo didn't like the sound of this interaction.

"OK, I will," PJ said, changing direction to head toward number 25. He looked back over his shoulder, suddenly lost.

The boys walked away giggling only to bump into a mass as solid as a steel door. The force of the impact threw them back and onto their hindquarters. Stunned, they looked up in unison to see Theo, the Hulk.

"Since you boys think you're so smart, let's have

you show my friend PJ to his classroom. What number did you say it was?" He loomed over them, his massive biceps popping out of his skin tight tank top.

"We're sorry," Petie blurted out. "We didn't mean anything by it. We were confused and we're sorry, right Billy?"

"Yeah, like, confused. We're sorry, man. Won't happen again. Hey PJ, I think your classroom is number 28, like you said."

PJ relaxed, a smile finding its way back to his face. "Yes. My room is number 28. Theo, my room is 28. I know how to get there. I will show you." PJ grabbed Theo's hand and began to pull.

Theo stopped momentarily and leaned down so that his face was almost touching the two troublemakers.

"I'll be watching you two. The next time I come here I better hear that PJ is your best friend and that you stick up for him. Do we understand each other boys?"

The offender's faces turned whiter than Casper the Friendly Ghost.

"Yes sir. We got it," they responded simultaneously.

"Hey PJ," Billy called. "Sit with us at lunch today, OK?" He gave a frightened smile to Theo.

PJ beamed.

"OK, I will." He looked up at Theo. "I eat lunch with my friends."

Theo gave the evil eye warning look to the twosome, picked up PJ with one hand, and tossed him into the air.

PJ giggled as Theo managed to catch him in the

palm of his hand. Billy and Petie were left sitting on the ground with their jaws hanging open as they heard the inside joke fade off into the morning.

"Little pig, little pig..."

≈

"Welcome to our classroom," Madison's teacher enthused, her vociferous manner somewhat contagious. "Today is such a special day, now that you, our special friends, are here to visit us. I'd like to start by reading a special poem I wrote for you, on behalf of our students." Her flowing beads, Birkenstocks, and dreadlocks in the making were an ironic contradiction to the Armani and Chanel crowd.

Tom glanced at Madison, and she returned his gaze with eyes half-mast. Clearly, she wasn't too interested in the special day or the teacher who appeared to be on Prozac.

The audience sat at attention so as not to miss a word of the poem.

"Welcome to our home away
From home and we hope you will stay.
Our students have so much to show,
So much to show you that they know."

Tom couldn't handle it. The effect of the poor prose was like watching paint dry.

"Oh my god, Madison!" Tom suddenly exclaimed. He spotted Madison's artistic self-portrait right away. Hers was a picture of a cereal box, an excellent self-portrait in water color of Madison eating a huge bite of Product 19 flakes from a bowl. *Breakfast for Champions* it said in bold red lettering. "A budding jingle artist, just like your mother."

Tom patted Madison affectionately on the back, a tear welling in his eye. He was so proud.

"Oh yes, sir, please, please speak out and be heard," Mrs. Cooper said joyously.

"Who, me?" Tom looked appropriately surprised as he laid his hand over his heart. He stood up to address his audience. "Well, hello, my name is Tom." The entire room shifted their chairs in his direction. "And this is Madison. I am her special friend, of course. Well, special in a brotherly, cousinly, uncley kind of way." Tom beamed at Madison affectionately.

Madison just sunk down in her seat. She looked totally embarrassed.

As if on cue, Theo walked in the room, having gotten PJ safely to the right classroom at his school.

"Oh, oh, and this is *my* very special friend, Theodore." Tom waved him over. "Say hello to all these lovely special friend people, Theo."

Theo looked around uncomfortably. Tom was sure he saw his partner notice the man with the chiseled chin and Ralph Lauren looks sitting a few seats away and not wearing a wedding band.

"Uh, yeah. Hi everybody." Theo was embarrassed, and Tom was the jealous type.

"Maybe you should come sit *down,* Theo," Tom motioned, a controlled strain in his voice. "After all, you *are* late. Did you get lost, forgot where your *home*room was?

"Huh, what? Oh yeah. Sit down. Sure." Theo made his way over to the seat saved next to Tom.

"You're pathetic," Tom whispered, crossing his legs away from his lover.

"Huh, what? What are you talking about? I got here as fast as I could. Hey Maddy." She gave him a pleading look of the *please help* variety.

Theo motioned to her that he had it handled

"That's right, pathetic. Or should I say, flirt? What, eye candy too tempting for you? I'm just not good enough anymore, am I?" Tom pouted.

"Welcome Theodore," Mrs. Cooper emitted with pure heart and soul radiance.

"Stop fighting," Madison insisted with a strong whisper.

"Yeah, come on Tommy. I didn't do nothin'. I just walked in the room. You know you're the only one for me." He gave Tom's knee an affectionate squeeze.

Tom abruptly wiggled out of Theo's grasp, only to lean into him seconds later with a big sigh.

"Well, alright then. I may have over reacted just a tad. Maybe I'm just tired. I think I need a Midol or something." Tom was slowly returning to his normal neurotic state.

Tom saw the best-looking boy in class lean over to Madison and whisper,

"How cool to have gay special friends. Didn't know you were so hip, Maddy." He quickly leaned back in his seat before the teacher saw his maneuver.

Maddy couldn't help but beam. The kind with all the pearly whites showing. "That's Dane," she mouthed to him.

Tom leaned forward slightly and whispered, "Not a total disaster."

Maddy gave him the biggest hug she could muster. Tom looked over at Theo, making sure he saw how much Tom was loved. Theo leaned in to Tom and whispered.

"Where's Trip? Wasn't he supposed to be here, too?" Tom's face turned an instant shade of red.

"Trip? Why are you so interested?" Tom went rigid and Maddy leaned over, talking in a low whisper.

"Trip called me on my cell phone and told me he had to go somewhere suddenly. You know Trip, he's always off to some crazy place."

Tom smiled smugly.

"See, he's busy. And so are you. So never mind." Tom was happy that he didn't have anyone else to compete with today for his lover's attention.

CHAPTER XXIV – *PLANE FLIGHT*

≈

Chatham and Camp arrived at the airport with a half hour to spare before their flight. They stood in the security check-in line with the rest of the air-bound passengers. The line was a little longer than Chatham expected. Don't stress, she told herself as she alternated her glance three times between her watch and the departure time printed on their boarding passes. She squinted to read the overhead monitors. Gate 88. Great. The gate was at the end of the double corridor. They might have to run if they couldn't get through the security checkpoint quickly.

Camp was pre-occupied with the whole process of putting items on the conveyer belt and having them disappear into the unknown, only to come out intact on the other side. Since multitasking was a part of Chatham's modus operandi, she decided to call Chloe. She dialed, only to receive Chloe's voice machine.

"I'm not available, Thank god. But I'd like to talk to you when I'm free so please leave a message." Giggling voices completed the recording.

"Hi Chloe, it's Chatham. Hope we're still on for dinner. I'll just come over when I get into town. Oh ya, Camp's with me. Hope it's OK to bring him too. See you tonight, bye." Chatham snapped the phone off just as the line was starting to move. Camp didn't seem to be in any hurry. He was dragging the toes of his merrills as he walked.

"Come on honey, pick up your feet when you walk," Chatham encouraged.

"Mom, do we have to go?" Camp asked, a bit anxious.

"Camp, honey, you love seeing Aunt Chloe and Grandpa."

"Yeah, I know. I want to go, I guess. I was just wondering what happens when stuff goes through the machine," he said, somewhat concerned.

"Oh, the x-ray machine? They just zap it with a magnetic laser or something. It's harmless."

Camp's eyes popped open.

"What's wrong, honey. Are you OK?"

Camp just looked down at his feet. "Nothing, it's fine." He let out a huge sigh and shuffled forward, not taking his eyes off the large Invision machine straight ahead. It was as though he was imagining that he would have to go through the see all x-ray machine himself.

Chatham couldn't help but notice the man in front of her. Double-breasted charcoal Armani suit with deep burgundy tasseled loafers and some sort of reptile skin briefcase in hand. He didn't have a ring on his wedding finger but he did have perfectly manicured fingers. Metrosexual, for sure, Chatham assessed. She craned to see what magazine he had tucked under his arm. GQ. Too perfect for me, she thought as she turned her attention elsewhere. Just then a boy about nine ran up to the walking clothes ad and gave him a big hug. A tiny blond haired woman clad in a fur-lined leather jacket, skin-tight jeans, and spiked heels was right behind him.

"Hey Jimmy," the man said scooping his son up and giving him a huge hug and kiss. "Ready for some fun?"

"Yeah, Dad. Sorry we're late." He nodded over to

the woman, presumably his mother.

"Yeah, sawry Phillip. We went out to breakfast at Silks with Stu, and it took forever for them to bring da bill." Her heavy Brooklyn accent hung in the air as she pulled out a metal emery board and began filing her slightly broken nail. The three of them were squeezed together in front of Chatham and Camp.

"For god sakes Janice, put that thing away. What are you crazy? They'll think you have a weapon or something."

"Oh my Gawd, do ya really think so? Does this really look like a knife or somethin'?" She started to wave it around.

He grabbed her hand and yanked it out of the air.

"Janice, go home to Stu. I'll have Jimmy home on Monday, just like we agreed. OK?"

Her personality did a 180.

"You better not fuckin' let him see anything wacky in New York. Ya got me? No Pink Pussycat or strip clubs or anything like that, alright?" She was practically spitting.

"Janice, he won't go to your old stompin' ground, don't worry. He'll be uptown with me at my new place on Park. I've come up in the world. Things are good." He puffed out his chest and pulled the lapel collar of his suit. He was clearly proud of his new image.

"Then ya better not be late on no alimony payments. I've got myself a lifestyle too that I needs to keep up. And I ain't hitched to Stu yet, so you're still on the hook." She leaned over to kiss her son. "Be good, Jimmy baby. Mommy loves you. I'll see you in a couple of days."

Chatham saw the little boy cringe from

embarrassment.

"Yeah Ma, OK. See ya." The flamboyant show girl wiggled her way down the airport promenade. She was made for attention.

The boy seemed happy to be with his dad but uncomfortable at the same time, like he was trying to convince his father to care.

"Hey Dad, I'm getting really good at Chess. They even asked me to be on the team at school."

"How did you learn to play chess? Your mother thinks chess is the name of a night club...the Ches(t) club." He laughed out loud.

"Yeah, I know. But Stu knows how to play. He taught me." The Armani man was suddenly tense.

"I don't want to hear a fucking thing about Stu, ya got me?"
The boy hunched his shoulders and cowered, like a wounded animal. Chatham heard him almost whimper.

"Uh, maybe you and I can play in New York this weekend," the boy said. "I hear they play at some park down in the village. Like you can bet on a speed chess game and win some bucks." The boy straightened up and inserted a hopeful expression on his face.

"Maybe I won't have to work too much this weekend." The father replied absently. He was already engrossed in his fashion magazine.

Not getting a favorable response from his father, the boy resigned himself to playing the Game Boy Advance he had stuffed in his cargo pants pocket.

Chatham felt sorry for the boy. She wondered which inflicted more psychological damage on a child:

having a divorced dad who wasn't emotionally available and whom you only saw once in a while, or one you didn't see at all because he wasn't available period. Chatham shook off the thought. She didn't want to wallow in misery in the middle of the airport.

Chatham glanced down at Camp. He was playing the same Super Mario Smash Brothers Game Boy Advance game as the boy in front of him. Chatham nudged her son and silently pointed to the boy's plastic blue companion.

"Hey, cool," Camp said to the boy. He was too secure to feel rejection. "Did you get to level 10 yet?"

The boy looked up at his dad who had practically climbed into the article he was reading about how to catch a rich woman in New York City. He looked back at Camp.

"Yeah, just yesterday."

"Sweet," Camp answered, completely impressed at the stranger's skill. I'm still at level 8. Super Mario hasn't totally demolished Kazooey yet. Well, he killed him five times, but to get to level 10 you have to –"

"Kill him seven times," the boy and Camp said at exactly the same time.

The father looked up and noticed Chatham for the first time. He seemed to like what he saw. Chatham actually thought about her wardrobe this time. Especially after the humiliating exercise outlet fiasco. She sported a silk black turtleneck, levis, a black and silver Donna Karan belt, and a pair of Cole Hahn knock-off black ankle boots. She would have liked to have purchased the real thing but the family was on a budget now, which meant no frivolous expenses.

The metro man scanned Chatham's hand so fast she

almost missed it.

"Solo trip?" he asked as suavely as he could. Well, that was a departure from his interaction with his ex, Chatham thought. Must be on the prowl.

"Well, no, actually. I'm with my son."

He clearly hadn't even noticed Camp. Too far below his field of interest.

"Business or pleasure?" he drooled. She didn't like how he raised his eyebrows and licked his lips as he said pleasure.

"Business, definitely," she answered as directly as possible. "And meeting friends," she quickly added. It had been so long, she didn't even know if she was encouraging or discouraging his advances. He reached into his pocket, pulled out a gold-embossed card, and handed it to Chatham.

"It's my new enterprise," he said, expecting her to be impressed.

She read it out loud. "Tower of Power Consultants. Sounds – powerful."

"Right you are, little lady," he said with a wink.

"And, what kind of consulting is it exactly?" she asked as innocently as possible.

"Why we advise top people on how to gain more power in their organization, of course. It's so they can make it to the top of the Ivory Tower. The pinnacle." He winked at her knowingly.

"Wow, sounds great. You must be quite good at it." She was hoping the checkpoint line would drastically increase its speed.

"Yep, think Trump will come crawling pretty soon.

He's heard of us. He'll be beggin' for our services. Think I'll charge him double. Perceived value they call it."

"Sounds like a great strategy," Chatham agreed. "Oh look, your turn." They had finally reached the front of the line. She couldn't wait to get through it and find the nearest trashcan to deposit the card.

The self-made man took off his tasseled loafers and prepared to lay them on the conveyer belt. Chatham couldn't help but notice his worn socks with holes in both ankles and Band-Aids on the blisters that his new shoes imparted. A little pain to accompany the new image. Fabricator was the only word that came to Chatham's mind.

The man's son put his items on the belt and the twosome were through in a flash. Chatham followed by laying her sundries on the belt. As soon as she stepped through the metal detector archway, the strange man pounced right in front of her.

"Keep the card, honey. The ball is in your court." He winked and was gone, his son practically running to keep up with the less-than-father-like figure.

Chatham was flustered as she put her ankle boots back on and gathered her things. She didn't even bother looking for a garbage can. She just dropped the card right where she stood.

Chatham turned around to wait for Camp, but he was nowhere in site.

It was Camp's turn to go through the security checkpoint, but he was glued in place. Fear clearly had overtaken him.

Chatham signaled to him, encouraging him to walk through. She cupped her hands around her mouth so that he could hear her above the commotion of the crowd.

"It's nothing, honey. Just come on through." She followed her gentle command with a smile and a wave for him to hurry up. Camp carefully removed his shoes and belt, placed them on the moving beltway and gingerly stepped through the arch. No sooner had he stepped beneath it than an ear-piercing alarm sounded, accompanied by a whirling flashing red light. Two armed security officials appeared instantly.

"Step this way young man," the head guard instructed. He was armed with a pistol, a can of mace and what looked like a stun gun.

Chatham couldn't believe what she was seeing. "Officer, that's my son," she protested. "He doesn't have anything to speak of. It must be your machine."

"Step back please, ma'am," the guard instructed.

"But officer, I am his mother. I am his legal guardian."

"I said step back ma'am, or I'll have you removed for disorderly conduct." The officer was serious. One of those minimum-wage power-hungry mongers.

Camp stared at her with big, scared saucer eyes.

Chatham mouthed, "It's OK" to her son and smiled weakly.

"What do you have there young man? Empty your pockets please."

"I don't have anything. Not anything. Uh, sir," Camp said, a look of guilt prevalent on his face.

"Nothing huh? Then what do I see bulging out of your pocket? Let's go, empty it." Camp looked at Chatham who nodded in agreement. He emptied the Game Boy

Advance he was coveting.

Chatham tried not to chuckle. From his perspective, the conveyer belt must've meant confiscation.

"Electronic contraption. Appears legal." The security inspector examined the game unit with a hand held electromagnetic wand and then handed it back to the boy. "Please walk through the security gate again, young man," the guard instructed. Camp hesitated but complied. The sirens went off again, this time accompanied by red *and* green flashing lights. Must be some color-coded heightened alert or something, Chatham thought.

"Ok, buddy, let's have it." The inspector was not amused.

"Have what?" Camp asked innocently. He was beginning to shake. Now two police officers had joined the security congregation.

"The other pocket, pal. Now."

"What other pocket? I don't have anything."

"Officers?" The inspector was looking for assistance. A policeman with bright red hair got down on one knee in order to deal with Camp on his own level.

"What's your name, son?" the officer asked with a friendly smile.

"Uh, Camp."

"Cool toy you have there. My son has one, too. Let's see, what game do you have here?" The officer examined the unit.

"Super Mario Smash Brothers," Camp answered automatically.

"What level are you on?" he asked, pushing the 'on' button.

Chatham knew this guy was a dad.

"Well I'm on level 8, but I'm trying to get to level 10, sir." Camp was starting to relax.

"Yeah, my son hasn't gotten there yet either. Long plane ride coming up?" Chatham didn't know where the officer was going with his line of questioning.

"My mom said it's six hours to New York."

"First class?" Camp looked at his mother.

"Coach, I think," Camp recited after reading Chatham's lips.

"Nice. Good snacks in coach."

"Yeah?" Camp liked the sound of that.

"Last time I flew it I remember good snacks and lots of soda."

"Cool," Camp replied.

"Can we get moving here?" the guard asked impatiently.

The police officer ignored him. "So, will you be playing your Game Boy during the flight?"

"The whole time," Camp answered proudly. I think I can get to level ten by New York."

"Cool. So, it takes a lot of power to play that game, huh?"

Chatham was catching on.

"Yeah, eats it up too fast." Camp was prepared for that though.

"Any chance you planned ahead and brought extra batteries. You know, in case you're about to make it to level 10, you don't want to run out of juice?"

Camp reached into his other pocket and pulled out a fist full of Ever Readies.

"I've got plenty of batteries. No way am I going to run out of power."

The police officer flagged over the security guard.

"Hey, do you mind if we just scan those? They won't go into cyberspace or anything."

"You mean the machine won't eat them?" Camp exclaimed, particularly worried.

"Nah. We'll use the wand though, just in case."

The inspector gave the handful a once over and returned them to the boy.

"Next," the guard commanded.

The police officer smiled at Chatham.

"Thank you," she mouthed as she grabbed Camp's hand and they sprinted for the gate.

≈

Trip knew he should be attending Special Friend's Day at Maddy's school. After all, he was a special friend to the Ross family. He just wished that the emphasis was more on special in Chatham's mind than actual friend. It's not like he planned it, falling in love with his departed best friend's wife. Was he betraying Peter by doing so? Trip wasn't even sure how it happened. When Peter died, it was the natural thing for him to step into the father role. He had been there for the wedding, the births of all the kids, and the death of his best friend. It all just fell into place after that. Heck, wasn't he sort of married to her already? He even had a key of his own!

But how did she feel? That was the question nagging at Trip, and he knew it was time he found out.

He booked a First Class seat to New York on the same flight as Chatham and arrived early at the airport so as not to run into her. Trip knew that Chatham tended to run late due to her crazy schedule with the kids and work. He had made a call ahead of time to his friend who did all the animal buying for the Central Park Zoo and arranged to meet with him over the weekend. It was an official business trip that happened to dovetail nicely with Chatham's travels.

When Trip arrived at the gate, Chatham and Camp were nowhere in site. Just as he had hoped. The flight attendant, who wore a large jeweled cross, took his ticket with a smile.

"Welcome to Vatican Air," she exhaled with perfect precision. "We get you there on angels' wings." She crinkled her eyes like a little cherub, making intimate contact with each passenger in an effort to make them feel special. It was a good campaign and each person seemed relaxed, knowing that they were being cared for.

Trip boarded the plane and took his seat in the last row of First Class. He was offered a crisp glass of champagne as the rest of the passengers filed onto the 767, taking their seats like a perfectly oiled machine. Everyone but Chatham and Camp. As the travelers passed by him, one after another, Trip began to get nervous. Did he get the wrong flight? He was sure he printed the correct information from her computer screen. Everyone was aboard and the doors about to close when he saw her. There she was in her stylish New York outfit, black turtleneck and jeans, with Camp in tow. Trip couldn't help but smile affectionately as he ducked down to pick up something on the floor that wasn't there. He didn't want to be recognized. Not just yet.

≈

Chatham and Camp were out of breath as they slipped through the closing door and quickly scurried down the aisle toward the next class of seats. They were about to exit First Class when Camp dropped his precious Game Boy. He had been gripping on to it so tight for fear that some other contraption would try to confiscate it that his fingers went numb. Camp quickly picked it up and turned just in time to knock over the glass of champagne precariously positioned on the passenger's tray. He knocked it right into the man's lap. Chatham saw it all happen, as though it were in slow motion. She leaned forward and reached, but not in time to catch the glass. As she lurched forward, her foot caught on Camp's heel and she fell right into the passenger's lap. She was horrified.

"Oh my god, I am so sorry. It was an accident." She struggled to get out of the faceless man's seat and upright again when he sat up and revealed his identity. "Trip? Trip! My god, what are you doing here?" His presence was more than a simple surprise.

Trip helped her up and tussled Camp's hair.

"Hey pal," he said affectionately as he wiped the pool of liquid off his pants and shoes. "Hi Chat. Fancy seeing you here."

"Please take your seat ma'am," the stewardess instructed. She had approached to see what all of the commotion was. "We have been cleared to pull away from the gate, but we can not until every passenger is seated."

Chatham could feel the other passengers' scowls as she stood rigid, not sure which way to go.

"What seat are you in?" Trip asked.

"Um, Um..." She looked at her tickets. "23A and B," she read from the two ticket stubs in her hand.

"Hey Trip, did you bring any cool animals with you?" Camp asked. He was oblivious to the need to move ahead and get seated.

"OK folks, you need to take your seats. Now." The flight attendant was determined to hurry them along. Chatham looked over her shoulder quizzically at Trip as they made their way to their proper location.

"Sorry," she mouthed as they passed through the curtains that separated the haves from the have-nots.

With all the commotion, Chatham didn't even notice the dark haired gentleman who had boarded the plane right behind her, finding his way to the front row of First Class.

CHAPTER XXV – *BI-COASTAL*

≈

Palio woke up at 9:00 a.m. east coast time in his suite at The Ritz, one of San Francisco's finest. Plenty of time for room service, a shower, and packing before he had to catch his flight back to New York. His eggs Benedict arrived, flawless as usual. It was the one indulgence he allowed himself. If he was going to be in two time zones in one day on a regular basis, he owed it to himself to sleep and eat well in order to stay healthy. The executive chef of the Ritz, Jean Pierre DuBre, was known for his exquisite food creations, right down to room service on the club floor of the hotel.

Palio's breakfast was accompanied by the *Wall Street Journal*. He liked to read it when he traveled. The newspaper made him feel connected to his home and, in his opinion, was the best-written paper anywhere. Especially the human interest section.

Palio downed a glass of fresh squeezed orange juice and opened the paper to a story about a local New Jersey man who made miniature wooden replicas of important landmarks like The Plaza and the Empire State Building. He made each one by hand in his workbench.

"I make these wooden replicas because I believe that everything in life should have remembrance, and it should be with a human touch. I also believe in things being accurate depictions of reality. So, I whittle away in my basement and ta-da, I get a tiny Rockefeller Skating

Rink," the article read.

"So how many of the skating rinks have you sold?" the newspaper interviewer had asked.

"Well, the first edition, only about 100. My calculations showed that there was a flaw in the rink so I called up Mr. Rockefeller and told him. They fixed the slope in the rink, and I made a new batch of 'em. You could say it's hard to keep up with the orders. I have a few of the guys from the senior center helping me with the raw cuts, but I do the rest."

"But you were in advertising, direct mail was it? What made you go into miniature wooden replicas?"

"Well, ya see, the Direct Mail business was good training. I created in that business, too. More like ways to convince people to try something, or buy something. After my wife passed on, god rest her soul, I decided that I wanted to create something a little more solid, ya know? So, I started whittling to pass the time. I wanted to see things for what they really were, not just what I wanted them to be, and I began to appreciate them, for the beauty they had, ya know? So, I decided to capture that. And, well, here I am."

"What other kinds of replicas have you made?"

"Mostly I do stuff for my grandkids and whoever pays me to, of course. Like the Empire State Building and the skating rink. Sometimes I do some for the tourists."

Palio reached into his buttery leather jacket pocket. He couldn't believe it. He actually had one of the man's creations. His friend who drove a carriage in Central Park had given him the horse and carriage creation just the other day, and Chatham had noticed it sitting on his office desk.

The little wooden passengers even had a tiny red blanket on their legs to keep warm. Palio read on.

"But I'm making a special one for my grandson; his birthday's coming up. It's an exact replica of the first carriage ever used in Central Park. It's a one of a kind."

"So you mainly stick to landmark buildings and tourist spots?" The interview continued.

"One time I did this job for a boat company. You know, the big boat guys that dock their giant ships off the South Street Seaport downtown? Well, this rich guy wanted a special one of his favorite yacht – the Sorbonne he called it. I don't know, twelve bathrooms or something on it. Piece of shit boat, if you ask me. Excuse my New Jersey accent. So I make him this exact replica and I figure that the hull needs a little shoring up. You know, at least another half inch of coated teak especially if he's planning to take it through the Bermuda Triangle where boats disappear and all. So, I tell the guy and he tells me I'm crazy. How could I tell him that his engineers are wrong, and I'm right based on an itty-bitty piece of wood? he asked me. Hell, I said. Do what you want. I'm just telling you is all. And I know because I know. Guess I didn't sound too convincing. He never called again. Last I heard, he lost the boat though. Guess where? That's right, the Bermuda Triangle."

"Do you think you were right?"

"Did we get in a fight? No. He just never called again. But I'm telling you. It was a hull problem."

And the article went on to talk about how this creative old man, who was hard of hearing, found his second career and passion in life. It was an inspiration for any senior who might think that life is over once they reached retirement.

Palio looked at his Rolex, gulped the last swig of coffee, and called down for his Mercedes to be brought to the front of the hotel. He stepped into the marble shower with its six shower heads and relaxed as the hot water massaged his sleep-deprived body from several directions. The time zones were taking their toll.

His mind wandered. He wondered if the old man would ever consider working for another boat company, his. The guy sounded pretty savvy and confident about his ability. Maybe he could help Palio's father with his new model designs.

His thoughts turned to the woman he had met twice now. The quirky suburban lady who was determined to make exercise a new part of her life. Chatham with the piercing blue eyes. She was witty and quick and vulnerable all at the same time, he thought. Her soft white skin reminded him of ivory soap. He wondered what it would be like to touch it. Palio realized that he had never met anyone quite like her before. And now he knew her name. But that was all.

The shower water began to cool. Time to get out. Palio grabbed the Egyptian cotton towel and dried off, the warmed marble floors inviting him to stay a while, to relax just a bit longer. He fought the urge. Something told him he may have been daydreaming a little too long. A quick glance at the clock across the room convinced him that he was, indeed, late.

"Shit," Palio exclaimed. He threw his clothes into his Ralph Lauren travel bag, grabbed his Rolex and wallet, and headed downstairs. His bill was automatically sent, so no need to stop at the registration desk. And thank goodness his car was waiting. Palio gave the valet a twenty-dollar tip, and headed to the San Francisco Airport in record time. Good thing the airport had valet drop off.

Palio ran through the airport at break-neck speed. He didn't want to miss the flight. It was a big weekend with his father's boat race, and he needed to continue negotiations with the olive oil princess.

The security check point was moving at a steady pace. It looked as though he would make it. As he approached the conveyer belt, Palio removed his shoes and placed them on the ramp. He overheard the security guards talking about some kid who had just gone through with an electronic toy and a pocket full of batteries.

"Pain in the ass, if you ask me. Stubborn little shit. Why didn't he just show me the frickin batteries? Who's gonna get docked for having to bring in the cops? Me, that's who. Little brat. I should send him a bill."

Palio couldn't believe what he was hearing. This kid must be a total terror. He hoped he wasn't on the same flight.

"Where did they say they were going?"

"You mean the kid and his mother?"

"Yeah."

"New York, I think. Yeah, New York. That was it. Not sure they made it though. The plane was about to go."

Palio looked at his watch. He had about two minutes. Now he had to sprint. And to make it worse, he undoubtedly had the troublemaker on his flight. Sleep would likely not be an option once again.

The pass through the security archway was uneventful. Palio put on his Cole Hahn shoes in record time and shifted into race mode as he dodged his way in and out of oncoming people traffic, toward the finish line. Palio practically threw his ticket at the lady and tore his way down the ramp and onto the plane just as the door was closing. He had to lean over and catch his breath. As he stood up, he noticed a woman sprawled over a passenger in first class. She looked so familiar.

"Please sir, please take your seat immediately. We are late for departure," the religiously clad flight attendant insisted with contained stress. She escorted Palio to his first row seat, a few feet away. He turned to sit down, but not before noticing a young child in the aisle with the woman. Must be the troublemaker, he thought as he sat down and grabbed the pillow from over head to put over his ears, just in case.

≈

Chatham was glad to take her seat as soon as possible, getting off the radar screen of potentially irate passengers. As soon as they were seated, Camp whipped out his Game Boy and powered it up.

"I'm sorry, young man," the attendant explained. "Electronic games are not allowed until ten minutes after take off." Camp looked defeated, but he complied with the order by putting the machine back into his pocket. He slumped down in his seat and covered his face with his jacket.

The flight attendant made her way back to the front of the plane as the captain's voice came over the loud speaker.

"Flight Attendants, prepare for departure."

At that precise moment, Chatham's cell phone rang. She had forgotten to turn it off amidst the earlier disorder. The attendants were seated with belts fastened already. Maybe she could quickly see who it was and then turn it off. Chatham crouched down with her head between her knees and pressed the send button.

"Hello?" she whispered into the mouthpiece.

"Chat? Is that you? Are you in the Broadway tunnel or something?" her friend asked. "I can barely hear you."

"Oh, hi Henrietta. Remember, I'm going to New York today. We're about to take off, and I shouldn't even be on the phone."

"Oh forget about it. It doesn't interfere with their radio commands anyway. That's a bunch of bull that the government tells you so that you don't figure out that you actually get free telephone calls when you're in the air. You go so fast through the different cell zones that they can't track the call. So it's free. I learned about it during one of my depos. Five cities were suing this guy who traveled every week up and down the coast. His long distance cell phone bills were always zero but every service showed activity on his telephone number. He only made long-distance calls when he was flying. It was cheaper to fly and call than to just call. Kind of cool, huh?"

"Wow, that is cool. Hey, guess who's on this flight?"

"If you are sitting next to Orlando Bloom, I'm coming right over."

"No, it's Trip. He's in First Class. He didn't even tell me he was going to New York. And he knew that I was.

Isn't that kind of weird?"

"You told me he's been acting weird lately anyway. Didn't he cancel Sunday dinner last week?"

"Yeah, he did. Do you think something's up?"

The passenger on the other side of Chatham stared at her as she continued to talk to her knees.

"Oh my god!" Henrietta blurted out with full emotion.

"What? What happened?"

"Chat, he likes you."

"What? Are you crazy? It's Trip we're talking about."

"Yeah. Mr. Dependable. He's always there for you and the kids. Ever since, well, you know… Everything is groovy until all of a sudden he starts acting weird. You know, not available, hard to get."

"No way." Chatham refused to believe her friend's outlandish claims.

"Yes way. Did anything happen on the plane?" Chatham thought about the interlude in First Class.

"Well, I sort of fell on him when Camp knocked over a glass of champagne."

"You what and he what?"

"Never mind, long story."

A voice came over the aircraft's PA system.

"Whoever has their cell phone on, please turn it off before you tell the rest of the story."

"Oh my god," Chatham said to her friend. "It's like they know what we're saying. I have to go. I'll call you tonight." Chatham snapped the phone shut and attempted to sit up. The passenger in front of her had decided to recline his seat completely. She attempted to nudge the seat so that she could at least slide around it. The passenger didn't budge.

Camp had his earphones on so that he could zone out to the Game Boy music, so he wasn't any help. Chatham looked down to discover a pair of assigned uniform shoes with a giant cross on the toe.

"Ma'am, you really must be in an upright position for take off. Please get up from…" She bent down to get a closer look. "From whatever contorted position it is that you are in."

"I can't," Chatham protested, her voice being muffled by the large in-flight mattress that was sitting on her head.

"Excuse me sir," the attendant said to the reclined traveler. "You need to wait until we are in the air before you tilt your seat back. Please put it back in its upright position until that time." She smiled at Chatham sarcastically.

The man grudgingly complied with the request, raising the seat so that Chatham could shimmy out. Chatham peeked through the crack between the seats. The passenger's popping eyes suddenly appeared in the sliver of space. Chatham visibly jumped at the site of the scraggly, sleep-deprived passenger. She looked around to witness several more frustrated passengers, their stares asking her if she was finally settled so that the plane could depart and they could get to their destination.

Chatham shrugged her shoulders, smiled weakly, and sank down in her seat as low as she could. When she looked over at Camp, she was now the same height as him.

Chatham was about to press the off button on her phone when a text message appeared. Leave it to Henrietta, always bucking the system.

"Good luck on the pitch," the text said. "Don't wear underwear." Chatham wasn't sure she read it correctly. She tapped in a quick response.

"Why not?" An answer came back just as the plane touched off the ground.

"Do you want the fucking account or don't you?"

Chatham laughed out loud as she pressed the cancel button and sat a bit higher in her chair. She was thankful for her close friend. She helped Chatham cope.

CHAPTER XXVI – *CHLOE*

≈

Chloe opened the French doors to the master state room on the Chamonix. It was a glorious suite. Sunshine poured into the room from her large window. The view of the ocean was absolutely breathtaking. She had slept in longer than she had expected. Chloe rolled out of her king-sized bed and slipped into her silk yellow robe.

As she went into the exquisite bathroom, she saw the set of fresh towels on the counter. A towel folded into a bird on top of the stack. Yesterday, it was a flower. She smiled, wondering how the staff learned to do that fancy and entirely unnecessary trick.

After a few minutes of freshening up, Chloe decide to explore the ship. She adjusted her robe, walked up the gleaming teak stairs, and emerged onto the main deck. The sun was so bright that she had to shield her eyes from its brilliance.

"Good morning, Miss Chloe," the South American butler greeted. He had a beautiful English accent and chocolate brown skin that made a sharp, attractive contrast to his white uniform.

"Good Morning," Chloe responded, a bit disoriented as to their location.

"I have breakfast for you in the Morning Room. Gabrielle is in a short meeting and will join you presently." He gently motioned in the direction where her sustenance awaited her.

"Thank you," Chloe replied, still a bit unsure. She followed the attendant toward the room with the buttery yellow walls, thick white molding and springs of fresh flowers adorning the mahogany breakfast table. Chloe looked around her. They must have sailed all night, she thought as she recognized the Statue of Liberty in the distance and the tall Wall Street buildings towering above their sparkling boat. When she arrived at the table her purse was waiting for her. She unzipped the Soho burlap clutch and pulled out her cell phone. It looked as though Chatham had called earlier this morning. Chloe pressed the call key, which automatically dialed the last number that had contacted her. She sipped her fresh squeezed orange juice as the phone on the other end of the virtual line rang.

"Hello?" came a whisper from the other side. Must be a bad connection.

"Chat? Is that you?" Chloe raised her voice a few decibels to be heard.

"Oh, hi Chloe. I was just turning my phone off. I'm on my way. Are we still on for tonight?"

"Of course, silly. I didn't listen to your message yet though. Pre-occupied if you know what I mean."

"I'm jealous. How was your sailing trip with boat boy?"

"Divine. Heavenly. Beyond compare. I don't know where the hell he is right now though. A meeting or something. I must have slept in."

"What did you say he did?"

Chloe picked up a sachet of velvet wrapped confections placed discreetly at the side of her plate.

"One of those fancy pants candy companies by the look of things," she said, examining the soft pouch that held three exotic truffles. There wasn't a label anywhere though. "He also mentioned something about boats. I don't know, I wasn't really listening." The comment struck Chatham as odd but she wasn't sure why.

"Sounds yummy. By the way, I'm bringing Camp with me. Is that OK?"

"When would it not be OK for me to see one of my favorite nephews? Just come on over when you get in."

"OK, we'll see you tonight. Oh yeah, I forgot to tell you. Guess who's on the same flight?"

"If it's Leondardo DiCaprio I'll make them hold the plane when it lands until I get there."

Chatham chuckled. Her two best friends were similar in so many ways, yet they were totally different.

"It's Trip. He didn't even tell me. I mean, don't you think he would tell me?"

"You sound like a jealous wife. Are you guys that close that he has to check in with you?"

"No, but you know he's part of the family. He's always around. And he knew I was going to New York this weekend. He was just over with some exotic skunk for the kids, and he never mentioned it. And he was supposed to go to Special Friend's day, and he blew that off, too. He never blows off the kids."

Chloe was still wondering why Trip needed to check in with Chatham. Or why he wouldn't if it was expected that he would.

"Oh my god!" she said, the idea suddenly coming to her. "He likes you."

Chloe grew up next door to Trip. He was her brother's best friend and she knew his behavior like a well-read book.

"That's what Henrietta said. You guys are nuts."

"Stops by. Finds out you're going to New York. Doesn't tell you that he is planning the same thing. Either he has a girlfriend in New York, or he wants it to be you but he doesn't know how to tell you. Yep, he's following you."

"Chloe, you must be seasick," Chatham responded, refusing to believe such nonsense. "Oh, my god, I have to go. The crazy attendant just turned into a devil, and she's headed my way. I'll see you tonight."

Chloe wasn't sure how to respond to the conversation she had just had with her best friend and old sister-in-law. She suddenly wasn't hungry. Does Trip really love Chatham? she wondered.

Chloe stared out of the window at the blur of people moving at a brisk clip across the Seaport Plaza, it was clear everyone was operating on New York time. As she scanned the crowd, she swore she saw Gabrielle at the foot of the dock, talking to what appeared to be a very exotic looking woman. Her long sleek legs, soft olive skin, and dark chestnut hair that swayed like a thoroughbred made her appear more like a work of art than a person. Was that his meeting, Chloe wondered. She saw her date give the woman a quick peck on both cheeks and head back to the boat.

"May I escort you to Mr. Gabrielle?" The butler appeared out of nowhere.

"Yes, thanks," Chloe responded, a bit off guard. Not that she was jealous. She had only been dating Gabrielle for a short time. Still, it's nice to know when you're important to someone, even if it is all just a game. Or was the game thing getting old? Always winning by dumping them before they could dump her wasn't exactly her idea of romantic. Was she afraid to commit to someone? Or maybe she was afraid that once she did, he would end up like her brother. Gone.

Chloe shook off her confusing thoughts and hustled back to the cabin to change. She selected olive suede slacks and a black cashmere turtleneck, something conservative that said, possibly unavailable. The outfit wouldn't be complete without her signature funky look, so Chloe added a tie dye vest at the last moment. She was slipping on her black ankle boots when she heard a familiar voice.

"My little Neopolitan ice cream, where are you going so fast? I haven't even had my coffee with you yet and I want to celebrate."

Chloe began packing her things. "You were up early and I'm late. It will have to wait until next time. And celebrate what?" Chloe wasn't sure if she was jealous or not, she still couldn't get the thought of Trip being in love with Chatham out of her mind.

"I am going to be a very rich man, my little Chloe. I will buy you many things."

"You're already rich," she said nonchalantly as though money was no big deal. She was curious, but didn't want to let on.

"Nothing like this. I will own all the candy in the world soon, and all the boats and boat designs. Perfect transportation from, I mean for, the masses. Just one more conquest, and now I know it will soon be mine."

Gabrielle came up behind her and circled her waist with his strong arms. Chloe couldn't help it; she melted right then and there. Maybe she was imagining things, she thought as he lifted her up and carried her back into the State Room.

CHAPTER XXVII – *PLANE FLIGHT CONT.*

≈

As soon as the overhead seatbelt light went off and it was safe to move about the cabin, Palio reclined his seat in an attempt to get some sleep. Lucky for him, he was in the front row window seat with no one next to him. He stretched his legs out over the imaginary border and leaned back for what he hoped would be a five-hour rest.

This back and forth existence was taking its toll. Palio was beginning to think he was delirious. He could have sworn that he recognized the woman in the aisle as the one he had unusual interludes with at the health club. Couldn't be, he reasoned to himself as he covered his lap with a blanket and tucked his head under the stiff airplane pillow. In no time at all, he was on an exotic island in his mind. A restful, warm, do-nothing place with a beautiful woman. Well, he couldn't really tell who he was with. Was it the olive princess? Was it his transformed childhood friend Maria? He couldn't quite make her out.

Palio kept hearing a voice in his dream, but it didn't fit with the montage.

"Just use the bathroom in front, sweetie. I know you're not supposed to. But if you have to go, then just go. The line is too long in the back. Don't worry, it's OK."

Suddenly there was a child in Palio's dream, running along the beach toward an outhouse that suddenly appeared. Problem was, he tripped and fell right into . . . Palio's lap.

"Sorry," the boy said, looking up at Palio's face.

"Huh, what?" Palio jolted out of his paradise.

"Sorry. I fell," the boy said, stating the obvious. "I didn't do it on purpose," he continued somewhat defensively as he got up and ran toward the restroom at the front of the plane. He was holding the spot between his legs just in case.

Palio was still in a daze as he watched the boy scamper off.

"I knew it," he said to his pillow. I knew that kid would find a way to cause trouble. "I must be psychic or something," he mumbled as he attempted to fluff up the stiff pillow and escape back to his dreamland.

He was just about there again. White sand beaches, cool to the touch. Crystal clear blue-green waters with little clown fish and searays gliding by effortlessly. Who was that in the distance?

"Excuse me," a voice from out of nowhere intruded, accompanied by a poking of some sort. "Excuse me, mister." The annoyance was insistent. Palio opened one eye half way to see Captain Trouble standing directly next to his little haven. "Could you help me?"

"Help you? With what? Can't you see I'm trying to sleep?" Palio replied, more than a little annoyed at the constant interruption.

"I can't get the bathroom door open, and I have to go," the boy said, holding himself and hopping from foot to foot.

"Did you ask the stewardess?" Palio inquired, not moving an inch from his comfortable position.

"She kept telling me, 'Just a minute' and if I wait another minute I am going to go."

Palio envisioned being the recipient of this

unfortunate event which sparked him awake enough to get up and escort the boy to the bathroom. He was right, it wouldn't open. Why? Because someone was in there.

Just as Palio launched his full body weight into the door, it opened as gently as a soft breeze. And Palio landed smack into the exiting gentleman.

"Gee, pal, in a hurry or something?" the patron exclaimed.

"Oh, sorry. I was trying to get the door open for this kid here."

The bathroom patron looked up and met eyes with Palio; instant recognition on his face.

"Oh, it's you. What are you doing here?" the man said with disdain. "Hey Camp," Trip said, addressing the little monster.

"Hi Trip. I have to go." Camp quickly slid past Trip and into the bathroom, closing the door behind him and locking it.

"You know him?" Palio asked, surprised anyone would admit to such a thing.

"Camp? Yeah, sure. I'm a good friend of the family you could say. There's his mother back there." Trip pointed to Chatham who was leaning over the edge of her seat watching to make sure Camp was OK.

Palio couldn't believe it. Chatham was here on the same plane as him. It had been her after all.

Trip knocked on the bathroom door.

"You OK, buddy?"

"Yes," came the response.

"Do you need anything?"

"No." The voice behind the door sounded tense.

"You sure?"

"Yes."

"OK, I'm going back to my seat. Come over when you come out, OK?"

"OK," Camp responded.

Palio offered to shake hands, but Trip just turned on his heels and returned to his back row first class seat on the other side of the aircraft. Palio shrugged his shoulders and took the three steps back to his front row seat near the restroom.

"OK," he said to the air. "We're done with that mess. Now, how about a little respite?" Palio snuggled down into his seat for one last attempt at traveling back to that special place in his mind.

"Uh, mister?" came a voice less than a minute later.

Palio was really getting annoyed at this point.

"What?" he said firmly as he opened his eyes yet again.

Camp was sitting next to him, holding something in his hand. He looked terrified. Palio felt bad for scolding the strange kid.

"Sorry, I was just trying to get some rest. I didn't mean to yell at you." Camp looked like he was going to cry.

"What have you got there?" Palio asked, trying to get the boy's mind off the tears.

"Don't tell my mom," the boy said.

"Don't tell your mom what?" Palio asked.

"Promise?" The boy wanted a commitment.

"Yeah, promise. What's in your hand?"

"Pinky swear?" Camp insisted, holding out the

pinky in his free hand to seal the deal.

What is a pinky swear, Palio wondered. Was he supposed to say a swear word and wiggle his pinky? He would just take the kid's lead. Palio offered his fifth finger for what he hoped wouldn't be some sort of bizarre ritual. Camp took Palio's pinky with his own and shook it hard three times. He then turned Palio's hand over and placed the hidden item into the open palm.

Palio was taken back by the interesting gift, but decided to maintain his composure.

"What do we have here?" he asked, even though he could tell without unraveling the item.

"I didn't mean to. Please don't tell my mom."

The urine-soaked underwear rested peacefully in Palio's hand. What to do. Palio reached for the airline sick bag, opened it with the same hand and deposited the soiled undergarment into the bag, never to be seen again. He handed the bag to the child.

"Look, I'm sure your mom will understand. She is probably a very understanding person." Palio did his best to appear convincing.

"Yeah, I know. It's just that all my other underwear is in the suitcase, and it's not here. It's been confiscated."

"Confiscated? What are you talking about?"

"They send everything through these giant machines that eat them. It almost ate my Nintendo DS 3D, you know." He pulled his precious toy out if his pocket to show Palio. He presented it like a valuable jewel.

"So that's a Nintendo DS," Palio observed as he reached into his pocket for a hanky to wipe the remnants of the original gift from his hand.

"Yeah, 3D, do you want to play? It's totally sweet."

Palio wasn't used to being around children. There weren't any young tikes in his family, although his father was constantly reminding him that he wanted to be a doting grandfather and how could he if Palio didn't get married…

Palio didn't want to offend the boy. After all, he did just have a totally unfortunate experience. Palio figured that if he didn't agree to a quick game the kid would probably lose it completely, and he would be arrested for child abuse or something.

"Sure. I'll give it a try. How do you play?"

"OK, I set it for two players. I'm Super Mario, and you're Kazooey. I have to kill you seven times to make it to level 10. I'm at level 8, which is pretty good but I have to make it to level 10 if I'm going to show up at school after vacation. I have a bet with a kid in my class that I'll get to level 10 first. As soon as I get there I have to call him so I'm in a hurry, you know? I get double points if someone else plays Kazooey, and I win instead of me just playing against the Game Boy. Are you ready?"

Palio wasn't sure what the kid was talking about. Kazooey?

"Yeah, sure. Let's do it," Palio answered, presenting a positive front.

It didn't take long for Palio to get the hang of the game. Super Mario would pass over gold coins or floating stars to get more power. The trinkets would help him run faster, jump higher and do all sorts of Tae Kwon Do type kicks and punches. As Kazooey, Palio had to find power to defend himself and use special weapons like giant punching gloves or magic kicking shoes to fight back and win points against Super Mario. The helpful items were hidden down secret passages or in underwater tunnels. Palio actually liked this game.

"Hey, get out of my way," Palio exploded at the game as he took his turn for the third time. "Those are my magic sneakers!" Kazooey punched Super Mario in the solar plexus which lifted Super Mario in the air and onto his back. Xs and Os spewed out from Super Mario to show that he had been defeated in that round. It was Camp's turn.

"Yah! Take that, Kazooey!" Camp made Super Mario pick up Kazooey, spin him around, and toss him over the edge of the highest precipice. Kazooey landed on his feet though and started to climb back up the mountain. "Oh no you don't," Camp yelled. Super Mario jumped into a race car and headed down the spiral mountain rode to confront his enemy.

"Hey, you can't do that!" Palio objected. "That's my car!"

"Was," Camp laughed as his character barreled down the hill in search of his prey. "I'm going to win," Camp cackled.

"Don't bet on it pal," Palio promised. "I have one turn left."

"Not," Camp retorted. "I killed you in the last round. See?" Camp quickly flashed the Game Boy screen so that Palio could see it. Zero power. "You used up your last life."

Palio was bummed. He wanted another turn. But it wasn't over completely. The game was tied. It was up to Camp to score in order to win and get to the next level. If he didn't score, it would go into overtime which meant one more turn each.

"No way, you're not going to win. I am the champion!" Palio was trying to psyche Camp out so that the game could continue.

Camp just laughed. This kid had confidence.

"I can win with my eyes closed," Camp claimed.

"Yeah, right," Palio answered in disbelief.

"I'll bet you a buck," Camp offered.

Palio liked a challenge as much as the next guy. "A buck? Do you do this kind of thing often?"

"No, I'm just sure I'll win, that's all."

"That sounds overly confident to me. You're on." Palio pulled a dollar out from his wallet and placed it between them as Camp closed his eyes as tightly as he could.

Palio watched the boy play the game by Braille. Within thirty seconds Super Mario had caught Kazooey and crushed him. Kazooey lay defeated at the base of the mountain with Super Mario standing on top of him doing a victory dance of flips and twirls.

"Unbelievable," Palio said to Camp. "You won." Palio bowed to him in awe.

"He got you, didn't he?" the soft voice asked. Palio looked up to see the mystery woman from the club. He was embarrassed that he couldn't control his outbursts.

"Oh, hi," Palio answered, standing up to greet the guest, slightly bent over due to the low overhead.

"Hi," she said, holding out her hand. "I'm Chatham. We met at the gym. I'm really sorry about this." Her cheeks were a soft pink color as though she had just run a short race. She was glowing.

"No problem. Really. He's a great kid." Palio couldn't believe he was complimenting the kid who was destined to make his travels miserable. But he was growing on him in an odd sort of way.

"I beat him, mom." Camp looked up with a large grin.

"You did? That's great, honey." She tussled his hair and looked back at Palio.

"Did he do the eyes-closed trick?"

"As a matter of fact, he did," Palio answered, opening his eyes wide at Camp in a light-hearted accusatory manner. Camp smugly reached for the dollar bill and tucked it in his pocket.

"Nice doing business with you," Camp replied. He picked up his barf bag and stood up to leave.

"What is that Camp? Did you get sick?" Chatham looked at Palio hoping for an answer.

"He's fine," Palio responded, winking at Camp. "Just a little garbage that he agreed to throw out for me in exchange for taking my money."

Camp let out his breath and grinned smugly.

"Thank you, by the way, for, well, saving me I think?" Chatham said.

"Oh sure, no problem. Do you have a bruise?"

"Don't even ask. I can barely walk."

"You're doing a good job faking it."

"Yeah, thanks."

"Nice of your boyfriend to take you home," Palio said. He was clearly fishing, but hoped she wouldn't catch on.

"Oh, Trip? He's part of the family." Chatham

looked over at Trip and waved. He didn't seem very happy watching the conversation.

An attendant approached the threesome. "I told you that you could retrieve your son and then go right back to your seat, madam."

"Oh, sorry. We were just leaving. Nice talking with you, sort of," Chatham said to Palio as she prepared to depart. "Have a nice flight." She was gone.

Palio wanted to go after her but he wasn't sure what he would say. He saw Trip signaling to Chatham and Camp that he would come back and visit with them. Part of the family. He wondered what exactly that entailed. The way it looked, he wanted to be more than that. Trip hadn't taken his eyes off Chatham, not that Palio could blame him.

Palio turned back to his seat and wondered if it was her he saw in his dream.

≈

Chatham hurried Camp down the aisle toward the curtains, the annoyed attendant directly on her heels. She made an OK sign with her thumb and forefinger, letting Trip know that he was welcome in the lesser class. Just as they were about to pass through the curtains, Camp leaned over to the boy on the aisle seat in the second to last row.

"Level 10, baby," Camp whispered.

Chatham recognized the boy from the security check point. His father was engrossed in the Sky Mall magazine. Chatham could have sworn she saw him tearing out the ad for Viagra.

"Sweet," the boy answered, holding out his hand to give Camp a high-five.

Chatham smiled at the boy and ushered her son

through the curtains and back to their little domain for what she hoped would be an uneventful remainder of the flight.

That man is beyond gorgeous, she reflected. But first class? How does a health club counter employee afford first class?

"Mom, can I use your cell phone?" Camp asked as he reached for his mother's purse.

"Camp, you can't use a cell phone on planes. It's against the rules."

"You did," he retorted.

"That was different. I forgot that it wasn't turned off."

"Yeah, but you still used it. You talked to Aunt Chloe and Henrietta. Why can't I call Stue from my class? I just got to level 10. If I don't hurry up and call him then I won't win. I have five bucks riding on it."

"Camp, are you betting again? You can't do that. If the headmaster finds out you are betting, you'll be like Pete Rose. He can never play baseball again, and they'll never let you back into that school again."

"Mom, relax. No one will tell. Come on, please. Just one call. I'll talk by my knees like you did and you can put a blanket over me. That bird lady won't see. I promise. Please?" Camp pushed out his lower lip as far as he could and gave his mother the saddest puppy dog eyes he could muster. Was it guilt or the youngest child syndrome that always made Chatham give in?

She looked around. The attendants were doing their job, attending to complaining passengers; they looked totally preoccupied.

"OK. But make it quick. And whisper."

"Thanks Mommy. I love you so much. You're the bestest mommy in the whole world." Camp reached over to give his mom a full bear hug. He reacted to his feelings so completely.

"I love you too, honey," she said returning the squeeze. "Now hurry up before that flying bird lady comes back here, and we get kicked off the plane."

Camp leaned down and Chatham covered him with a blanket. She quickly pulled out the Inflight Magazine and opened it to mask her son from view. She didn't even notice the title of the article: "Italian Wonder Family: How the Capriatti's Made Manhattan." She was too busy wondering if Henrietta was right. The call would probably be free and no one would ever know.

≈

Trip wiped his sweaty palms on the sides of his pants. What would he say to her? Now that she knew that he was on the same flight, his game plan had changed. Should he tell her the truth – he was following her because he had to tell her how he felt? No, don't want to give her a heart attack in mid air. He decided that he would offer her a ride to her hotel. But how would he explain that he just happened to be staying in the same hotel? No, that won't work either. He would just have to continue playing hard to get and run into her somehow. Yes, that would have to do.

Trip took a deep breath, stood up, and headed back to coach to visit with his pseudo family. He knew he had to sound coincidental, nonchalant, and pre-occupied. He had never been so nervous in all his life.

CHAPTER XXVIII – *THE CHASE*

≈

The limousine driver picked Maria up at 8:00 a.m. She was inconspicuous this morning in her black Calvin Klein jeans and a cream colored Donna Karan cashmere sweater; it was the perfect attire for today's mission. A precise breakfast of a hard-boiled egg, sourdough toast flown in fresh from San Francisco, papaya, and Columbian coffee awaited her. She settled in for the drive down to the Seaport.

"So give me the rundown. What happened last night?"

She was having Georgina followed. If the Capriatti men were going to do business with this ice woman, she wanted to make sure they were making the right decision. Maria protected what she believed to be her own, or hoped to be if she played her cards right.

"Uneventful evening, Miss Porticello," the driver answered.

"What do you mean 'uneventful'? Didn't she do anything?"

"Was in her suite at The Pierre by seven, ordered room service, read that other DaVinci Code book, *Angels and Demons*, and turned out the lights at 9:52. The guys hung around until one and nothing, nada, she was out for the count."

"Did you cover all the exits?"

"Just like we agreed."

"I don't believe it. It just doesn't add up."

"Yeah, I know what you're sayin'. But I'm tellin'

ya, she never left her room."

Maria thought something was not quite right about it, but what could she do? "And we know where she's going? Are we sure she'll be there?"

"Oh yeah. We tapped her line like you said. She's meeting some bald guy at the Wharf who pulled in at dawn this morning on his mega boat. I hear it's a beauty."

"What do we know about him?"

"Seems his yacht is registered in the Caymans, and he's from Sweden or Norway; we're not quite sure yet. He has passports from both countries."

"Business?"

"Runs a large European chocolate company and owns lots of big boats. We're running some checks on what else he's into."

That's odd, Maria thought. Boats and candy, extremely close to what the Capriattis do. Maybe it was just a coincidence. "Any real estate?"

"Has a five thousand square foot co-op on lower fifth. It took a while to find it."

"Significant others?"

"He's been dating this organic Soho chick for a few weeks. Works part-time in a modeling agency. Not a model or anything; she does the bookings. Has a decent apartment, and she lives alone. Don't know how she does it on a part-time worker's salary with no benefits. We think she has a trust fund or something."

Maria was getting more interested by the minute.

The driver pulled into an open spot alongside the street closest to the Seaport. They had a perfect view of the gleaming white ship that had arrived as silently as the rising sun. They waited patiently.

"There she is!" Maria said suddenly. She grabbed the binoculars out of the side paneled cabinet and focused them. She didn't want to miss a thing. The olive princess approached the dock, immediately met by a short, stocky, bald-headed man. Maria peered through her looking glass as they delivered the customary greeting, cheek to cheek, three kisses.

"He must be from Belgium, not the Netherlands," Maria commented as she continued to observe the interlude.

"Why is that, Miss?" the driver questioned.

"In Belgium, they kiss three times, not two." It was her job to know the nuances of international customary behaviors. It was one of the reasons that her undercover surveillance business was so successful overseas. "And Belgium is known for their chocolates," she added. Maria found the activities of this foreign ice princess to be quite intriguing.

The conversation seemed to heat up mighty quickly.

"Can you pick up what they're saying?" Maria asked impatiently.

"I'm trying. These damn concrete buildings block most microwave signals. Let me switch to digital." The driver pressed a few buttons and suddenly, two voices were as clear as if they were sitting inside the limousine having coffee together.

"I told you my price. You take it, or I walk," Georgina said.

She really knows how to hold her own, Maria thought.

"Georgina, we had a deal." The Kojak double seemed slightly annoyed.

"My ass we did. I'm the one wearing the pants, and we don't have a deal until I say so."

"You seem awfully sure it will be yours to offer."

"Give me a week. Besides, how can he resist?" She shook her head sensually from side to side, emphasizing her ability to charm.

Maria couldn't believe how the woman's ball-busting exterior could change instantly to soft and sensual. She was a master of manipulation.

"How can he resist? How can I resist?" the bald man mimicked her. "Alright fine. I'll give you your price. But I want all of it, the entire empire. That includes all the plans for future. I don't want any more competition."

"The world is your oyster, darling," she said as she leaned into him to seal the transaction. He leaned over and kissed her on both cheeks three times again. Without so much as a goodbye, the bald boat man and the olive princess went their respective ways.

Maria flopped back onto the soft leather bucket seat in the rear of the stretch. Who was this woman? she thought. And what the hell was she up to? Maria looked up in time to see the man wrap his arms around a woman who looked pretty normal, except for a psychedelic vest she had on. Must be Miss Soho, Maria thought.

"Who the hell is that?" Maria blurted. Her binoculars had accidentally slipped due to the sweat on her brow to reveal the dock next door. There was a man, about her age, standing on it, discreetly observing the activity on the large boat that rested one ship over. "He looks so familiar, who is he?" It was on the tip of her tongue.

"Looks like a cop," the driver said casually.

"Cop? You've got to be kidding. I've never seen cop muscles like that before." She thought his muscles looked pretty good. "I've seen him, I just know it."

Maria pushed the zoom button on the binoculars so that she could gain a closer look.

"Oh my god!" she said suddenly. "It's the guy from the Laundromat!" It was all coming back to her.

As if in slow motion, the good-looking surveyor turned and stared right into her line of vision. Maria gasped and lowered the magnifying lenses.

"Get me out of here, now!" she exclaimed. She had been seen by the gorgeous muscle man. The driver screeched out of the metered spot and was gone in less than five seconds.

≈

Chatham was about to fold the magazine that she hadn't been reading when a picture caught her eye. It was of a father and son. The son had an uncanny resemblance to the health club worker sitting in first class. She quickly ripped out the article and stuffed it into her purse. Just then, Trip showed up. Chatham wondered why Trip had been so awkward on the flight. He only came back to sit with them for a few minutes and he seemed so aloof, unavailable, definitely not his normal self.

"Trip, hi. Come sit down." Chatham motioned for him to take the empty seat next to Camp.

"Where's Camp? Back in the bathroom?" Trip asked, not noticing the blue lump next to him.

"No, he's here," Chatham answered softly, pointing

to the mound.

"What is he doing under there?" Trip asked.

Chatham lowered her head below the seat top so that the stewardess would not see her response.

"He's on the phone," she mouthed silently as she put an imaginary phone to her ear.

Trip chuckled. Humor helped calm his nerves, Chatham knew.

"What are you doing here?" Chatham had been dying to ask him, all the while wondering if what Chloe and Henrietta claimed was true. She analyzed his every move for hints of interest.

"This is a buying trip. You know, I'm always going somewhere." He retrieved the Inflight Magazine from the seat pocket in front of him and flipped through it absently.

"Oh you never told me."

"Was I supposed to?"

"Well, no. But you did know I was going, and I thought you might just say something like: 'Oh, what a coincidence, I'm going to New York, too. On the same day. And on the same flight.'" She looked at him awaiting an explanation.

"Oh, yeah. Sorry. It was a last minute thing." Trip went back to reading.

Chatham was a little annoyed. Was even reading that? And why did he refuse to look her in the eye? "Oh, OK. Well, how long are you in town for?"

"Just a day or two. Completely booked. Meetings, meals, every minute really."

"So – no time, huh?"

"Yeah, sorry. You sound like you're really busy,

too."

"Yeah, I guess so. I have a meeting tomorrow morning for sure. And dinner with Chloe tonight."

"How is Miss Chloe?" Trip had always called his best friend's sister Miss Chloe.

"She's great. Off on some exotic cruise with a mega rich candy company guy or something. I just talked to her actually."

"Well, hey, say hello for me. I should get back to my seat." He motioned to the head attendant who had a disapproving look on her face. She turned abruptly on her heels and passed back through the black curtain.

"Yeah, OK. Good seeing you. Do you need a ride or anything? I have a car service coming." Chatham wanted to offer. After all, Trip was family, even though he wasn't acting like it.

"No thanks. I've got a ride. Say hi to the little guy and good luck in New York." He stood up to leave.

Chatham wasn't sure what to make of their brief visit.

"Thanks. You, too. See you at home."

Trip looked at her strangely for a moment and then nodded his head. He turned to walk back to his seat.

≈

The plane pulled into the gate and came to a full stop. Passengers gathered their things and began to file out as soon as the seatbelt sign turned off and the aircraft door opened. Palio reached up into the overhead storage bin to retrieve his leather jacket. The miniature wooden figurine of the Horse Drawn Carriage fell out of the stored coat. Palio picked it up and was about to place it back in his jacket pocket when he heard Camp's voice.

"Hi," Camp said as respectfully as he could.

"Hi, Camp. What's up, pal?" Palio was glad the boy came to say goodbye.

"I just wanted to say thanks for not ratting me out with my mom."

"No problem. It will be our secret, OK?"

Camp grinned. "Deal."

"Just make sure you get a new pair when you get to your hotel, OK? I'm sure they sell them there in case the machine ate them. You know?"

"Do you think so?" Camp was relieved. "These pants are kind of itchy." Palio laughed. "Hey, I have something for you." He handed Camp the miniature as a gift.

"Wow, thanks. My grandpa makes these. Well, see ya." Camp ran back to find his mom.

That's odd, Palio thought as he made his way off the plane. His mind went back to Chatham. Palio hoped to get a chance to talk to her once more.

CHAPTER XXIX – *DISCOVERY*

≈

PJ came running out to carpool at break-neck speed. He had a huge grin on his face. He was waving his hand until it was practically flying off his arm.

"You found me," he yelled to Tom, Theo, and Madison who were all waiting in the car at the front of the carpool line.

Theo leaned out of the front passenger window and waved back just as frantically. "Hi, PJ. We were waiting for you."

Tom beamed. In many ways Theo was just a giant kid. It was endearing.

PJ jumped into the back seat of the SUV, put on his seat belt, and paused to catch his breath.

"How was school, PJ?" Tom asked, trying to act like the perfect uncle.

"Fine."

"What did you do in school?"

"Billy pushed me in the line," PJ answered, using his sweatshirt sleeve to wipe the tears that suddenly welled up.

Theo looked at Tom, giving him a knowing look.

"What happened?" Tom asked as he pulled away from the curb and back into the line of departing cars.

"Billy said, 'I'm first dummy.'" PJ was reliving the moment. "I said, 'No, I'm line leader.' He pushed me down, and I got an owie," PJ lifted up his pants leg to show a Band-Aid covering his scrape.

Tom could tell that Theo was heated. He placed a

hand on his partner's giant shoulder in an effort to calm him.

"There they are," Theo whispered. As luck would have it, Billy and his friend were walking down the sidewalk near the back of the carpool line.

"I'll be right back," Theo said, opening the door and exiting before Tom had a chance to slow down or object.

"Where the hell is he going?" Tom said, alarmed at his lover's irrational behavior.

They watched Theo approach the two boys. The boys seemed to recognize him and stopped dead in their tracks. After about a minute of watching them cower, nod their heads vigorously, and then leave, Theo made his way back to the car.

"Now what the hell was that all about? Who do you think you are? The Hulk or something? Scaring those boys like that. I am so embarrassed. What am I going to do with you?"

"They're bullies, Tommy. I already talked to them this morning, and they didn't listen. They'll behave now, I guarantee it."

"What did you say to them?" Madison piped up from the backseat.

"I just told them that I was thinking of volunteering in their classroom and coaching their soccer team."

"And that scared them?"

"I also told them that if they ever touched PJ again, I'd turn them into lunch leftovers."

"Oh my god, Theo! You threatened them?" Tom felt faint.

"No, I promised. It's up to them if I keep my

promise." He looked back at PJ. "PJ, I told Billy that you are first in line. Every time. He said OK."

"OK, Theo. I will tell Billy. I am line leader. Theo told me." Tom could see PJ's tears disappeared almost instantly from the rearview mirror. Maybe Theo had done the right thing after all.

Tom parked the family car in the garage and instructed his brood to get their homework done. Maybe they'd have ice cream after dinner if everyone was done in time. P.J. and Madison were out of the car and up the stairs in about five seconds. P.J. pulled his 'News For You' adaptive packet out of his backpack as he ran.

Tom looked over at Theo with pride.

"Piece of cake."

"Yeah, when you use bribery," Theo retorted.

"It wasn't bribery; it was a promise. You're just jealous that I don't have to threaten children to get proper behavior. Like a Neanderthal." Tom closed the door behind him and headed into the house.

"Awww, Tommy. Come on. Those kids were mean to little PJ. He needs a guardian angel." Theo followed Tom up the stairs and into the kitchen.

Tom had already pulled out the chicken, a box of Rice-A-Roni, and some frozen vegetables for dinner. This was the one day of the week that Madison didn't have ballet, and PJ didn't have speech. Hopefully it would be a calm and relaxing evenings.

Theo started to unload the dishwasher when he noticed a pass on the counter, near the phone. One free week at Exercise Anytime.

"Hey, I know this place. I've worked out there

before," he said to Tom as he quizzically showed him the pass.

"Well, what do we have here? Our little Chatham trying to beef up? What a surprise."

"She's not fat," Theo responded.

"You stupid oaf," Tom scolded. "Don't you get it? She's trying to shape up to get herself a man." Tom just smiled to himself. He was glad to see Chatham take an interest in herself for once. It had been a long time.

Madison walked into the kitchen to see the two lovers huddled around the laminated freebie.

"Hey, get a room, will ya?" Madison opened the cabinet and pilfered through it until she found the marshmallow puff.

Theo and Tom watched her as she opened up the white fluff jar, stuck her finger in, and retrieved a large glob of white meringue. She proceeded to lick it off her finger without giving it a second thought.

Tom's mouth was wide open.

"What? You've never seen anyone eat out of a jar before?"

"Pure sugar? Madison, that's just… well, that's just gross," Tom said, not able to look any longer.

"Yeah Maddy, you'll lose your teeth by the time you're eighteen if you keep on eating that stuff. I know. I used to workout with a guy who lived on cotton candy to keep his energy up. His teeth were so cavity infested that he has to wear dentures now. And he's not old."

"Whatever," she said as she tossed the remainder of the confection into the garbage.

Tom gave Theo the eye. Watch this, he silently

communicated.

"So, Maddy... I don't think mint chip ice cream does the same thing."

Madison ran over to Tom and gave him a huge hug.

"Homework will be done in no time."

"OK. Dinner in a few, and then we will go to Baskin Robbins."

Tom smiled at Theo triumphantly. He was king of this household.

"So what were you guys looking at?" Madison asked, walking over to the counter where the plastic paper lay.

"Well," Tom said with a little swivel in his hips. It was the kind of move a typical girl made before she was about to deliver some devastating gossip. "We found a free pass to a health club that your M-O-M was using. Hmm?"

Madison looked at him like he was a freak. "Yeah, so?"

"Yeah, so? Do you know what kind of health club this pass allows entrance into?" He shifted his weight to the other hip for emphasis.

"What are you talking about?"

"Your mom wants to be a body builder, Maddy," Theo said, getting right to the point, minus the drama.

"Why didn't you let me tell her?" Tom complained.

"Because you take too long, that's why."

"A what?" Madison said in shock.

"That's right, a steroid-enhanced weight lifter. Theo's people," Tom answered with a huff.

"Tommy, come on. Why do you always give me such a hard time?"

"Hard time, let's talk about hard time. You bully PJ's classmates. You totally embarrass me at Maddy's special day. Now you spring this devastating news on the poor girl. I mean for god's sake, what is next?"

"Let's go," Madison said suddenly.

"We are going, Maddy dear. After dinner and homework. You can get any flavor you want." Tom proceeded to shove the frozen vegetables into the Pyrex container and insert it into the microwave. He was still pouting.

"No, I mean the club, where Mom goes. Can we go?"

Tom stopped and turned to examine Madison's odd request. "Go, to a muscle mania mausoleum? I have vowed never to step foot into one of those. Disgusting." Tom squished up his face and turned his attention back to meal preparation.

"Then how did you two meet?" Madison asked.

Tom suddenly looked at Theo with true love in his eyes, and Theo seemed to welcome the advance.

"Well... Theo was in the grocery line, and I was behind him. You can imagine that I would notice him and his muscles and all."

Theo took in a deep breath and puffed out his chest a bit more.

Tom continued, "I think I accidentally put my asparagus spears on his lemon tart and, well, the rest is history as they say." They started to lean toward each other.

"Good story," Madison responded, inserting herself between the converging lovers. "So, can we go?"

"It would be fun to check it out, Tommy," Theo

suggested as gently as he could, making sure Tom felt in control of the situation.

"Now? But what about homework and dinner?"

Tom looked at the food he was about to prepare. At least he hadn't turned the microwave on yet.

"Come on, Tom. We can just check it out. It will be fun," Madison egged him on. "Besides, you can watch Theo lift weights. Right, Theo?"

Tom was hooked. "Well, OK. Go tell PJ to get in the car. What do you people take me for anyway?"

≈

Exercise Anytime was hopping on a Friday night. Scantily clad women were prancing around with their spandex jog bras and tight workout shorts, giggling and flirting with men three times their size. Madison had never seen so many piercings in all her life. Noses, eyebrows, tongues. One woman had even pierced her cheek.

"If mom is going to be part of this crowd, she will definitely have to let me get a belly button ring," Maddy smiled to herself.

"Welcome to E. Anytime. It's our spec-i-a-li-ty, day or night," the manager recited the slogan monotonously.

Madison, Theo and Tom all cringed as if on queue.

"Must talk to Chatham about that one," Tom whispered to Theo.

"What can I do you for?" the counter attendant offered.

"Hi, I'm PJ. We want to exercise." He was eyeing the mini trampoline in the corner of the gym. "I got a trampoline for Christmas."

"You did? Well, we have one, too."

"May I jump?" He looked at Theo intently as he stepped toward the carousal entrance bar.

"Whoa, hold on buddy. You need to be with an adult."

"I'll go with him," Theo offered. "He'll take care of it," he said to the employee pointing to Tom and followed PJ into the gym.

Tom presented the free entrance pass and escorted Madison into the active exercise facility.

"I didn't know Mom was so cool," Madison commented as she glanced around. "Oh my god, there's Dane." She smoothed out her sweats and t-shirt and let her ponytail out, so as to accent one of her better features. She was gone in a flash.

"Well, that was quick," Tom said as he scanned the room looking for Theo and PJ. "Oh my god, no!" Tom said, skittering over to Theo at break-neck speed. He grabbed the giant red bouncy ball from Theo's hands. "What the hell are you doing?"

Theo and PJ were jumping on the two mini trampolines while tossing a red therapy ball between them. They were giggling uncontrollably.

"This is a serious place, you imbecile! I just can't take it. I have to sit down."

"Tom, catch!" PJ yelled out as he threw the giant bouncy ball in Tom's direction. It bounced off Tom's head and back toward Theo. "Monkey in the middle," PJ laughed as he continued bouncing up and down.

"Give me that ball this instant," Tom demanded from Theo. Theo just laughed and tossed the ball to PJ, just out of reach of Tom's outstretched hands.

"Got it," PJ claimed. "I win!"

Tom let out a huge sigh. What was the point of trying?.

"Come on, Tommy. Lighten up. This is fun!" Theo and PJ continued their game of keep away until Tom suddenly sprung up and confiscated the giant ball. Theo and PJ stopped dead in their tracks, waiting to see if the game was over. The fifteen-second silence seemed like an eternity.

"I win!" Tom yelled. "PJ is in the middle." Can't beat 'em, he thought as he bounced up and down on the black nylon mesh. It was actually kind of fun.

Tom saw Madison wave over from one of the machines. She was with a tall boy. "Where is she going now?" Tom said to Theo.

"Looks like she's taking a class with her boyfriend."

"Boyfriend? I don't think her mother wants to hear that word yet. Twelve-year-olds don't have boyfriends, do they?" Tom couldn't quite remember.

"Oh Tommy, don't worry about it. It's only an exercise class."

"Well, you go with her. I don't want any shenanigans. I have to report back you know."

"Alright. Oh, PJ wanted to do the pull-up bar, but you'll have to help him."

≈

Theo jogged across the gym floor and into the padded exercise room.

"Hi, Theo. This is my friend Dane."

Dane looked at Theo, clearly in admiration. "Nice

to meet you. You're in great shape."

"Me? Nah. Just like to lift sometimes, that's all." Theo was modest.

"He's training for a championship next month, right Theo?" The Ross family was his biggest fan, other than Tom.

"That Mr. Universe thing in San Jose?" Dane asked. "I saw something about it on TV. Didn't the x-governor of California win that once?"

"Yeah. Before he became an actor and then governor."

"Cool. Can I have your autograph?"

Before Theo could respond, music started blaring in the room. "OK people. You were brave enough to come back so I'll be brave enough to teach once again," the dikey woman yelled through her Madonna style head set.

Just then a slimy-looking guy entered the room and took his place near Madison.

"Lizard, you know the rules." The instructor aimed her directions at the scaly patron.

"Yeah, Mirella baby, I know." He turned his attention to Madison. "Hi princess." He had already picked his prey.

Good thing Theo knew his type. There was one like Lizard at every gym. The guy who wore outrageous outfits and hit on anything female within a five-mile radius. Theo wasn't about to let the slimer get near his family.

"OK people. Pair off." Lizard turned directly to Madison before Dane had a chance. Madison appeared scared. Theo wasn't about to let this happen.

He tapped the creep on his shoulder.

"Hi there, pal. Let's you and I team up," Theo said. Lizard's eyes traveled up and outward for a full ten seconds in order to take in Theo's massive body. Theo had him by at least a hundred pounds.

Madison mouthed thank you to her good friend and turned back to partner with Dane.

"OK, are you angry?" the woman yelled her neck veins popping out from her skin. "I said, are you angry?"

Madison and Dane looked at each other sheepishly. Theo wondered what the point of this class was.

"Yeah!" the entire class yelled in unison.

"Well, that's not good," she said suddenly, blasting the music. "A good life is not about anger. You can only be peaceful and serene, thereby whole and complete, by managing your emotions." The teacher seemed effected. "Today's class has been altered to give you a more complete body, mind, and soul experience. Welcome to yogasize." She smiled with giddy delight. "It's a full workout with fun steps and smooth stretches." She looked over at Lizard. "Lizard, I recognize and bow to the divine in you, and I recognize and bow to the divine in myself. Namaste." Lizard returned the bow. "Now, please bow to your partner and wish them Namaste," the instructor guided.

Madison and Dane bowed to each other. Lizard looked at Theo and decided to bow extra low.

"We'll start by putting feet together with toes touching, hands in prayer position. Let's begin our practice by joining our voices together, our internal vibration and the sound of the universe."

Everyone joined in. Once the chanting was

complete, *Let's Dance the Last Dance* blasted out of the sound system and everyone followed along with the teacher. "Namascar A, sun salutation."

The class bent and twisted and hopped and stretched to the beat. Before long the entire group was in sync; bobbing and elongating to the newest fitness craze that was spreading across America.

Through the window, Theo could see Tom hoisting PJ up on his shoulders to reach the pull-up bar. Theo's broad smile let anyone know that he was proud of Tom for going with the flow for once in his life.

After the class was over, Tom, Theo, Madison and P.J. headed straight to Baskin Robbins for a much-needed treat. Tom figured it was ok to break the homework routine for a little fun just this once. Besides, they were all very curious as to what Chatham was up to with her new interest in body building. It couldn't be the slimy dude, Tom thought as he ordered a scoop of rainbow sherbert.

CHAPTER XXX –*THE THREAT*

≈

Palio was taking his time exiting the plane, hoping that Chatham and her son would catch up with him so that he would find an excuse to offer them a ride. He looked across the aisle at Trip and saw that the pair had already teamed up with their escort. Palio was actually disappointed. He was hoping to spend some more time with the little guy who was pretty fun, and maybe even get a chance to visit with the mom for more than an awkward moment. Palio went on ahead and made his way to the airport exit where his ride was waiting.

"So?" Gino said, as Palio climbed into the passenger's seat.

"So what?" Palio answered.

"So do you want to hear what happened while you were jet setting across the country?" Gino seemed particularly pumped up.

"I can tell you're dying to tell me. What happened?"

Gino signaled to the taxi next to him as he passed by.

Palio glanced over at the driver. "I know that guy," he said. "He's that taxi actor. Piece of work." Palio let his eyes drift to the back seat. His heart stopped. It was Chatham. She was staring back. Their eyes locked for what seemed like an eternity. As Gino floored the gas to pass the taxi, Palio smiled and casually waved to Chatham. She didn't wave back. Palio was disappointed.

"She's spoken for, I knew it," he said under his breath.

"Haven't you been hearing a word I'm sayin'?" Gino insisted.

"Huh? What?" Palio brought himself back to the here and now as he watched the taxi drive away. He wondered if he'd ever see her again. "Go on, I'm listening," he encouraged his friend to continue.

"Well, ya know that Italian painting chick you were meeting with at The Plaza?"

"Yeah, she keeps popping up it seems."

"Well, it didn't sit right that she was so interested in you, even more than the sale of her damn painting."

"And?"

"And, nothin'. After I dropped you off at the airport, I kind of, well, I sort of..."

"Kind of, sort of, what Gino?"

"OK, so I followed her. OK?"

"Geez, Gino. What are you trying to prove? We don't even really know her. Next thing I know I'll get a phone call that you're in the slammer or, even worse, in a fish tank somewhere being turned into shark bait."

"Aww, don't worry. I was careful." Palio had to admit he was curious.

"And what did you see?"

"Well, she had a pretty intimate meeting with the soon-to-be Head Mafia Boss from the lower east side." Gino gave Palio a knowing look.

"Bambini?"

"That's the one."

"What was she doing?"

"Whatever it was, she sealed it… if you know what I'm sayin'."

"No I don't."

"With a big fat wet kiss, and I'm not talkin' a simple lip lock."

"Really?"

"Yep. Something's up with that one. I can feel it."

"Interesting. One of Bambini's hoods paid me a visit today. Although by the look of him, he was more like a little squirrel. He told me to do the deal with Georgina, sell her everything, including my soul, whatever that means, and Mr. B will make sure that the family businesses stay status quo. Like Pop has ever made a deal for anything before."

"You sayin' he threatened you? I'll kick his fuckin' ass."

Palio knew he had to convince his friend otherwise. "Gino, listen. I went along with it."

"You what?"

"I know, I know. I need to know what's going on and how it could affect Pop and the businesses. Look, I'll have to pay attention, that's all. You know I'm taking her to the race tomorrow."

"Yeah, I think you're nuts. I don't care how good looking she is....She's a piranha fish, I can tell." The two were silent for a few moments, trying to figure out how to head off what could be a disaster in the making.

"The other weird part was this other outfit was watching the place. I'm tellin' ya, that cop was some hot number."

"Oh yeah? So there was a full unit on the stake out?"

"Unit in a limo, yeah."

It didn't make sense. "Since when do police drive around in limos?" Palio wondered.

"Exactly," Gino responded, already a step ahead of him.

"Is there anything else?" Gino looked away sheepishly. "You followed her again, didn't you?"

Gino decided to face his infractions head on. "Yeah, yeah I did. I told you I was suspicious. Followed her to the Seaport."

"So, you went to the docks? The center of mafia activity?"

"Right you are. This morning."

"And?"

"And it was good."

"Gino, for god's sake. Would you just tell me?"

"Alright. So there she was meeting with some dude who pulled in on a mega boat. I'm talkin' huge, gargantuan."

"Like a cruise ship?"

"Not that big, but big, yeah. And she talks with this short bald-headed guy on the dock. Well, at first it was nice, lots of cheek kissing and all. But it turned nasty pretty fast."

"Did you hear what they were saying?"

Gino looked at Palio like he was simply not cut out for surveillance work.

"I wasn't that close, I was a dock over."

"You were on the next dock? Doing what?"

Gino smirked. "I was pretending I was waitin' for a boat to come in. You know, fixin' the ropes and all."

"So what did they say?"

"All I heard was empire. He wanted the whole empire. And she was pretty darn sure she was going to have it to give to him."

"Interesting," Palio responded as he stroked his chin in thought. What is she up to, he wondered.

"Yeah, and remember the limo?"

"From the Laundromat?" Palio asked.

"That's the one."

"It was there? At the fish docks?"

"Yep, and as soon as I looked at it, it peeled away."

"Do you think they were following you?" Palio asked, concerned for his friend's safety.

"Nah. Same cop inside though. She had the window cracked, and I got a good look at her. Stop a mac truck dead in its tracks, she would."

Palio and Gino remained deep in thought as they pulled up to Monte's to meet Palio's father for the evening meal.

≈

Georgina's visit was progressing perfectly. She had made contact with the new crime boss who guaranteed that her olive empire would be number one in the eastern United States in exchange for her half of the Capriatti businesses. She agreed if he could guarantee that Palio marries her so that she would own half of the family empire. Then they would be true partners. He didn't mind the demand; it meant that he could finally exert his influence over the Capriatti family without them even realizing it. And this morning she had completed an accord to sell the Capriatti confectionary, health club franchise and miniature boat company to the bald-headed candy man, as well, right after she had completed her side of the plan. If she was going to own half of the Capriatti fortune, she would make sure to sell it to whomever she wanted, and splitting it between both of her partners made perfect sense. The combined transactions were sufficient to make her the second wealthiest woman in Italy. Add on a million or so bonus from Capriatti senior for the religious painting, that she never really owned anyway, and she would be a genuine contender on both sides of the English Channel. All she had to do was convince Palio to marry her with a little help from her new mafia friend. She didn't really believe that she needed the help that she requested from Bambini, after all, she was so close on her own - but just in case.

Georgina was in the mood to celebrate. One of Bambini's thugs was at her disposal for the remainder of her stay. She spent what was left of the day being escorted to Bergdorf's, Journelle Lingerie, and Ralph Lauren so that she could purchase the perfect outfit and accessories for her pending excursion with Palio. A long soak in the whirlpool tub in her suite at The Pierre followed her shopping spree and a restful nap served her well as she prepared for her surprise evening rendezvous with her prey. Georgina needed to set the bait early so that tomorrow was a guarantee.

"Your dinner guest awaits you, Miss," the driver informed, as she stepped into the back of the Hummer stretch which fit fifteen comfortably.

"Wonderful." Georgina smiled as she sampled the gift of imported chocolates and sipped the glass of chilled French champagne that awaited her inside the luxurious vehicle.

CHAPTER XXXI – *CONFUSION*

≈

Chatham waved to Trip as he exited the airport. Was he purposefully ignoring her? She wondered.

"Oh well," Chatham said out loud as she guided Camp to the taxi line that seemed to grow almost instantly. "We'll just wait in line for a taxi Camp, OK?" Chatham was talking more to herself as she debated the reasoning for Trip's odd behavior. How can he care for me like Chloe and Henrietta said if he's acting so rudely? She had no clue. Lost in her thoughts, she didn't notice that the horrible GQ father and his disconnected son were directly in front of her and Camp.

"Care to share a ride, doll?" the overly attentive stranger inquired.

Chatham just wanted to be rid of this anathema. "Oh, how nice of you to ask. We're fine though." She pretended to look for a phantom object in her purse.

"I'm going the same way," he continued with a slight lift of his eyebrow. He had totally forgotten that he was a "we," not just an "I."

The son looked down with embarrassment. He was clearly used to his dad trying to pick up on women, any woman that looked like she might provide a meal ticket.

"No, really. We're fine. But thank you though. Have a nice trip."

A taxi pulled up and the porter opened the door for the father and son. The pick-up artist didn't bother tipping. The man was about to step in when he turned to address Chatham.

"I'm at 540 Ninth Avenue Unit 1A. Hell's kitchen. It's *the* place to live. Stop by any time." He winked and was gone.

Sure, if you want to be knifed, she thought as another taxi arrived at curbside.

Chatham tipped the porter, who loaded their bags into the trunk while she and Camp slipped into the back seat. They were more than ready to get to their hotel, it had been a long and confusing day. Chatham let out a deep sigh, settled back into the taxi, and glanced out the window. As the driver pulled away, Chatham happened to notice the car directly next to them. Could it be? She was looking directly at the Italian health club employee. Her heart skipped two beats at the sight of him. He must have felt her eyes on him because he glanced over and waved. Chatham tried to lift her hand in response, but she was rendered immobile. And that was that. He was gone. Would she run into him again? she wondered as her driver exited the airport and headed toward Manhattan.

"The Pierre, please," she said politely to the anonymous man behind the wheel.

"Not a problem, lady," he responded in a perfect Queens accent.

Chatham lifted the laminated sheet from the seat pocket in front of her and read. "Your resume says that you're from Texas, but you have a pretty strong New York accent. Was that Queens I heard?"

"You a director or producer or casting agent? If you are, I can do Manhattan, east side or west, Brooklyn and Staten Island. Waddya wanna hear?"

"Can you still talk like a Texan?" she asked,

wondering if he'd be worth an audition.

"Shit, yeah. Oh, sorry kid," he offered to Camp. "Why I was weaned off the tit of a cow in the backwaters of Flower Mound, before it was populated and all. I'm a native Texan. Born and raised. Can't go anywhere without my Stetson," he added, positioning it on his head where it seemed to have rested its entire life. "Can't always wear it while taxiing though, New Yorkers get pissed off. I can shoot an elk with one shot of my high-gauge, single-barrel shot gun too. It's in the trunk, do you wanna see it?"

"Uh no, thank you. I appreciate the offer though."

"So, you a director?"

"Not exactly," she responded. Chatham liked this guy. He had the perfect Texas twang, and he had attitude. He would have to be if he had a chance of replacing the owner's voice in The Idle Spur restaurant commercials.. The owner Hank was one giant attitude and there wasn't room for a weakling in the same room. "I see you've done a shampoo commercial. How did you get that gig?"

"It was a piss ass commercial. I only auditioned because it said the actor needed to have a receding hairline, must be under thirty. That's me, see?" He leaned his forehead into the rearview mirror so that Chatham could see it through the plexiglass barrier. "So what the hell, I said. They lathered me up with some hair growth shampoo shit and made me sit there for ninety friggin' minutes while they filmed the suds on the shampoo to see if they collapsed more on the bald hairline than the rest of my head. I had to pee like a dog after his bone, but hell, I sat there. I wanted to be paid."

"Sounds like quite an experience," Chatham

chuckled.

"Yeah, I made a couple hundred bucks. What the hell, right? I was also in a film, did you read that part?"

"The Return of the Alien Worm Eaters?"

"Yeah, dumb ass title if you ask me, but I heard it did real good in Cambodia. I had to dress up as one of the worms."

Chatham laughed.

"Yeah, I know what you're thinkin'. They ate me."

"Well," she read the name at the top of the resume, "Billy Bill. What kind of name is Billy Bill?"

"Yeah, I know. Sounds like your stutterin' or somethin'. I was named after my grandpa and my pa. Grandpa was Billy and pa's Bill. So, you get Billy Bill. But you can just call me Billy B. Hell, call me whatever you want. Just call me if you're lookin' for a Texas or New York actor. So what did you say you do?"

Chatham had an idea. "What would you say to an audition on the spot?"

"Not until you tell me what the hell you do," he laughed.

"I'm sorry Billy B. It's been a long day. I'm in advertising."

"Not another friggin' shampoo spot."

"No," she chuckled. "Don't worry. This is for a chain of Texas Barbeque restaurants. I need to find the perfect someone to be our new spokesperson now that our current spokesperson, the president of the chain, will be moving on to play the back nine you could say."

"Hell, where do I sign up to replace Mr. Washed Up? I love that barbeque shit. Wish they served it in this concrete jungle.

Chatham looked over at Camp; he was into Level 10 on his Super Mario game and was oblivious to the world around him.

"I'm going to make a phone call to Hank and when I say go, you say, 'Come on over to The Idle Spur all you hungry bumpkins. But don't come over if you're not, cause we're all beef and no bull. Thanks for listening. We'll have the baby back ribs waitin' for ya.'"

"Hell yeah, I can do that. All beef, no bull. I'm ready. Hell, you never know when you're gonna get your break."

"That's right, Billy B, you never know."

≈

Billy Bill pulled up in front of The Pierre to deposit his fare. He jumped out of the front seat, opened the trunk, and handed the bags to the bellman who was waiting to greet the hotel guests.

"Hell lady, that was one tough son of a bitch you had on that phone."

"I told you he had attitude. But I think you did just fine. Now the job pays one hundred dollars an hour plus residuals when it airs. You might even make enough to be able to give up driving a taxi."

"Now what would I want to do that for? Once I'm on this spot, everyone will know who I am and every director or producer in Manhattan will be dying to get in my taxi. I'm gonna put a huge sign on the side. Driver is spokesperson for The Idle Spur. You betcha, I'll be double dippin' and probably get a lead in a movie or something. Well, I hope so anyway."

"OK, Billy Bill," Chatham smiled as she handed him the fare plus a ten-dollar tip. "Here's my card, and I have your number, uh, your resume. I'll be in touch as to when we shoot the first spot. I'm not sure yet if we'll fly you to Texas or San Francisco, but either way, we'll pay, don't worry."

"Well, Miss, I can honestly say this was the best cab ride I have ever had. Thanks for your company." He tipped his hat to Chatham. "And to you too little fella, and that crazy game you seem to have climbed into. Well y'all, I'll be seeing you. If you find yourself needing a personal taxi while you're visiting this special city, then don't hesitate to call. I'm outta here," he waved as he jumped into the front seat of his taxicab and floored the gas.

As he drove away, Chatham could hear him let out a scream of delight.

"Yee-haa!"

Chatham and Camp followed the bellman into the lobby of The Pierre. The mahogany paneled walls, paisley couches, and hunter green club chairs in the sitting area spelled out class and elegance – all part of the club.

"Good evening, how may I offer my services?" the registration clerk inquired as Chatham stepped up to the calcutta marble slab counter. Fresh gardenias and orchids were generously dispersed throughout, and Vivaldi was being piped through the high end sound system. Chatham felt instant relaxation overtake her.

She was handing the clerk her American Express card when she heard a familiar sound.

"Hey sport, are you following me?" Chatham looked over her shoulder to witness Trip hoisting Camp up onto his shoulders. Chatham completed her check-in and walked over to join Trip and Camp. She was flabbergasted to see him and confused.

"Trip, oh my gosh! You didn't tell me, I mean, I had no idea that you were staying here." She wanted to respect his privacy.

"Didn't I mention it?"

"No, you didn't, but that's OK. Hey, we're having dinner with Chloe and Dad tonight, after we get settled. Would you like to join us?" "Oh, thanks. Uh, sure. I actually don't have plans tonight."

Chatham fiddled with her purse. "Great. So, we'll see you downstairs in about forty-five minutes."

Trip set Camp down and tussled his hair. "Sounds like fun."

"OK, see you soon," Chatham added as she took Camp's hand and headed to the elevator bank.

Chatham was at a loss. Trip shows up on the same flight, acts totally aloof, and now ends up at the same hotel? Something was off here, and she was beginning to think that Henrietta and Chloe might be on to something. But how to feel about that? It was Trip after all. Why he was practically family already! But attraction, desire, love? Chatham was completely confused and not at all sure how she felt.

CHAPTER XXXII – *INTERSECTION*

≈

Gino pulled up to the reserved parking spot in front of Monte's. It was one of the benefits of the Capriatti-Monte relationship even though taxi was the normal modus of travel in New York City. Still it was nice to have and the Capriatti clan appreciated the kindness of their good friend Monte. The two friends entered the restaurant and scanned the room. They heard Monte call out from across the restaurant.

"Palio, Gino, my boys. Come in, come in!" Monte made his way through the tables, stopping to kiss a hand or pat a shoulder as he weaved his way to the front door. He met Gino and Palio at the top of the stairs with a giant bear hug. "Where have you crazy boys been? Palio, are you still traveling to the left coast every other day? Now don't you be spending too much time in that San Francisco city, my boy. I don't want you to be influenced by the crazy marriage laws." Palio laughed and returned the hug.

"Don't worry about me, Monte. I'm as straight and boring as they come."

"Well, when two nice-looking, eligible men come in to a restaurant in my town, it's a whole different story. Women will swoon." He turned to Palio's pseudo brother. "Gino, can't you convince this brother of yours to settle down already? Roberto and I have the perfect match for him, eh Palio, my boy?" He elbowed Palio with a wink.

"Match? What match?" Gino asked.

"Never mind," Palio said. "There will be no wedding," he gently reprimanded his old friend. "If you and my father had your way, I'd have ten children by now."

"Grandchildren for your papa and grand-uncle children for me. I will give them all the pasta they could ever desire." Monte let out a genuine laugh filled with love.

Palio couldn't help but grin. The man was crazy, but he had a heart of gold.

"And you," he said, nudging Gino. "What's your story in the romance department? What, are you waiting for your brother to take the plunge first?"

"Oh, he's hooked on some mysterious police officer or detective or something," Palio answered on Gino's behalf.

Gino stared at the floor.

"What's this I hear, Gino my boy? Your heart is aching for someone you haven't even met? What a love story, I have to tell Roberto."

"Shut up, Palio," Gino retorted, elbowing him in the ribs.

"OK, OK. I'm shutting up." Palio saw his father waving from their favorite table. "There's dad."

"Come, I will take you," Monte offered as he led the boys to their usual table.

Palio thought he recognized the auburn-haired woman across the room at the corner table, whose back was to them, but he couldn't be certain. He strained his eyes to see who she was with, but the man was shielded by a large palm frond. Palio made a mental note to take the seat facing their direction.

Palio's father embraced his son and his pseudo-adopted son.

"My two favorite boys. It's good to see you." He

kissed them both on each cheek and turned to address Palio as they took their seats. "So you're back from California. How is my little health club chain doing so far?"

The thought of Chatham lying in his arms came instantly to Palio's mind. "Oh, the club. Papa, it's not a chain yet. It's one club with a franchise ready to grow."

"Ahh yes, and it will be a chain in a blink of an eye now that you are its captain. What will be your next city?"

"I was thinking of New York actually," Palio responded. "The New York athletic clubs are up and down the Upper East Side so I thought we'd focus on the Chelsea area and maybe the Village."

"Such a planner you are. I love it. And have you found the club in San Francisco interesting so far?"

"Pop, it's in Marin, which is not exactly San Francisco. And, yes, I have found it interesting to say the least." Palio took a sip of his water to mask his flustered face.

His father leaned across the table. "To say the least? What is that supposed to mean? Why are you being so coy? So have you found something or *someone* particularly interesting?"

Palio figured that he should give his father some hope, it was basically what he lived for, other than his precious sailboats and candy expansion.

"Actually, I did meet someone," Palio offered as he wiped his mouth with the linen napkin.

"Glory hallelujah!" Mr. Capriatti exclaimed loud enough for the entire restaurant to hear.

"Thanks for telling me," Gino sulked.

"There's nothing to tell, really. She's taken." The

conversation stopped in its tracks.

"Well," Palio's father continued, "let's talk about my precious painting."

Mr. Capriatti's outburst had attracted the attention of the entire restaurant. Palio was about to fill his father in on the painting negotiations when he saw the woman across the room turn full around and lock gazes as though she knew he'd been there all along. It was now or never. Georgina whispered harshly to the bodyguard across from her while maintaining eye contact with Palio.

"Here goes nothing. Now leave after I do."

Palio smiled and waved casually. She responded by rising out of her seat and swishing her way across the restaurant to their table. Her black sequined dress with the plunging neckline clung to her as she approached the three seated men. Palio stood to welcome her, and assuming an invite, Georgina leaned in and planted a somewhat lingering kiss on the side of his mouth.

"Gentlemen," she offered with perfect grace and sensuality.

Mr. Capriatti followed his son and stood to give her a hug. "I could tell by the sound of your voice that it was you," he added, stealing a quick approving glance at Palio.

"Yes, Roberto, so good to finally meet you face to face."

"You know Palio, of course," Mr. Capriatti offered with a gesture of his hand. "And this is his best friend, well, brother really, Gino."

Gino lifted his head with a slight nod. "Nice to meet you," he said before he went back to dipping his bread in the extra virgin olive oil.

"Come, please. Sit," Palio's father offered. "We have so much to talk about."

Georgina accepted the chair that Palio pulled out for her. "Actually, I have plans this evening." She nodded in the direction of her table.

Palio looked over but still could not make out her dinner date. "I think I can stay for a few moments, though." She looked over at Palio with dreamy eyes. "And how are you, Palio? Back from your travels?"

From his peripheral, Palio could see that Gino was studying her intently. It was clear that he didn't trust her. "Yes, just in. I'm on the earlier time zone so I don't think I'll fall asleep in my meal."

She laughed genuinely. "That's OK. I'm used to it." She patted his shoulder gently. "Be sure to get some rest before our date, I mean meeting, tomorrow," she offered.

Palio's father raised his eyebrows in his son's direction.

"I'm taking her to see your boat race tomorrow, Papa," he acknowledged, widening his eyes at his father in a gentle reprimand.

"Ah, yes. And I will win tomorrow if I have my way."

"His biggest competition is a ten-year-old red head," Palio chuckled.

"Don't trust him as far as I can see him," Palio's father responded with certainty.

"Do you know boats?" Gino interjected suddenly.

Georgina smiled coyly. "All I know about boats is how to pull the silk cord to order breakfast from the master state room. And you? Do you work on boats?"

Palio saw Gino's face flush. He could tell his brother wasn't pleased with the beautiful olive princess. "No, I don't know much about boats either. Other than watching the large ones that pull into the Seaport and seeing the kinds of people that visit them, that's all really." He met her gaze and smiled completely.

Georgina laughed uncomfortably.

Palio tried to take control of the conversation before Gino's blood really did boil and he gave away more information than he needed to. Probably best to leave Georgina in the dark as much as possible.

≈

Trip, Chatham, and Camp stepped into the complimentary sleek black, stretch limousine, a fringe benefit service offered by The Pierre.

"This is so totally cool," Camp exclaimed, looking around at the soft black leather bench seats, mirrored cabinets, and shiny crystal decanters that lined the sides of the vehicle. "Look at the cool stars on the ceiling! They change colors. This is totally awesome!"

Chatham smiled lovingly at her son. His innocence and joy was so real, so spontaneous, traits she had forgotten over the past five years. But she was here, in New York City, about to have dinner with a man who might, in fact, be in love with her, and she, well, she thought that maybe she could try again. She was willing to open up to the possibility. That's a good sign of recovery, isn't it?

"Hey, Mom, can I have some Coke?" Camp asked as he reached for the decanter filled with cognac. Chatham intercepted his prize as he was about to take a swig.

"Camp, the coke is in the mini fridge over here,"

she offered, opening the mahogany covered panel to reveal a cool chest filled with every flavor of Coke available.

"Cool," Camp cooed. Chatham laughed lovingly at the site of her son's pure joy in discovering the plethora of choices. "Can I have a cherry Coke?" he asked enthusiastically.

"Sure," Chatham said, opening the can and pouring a small amount for the three of them, handing one each to Camp and Trip..

Chatham sat up straight and lifted her glass. She could feel Trip staring at her as though he was studying her every move. Never before had she been so hyper aware of Trip's movements. Never before had she felt even the least bit uncomfortable around him. She willed her face not to flush.

"A toast! To us," she offered somewhat nervously. "May we both win what we're here for." She had to know what Trip truly was here for. Her curiosity was almost painful. Was it really business or was it her? Chatham needed to settle this emotional dilemma once and for all, and she was determined that this trip would reveal the inevitable. She only wished it would happen sooner rather than later. The sooner they got this over with, the sooner life would get back to normal. Or would it? If she and Trip got together, surely life could never be the same. But that might be a good thing, she surmised. On the other hand, what if it didn't work out? Would they be able to remain the same, tight-knit family they were now, even after everything was out in the air? She couldn't bear to think of life otherwise.

"Yes, may we both come out winners," he smiled,

returning the toast with a gentle clink of their glasses. They held their gaze.

"Mom, Mom! Your phone's ringing." Camp was tugging on Chatham's cream silk shawl.

"Oh, oh, I'm sorry," Chatham responded, reaching for her bone-colored clutch. She retrieved her telephone and flipped it open to accept the incoming call. "Hello?"

"Well? When were you going to call me? Ever? What the hell happened with the Tripster?"

Chatham looked over at Trip and smiled weakly. "Oh, Henrietta. Nice to hear from you."

"What? Nice to hear from me? Where the hell are you? In a limo with some guy or something?"

"Well actually, yes. Yes, I am glad to hear from you."

"Oh my god. Who?" Henrietta was not going to hang up without an answer.

"Great. Trip says hello to you, too."

"How did she know I was here?" Trip whispered.

Chatham just shrugged.

"What did I tell you? I was right. He's crazy about you. Now what the heck are you going to do about it? Do you love him?"

"Henrietta!" Chatham exclaimed, shocked at the direct affront.

"Is everything OK?" Trip asked, leaning forward with concern. Chatham waved him off nonchalantly. "OK then, Henrietta. I will give you a call later, OK? Thanks for calling and have a nice night."

"Thanks for calling? Have a nice night?! What is this, Cotillion practice or something? You better call me tonight, or you know I won't sleep. I have to live vicariously through somebody. It's not like my husband would show up suddenly and whisk me off in a limo. In my dreams maybe, but definitely not in reality."

Chatham gently clicked the telephone shut during Henrietta's mid sentence.

"Is everything OK?" Trip asked again with genuine concern.

"Oh, you know Henrietta. True drama queen. Always has been." Chatham attempted to change the subject. "Oh look, we're here." She looked out of the darkened window. "Monte's. The Concierge said it was the best Italian restaurant in Manhattan. A particularly genuine local dining establishment was how he put it, I think."

She and Trip both laughed. The Pierre was so formal and perfectly mannered.

"Well, I would particularly enjoy dining here then," Trip offered, opening the door for Chatham and Camp to exit.

The limousine driver gave Trip his card and told him to call whenever they were ready for their return. Trip handed the driver a twenty-dollar bill, which he politely refused.

"I really like this hotel," Trip concluded as he, Chatham, and Camp entered the restaurant. A portly fellow with a balding head and jolly smile immediately greeted them.

"Welcome to my home away from home," the man offered as he shook Trip's hand and gently kissed Chatham's. "And you are my special guest tonight," he said to Camp as he handed him a chef's hat. "You can create any dish you want as my guest chef and it will be done for you."

"Cool," Camp said. He was clearly still in a state of awe at the entire evening.

"Please, your father is waiting for you," Monte said as he gestured for them to follow.

"How did you know?" Chatham asked as she trailed behind the maitre de.

"Monte knows everything," he answered as he held out a chair for Chatham. He leaned down and whispered in her ear. "He saw you come in." Monte smiled and snapped his fingers twice. "Alfredo! A bottle of our best Pinot Grigio for my new friends. On the house." He kissed Chatham's hand once again and was gone.

Chatham leaned over and gave her father a kiss. "Dad, how are you? Where's Chloe?"

"Well I'm just dandy now that I'm here with my favorite daughter and her friend." He shook Trip's hand and winked at Chatham. "What a nice surprise to see you, my boy."

"Hi, Mr. Ross," Trip returned, shaking his hand. "Your daughter and I, uh, met up completely by coincidence. Right, Chat?"

"Yeah, complete coincidence. Kind of crazy really."

"Kind of crazy indeed," Mr. Ross responded, eyeing the two suspiciously. "Chloe called to say she'd be a few minutes late," Chatham's father explained. "Something about unpacking after a little boat ride?" He looked at Chatham to see if she'd break the secret code. Chatham just smiled as she recalled Chloe's described adventure with the infamous Gabrielle.

"Oh, yeah. Chloe went for a little outing with a new friend of hers." Chatham decided to offer no more.

Camp was sitting patiently, waiting for his turn to be addressed. Chatham's father pretended to just notice him. It was a joke between them. Mr. Ross would pretend that each time he saw Camp, he had changed so much that he didn't recognize him. And then he would shower him with love.

"And who is this sprouting young athlete? Is this a new grown-up friend of yours, Chatham?" Mr. Ross said staring at Camp with saucer eyes.

"Hi, Grandpa," Camp squealed, knowing the secret signal to run over and give his favorite relative a giant squeeze.

"As strong as Atlantis, too," he exclaimed as he returned the bear hug to his grandson. Chatham's father reached into his navy blue cardigan sweater pocket. "I have a little something for you," he said, hiding the gift between two palms.

"Let me see, let me see!" Camp insisted, attempting to pry his grandfather's hands apart.

Mr. Ross opened his interlocked fingers to reveal a small wooden carving.

"Hey Grandpa, I have one too," Camp said, pulling out an identical horse and carriage from his own jeans pocket.

"Well would you look at that?! Where did you get that, son?"

"Oh my gosh, I've seen that, too!" Chatham exclaimed. "In a health club in Marin."

"What the devil is going on here? Is someone

duplicating my creations?" Chatham's father was not amused.

Camp stood up and pointed his finger at a table across the room.

"I got it from him," he said, pointing to Palio who was sitting comfortably with a man about Mr. Ross's age, another man about Palio's age, and a gorgeous exotic woman who was gazing at Palio with lust and determination as her gaping neckline practically fell open.

Chatham's heart sank. She now knew that there could never be a chance.

"Who the devil is that?" Mr. Ross demanded.

"The competition," Trip said under his breath. Chatham wasn't sure she heard Trip correctly.

"The what?"

Camp grabbed his grandfather's hand and dragged him across the restaurant before Chatham could stop them.

"He's my friend, grandpa. He almost beat me at Super Mario Smash Brothers, level 10. But I won."

"He what? Super who?"

≈

Camp and his grandfather arrived at the Capriatti's table. They were met with stares and looks of confusion. Palio observed the blank expressions on his tablemates' faces and slowly turned around.

"Camp!" he smiled, scooping up the young Ross boy and hoisting him up on his lap. "Did you bring my favorite game with you?"

Camp reached into his back pocket and pulled out his Game Boy. "Don't go anywhere without it," he smiled. Camp looked over his shoulder at his mother who didn't normally approve of him carrying his Game Boy to dinner. He quickly slid it back into his pants pocket.

"This is my grandpa," Camp said proudly. Palio set Camp down and stood up to shake Mr. Ross's hand.

"My Grandpa gave me a toy just like the one you gave me, see?" Camp pulled both of the wooden carvings out of his pocket and showed them to Palio. One had a white horse and the other had a black one.

"Well, I'll be. So you're the creator of these incredible miniatures," Palio exclaimed with complete admiration. Mr. Ross was caught off guard, but he didn't mind the praise.

"As a matter of fact, I am. But what I don't understand is, how did you get one, and, if you don't mind me asking, who the devil are you anyway?"

Palio laughed with childlike joy. Camp brought out a side of Palio that seemed young, happy, and carefree. "I know it seems peculiar Mr. ...Camp, you never told me your last name."

"It's Ross. There's my mom over there; you met her, too. And her friend Trip."

Palio looked over at the table and smiled. "Yes, so it is." His heart leapt when he saw Chatham again. Spoken for or not, he still couldn't help how he felt when he saw her. Palio forced himself to focus. "Mr. Ross, I am very sorry for the confusion. Let me try to explain. Camp and I, and your daughter, met on the plane flight out here today under a most interesting circumstance. Actually, I've met your daughter before, twice."

"Yeah, Grandpa. I took my seatbelt off because I had to go to the bathroom, and Palio smashed the door in on Trip and..." Camp leaned over to whisper the rest of the story. "And I didn't get in trouble or anything," Camp finished proudly.

Mr. Ross nodded with amusement at the entire story. "Don't tell Mom about the, you know. Promise?"

Mr. Ross conspicuously offered his pinky to seal the agreement.

Palio smiled in recognition of the family ritual. He felt honored to have been included.

Mr. Ross let out a hearty, belly laugh. "Well I've never heard a story quite like it, but I'm convinced that sometimes, things are just meant to be. So, Polio..." he said.

"It's Palio, but you can call me whatever sounds right," Palio said smiling.

Mr. Capriatti cleared his throat. "Oh Papa, I'm sorry. This is my new friend Camp, and his grandfather, Mr. Ross. And this is my brother Gino and our family guest, Georgina."

"I've heard about your wooden sculptures," Mr. Capriatti replied. "You're in demand."

"Well, thank you I suppose. I try to make each one special. And I am especially curious as to how you came across one, Paa... Palio."

Palio smiled at the correct pronunciation. "It looks like the model I gave to my friend in Central Park."

"Yes, Marco. He's my friend also. It was a gift."

"Marco has always been a generous man," Mr. Ross agreed.

"Ever consider making one-of-a-kind boat models?" Mr. Capriatti inquired.

"Tried to once, for that big boat company in the city. They had a model called The Sorbonne. I told them that they needed to add to the hull, and they told me I was crazy. That damn boat sank in the Bermuda Triangle, just like I predicted." Mr. Ross was clearly proud of his ability to determine exact measurements. Palio wasn't sure where the conversation might be going. After all, his own father had modeled his last miniature sailboat after that exact model.

"I heard about that boat. Piece of shit."

"Tell me something I don't know," Chatham's father added in complete agreement.

"But Papa," Palio objected. "Your last boat was designed after that very model."

"That's right, and I lost." Mr. Capriatti cracked a sly smile. "Fixed the problem though. Something with the design of the hull."

Mr. Ross nodded knowingly.

"I'll tell you what. How about you, and your family, come to my little boat race tomorrow in Central Park and tell me what you think of my newest gem. It's my secret weapon." Mr. Capriatti looked around and lowered his voice. "It's called Lucia, for after my wife who has passed away."

"God rest her soul," Mr. Ross added.

"Thank you. The keel is an exact duplicate of the winning America's Cup Boat, except for one thing." The entire table seemed to lean in closer. "It's made out of the newest, sleekest titanium alloid. The stuff isn't even on the market yet. My little Lucia flies in the wind." Mr. Capriatti sat back in total contentment.

295

"How does it perform in cross wind turbulence?"
Mr. Ross asked.

Palio gave Camp the google eyes. Neither had any
idea what secret language the two old men were speaking.

"Like a charm."

"Hmm." Mr. Ross looked over at Camp.

"Can we go Grandpa, please? Can we? I want to see
the boat race; it sounds so totally sweet."

The entire table laughed.

"Sweet it will be, my boy," Mr. Capriatti added
with a twinkle in his eye. "Totally."

The table exchanged handshakes once again and
Camp and Mr. Ross returned to their table.

≈

"Dad, Camp, what was that all about?" Chatham
demanded when they got back to the table. She had no idea
what was going on at the table between laughing and
whispering and handshaking. And that woman with Palio.
Was it his wife?

"My dear, tomorrow Camp and I are going to a boat
race. A fantastic little boat race, that is if it's OK with you."

"Tomorrow? Well, I have my presentation
tomorrow and then I thought I'd meet up with you two."

"You're invited," her father said, letting her know
she wasn't being left out.

"Did, um, did he invite me?" she asked as casually
as possible.

"He? You mean Paa, Paal... what the heck was his
name again?"

"Palio," Chatham answered softly.

"Right, that's it. And his father. He wants me to see

his newest race model. Sounds like he's a boat nut who likes to win. And I like that."

Chatham looked up casually at Palio's table. He was laughing with the foreigner. The woman was practically sitting in his lap and Palio didn't seem to be mind. The older gentleman seemed pleased with the interaction as well, but the body guard type had a bit of a disapproving ';.scowl on his face. Chatham decided not to be depressed. After all, she was invited as part of the family. She decided that she would just go see, what, if anything, might come of it. Besides, Camp really wanted to see the race and her dad was asked for his expertise. She might as well support their interest.

Chatham looked over at Trip. Trip hadn't taken his eyes off of her all night, and it didn't look like he was about to. Chatham found herself blush at the acknowledgement of his interest just as the restaurant owner approached the table with a skip in his step.

"So I see you've met my good friends, Roberto and Palio. Me and the Capriatti family, we go way back, we do. I had a little investment in his confectionary company, and voila! I have this beautiful restaurant to share with all of my friends, old *and* new." The group smiled gratefully.

Chatham was curious about the story the restaurant owner was telling.

"Would those confections happen to be jellybeans?" Chatham asked out of the blue.

"Why Miss, how did you know? Blueberry meringue cheesecake is their number one flavor. Every time you eat one, you know it's from the Capriatti Candy Factory. No better jellybeans anywhere in the world. Be sure to take a handful from the hostess stand when you leave tonight."

Chatham remembered the jellybean contest at the health club. She thought it was odd at the time, but things were starting to make more sense to her. Who was this Palio Capriatti anyway? She thought he was simply the extremely attractive counter attendant at the local exercise outlet.

"So, my little chef. Have you decided on a special dish of the night?" Monte asked Camp with full attention.

Camp took the task seriously. "Can I have spaghetti with peanut butter and chocolate ice cream?"

"Camp!" Chatham admonished. "The chef isn't going to make noodles like that. Why not ask him to make your favorite red sauce?." She smiled at the restaurant owner with apology. Monte held his hand up gently.

"Anything my little chef desires he gets. We will call it peanut butter spaghetti a la mode in honor of my new friend. I will have it out to you promptly." Monte proceeded to take the remaining orders and was off to the kitchen to convince the chef to create the unusual concoction.

Chatham's telephone rang from somewhere below the table. She reached under the white linen tablecloth and plunged her hand into the darkness in search of the intrusive noise. It didn't take her long to identify the piece of equipment that was often found glued to her ear.

"Hello?"

"Hey Chat. I am so sorry, but I will not be able to make it tonight. Gabrielle just showed up with a room full of roses and two bottles of Crystale. Chatham heard affectionate noises in the background. She could only imagine where Chloe's friend was delivering his caresses.

"Can I see you and Camp tomorrow?" Chatham knew that Chloe must be serious about this one to cancel on family. But she was happy for her sister in law. It was time that she met someone that really mattered.

"Sure Chloe, no problem. Camp is staying with grandpa tonight and then they're going to some boat race tomorrow in Central Park. I have my presentation and then I was going to join them."

"Oh, the Little Boat Race Championship. I know all about it. Everyone goes. I'll meet you there! About noon?"

"OK, that sounds good. Have a great time and you know I can't wait to hear about it." She heard Chloe giggle. "See you tomorrow."

Chatham flipped her telephone shut and rejoined the conversation in progress.

"He told me that he would consider selling it to me for the right price so I agreed to meet him in person to discuss it, which was why I jumped on a plane and came out here." He looked over at Chatham and smiled.

"What is it this time, Trip?" Chatham asked. "I hope it doesn't smell," she said with a mock reprimand.

"OK, OK, so I was a little off on the skoonard. This is an almost extinct Numbat. It's extremely rare. I don't have a buyer yet but I'm sure I won't have a problem finding one."

"Well, my boy," Mr. Ross interjected. "I have no idea what a skoonard, woonard or numbat, wumbat, fumbat are, but I do know that I am starving."

Almost as if on cue, the chef himself appeared with

the table's order.

"For you my junior chef," he said to Camp as he placed his concoction of peanut-butter flavored noodles with small scoops of chocolate ice cream on top, directly in front of him. "Voila, the perfect meal."

"Gracie," Camp responded reaching for the chef's hand and kissing it.

The table chuckled.

"You know Italian, my little bambino?" the chef inquired with a smile.

"No, I just heard the big man with no hair saying it a lot." Camp disregarded the reactions around him and dug into his feast.

"And for you, madam," the chef said placing a plate of Fettuccini Alfredo in front of Chatham. She realized that she hadn't eaten anything since morning. The delicious smell alone was enough to satisfy her pallet.

Before she began devouring the delicious meal, Chatham casually glanced over her shoulder to see Palio. She was thankful to see that the beautiful woman was no longer with them. Just then, as if on queue, Palio met her gaze. He smiled warmly and tipped his head to her. Even from across the restaurant, Chatham's stomach flip-flopped and her heart turned over in response.

CHAPTER XXXIII – *THE SPY*

≈

Maria crouched under the window to the tiny Italian Restaurant. She was clad in her typical all black from head to toe, including sunglasses and a black scarf to mask her identity. She was determined to fully understand what the olive princess was after. She had to squash it at any cost. Her legs were beginning to cramp at having been in the same squatting position for the past hour. And she was getting hungry. If it wasn't for her own personal stake in this escapade, she would have assigned one of her thugs to the surveillance. But she just couldn't help it. She loved Palio and nothing was going to stand in the way of getting him. Maria decided that she would protect what was hers, at any cost.

"Can I help you, Miss?" an employee asked from behind her.

Maria stood up quickly and almost fell on him due to the weakness in her joints that resulted from her unusual position.

The boy caught her just in time.

"Oh my gosh, I am so embarrassed," Maria offered, turning on her dumb brunette character. "I was looking for my belly button stud. I think I lost it here earlier. You see I was dining here and I came out for a smoke, and well… gosh, can you help me find it?"

The bus boy immediately got down on his knees to scan the ground, attempting to sift through the pebbles and differentiate between a pebble and a naval piercing trinket. Maria was so into character, directing the boy as to where she might have lost the bauble, that she barely caught the restaurant's back door opening for the second time.

Maria looked up and gasped. It was him! The police man or undercover agent, or whoever he was. Right there in front of her and eating at the same restaurant as her precious Palio. She ducked into the shadow of the restaurant wall and studied him. Funny, he was dressed in a similar manner as the gentleman who's back was to her in the restaurant. Was he actually dining with them? How did he know the Capriatti men? Who was he to them? Maybe he was filling them in on the activities of the olive princess. But she was there too, fawning over Palio, so it couldn't be that. Maria had no idea who he was and now; she was totally and completely confused.

"What are you doing there?" the handsome man asked the busboy who was down on his hands and knees sifting through the broken glass and dirty pebbles of the back alley.

"Damn," Maria said under her breath. She did not want to be noticed, not even by this godlike being standing less than twenty feet away from her.

"Yes sir," the boy said standing up and brushing off his pants. "I am helping one of our earlier guests attempt to retrieve a lost stud, I believe." He was quite respectful.

"A stud?" he asked as he lit a cigarette. "Out here?"

Maria noted the disbelief in his tone.

"I'm sorry, ma'am. I don't see anything," the innocent bus boy answered.

"Who are you talking to?"

At this point Maria really had no choice. She slowly stepped out from the dark shadow, remaining in character.

"Oh my gosh, can you believe it?" she said dramatically while bending down. "Here it is! My precious diamond belly-button stud! My mama will be so very happy that I haven't lost it forever. I got it for my first communion, you know." Maria regretted that last statement almost immediately. What seven-year-old girl gets a belly button piercing for her first communion?

She could practically see the gorgeous man's antennas go up.

"Really? You got your belly button pierced at – seven?"

He must be Catholic, like me to know about communion, Maria thought. Bad sign. Must divert from subject matter now.

"Thank you so much, you wonderful bus boy," she added, giving the boy a hug and quickly making her way past the mystery man. As she brushed by him her breath momentarily stopped and her knees grew limp again. The shadowy figure caught her just in time.

"Are you OK, Miss?" he asked as he helped Maria back up to standing.

Maria reminded herself to stay in character although she wondered why she had the sudden urge to deliver a passionate kiss to a man she didn't even know. "Yes, yes, thank you. I'm so sorry. It's just that I was looking for my diamond, and my knees grew weak from crouching and all."

"Awfully dark for sun glasses, isn't it?" he asked amusingly.

"Oh, these old things. Well, I do have sensitive eyes. Um, even at night." She quickly stood up and attempted her exit. "Thank you again for your help," Marie added as she scampered down the back alley and hopefully away from the embarrassing scene as soon as possible.

"Here let me walk you," the man offered as he stomped out his cigarette and jogged to catch up with her.

The strong, protective hand gently held the edge of Maria's elbow, which almost caused her to faint into his arms once again. Focus Maria, she told herself.

"Where is your dinner date?" he asked, fishing in a concerned citizen sort of way.

Maria debated with herself. If I say *He* then this gorgeous hunk of a man will think I'm taken. Well, I am, aren't I? If I'm going to be with Palio, I'm definitely taken.

"My sister had to get home to her kids." What am I saying? Maria snapped at herself.

The man smiled. Maria couldn't tell if he was pleased with her response or not. Not that it should matter, she reminded herself. Remember Palio?

They walked out to the front of the restaurant and like Adonis, he lifted one perfectly sculpted arm into the air and hailed a cab.

"Wait a minute," Gino said lowering his flagging hand. "If it's alright with you, I would be happy to give you a ride home. I was just having dinner with my brother, I mean, my best friend and his dad. We call one another brother. You know, have known each other forever kind of thing. Anyway, I can just tell them that I'm giving a friend a ride, and I'll be back in a flash."

Marie froze, her mind and body benumbed. An instant revelation came over her. "Oh my god!" she blurted out. "You're Gino!" She pulled down her scarf and removed her sunglasses so that Gino could see her fully.

"I'm sorry, I don't understand," Gino replied as he stood eye to eye with the dark haired beauty..

"Gino, it's me. Maria," she said softly, and lowered her eyes humbly.

"Maria Porticello? The same Maria who's running the candy factory? The family Maria who I haven't seen since we were kids?" The shock on Gino's face was priceless.

Maria nodded in response to each of his direct questions.

"Wow," was all Gino could conclude.

"Yeah, wow," she responded with authentic surprise.

They stood staring at one another for a full minute. The electricity between them was so powerful it could have lit up all of Manhattan.

Gino snapped himself out of his trance.

"So, I'll just tell Palio and Roberto, if that's OK with you?"

"Sure," was all she could say. Maria suddenly became very warm.

"OK then, I'll be right back," Gino added with an affectionate smile. As he was about to enter the restaurant, he momentarily turned back to Maria. "Do you want to come in and say hi?" After all, she was family, too.

Maria wanted to accept but how would she explain her reason for being there, in the back alley, spying? "Oh no, that's OK. Tell them I'll speak with them tomorrow if you would. I'm a little tired."

Gino nodded and disappeared into Monte's as Maria waved off her bodyguard thugs so that she could accept the ride from Gino. This evening had definitely taken an interesting turn. What was even more peculiar, Maria didn't mind it at all.

≈

Chatham looked up in time to see Palio's friend enter the front door of the restaurant. Didn't he disappear out the back way a while ago, Chatham wondered. She wasn't sure. In fact, she wasn't sure of most things right now. Maybe she still had jet lag.

"Are you ready, my boy?" Chatham's father asked after the tiramisu, hot fudge sundae, and coffee were emptied from the dining table.

"I'm ready," Camp answered as he licked the last heaping of hot fudge from his spoon.

"Wait Dad, we can go with you and you can drop us off at the hotel." Chatham looked to Trip for approval of her plan. It was getting late and Chatham knew she needed a good night's rest if she was to perform well tomorrow.

"We can do that, but Camp here looks pretty beat, huh pal?" Mr. Ross winked at Camp.

Camp yawned and stretched as if on queue.

"Yeah, Grandpa. I'm beat, totally. Can I sleep in the workbench tonight?" It was Camp's favorite room. Mr. Ross's workbench was filled with partially made miniatures of everything from exact replicas of full-sized jet airplanes to bone-for-bone duplicates of extinct dinosaurs like the T-Rex. Each miniature was for some project that Mr. Ross had been hired for, except for the special shelf. The long white mantelpiece above the bench was saved for the carvings he was making for his family.

Camp was practically to the front door, before he came racing back across the restaurant, almost tripping Monte in the process. He threw his arms around Chatham.

"Be good for grandpa, OK?" she asked sweetly.

"I will, mom!" Camp gave Trip a hi-five and dashed back to the front door by way of Palio's table.

Chatham saw her son, for the second time that evening, bother the handsome Palio and his table.

"See ya tomorrow," Camp said as he paused to give his regards.

"Hey," Palio responded. "Bring the game. If we have time, I'm going to beat you this time. I have five dollars riding on it."

"Five bucks? Promise?" Camp asked.

"Promise," Palio answered, offering his pinky to seal the accord.

Chatham saw the entire interaction unfold, and she couldn't help but smile. One glance to her left, and she knew that Trip saw it, too.

Trip flagged down the waiter as Chatham watched her father and son depart.

"A bottle of Dom Perignon, please," Trip instructed.

Chatham looked at him with wide eyes. "Trip! I have a presentation tomorrow."

"Exactly. And a bowl of strawberries with chocolate dip as well." He shut the menu and turned his full attention to her.

Chatham was instantly nervous. Where was he going with this?

"Actually it is good luck to have a glass of champagne before a big presentation. It relaxes you and makes you happy. So be quiet and go along. Tonight, I'm in charge."

Wow, Chatham had never heard Trip speak like that before. Was this a side of him that had always been there but that she had overlooked? He suddenly displayed a more assertive, take-charge attitude, which was way out of character. Trip had always been Mr. Accommodating. He was simply there, for whatever, whenever it was needed. She wasn't sure what to say.

"Oh, OK," Chatham responded. Her body involuntarily tingled at the thought of being taken care of for once. It felt good. Chatham glanced in the direction of Palio's table. They were leaving, and it was clear to her that Palio was definitely escorting the exotic woman. Chatham watched as they said their goodbyes to Monte.

"Palio, I will go on ahead," she heard his father say. Why don't you take our friend home? I need to rest up for tomorrow's big race, eh?" He kissed Georgina on both cheeks and left. Just as Mr. Capriatti was about to exit the restaurant, he turned around and looked over the customers heads until he found Chatham's table. Chatham and the older gentleman locked gazes for an instant. She could have sworn that he winked at her before he turned back around and departed.

Chatham watched as Palio helped the woman with her coat who, in return, planted a gentle kiss on Palio's cheek. Chatham sighed to herself. What was she thinking? She was dreaming of some man who she shouldn't be dreaming about because she knows nothing about him, while the man who has been there for her all along, ever since her beloved Peter died, was right there in front of her offering her champagne and chocolate-dipped strawberries. Get your priorities straight Chatham, she said to her alter ego. It's time to move on and move on you shall.

Chatham glanced over at the man seated alone in the corner, partially blocked by a large palm frond. He was watching Palio and the exotic woman intently as they departed the restaurant. The heavy set man had a look of smugness on his face, as though he was watching a secret unfold exactly as planned. She thought she saw him whispering into his lapel, but she couldn't be sure. As the front door of the restaurant closed behind the couple, the solid muscle figure put down several hundred dollar bills and left without as much as a glance at the check. It was as though he planned to follow them.

≈

The man on the other end hung up the phone, satisfied with how the evening unfolded, and went back to join the sumptuous Chloe.

≈

When the champagne arrived, it was Trip who lifted his glass first.

"To you," he said softly. The smile in his eyes contained a sensuous flame.

"To us," she returned, just as kindly. The candle's light reflected a depth of emotion that neither had been brave enough to show – until now.

"I like the sound of that," Trip added. The close friends beamed as they dipped their strawberries into the warm chocolate sauce that accompanied the delicacy. At that moment Chatham erased all other thoughts from her mind. She was here with Trip, where she was supposed to be and it was time for her to let it be.

CHAPTER XXXIV –*SURPRISES*

≈

Palio stepped out onto Bleeker and hailed a cab for him and his unexpected guest.

"Are you sure you don't want to leave with your dinner date?" Palio asked one more time. He wasn't too sure about giving Georgina a ride home. Something felt dangerous about the sudden arrangement.

"No, no, really. It was a business meeting, and he was heading to the airport. Now I don't have to ride home alone," she smiled as demurely as possible. Modestly did not come naturally for a woman with laser focus.

I'll just drop her at her hotel, Palio reasoned with himself. He didn't believe in evening negotiations, especially after consuming a few glasses of good red wine that had significantly warmed his senses. Besides, he couldn't get Chatham out of his mind. If only they could meet under normal circumstances.

Palio's thoughts drifted. A single mother with a boyfriend living on the opposite end of the country. It didn't really make any sense, but something told him that Chatham was exactly what his mother would have wanted for him.

The cab pulled up to the curb and turned off its rooftop light to demonstrate that the fare was spoken for. Georgina quickly grabbed Palio's arm.

"I think that other cab was here first," she said pointing to a taxi less than half a block away. She guided Palio in its direction.

"Hey pal," the first taxi driver said as he opened his

window. "What's your problem?" Palio just shrugged his shoulders at the driver.

"Women, can't take 'em nowhere. They're always drivin' the boat," the driver said as he flipped the rooftop light back on and sped away.

Palio held the door open for Georgina who slid into the back seat about half way. She scooted closer to Palio as he climbed in and shut the door.

"The Pierre?" Palio asked, remembering where he was to pick her up the following day at the appointed noon hour.

"Yes, thank you," she said, demurely. "I am so happy to have finally met your father in person. He is so very charming, as is his son," she added with a fluttering of her eyelashes. Palio didn't take the bait.

She slipped out of her spike-heeled shoe, untucked her bare leg from under her sable coat and crossed it in his direction.

Palio noticed. Her leg didn't have a flaw on it. "So tomorrow, the race. It should be quite good," Palio said, hoping to change the direction the interlude was headed.

"Yes, the little boat race. I know so little about boats, you know. Tell me about your father's boat. The Lucia, did he call it?"

"Yes, after my mother."

"The company must be worth so much. Well, I have no idea really," she quickly said, "but based on his passion, he is probably very successful."

"Let's just say that my papa's little boat company could buy you many Park Avenue apartments. I mean, could buy *a* person." He didn't want to give her the wrong idea.

Georgina blushed. "Me? On Park Avenue? Why I hear it's very nice."

"I think you could handle yourself," Palio smiled, not doubting for a minute that this very capable, gorgeous creature could get just about anything she wanted. Palio glanced away, hopeful this ride would be over soon.

Just then Palio noticed the head shot affixed to the back of the taxi seat with masking tape, and a message written in black magic marker below it: New spokesperson for The Idle Spur Restaurants. Yee haw!

"It's you again," Palio said to the back of the driver's cowboy hat.

"Hey, how's it goin'?" the taxi driver said with a little more confidence than last time.

"I see you got a new gig," Palio observed. "So how does a taxi driver who seems to work at all hours manage to get such a high-profile acting job?" He was impressed with the driver's ingenuity.

"It's all in the marketing, pal," the driver responded with his New York voice. "This lady was sittin' in the back, just like you and your little Mrs. here."

Palio glanced at Georgina as she reached over to touch his hand ever so gently.

"Do you want an audition, she says to me? I mean, right there on the spot. Had to say some line about Bull Shit, no offense lady, to one of my very own – over the telephone even. He was a bit of a hard ass. Asked me where I was born and could I shoot an elk in one shot and shit like that. He didn't know who he was messin' with. I won the Elk Bustin' Championship in my hometown of Flower

Mound when I was ten. Yeah, so I got the job and they're flying me to San Francisco or something for the shoot. I'm a real actor now," he said, sitting up a little straighter.

"Guess you'll be giving up your role as taxi driver," Palio chuckled.

"Hell no! Like I said to Miss Ross, she's the one that hired me. He handed over the card for Palio to see.

Palio was suddenly at a loss for words. This woman just kept showing up!

"I told her, what are you crazy? Look what kind of work I got from you. Next thing you know it, Stephen Spielberg will be riding in my cab and will want me for the next E.T. or something. I'm good with costumes. I did this worm film once."

Palio wasn't listening. He simply stared at the card he was holding between his thumb and forefinger. Could it be the same Chatham that he had met at the health club, on the plane, and, just tonight, had seen in the same restaurant? So she's in advertising, he summed up. No wonder she changed the slogan on the club outfit I gave her. She's clever and absolutely intriguing, Palio concluded to himself, oblivious to the world around him.

≈

Georgina watched Palio, somewhat worried. She wasn't gaining any ground. He was on another planet and she would have to bring him back to earth – her earth. She knew she needed to forward their relationship along, and fast. She couldn't afford to waste any more time. All she really had was this opportune cab ride to make her move. Tomorrow's event would be crowded with people and she would have too much on her mind.

The driver was turning out to be a total disaster. She specifically requested an actor that would create a romantic mood during the ride, and here he was... completely butchering it. And it cost her a two-hundred-dollar fee to the agency. Georgina caught the driver's eye in the rearview mirror. She made sure her feelings were clearly expressed. .

The Texas actor seemed to understand. He quickly turned on the radio to the local classical music station and turned on a fake candle the agency had given him for this particular fare. He placed the mood enhancer on the dashboard and turned off the internal taxi light.

The driver took a sudden turn off Fifth Avenue and onto 47th street, the heart of the jewelry district. He slowed down to make the drive last a little longer. The taxi glided past non-glare windows filled with diamond engagement rings, necklace, and bracelet displays. Georgina recognized where they were. On this street you could buy a three-carat diamond for half of what you'd pay at Tiffany's and you wouldn't forfeit anything by way of quality. Most of the world shopped there.

Georgina subtly shook her head at the driver. This wasn't good enough. Change of plans. The driver took the next turn back onto Fifth and slowed down as they approached Tiffany's. She nodded her head with approval.

The taxi driver suddenly needed to fix an indicator on the control dashboard. "Damn thing, mind if I pull over for a quick second? I won't charge you."

"Sure," Georgina replied, a little too quickly. The driver swerved in front of a large Lincoln and came to a sharp stop directly in front of Tiffany's silver doors that looked like a large present waiting to be unwrapped.

"So, where ya'll from?" the driver inquired casually as he pretended to fix a wire. If he was going to earn his fee, he had to make sure there were no more slip-ups.

Palio seemed to snap back to the here and now. "Oh, here. Manhattan, actually," Palio answered. The business card was still in his hand. He looked over at Georgina who was intentionally cooing at the diamonds in the windows. "And my friend here is from Florence, as in Italy."

Georgina put her hands together and leaned her entire body toward Palio, allowing her coat to drape open and her legs to part slightly.

"Oh Palio, can we? I mean, unless you have other plans. I so rarely get to see New York other than when I'm in meetings with Sotheby's or the olive oil importers. I've always wanted to see Tiffany's." She batted her eyes beseechingly, practically begging for Palio to step into the role of adoring, doting husband. She was making it incredibly easy for him to pamper his vulnerable little wife.

Palio looked at the driver, eyebrows raised.

"Yeah, sure, I'll wait, no problem."

"Well, OK. I guess that will be alright," Palio answered somewhat uncomfortably.

"Perfect!" Georgina exclaimed. They made their way to the dangerous retail establishment. She was beaming. If all went according to plan, this would be the first of many trips to this wonderful little store.

CHAPTER XXXV –*MAD DASH*

≈

"May I take my seatbelt off?" PJ asked, squirming in his seat. Theo turned to see PJ holding his privates.

"Do you have to go to the bathroom, PJ?" Theo asked.

"I have to get out," PJ insisted, attempting to open the car door before they were even in the driveway.

"PJ no, you have to wait," insisted Tom. He pressed the garage-door clicker and kept his foot on the brake as the garage door raised.

"I have to get out!" PJ demanded, manually lifting the door lock and flinging the door open. He ran into the garage and up the stairs like a lion after its prey.

"Theo, I told you to make sure the childproof lock was on. I could have run him over!" Tom always blamed Theo when he was stressed.

"Sorry Tommy, I thought I did." Theo looked down, and sure enough, the little stick figure was visible, which meant that the locks were supposed to be child resistant.

"Then how did he get out? Hmm? Tell me. What is he the hulk or something?"

"Well, we did lift some weights tonight. Maybe."

Tom darted his face toward Theo with an intense, disapproving stare. "Please."

Madison jumped out behind Theo and dashed up the stairs. She secretly hoped that Dane might have left her an instant message on her computer.

"Aaahhhh! Tom, Theo, come quick!" The scream was deafening.

Tom and Theo raced up the back stairs and hurled into the kitchen, only to be met by a pantry cabinet completely covered in ants.

Tom's hand went right to his mouth in a very feminine, weak gesture. "I think I'm going to faint."

Theo caught Tom as he was about to fall.

"Oh my god, get them out of here!" Madison screamed as she jumped onto the counter top for protection.

"Maddy, relax. They're only ants, not piranhas," Theo retorted, waving a paper plate in front of Tom's face until he regained his composure.

Tom stood up and glanced at the ants. "Disgusting. Theo, get rid of them! I have a terrible headache." He marched out of the kitchen and into the master bedroom. The door slam meant stay out.

It took Theo a good hour to wipe up all of the ants. There had to be at least a million of the tiny invaders. Theo followed the trail from the top of the pantry to the back of the bottom shelf and reached his Popeye arms into the darkness of the food closet to pull out the offender – a jar of marshmallow puff. Theo held up the incriminating evidence, but didn't say a word.

Madison fidgeted uncomfortably. "Well, I better finish my homework. I'll see you later, Theo."

Theo knew something was up. "Homework on a Friday night?" he asked innocently. "You're pretty dedicated with the books there, Maddy."

"Theo, it's my fault," she blurted out." I was eating that stuff for breakfast the other day and didn't put the top on the jar the whole way, and Mom grabbed it from me and, well, you can see what happened. I'm really sorry. Please don't tell Tom."

Theo winked. "Why don't you help me clean out the back of this shelf then; I think it's the last of them." Madison wet a paper towel and reached into the back of the shelf to wipe it clean.

"Can you shine a flashlight in here Theo so I make sure to get them all?" Maddy sprayed and wiped the little insects until not a single one remained. Theo was proud of her.

"Hey," Maddy commented. "There's a big hole back here." She shimmied out of the pantry to give Theo a look.

Theo shined the flashlight into the hole, assuming that it would contain the ant nest. Instead, he could see the outline of a soft leather pouch, tied neatly with rawhide string. But how did it get there? The hole wasn't more than the size of a silver dollar. He tapped the end of the flashlight around the hole until he heard a soft click. With a gentle nudge, a small panel opened and the pouch was easily scooped up from its hiding place. Theo tucked the parcel into his pants and made his way out into the brightly lit kitchen.

"What is it?" Madison asked, anxious to know if they had finally eradicated the pests from the source.

"Yep, it was the nest. I think they ate right through."

Madison scrunched her nose in disgust. "Eww. Well at least now I can sleep. Thanks Theo. And thanks for not spilling the beans." She gave him a quick hug and headed up the stairs to change.

Theo examined the leather holder and removed its contents. After reading what was inside, he decided that Tommy would know what to do. Nervously, Theo made his way to the master bedroom.

"I told you I have a headache," Tommy scolded as Theo entered and closed the door firmly behind him. He approached the bed where Tommy lay, a chilled gel pack on each eye. Theo stood silently.

"You've got to be kidding. I am not in the mood, can't you see that?" Tom whisked the coolants from his face and sat up.

Theo just stared at Tom in silence. It was amazing to him how little his partner knew him sometimes.

"What? What is it Theo?"

"You should look at this, Tommy," Theo suggested, offering the folded pouch.

"Look, at what? What is this?" He accepted the folder cautiously, unfolded the contents and skimmed the prose.

"Oh my god," Tom mumbled. "We… we have to go. We have to go to Chatham, now, tonight."

Theo shook his head. "Can't we just call her?"

"Call her? Call her? What's wrong with you? Of course we can't call her. She's about to fall flat on her face, and we have to help her. We have to save her."

"I guess you're right, but she's on a business trip. Can't this wait until she gets back?"

"Of course I'm right. And no, Theo dear. This can't wait a moment longer!" Tom hopped off the bed, suddenly cured of his headache. "Maddy, PJ!" he shrieked commands at lightning speed.

Within a half hour the four musketeers were on their way to catch the red eye to New York City.

≈

Chatham had had a little too much champagne. As she exited the taxi she practically fell into Trip's waiting arms, unintentionally, of course. Or was it intentional? Trip couldn't tell.

"Come on, I'll walk you to your room," Trip offered, taking her hand under his arm to steady her. So much for his plan of attack.

"Oh no, I'm fine, really. I think I just have jet lag or something," Chatham objected. "I can make it, really."

"Are you sure?"

"Yes, Trip, for God's sakes alive. I'm not drunk. A little tipsy maybe, but definitely not drunk." Chatham weaved through the lobby of The Pierre. "Damn, these shoes are killing me," she said suddenly.

Trip watched her sit down in the middle of the lobby, take off her heels, and toss them his way. "Can you carry these for me?" she asked.

"I can do better than that," he mumbled as he scooped Chatham up into his arms and made his way toward the lift.

"Oh, Trip! A ride. How nice of you." Chatham buried her face into Trip's neck.

Like something out of a Cary Grant film, Trip glanced down at Chatham just as she angled her face to get a closer look at her prince charming. The kiss was ever so soft. The couple lingered, their lips brushing and breath connecting. Trip shuttered with pleasure, amazed that a kiss could conjure up so much feeling.

Chatham smiled a thin, content turn of her lips and fell asleep.

≈

Gino loved surveillance. After all, he was a protector, part of the family, a loyal friend to the core and he had a bad feeling about this Italian import.

"Come on, Gino," Maria said firmly. "Let's go in."

He looked over at Maria. How could he not have met up with Maria in all these years? Why hadn't their lives intersected? At that particular moment, he didn't really care why. Gino was on an adventure with the most gorgeous woman he had ever laid eyes on, which made it hard to concentrate on the task at hand.

"I think we should stay here, the taxi is waiting for them and he might see us if we get out," Gino offered.

"Don't worry about it," Maria promised. "Take my lead." She reached for the door handle and slid out of the passenger side, ducking just out of sight of the taxi driver.

Gino followed close behind, wondering why he needed to be crawling on all fours at night in the middle of Manhattan. It didn't matter. It was as though he was on a leash being led willingly by his lord and master. He knew he would give Maria whatever she wanted – he was smitten.

Maria and Gino ducked into Tiffany's and quickly scooted to the far corner of the room, far away from where Palio and Georgina were perusing.

"What are you doing?" Gino whispered as they pretended to look at rows and rows of Tanzenite bracelets.

"It's called audio spy. Newest stuff on the market. All I have to do is put this little Statue of Liberty pin on."

"Here, let me help," Gino proposed. He retrieved the pin from Maria's hand and took his time affixing it to her sweater, right above her heart. Gino quivered as the back of his hand accidentally brushed against her breast. "I can't get the clasp to work." He wondered if she was already annoyed with him, or if he was being entirely too obvious. "OK, there we go. Now what?"

"Huh? Oh, yeah. So, here is the receiver. It goes in my ear and threads down through my clothes and into the pack that hooks to the back of my slacks." Maria began to fiddle with the apparatus.

"Can I help again?" Gino asked. Maria almost dropped the device.

"That's OK. It's pretty easy to get on."

Damn it, he thought. I'm being way too forward. He felt slightly defeated but acquiesced.

"Then you press the torch and voila, instant access." Maria was suddenly deeply focused as Gino wondered how she could know so much about surveillance when she only ran a candy factory. Something else was up, and he wanted to find out what it was.

He glanced over at the entrance to Tiffany's and saw the same two massively built body guards who had been trailing them as they trailed Palio. Maria was clearly someone very important; and now she was quickly becoming important to Gino.

"Oh my god," Maria blurted abruptly. "Palio, no!"

Gino didn't like how vehemently Maria objected to whatever it was that she was hearing. It was as though her protection of Palio was way too personal. How much did she care for him anyway? "What? What's going on?" Gino insisted. "Let me hear." The couple looked like exactly that, a couple in love, their heads pressed closely together as they listened to the conversation across the store aisles.

"I've always wanted to get married, Palio," Georgina purred. "It's just that, well, it's just that I haven't found the right person – until now," she added softly as she tilted her head and looked up at him with her saucer brown eyes.

Maria and Gino turned their heads in unison to witness the exchange. They watched as Georgina pretended to trip so that she would fall quite perfectly into Palio's embrace. She wrapped her hands around Palio's neck and pulled him close, attempting to get her footing.

"I must have slipped…. Palio, thank you so much for saving me. A real knight in shining armor." She leaned up and planted an intimate kiss on Palio's mouth in feigned gratitude.

Maria's face scrunched up into a ball of jealousy as she quickly averted her eyes. Gino wondered how deeply Maria felt toward Palio. After all, Palio did mention that he had taken her out after many years and that she had completely changed, for the better. Gino recalled something about joining the families together or something like that. Better move fast, Gino concluded. This girl is my match, and I'm not going to let her get away.

"I think I'm going to faint," Maria blurted, not sure if she could steady herself.

Gino had to act quickly. "We need to move," he commanded. "They're coming over."

"What?" Maria snapped to. "We can't let them see us, it will blow the whole thing."

"OK then, let's pretend I just gave you an engagement ring and you are thanking me." He turned toward the man behind the glass display. "Sir, can my fiancée try that ring on?" Gino pointed to a four-caret, cushion-cut diamond with one carat trillions on each side. It was stunning.

He placed the ring on Maria's wedding finger and wrapped her in his arms. "Now kiss me," he instructed. "Like you mean it."

Gino's lips met hers with a gentleness that a man of his size couldn't possibly deliver. He felt her respond to his kiss as she leaned her entire body into his with a fervent passion. For a moment, nothing else mattered. Gino forgot why they were there and who they were following. All he could see was Maria. Beautiful Maria in his arms.

When they finally parted, they discovered that Palio and Georgina were nowhere to be found.

≈

The bodyguard smirked as he watched Bambini's puppet and her soon-to-be betrothed make their way out of Tiffany's and into the waiting cab. But he didn't like the looks of the two sulkers that were following his prizes. Nothing was going to get in the way of his boss's plan to own the Capriatti family fortune. If they turned out to be a glitch, well, then he would simply get rid of them. He watched Georgina casually put her left hand on Palio's back. She turned her head around and smiled directly at his car. All was going according to plan.

"Let's go," he commanded. The jet black Bentley peeled away from the silver spoon curb and made its way down Fifth Avenue toward the seedier part of town.

≈

Harlan knew he should have gone to the restaurant to see how his plan was unfolding, but the crazy organic girl had a spell over him the day he walked into that SoHo dress shop and he simply couldn't help himself. He wasn't the kind of man that let his emotions rule, but something came over him as he watched her dance in the mirror, scarves flowing to her swaying movements. How did she fit in to all of this? He was focused on owning the Capriatti family businesses, and nothing was going to stand in his way. He would compartmentalize Chloe, just like he did with each area of his life. She was only a source of amusement, that's all.

All that mattered to him was building his empire. The merger of the Capriatti candy company with his own would give him a monopoly on the worldwide candy market. The health club he would sell off, or maybe have a friend run it. His favorite gem was the miniature boat company. Once he had it, not only would he have the largest yacht company in the world, but he would control every toy-related boat product. He had the manufacturing to grow the company into the largest toy company in the world, which would make the transporting of all goods, legal or not, as easy as pie. Harlan knew that Georgina was the one to get it for him and he was going to make sure she succeeded. If she married Palio, then she had agreed to sell him the entire empire.

There was no other way. The Capriatti's would never sell. Mr. C will not be around forever, and Georgina was his way to Palio. He knew that Georgina didn't give a hoot about Palio Capriatti. It was all business. He was simply a challenge that she would soon conquer. Harlan had heard rumors that Georgina was dealing in olive oil with Bambini, but he didn't see that as a conflict. He would get his empire and that's all that mattered. Little did Harlan know that Georgina was double dipping her way to elite wealth status. Along with wealth came power and down deep, that is all that mattered to her.

Harlan was glad he had met the infamous olive princess when he was in Italy last year for the yacht show. When she approached him and told him that she could make him an offer that he couldn't refuse, she definitely had his attention. How did she know so much about the Capriatti family, he remembered asking her.

"It all has to do with a little painting I happen to have," she had replied, a smile of victory on her lips.

CHAPTER XXXVI – *MORNING AFTER*

≈

Chatham woke to find herself tucked into a king-sized four-poster mahogany bed with mounds of down piled high atop 1,000-thread count sheets. She slinked lower into the luxurious sleigh, wishing she could sleep the day away and the headache that greeted her when she opened her eyes. Chatham reached down to feel something at the base of her feet when she realized that she had no clothes on. She sat up suddenly.

"Oh my god, how did I get here?" she asked the empty air.

Trip entered the room from the bathroom as if on queue. "Good morning," he said cheerfully.

"Trip, oh my gosh, what are you doing here?" she blurted out while grabbing the blankets for cover.

"Came to check on you. You were a little out of it last night."

"Out of it? What do you mean by out of it? I don't remember a thing." Chatham rested her head in her hands. "My head is killing me."

"I had an inkling. Here, two Advil and a cool cloth for your forehead should do the trick." Trip handed her the pills and a glass of water and proceeded to fold the cool cloth. "Lay down and rest, Chat, you have time."

Chatham suddenly remembered.

"Time, time, what time is it?" She shot up again, forgetting to cover herself in the process.

Trip respectfully turned his head away. "It's 8:30, why?"

"Oh my god! I have to be at my client's office in thirty minutes. I mean *in* his office, not on my way to his office. He's a freak for promptness. Where is my dress?" She began to get out of bed and then remembered her lack of attire. "Trip, did you, I mean... did we... what the hell happened last night?"

Trip chuckled as he braced the sides of the tufted chair. "Yes and Yes. You asked me to help you get ready for bed, so I did." Trip smiled slyly. "And, yes, I slept with you." Chatham's mouth dropped open, at a loss for words. Trip adopted a more serious tone. "And no, we didn't do anything. You wanted to, but I didn't want to take advantage of you. I just wanted to make sure you were OK."

"I, I asked you to make love to me?"

"Several times in fact. Can't say I didn't think about it." He smiled again.

Chatham was a little more than flustered. Oh well, no time for that; she had to get to her appointment. She needed this account.

"Trip, I don't know what to say. Can we talk about this later? I mean, I have got to go, but I'd really like to talk about this more."

"Chatham..." He stood up and crossed the carpet toward her. Trip leaned down to meet her face to face and whispered, "I am here for you; I've always been here for you." He gave her a quick kiss on the lips and turned toward the door. "I'll meet you downstairs."

Now she was in a pickle. Did she want this sudden change in their relationship? After all, it sounded like she practically begged him to have her last night. So much for playing hard to get. She was so confused – where was this going?

"OK, I'll hurry," she answered, wrapping the luxury sheet around her as she headed toward the bathroom.

Chatham took a thirty-second shower and was in the middle of drying off when her phone rang. She grabbed the extension in the bathroom while attempting to apply a Marilyn Monroe type mole to the correct spot on her face. She had downloaded a picture from the Internet of Marilyn Monroe in the famous white dress before she left. Now to just get it right.

"I've only been calling you all night. Where the hell have you been?" Chatham answered without skipping a beat. "Oh, hi Henrietta. I am so sorry. I passed out. Literally."

"On who?"

"What do you mean on who?"

"Well if you passed out, you very well didn't get into your room on your own, right?"

"Were you here?"

"Chat, I know you. You don't drink alone, so I know you didn't sit in your hotel room downing a bottle of champagne and pass out on the fancy-pants bed while saying goodnight to the television set. So, who did you pass out on?"

"You won't believe me if I told you."

"Try me."

"Trip."

Silence. "Nooo."

"Yes."

"Can't be."

"Is."

"Your choice?"

"Sort of, I think so. At least that's what he told me."

"OK, I'm missing something here. Did you ask him what the hell is he doing in New York anyway?"

Chatham continued to apply the black eye pencil to her lids. She steadied the phone between her shoulder and chin and drew on thick swipes of color to match Marilyn. "He said he had some meeting with the Central Park Zoo. It was a coincidence that he was even on the same flight."

"Yeah, right. Wasn't he over at your house when you booked your ticket?"

Chatham tried to remember. "Actually, I think so. I left the reservation on the computer and then had to dash out to pick up the kids. He could have read it; it's possible."

"Totally conniving. And what did you say to him last night?"

Chatham was embarrassed to repeat it. "Well…"

"Chat, what did you say?"

"He said I asked him to sleep with me, and, well, he did."

"What!"

"But he said we didn't do anything," she added quickly.

"OK, how were you dressed when you woke up this morning?"

"Um…"

"Chat, come clean."

"Exactly."

"Clean?"

"As a whistle."

"Nooo."

"Yes again."

"He's a liar. All men are liars. He definitely fucked you."

"What? Are you sure?"

"Come on. Trip has had the hots for you since Peter died. Sorry honey, you were too depressed to notice. Now he had his chance, and he took it. They're all scumbags."

Chatham wondered. "Do you think so? I mean, I can't remember a thing. Last thing I remember was Trip ordering a bottle of champagne and chocolate dipped strawberries at dinner, and I went along with it."

"Need I say more?"

"Henrietta, what do I do?"

"Do you love him?"

"I... don't know."

"OK, what about the gym rat guy?"

"You'll love this. He was on the same flight, and, he was at the same restaurant last night."

"OK, so you have the boy next door and a stalker. Hmm, tough decision."

Chatham was completely confused, and now she was going to be late. "Look Hen, I've got to go. This is my big presentation, and I'm going to be late as it is."

"Are you going to wear the dress?"

Chatham was attempting to zip it up without dropping the phone. "As we speak."

"What about the wig?"

"Well I have to now. I have no time to do my hair. OK, wish me luck! I'm off."

"Knock 'em dead. Oh, one more thing."

"What is it?"

"Tricky Vicky asked me to ask you to get the yacht guy to donate a week for two to an exotic island for the auction."

"You've got to be kidding. How did I let her rope me into chairing that thing? I have no time for that."

"Honey, you've got bigger problems to worry about, but I'm only the messenger here. I'll report back to the trickster that you said no problem, glad to do it. Maybe she'll give you a few gold volunteer stars."

"You know what I want to tell her to do with her stars?"

"Don't worry, I already have. I'm off the committee."

"Great, thanks a lot."

"You're welcome, now go get 'em."

Chatham planted the wig on her head, lathered on deep red lipstick, threw the container of Advil into her matching white purse, and sprinted out of her hotel room to join Trip in the lobby.

≈

"Can you step on it?" Palio asked the cab driver. He was already thirty minutes late to pick up Georgina, and he didn't want to blow it. The evening before had lasted much too long, and he had overslept. Palio reflected on the series of events the night before. It seemed as though the taxi driver had almost planned for one delay or side trip after another. Before he could say no, Palio found himself being talked into several drinks with Georgina at The Pierre before he was finally able to excuse himself well after midnight. And how he let himself get roped into a visit to Tiffany's, he'll never know.

All he wanted on the ride with Georgina was to see if they could come to some sort of agreement on the painting his father had his heart set on, to honor the memory of his mother. Before Palio knew it, he was agreeing to buy her a flawless, five-caret diamond ring in exchange for the painting. At least she wore it on her other ring finger.

Palio thought he had seen Chatham being carried up the stairs as he was leaving The Pierre around midnight, but he wrote it off to having had too many nightcaps at Georgina's insistence. And to top it off, he agreed to take her out to brunch before the race. Palio had no idea how he let himself get talked into what he didn't want to do. When would he get to do what he wanted?

He tossed a twenty over the seat and made his way out of the cab.

"Thanks pal," the driver yelled through the open window. Palio dashed through the entrance of The Pierre. As he was going through the heavy-leaded door he noticed a Marilyn Monroe look a like coming out the other shiny brass exit. She looked so familiar.

The woman opened the door gracefully. It was perfect timing. Just as she walked through the exit, Palio entered. With grace equal to that of Grace Kelly, she gently lifted her head and smiled.

Palio was at a loss for words, so much so that he stopped in his tracks. All he could do was stare at her. She looked just like his beautiful Chatham, the woman who plagued his thoughts, but this woman was a Marilyn

Monroe double. He stood there, frozen, as the heavy door followed him and knocked him strongly into the lobby of The Pierre and onto all fours on its plush, deep burgundy carpet.

"Miss," the doorman said to the woman, as though this was an everyday occurrence. "May I help you into your taxi?" He practically lifted her out of the air and whisked her into the open taxi door awaiting her. It all happened so quickly that Palio didn't have a chance to say anything.

Palio staggered to standing and brushed off his wool slacks before proceeding to the lounge area where he expected to find Georgina, incensed at his delay. But she was nowhere to be found so Palio claimed a deep leather chair right next to the oversized fireplace and settled in to wait. As he sat gazing into the dancing flames, it occurred to him.

"Oh my god," he exclaimed, a bit louder than expected, "It's her!"

"Why yes it is Palio, my love," the sensual Georgina answered, assuming that his shock was that of approval of her chosen attire.

Palio smiled slightly, but he was too distracted. He couldn't get Chatham's face out of his mind and he knew that he had just seen her again. But why was she dressed up as Marilyn? Where was she going?

Georgina casually sat on the arm of the wing backed leather chair, leaning back onto the curve of the brass studs. She rested her left hand on the black cashmere miniskirt accompanying her black leather riding boots that hugged her shapely calves like a second skin. Her sheer cream blouse didn't leave much to the imagination. "So where to?" she asked Palio, with a light laugh.

Palio's thoughts were brought back to the present when he noticed the ring that had made its way to Georgina's betrothed finger.

"Palio? Didn't you hear a word I was saying?"

Palio shifted uncomfortably in the chair to face her. "Sorry I'm late," he said, almost like a robot. He was still figuring out how to handle the situation.

"Oh, that's all right. I was still getting ready. I guess I had such a good time last night that I was in some sort of a dream state or something." Georgina leaned over to rub a smudge off her boot. It just so happened that she was at the perfect angle so that her shirt gaped opened to Palio as she reached down, her breast brushing against his knee ever so gently.

Palio didn't know what to do. This woman was obviously making a full-court press to gain his admiration and all he could think about was how to gracefully get out of it and go find the Marilyn Monroe double. But the painting. He couldn't mess up the painting, even if he did have to deal with a gorgeous psychotic woman who was apparently his new fiancée. It meant the world to his father.

Palio leaned down to help Georgina wipe the imaginary smudge off of her boot. The two were huddled together like lovers sharing an intimate secret. As Palio lifted his head to prepare to leave, he saw Marilyn rushing by, her pointy white shoes wobbling along the slate floor at lightning speed. Palio's heart rushed with adrenaline at the site of her. He had no choice but to listen to his soul.

"Excuse me for a moment, will you?" he asked politely, offering his chair to Georgina as he stood. "You see, I know the chef and was hoping to have had something prepared."

Georgina purred with anticipation. "Prepared, for me? What is it?"

"If I told you, it wouldn't be a surprise now would it?" Palio took Georgina's hand and brought it to his lips. "I won't be but a moment," he promised, dropping her hand suddenly and dashing off toward the elevators. Two can play at that game, he thought.

Palio watched the numbers above the classic mahogany elevator door until they stopped at 12. He pushed the up button of the other vintage hotel elevator, secretly hoping that he would have time to head Chatham off before she returned. The door opened to an empty lift, and Palio stepped in.

"Twelve, please," Palio requested of the lift operator.

"Yes, sir. Staying with us this evening sir?"

"Not this time, no. Meeting a friend."

"Yes sir," the operator responded. No sense in continuing the imposition, one never knows the reason for a morning visit to a friend's room and one simply should not ask. Palio's heart began to race again. What would he say to her? How could he casually explain his presence in a luxury hotel at the start of the day and ask her out at the same time? Well, he'd think of something.

The door opened to the twelfth floor and as Palio was about to step out onto the crown patterned plush carpet, he saw her. Chatham was just exiting her hotel room with her cell phone in hand. She had taken her shoes off and was running in his direction.

"Hold the door, please," she called out. "Please hold the door." Palio was hoping to have time with her other than the quick elevator ride so he stepped out and thanked the liftman.

"OK then, on your way," Palio offered, doing his best to block the view of Chatham while helping to close the door with his foot.

"No, wait," Chatham screeched.

The lift operator inserted his arm to prevent the doors from closing and peeked out onto the floor.

"Yes, ma'am. Sorry, ma'am. I didn't quite hear you. Please step in."

Palio let out a defeated sigh as Chatham stepped past him and onto the lift. She was in too much of a hurry to pay attention. Palio stood there, frozen, just staring at her. He was about to let this woman drift out of his life yet again, but his heart took over. Without realizing what he was doing, Palio yelled out.

"Wait!" He used both hands to pry open the door so that he could quickly step in.

"Sir?" the elevator attendant inquired. "I believe you were meeting a friend?"

"Yes, um… yes. Wrong floor." Palio was winging it, which was quite out of character for him.

Chatham was in shock. Right next to her was the man she couldn't stop thinking about at every turn. But what was Palio doing at a hotel at 8:45 on a Saturday morning? Was he with the foreign woman? Or, just maybe, could he be there to see her? Regardless of his intentions, Chatham didn't want him to see her in her silly costume so she quickly looked down, but not before a slight smile filled her lips.

"Which floor, Miss?"

"The lobby please," Chatham answered.

"Yes, me too," Palio followed. He glanced over at Chatham with a smile.
"Forgot something?"

"Yes, I did unfortunately. I'm on my way to a very important meeting, and I forgot my mobile. I am already so late. I guess I'm not getting a very good start, am I?"

"Nice dress though," Palio said, smiling with amusement.

"Don't ask," Chatham responded. "It's part of the meeting."

"Wasn't planning on it," Palio responded. OK, he only had about forty-five more seconds. Here goes. "Do you remember me?" he blurted out. "Last night, the restaurant? The plane?"

Palio noticed the doorman stiffen his lip before he pressed a blue IOP button embedded into the walnut wainscoting.

Before Chatham could answer, the elevator stopped at floor number ten and the door opened to allow a very mismatched couple in. He was about four-hundred pounds, and she easily over six foot and as thin as a candy cane.

"Excuse me, pardon me," the heavyset man said as he turned sideways to enter the elevator, squishing Palio and Chatham together in the back corner of the elevator. The lift moved visibly with the added weight, which gave the operator concern. The posted maximum weight for the ancient lift was 800 pounds. They were definitely over.

The tall, beanpole entered next. Even though she

was only about 80 pounds, it was enough to put the allowance too far over. Suddenly the elevator dropped. Skinny Mini jumped up on Heavy Harry's girth and wrapped her arms around his neck, hugging him for dear life.

Chatham had also jumped up in fear, wrapping her arms around Palio. They were cheek to cheek and Palio had to admit to himself that he didn't mind the free fall at all.

The operator grabbed the old fashioned manual arm of the carrying cage and, with all his might, attempted to shift it to the stop position. As hard as he tried, he couldn't quite get it there. Heavy Harry grabbed the man and pushed him toward the lever's edge, which enabled the handle to click into place and the lift to stop. The elevator froze with open doors about a foot below the fourth floor.

Chatham grabbed Palio's hand and pushed their way past the very large man and climbed up and out of the elevator.

"We'll walk, thank you," she offered as she helped Palio step up and out of the potential disaster.

"Yes, enjoy your ride," Palio added. He could tell that the elevator operator was not happy.

Palio and Chatham watched Skinny Mini and Heavy Harry hug and kiss intensely out of gratefulness as the doors of the elevator closed for good.

Suddenly they were completely alone, for the very first time. Palio turned to Chatham.

"So, are you going to join me or not?"

"Join you, where?"

"At the boat race today."

"Gosh, I was hoping to. I mean, I'd like to. It's just

that." She kneeled down to put on her high heels. She looked at her watch and panicked. "Oh my god, I am late, certifiably. I've probably lost the account and this whole trip was useless."

Palio couldn't stop himself. He helped Chatham up and pulled her close to him. He knew the attraction was undeniable. "Useless?" Palio asked, inches from her face.

Chatham simply melted into him, giving way to the emotional surge. "Well no, not useless. I mean, I get to see my dad and bring one of my kids on a trip to New York to see the city and..."

Her warm breath and flushed face drew him in as he brushed his full lips against hers in a soft kiss filled with soulful connection. The kiss quickly turned into a full-body expression of love, passion and attachment, as though they were predestined and ordained. Time definitely stood still.

≈

The slam of the stairwell door snapped Chatham and Palio out of their embrace. In unison, they looked over at the approaching figure. It was Trip.

"Chatham! For god's sake... there you ..." his voice trailed off.

Chatham quickly stood back and smoothed out her dress. She was horrified. "Trip, do you remember Palio? From the health club and the airplane and... the restaurant?" She looked at Palio for assistance.

"Trip, how are you?" Palio asked, extending his hand.

Trip didn't bother. "What are you doing? You're going to be late for your meeting, remember?" He eyed

Palio suspiciously. "Did you get your phone?" he asked from a forced jaw.

Chatham held the tiny flip phone up with a weak smile.

"Looks like you got something else along the way, too." Trip added, clearly resentful of the situation.

"Actually Trip, Chatham and I happened to bump into each other in the elevator and it stopped due to an outstanding force you could say and, well, we had to climb up and out of the lift and, well, here we are."

"Yes Trip, that's right. We were just on our way down the stairs."

"Looked to me like you weren't in a hurry to go anywhere."

Trip was acting like a jealous boyfriend, and it was beginning to affect Chatham. Did he have any right to act this way? Did she have any right to think that he had no right? After all, they did sleep together and she had known Trip forever. Chatham was totally and completely confused. She gathered her purse and addressed Palio as distantly as she could out of respect for Trip even though she wanted to rush back into his arms.

"Thank you very much for your help today, Palio. Hopefully we will be able to attend the boat race this afternoon. If not, I wish your father well." Chatham turned her back to both men and opened the stairwell door. She saw Trip give Palio one last cold stare before following her down to the waiting cab.

As Chatham exited the hotel she couldn't help but look over her shoulder. Palio was watching her from among a very crowded group of men who seemed to have a sudden interest in Palio and his reasons for being in the hotel.

Chatham felt her phone vibrate.

"What's that noise?" Trip demanded.

Chatham cringed at his tone. He was acting incredibly harsh. She flipped her phone open to see that she had a voicemail. Chatham climbed into the cab and dialed her voicemail retrieval number. She prayed it wasn't Harlan, already pissed.

"You have one message. Yesterday, 10:00 pm."

"Oh, hello Chatham, this is Annette from up the street. I just wanted to let you know that I will need to switch carpool with you tomorrow morning for soccer practice because I've made it to the semi finals at my tennis club and, well, I have to play in the tournament. It starts at 8:00 a.m. sharp, so of course I will not be able to drive. I'll just send my little darlings down to your house at 7:15 because I'll need to get to the club early and warm-up; you understand. Oh, Herby likes pancakes and Sarah likes sunny-side eggs mixed with bacon and toast in a cup. Alrighty, thanks so much."

Chatham flew into a panic. She had no time for this. She quickly dialed home – it was 6 a.m. there – hopefully Tom and Theo were awake.

"Listen Chat, about last night. Nothing happened, really." She smiled blankly at Trip; why wasn't anyone picking up?

"Tom? Theo? Are you awake yet? It's Chatham. Hello? Well, hopefully you're in the bathroom or something. Listen, my goofy neighbor up the street has blown off carpool for soccer practice this morning so you

343

have to drive, OK? Her two kids will be at the house in an hour so if you could add them to your breakfast preparation, that would be great. Sorry and thanks. Are you there? OK, call me. Bye." Chatham hung up and looked at the phone.

"That's weird, no one answered."

"Chat, the sun is barely up yet, and it's Saturday. Don't worry about it. I'm sure everything is fine."

She tried to shrug it off. "You're probably right." She looked at her watch. "Can you drive a little faster please? I am late for a meeting."

"Look, Chat. I need to talk with you about something. I mean, I want to ask you something. About you, about me, about us." He gently lifted her hands and held them in his own. Chatham was in a panic. Is this what she wanted? She had no idea. She had just made out with Palio, and now Trip was about to confess his feelings for her? It was so much, so soon. And she was late for one of the most important pitches in her career.

"Trip, listen. Can we talk about this some other time?"

"No, it has to be now!" He was insistent.

Chatham was stunned into silence.

"OK, so here it goes."

Chatham held her breath as the car came to a sudden, screeching stop.

"That'll be seven bucks, pal," the driver stated.

Chatham opened the car door and mouthed sorry as she quickly exited and began to run toward the building.

Trip threw a ten-dollar bill at the driver and jumped out of the taxi.

"Chatham, wait!"

CHAPTER XXXVII – *DIVERSION*

≈

Georgina watched as Palio exited the stairwell directly behind the Marilyn Monroe double and her escort. The trio looked quite peculiar exiting one after another, almost as though there was existing tension between them. She made her way across the lobby to greet Palio when something she saw made her stop cold.

Out of every available nook and cranny emerged a group of men wearing dark blue suits and dangling earpieces. Georgina feigned interest in a magazine on a nearby table. FBI? CIA? She knew she should be careful.

Maybe the government had made the connection. But how? Georgina was sure that she had covered her bases and that no one would guess her real identity. Yes, it was true that she was simply the daughter of an olive oil plantation worker. Her family lived on the wealthy owner's land and earned their keep. The fact that her entire extended family had been beholden to others for generations infuriated Georgina and she would no longer stand for a slave existence. She was determined to live life on her own grand terms. After much research, she was convinced that the best way to gain wealth *and* power was through marriage. The rest of her plan was dependent on it. Palio Capriatti was one of the most eligible, wealthy bachelors in New York City, and with the exact type of empire that she required to ensure her success. He was the perfect target.

The commotion around Palio was definitely increasing. Georgina decided that the potential for discovery was too dangerous and that it would be safer if she left. Catching Palio's eye amidst the chaos, she pointed to her watch.

"Meet you here later," she mouthed as precisely as she could. Palio nodded and simply put his hands up in the air.

Georgina flagged the first cab she could find. The doorman was immersed in the Palio situation as well, so she was on her own. She preferred it that way at this particular moment.

The bright yellow motorcar screeched to a halt directly in front of her. It just so happened to be the same cab from last night's episode. Georgina slid into the back seat quickly.

"Well howdy, ma'am. Good to see you," the Texas driver greeted.

"Did I hire you again? I didn't think I did." Georgina was somewhat preoccupied and annoyed.

"Where to, ma'am?" the driver asked as nicely as he could. He could tell that the woman was on edge.

"First of all, do I look like a ma'am, you idiot? I am a Miss, as in M-I-S-S. Do I look like I'm married for god's sake?" She was annoyed that her plans were yet again interrupted.

"Sorry, ma– I mean Miss. It's just that that there rock on your wedding finger sure sparkled when you were climbing into the car. I was sure it was given to you by your husband, that's all."

Georgina looked down at the painting purchase price. She took a moment to admire it. "Well, engaged. Not married." She continued to gaze at her prize. "So I'm not a ma'am yet – got it, pal?"

"Yes, Miss, I do. At your service, for sure. So where can I take your newly engaged self?" he asked cheerfully.

"Park and Seventy Second and step on it," she ordered.

The Texas taxi driver peeled out from The Pierre and took a quick right at the corner. Georgina's telephone rang as if on cue. She knew who it was.

"Yes, I'm on my way. No, he's not with me. Why? Because I think the feds are on to us you asshole." She looked up to make sure the driver wasn't listening. He seemed to be talking to himself. What an idiot, she thought.

"Yep, if you come on over to The Idle Spur for dinner tonight, you'll get all beef, no bull. You betcha we'll be waitin' for ya. Yeehaw!"

Georgina took her voice down a few octaves. "Listen to me, you fat fuck. I'll marry Palio Capriatti, you can bet on that. And then we'll own the whole fucking empire. Trump will be wishing I never stepped foot in the big apple. Have it ready," she ordered and snapped the phone shut.

The taxi driver pulled right up to the imposing building and ran around to open her door.

"Keep the change and wait here," she said, tossing him a hundred-dollar bill.

≈

Billy Bill watched the gorgeous woman storm up to the building. Crazy lady or not, the cabbie was not minding this sideline at all. But her conversation disturbed him. Was she talking about the guy from last night? He seemed like such a genuine fella, although it was clear that he was not interested in her like she was in him. She had practically tried to screw him right there in the back seat.

Best of all, Billy Bill couldn't help but remember the look on the man's face when he handed over his new boss's card. It was as though the guy had just seen, in print, the name of the woman he had loved since birth. He was paying more attention to the card in his hand than the beautiful, but desperate woman cuddled up next to him.

Maybe he should tell Miss Ross about all this, the Texan thought. He reached for his ten-gallon hat, ready to settle in for a while when he saw her – the movie star. She looked just like Marilyn Monroe. She scurried across the street, clutching her dress and several papers. Following right behind her was some lapdog dude who was hanging on her every move.

"Hey lady," the Texan called. "Need a ride?"

"Oh hi Billy Bill, how nice of you to be here, and I didn't even set an appointment with you." The driver tried to cover for his mistake.

"Oh, heck, you know me. I'm everywhere I need to be."

Chatham's face lit up. "That's a good one, do you mind if I use it?"

"Hell no. You gave me a real live actor job now didn't ya? I'm only glad to help out when I can. I got some other ones too, wanna hear 'em?"

"Not now. Listen, maybe you can do me a favor. My friend over there."

Billy Bill followed her gaze. "You mean the one attached to your spurs?"

"Well, yes, sort of. He likes to watch out for me. Anyway, he is supposed to be at the Central Park Zoo. Can you take him there for me? I kind of need some space while I put on this, well, performance, to see if I can get this business."

"Why the dress?"

"Long story. The client is kind of eccentric."

"Ex. . . what?" Billy Bill asked, not understanding his boss's fancy language.

Chatham shook her head. "Never mind. Can you help me out?"

"Sure as hell can. Send that feller right on over to my express service, and I'll done get him where he needs to be."

Chatham smiled thankfully, and Billy Bill winked in agreement.

Billy Bill watched as Chatham spoke to the man following her, promising that she'd be fine and that she'd see him later at the boat show. She practically pushed him into the taxi.

"OK then Trip. Thanks for the ride and I'll see you in a few hours, OK?" Trip didn't answer. Chatham made an abrupt turn and disappeared into the client's office building, her white dress blowing in the wind.

Billy Bill figured he could drop Trip off and make it back in time for the dragon lady. And he'd earn an extra fare in the process. Everybody wins.

"So what you in town for, pal?"

"What's that?"

"I asked what's up?" Billy Bill had placed his hat

on the seat next to him and shifted back to his local dialect.

"Weren't you just talking with a twang a few minutes ago?" Trip asked.

"Aww heck, do I sound all that bad?" Billy Bill asked, resorting back to his native tongue.

"Don't worry about it," Trip responded absently.

"What's wrong? Had a bad day already or something?"

"Bad day, yeah, you could say that."

"Did it have anything to do with that pretty lady?"

"Everything."

Billy Bill pushed his hat back on his head. "Well, I just might have an idea for you if you're willing to hear it."

"You, an idea? Why should I listen to a Texas taxi driver in the middle of New York City?"

"Because I'm an actor, and I know how to put on a good show."

Billy Bill saw Trip's disbelieving gaze in the rearview mirror. "According to who?"

"The pretty lady," he answered smugly.

"You know her?"

"You could say that. She hired me as the new spokesperson for The Idle Spur restaurant chain. I think we're doing the shoot in San Francisco or something real soon."

"Well I'll be," Trip laughed. "She does get around, doesn't she?"

"Sure does. She's a classy lady she is."

"That she is," Trip agreed, gazing off to the horizon.

Billy Bill turned left, entering the busy morning traffic. "Ah, the joy of New York," he muttered. "So you like her, don't cha?" he inquired. He didn't want to pry too much, but his passenger was wearing his heart on his sleeve.

"Only forever," Trip sighed. "I thought we were close, I mean real close. Now I'm not so sure. She seems to keep running into this Italian guy, a local. Palio's his name. Good looking and probably just as rich. How do I compete with that?"

Billy Bill knew he was really just talking out loud to himself. "Yep, and he's a nice guy, too. I even know his papa."

"You know him?" Trip snapped.

"Course I do. Give him and his papa a ride every now and then again. Heck, I even gave Palio a ride with his girlfriend last night. She's got some huge rock on her finger. I think they're engaged."

Billy Bill saw Trip practically jump out of his seat. "Engaged?"

"Yep, as sure as the day is long. She told me herself. Set up the whole date, and I was hired as the actor taxi driver to slow down their trip so that she could talk him into going into Tiffany's. What did she come out with? A great big honkin' diamond on that there weddin' finger. Then they was huggin' and smoochin'. Well, she was doin' most of it anyway."

Trip leaned forward in his seat. "You've just made me a very happy man, my friend!" he said, hitting Billy Bill on the shoulder.

"Glad to hear it, sir," he said. He was glad to help out this down-in-the-dumps man.

"So you say you have an idea?"

"Yeah, and it's a good one. Works every time to win the heart of the girl of your dreams. Here's what you do…"

CHAPTER XXXVIII – *THE ZOO*

≈

Chatham's phone rang as she stood next to the elevator bank. She was used to all the stares by now. In fact, she was almost beginning to enjoy the attention her Marilyn costume provided. It was nice to be noticed for the right reasons.

"Hello?"

"Sorry, Chat," came the voice from the other end.

"Chloe? What happened to you last night?"

"I kept waiting, that's what. My friend showers me with champagne, that's when I called you, and five minutes later he asks me to wait for him while he makes a call. Well, I waited and waited and waited. The call took hours. Before I knew it, it was too late to join you and then he shows up well after dinner with a bottle of Dom Perignon to make up for it. I wasn't in the mood at that point. Yeah, I'm still mad at him so I left this morning, after breakfast."

"Look, I'm about to get in the elevator. Trip just went over to the zoo to make some deal on a zorbat creature or something."

"A what?"

"You know Trip. He's always dealing in some sort of exotic recluse."

"Central Park Zoo?"

"Yeah, why?"

"No reason. So… have you been hanging out with Trip a lot?" Was Chloe interested in Trip? Chatham wondered. She quickly dismissed the thought as nothing but paranoia. "Well, we ended up sleeping together last night. Long story."

"You what?!" Chloe blurted out. "I mean, that's great."

"It's not what you think. Look, I have to go. I am so late! They probably won't even let me in. I'll call you later, OK?" Chatham quickly hung up, wondering if she had detected deflation in Chloe's tone, or if she had just made it up.

≈

Chloe just stood in place, staring at the phone. Had she really heard that right? It was then that she decided to take matters into her own hands.

Chloe walked the two blocks to the Central Park Zoo at a clipped pace. She hadn't seen Trip in a very long time, but she could still recall as a kid how excited she felt each time he walked into her house to see her brother Peter. She remembered seeing him at Chatham and Peter's wedding – wow! He didn't really notice her then. Chloe did her best to make him notice her on future visits by creating a boehmian style of dress and developing organic ways. It didn't work. To Trip she would always be Peter's little sister.

Then her brother died. It was after the funeral that she decided to move to New York to see what life would bring her. And, for now, it was Gabrielle, the older, rich, bald, doting New Yorker who treated her like a queen. A caged queen sometimes, but one that could have the brightest feathers money could buy. But she was pretty mad at him right now, and Trip was in town, only two blocks away - so why not? Even if Trip was already taken, it wouldn't hurt to say hello.

Chloe paid her five dollars and made her way over to the monkeys. Was a zorbat a monkey type creature or some kind of lizard? She turned the corner around the emperor tamarin cage when she saw him. Just like that. It had to be him because her heart stopped and her legs grew weak. Chloe looked down at her outfit. Typical. Speckled wool knickers, neon orange spandex, long-sleeved top, knitted vest, and a skull cap. A crocheted tie die scarf hung loosely around her waste.

"It will have to do," she said to the tiny monkey jumping to and fro around its cage. "Yeah, I feel like that sometimes, too. But I'm about to break out, wish me luck." She blew the wise faced monkey a kiss.

≈

"He's a feisty little bugger, isn't he?" Trip said to the zoo owner. "Does he get any bigger than my hand?" Trip switched from hand to hand as the little creature hopped and crawled over him. He was really fast.

"Not a stitch. And he loves small spaces, too. Especially when they're moving."

"Like a toy train on a track or something?"

The burly man nodded. "The only thing is, if he really gets going, you know zippin' along the freeway or something..." The zoo keeper looked around to see if anyone was listening.

Trip leaned in closer. "Yeah?"

"Yeah, well. He gets a little troublesome, if you know what I mean." The keeper raised his eyebrows in a "you know" expression.

"I'm not sure I follow you," Trip responded in a

low spoken tone.

"He digs," the man whispered, quickly standing and stuffing his hands in his pockets.

"He what?" Trip didn't understand.

"He digs, man. You know, burrows, scoops, tunnels? It's some sort of genetic molecular reaction to speed or something. Anyway, it's no big deal, just keep him in his cage with the flap over it when you're driving, and you'll be fine."

Trip pondered the unusual caveat to the creature. "Well," he said, stroking his chin. "I guess I can handle that. I hope my buyer can," he added off handedly.

"So we have a deal?"

Trip reached his hand out to scal it.

A good-looking woman one cage over suddenly diverted the zoo owner's attention. "Mmm, mmm," he said lustfully. "If only I could trade this creature for her."

"Alright, little guy," Trip said to his new furry friend. "You ready to get out of here?" As he slowly moved the creature to his right hand, Trip noticed something familiar, something comfortable about the young woman in front of him, yet he couldn't put his finger on it.

She lifted her eyes to notice the furry animal. "What a sweet little creature," she said, reaching out to offer her forearm to the little mite. "What's his name?"

The zombat took to her immediately, nuzzling its long white mustache into her crocheted scarf.

The woman giggled. "I'm not sure I can get him to come out."

Trip peered at the stranger. There was no mistaking those sable brown eyes.

"Chloe?"

"Oh my gosh, Trip?"

"I knew you were living in New York, I mean, I knew you were here at some point. Wow! I mean, hey, it's great to see you." Trip could not believe it. Standing before him was his best friend's kid sister who quite obviously wasn't a kid anymore.

"Seems to have stuck on me, this crazy old city. I love it here, actually. And you, how are you? I mean, what are you doing in the big apple?"

"Who me? Um, business," he added a little too quickly, looking down as he recalled the real reason he was in town.

"Still dealing in one-of-a-kind critters, huh Trip?" she asked.

Trip appreciated the diversion. "Yeah, well, you know me. I've always loved animals, and this one is a real beauty." He stepped closer to Chloe, offering to relieve her of the squirrelly being. Trip felt an eager affection coming from her and was caught off guard when he found himself wanting to return it.

The zoo owner stepped back toward Trip. "And remember what I told you," he said. "When you are moving fast, OK? Cover the cage."

Trip nodded, only half listening.

"OK, then. So our meeting is over. Here is the cage, congratulations. Do not call me if you have a problem." And with that, the zoo keeper was gone.

Chloe and Trip stood silently, each with a heart rendering tenderness of gaze for the other.

"Say," said Trip, suddenly remembering the advice

from the cab driver. "Are you in a hurry?" Trip had no intention of betraying his feelings for Chatham, but he couldn't deny that his heart was beginning to feel like a jack hammer. "Would you like to come with me somewhere?"

"Love to," Chloe answered quickly. "I mean, I think I can squeeze it in. That is, if you let me carry the little bugger."

They both chuckled, falling into perfect step as they headed out the south entrance of the park toward The Plaza.

CHAPTER XXXVIX – *INFORMATION*

≈

Billy Bill made his way back to 72nd and Park to wait for the olive princess, as instructed. He hadn't been there more than a minute when a little poindexter of a man came skidding up to the car.

"Um, excuse me, Mr. Taxi man."

"Uh, yeah, that's me," Billy Bill answered.

"So, yes, um, Miss Georgina said she doesn't need your services anymore. OK?" He turned to leave.

"Are you sure? Cuz she told me in no uncertain terms to stay put until she came out. It's a bit of an inconvenience in that I skipped other fares just so as to wait for her and all."

The man pondered the predicament. "Well, she seems to like you for some reason, so she told me that if you are upset, then to give you this." The man tossed Billy Bill his second one-hundred dollar bill in less than an hour. "Will that do?"

"Hell, ya," Billy Bill exclaimed. "Maybe I'll just become Miss Georgina's personal attaché as they say. She's still a Miss, isn't she? I mean, she's only *about* to get married, right? I wouldn't want to mess that up again."

The pointy man looked confused. "Miss Georgina, getting married?" He began to laugh a hyena type howl. "She's already married, silly taxi man. Goodbye." And with that, the man scampered away.

Billy Bill was sure the man was mistaken as he pulled away and headed toward JFK airport to find a long fare. He needed to think about all of this.

≈

Tom looked at the obnoxious cab line. "Come on Maddy and PJ! Let's walk to the end of the terminal and hail one from there." Tom took off at a clipped pace, making the rest of the foursome jog to keep up.

"I will carry my pack-pack," PJ proclaimed, leaving his suitcase for Theo to haul. Theo scooped up the Barney case without breaking his stride.

Maddy had her Roxy suitcase on rollers, which left her free to stroll with style, her skinny knit scarf wrapped around her neck – the current trend.

"Tommy, are you sure we can't just call her on her cell phone or something?" Theo asked. In spite of the recent developments, he didn't understand the need to bother Chatham when she finally had a weekend away.

"Theo, don't you get it? If I told her over the telephone, she'd probably have a heart attack because all would be lost, and I just can't have that on my conscience."

"Well, why not just wait until she gets back from New York?"

"Because, idiot! She has to sign the papers by today and then they have to be dropped off at the offices in New York, or it's gone – all gone." Tom's emotional display was in full force. "Besides, we're already here!"

Theo grimaced. Sometimes his partner was too harsh on him. "What offices?" Theo asked.

"The lawyers, stupid." Tom replied with exasperation.

"Well, couldn't you fax it or something?"

"It has to be the original."

"What about sending it, like overnight or

something?" Theo was proud of his ingenuity.

Tom stopped in his tracks to reprimand his lover. "Theo, what am I going to do with you? If I sent it overnight, it would get to her hotel no earlier than 10:00 this morning. Her meeting is at 9:00, so she'd miss it. And who knows if she'll be back to her hotel by 6:00, which is actually too late, because the papers have to be at the lawyer's office by 6:00. That means she would have to be back to her hotel by 5 at the latest and actually see the papers, sign them, and then get them to the church on time – get it?" He sharply turned on his black leather boot heels.

"Church?"

Tom was back to his roadrunner pace. "Never mind, you oaf. The only way this is going to work is for me to deliver them, personally, myself, by hand. Otherwise. . ."

"Uh, um, all is lost?"

"Exactly. Now, can you please get us a cab? I'm beginning to perspire, and it's ruining my ph balance."

"When are we going to see mom?" Maddy asked.

Theo put his hand on her shoulder. "Soon, sweetie."

As if on cue, a yellow cab zipped up to the curb. The driver leaned over and shouted out of the open passenger window.

"Hurry up, or I'll never get ta drive in dis airpawt again." He pressed a button, which opened the trunk and in one fell swoop, Theo had the bags packed and the kids in the cab.

"You are a sexy piece of man, aren't you?" Tom purred at his friend.

Theo smiled. He knew Tom loved to watch him carry heavy things. "Glad to see you're relaxing a bit,

362

Tommy. Now hurry and get in so we can go find Chatham."

"Where to?" the driver asked.

"72nd and Park," Tom responded. "And please, step on it."

"Yes, sir."

Tom looked at his watch and then at Theo. "She has to be at her presentation by now. I hope that Monroe dress works for her. It hadn't been blown after the dry cleaning. I wish she had bought the tulle to put under it."

"Don't worry, she'll be fine," Theo assured with a pat to Tom's knee.

Theo noticed that the driver had a quizzical expression on his face as he peeled out from the curb.

"Ya'll wouldn't be talkin' about a nice lady named Miss Ross, now would ya?" he asked.

Tom and Theo exchanged a surprised look.

"Do you know her?" Theo asked.

Tom slapped Theo's forearm and hissed, "Shut up, will you? Don't you know anything about New York? I'll handle this." He elevated his voice forward. "Who wants to know?" Tom tried to cop an attitude which didn't come across too well.

"I was just askin' is all. I happen to know where she is cause she's my boss."

"Your boss!" Tom and Theo answered in unison.

"You work for my mom?" Maddy asked. PJ was too busy ogling the bright lights of the big city.

"Tom, look. Times Square. It has lights!" he exclaimed.

"Hey, PJ," Maddy said, pulling the sleeve of his

sweatshirt. "Look at that giant lady on the sign."

"She has on her underwear – she's naked," PJ said, laughing out loud. Maddy and Theo laughed along with PJ. The Victoria Secret model on the sign was barely clad in black lace.

"Be quiet everyone," Tom insisted. "Now, Mr. Taxi Driver, you were saying?" Tom and Theo leaned forward to hear more clearly.

"You heard me right, I done work for Miss Ross. You are sitting in the very cab of the new male spokesperson for The Idle Spur restaurant chain. Hell, I'm gonna be making like a 100K a year when that spot airs."

Tom looked over at Theo. "Chatham never told me about this," he whispered with suspicion. "What has she been up to?"

"Yeah, dropped her off this morning in fact. She and that boyfriend of hers."

Theo relaxed with a sigh; he knew there had been a mistake. He listened to his partner address the taxi driver as a school teacher would a child who didn't quite understand the lesson.

"Oh no, you see, you must be mistaken. Chatham doesn't have a boyfriend. Not at all."

"Maybe she didn't, but she does now. Called him Chip or Drip or something like that." "Mom is going out with Trip? No way," Maddy piped up.

"Look, I'm not trying to say nuthin' about nuthin'. I just picked Miss Ross up and her, um, friend, from The Pierre this morning. I figured he was her boyfriend because he ran after her when she and some good-looking Italian guy came out of the stairway. The Tripster knew the guy, and he wasn't happy. But then he was."

"Was what?" Tom demanded.

Theo scratched his head. This wasn't making any sense.

"He got happy cuz I gave him some good 'ol Texas style advice. Works every time."

"What, you told him to take her to a barbeque or something?" Tom asked with a condescending snicker.

Theo poked his lover in the ribs.

"Hell no. Look, don't you know nothin'? Every Texan knows that it's books that work with chicks."

"Books? What are you talking about?" Theo asked.

"Yeah, books. See, there's this very cool little hotel right by the New York Public Library where famous writers stay when they're in town. I just told him to take her to the lobby and pretend he had forgotten a book. Pull a sappy one off the shelf, and I guarantee you'll see someone worth knowin'. I'm tellin' ya, it works every time."

Tom closed his eyes and breathed in deeply. "That is the stupidest thing I've ever heard."

"Be nice," Theo whispered.

"Maybe," Billy Bill said, "but I bet you're wonderin', aren't ya? I'm tellin' ya, it works every time, every time."

"I like books," PJ piped up. "Old hat, new hat, red hat, blue hat; it's my favorite."

"Do you like my hat?" Theo asked PJ.

"Yes I do. I do like your hat."

"You two hush," insisted Tom. He turned his attention back to the driver. "So you dropped Trip off at this famous writer hotel?" Tom asked with disbelief.

"Nah, Miss Ross told me to take him to the zoo, so I did. That's about it." A Lincoln town car honked loudly behind them. "Yeah, same to you pal!" the driver yelled. "Think you're so important. Got some place to go do ya? Well so do we, pal," he mumbled, weaving back and forth so as not to let the aggressive car pass.

"I feel sick," PJ said.

Before Tom could move away, he had the pleasure of wearing PJ's airplane food over his entire sleek black jeans and turtleneck.

"Eww! Gross," Maddy cried, sliding as far to the corner of the cab as possible.

"Aww, come on. He couldn't help it," Theo defended. He began to wipe up the mess with his sweat-suit jacket.

"Get me to my hotel, now!" Tom demanded.

"You bet pal, where you staying?"

"The Pierre, of course. You should know that one by now. And hurry damn it!"

"But what about the papers, Tommy?" Theo asked with concern.

"Oh, shut up and leave me alone. I'm covered in puke!"

The driver opened all the windows to their fullest extent and raced his way up midtown toward the luxury destination.

Theo wasn't sure what to make of the situation. Chatham and Trip? How could that be?

CHAPTER XL – *DEFLATED*

≈

Chatham flipped her cell phone shut just as the elevator opened. She was glad that Chloe was OK and not totally swept away by the balding candy store man.

Chatham didn't even notice when the populated elevator bank stared at her as though she had risen from the silver screen. She was getting used to her disguise, and, in a way, was gaining a new strength by wearing it. The last man to leave the boxcar stepped to the side and swept his arm toward the opening.

"Miss Monroe, if you please," he gestured.

Chatham smiled shyly. He's certainly doing his best to look debonair with that gelled hair and the fitted leopard fur pants, she thought. Have I seen him before? she wondered. But she was a bit hung over, so it was quite logical to assume she was simply imagining things.

Chatham stepped into the lift and pressed floor number 12. Oops, she meant to press Penthouse. Just as the doors were about to close, the leopard man and the woman from The Pierre slipped into the elevator and pressed the top floor button. Chatham thought she had seen the woman before, but wasn't positive. Was that Palio's mysterious woman? She quickly put her head down and pretended to look for something in her purse. She didn't want the woman to recognize her, although she highly doubted she would with her ridiculous outfit.

"I told you I wanted all the information about the club, not just who pumps iron there, you moron," Georgina hissed at the jungle man. "And who do you think you are,

Tarzan?"

"That's right," he answered with control. "I'm going to the ball."

"And that's the bride of Frankenstein over there. What is she, your date?" Georgina snapped.

The creepy-looking man glanced over at Chatham. She could feel his eyes on her. Looking up, she met his gaze. Lizard! Here was the man responsible for the giant bruise on her gut. She brought her hand to her mouth to stifle an audible gasp.

He turned to Chatham and winked. Clearly, he remembered her.

"So sorry, Georgina. I know you set me up with the confectionary store and the tiny strip mall to make me legitimate so that I could *weasel* my way into Mr. Capriatti *junior's* life." He emphasized weasel and junior almost as a signal to Chatham.

"And you wanted me to find out which clubs Mr. Capriatti was planning to buy in New York City to expand the new fraction in his little empire, and, you wanted me to insert said research so that he opted for the dilapidated health club chain that your Italian mafia friend owns. That way, everyone wins."

"I'm aware of what I've asked you to do, idiot."

But Lizard wasn't finished. "Mr. Capriatti buys a crummy club line that you get a piece of at top dollar. Then, after you marry him, you show Mr. Capriatti the error of his ways, and you sell back to said mafia friend at a rock bottom price, of which you get all of that money plus a fee from your mafia friend for the transaction. I think it's called *double dipping*, and you're already good at that."

Lizard's eyes moved to look at Chatham without even a flinch of his head as he licked his lips. Chatham interpreted it to mean that she had her claws in others besides Palio.

"Shut up, you worm."

Chatham felt incredibly uncomfortable. She glanced at the top of the elevator door. How much farther?

"I, of course, get to keep the strip mall that contains the cute confectionary store where people come to buy donuts and coffee and *muffins*?"

Lizard's emphasis was not lost on Chatham. She remembered when he had stood up for her at the donut shop. "And the other business *partner* gets the candy empire and the miniature boat company. Isn't that how the plan goes my dear? Or do you sell everything to both of them? It is all a bit confusing for a worm."

Georgina stuck her nose in Lizard's face. "Listen, slime ball. Do you have diarrhea of the mouth or something? You know what you're supposed to do and you better have a good reason for Harlan why it hasn't been done yet. You are way over valued. Do you understand me?"

Chatham gasped. Harlan? Her Harlan? What did he have to do with this whole mess? Was he involved with the mafia? Questions came to her mind at a rapid-fire pace. She needed to get out of this small elevator. She needed fresh air.

"I said, do you *understand* me?" Georgina repeated, her voice a scary decibel.

Lizard's whole demeanor suddenly changed from confident to subservient. He bowed his head, nodding cowardly. "Look, I'll do it. I'll make it happen, OK?" he whined.

Chatham shivered.

Georgina didn't move. "You better. I'm going to own Palio Capriatti, you can bet on it, and everything in his little empire. I'll be the richest woman in the United States, and I won't have to answer to that Italian thug or bald bastard any more." She flashed her enormous diamond ring, which bounced its light off the pearl white walls of the lift. "My plan is already working."

The door opened on floor twelve but no one got off. Georgina and Lizard turned to Chatham at the same time, parting for her to exit. She didn't. The doors closed to dead silence as the elevator finished its rise to the Penthouse. Chatham could literally see the tension in Georgina's back and shoulders rise at the thought of revealing such intimacies to someone destined for the same location.

Chatham was thankful when the doors opened. She whisked past the dynamic duo and stepped out of the transport. Just great, she thought. Her secret fantasy was only just that, a fantasy. Something that could not, would not, ever come to fruition at any point in her entire life. Who did she think she was, dreaming about a man she didn't even know? Thinking that he would whisk her off her feet to an exotic island or something?

She bit her lip, forcing herself not to lose it completely. The overload of information she had just received was beyond her comprehension at this point. She didn't know what to do. Palio's touch was the only thing she could focus on. His tender kiss from that morning, only minutes ago, had already lost its tenderness. Why did he kiss her so passionately in the stairwell if he had a fiancée? More importantly, how could someone as wonderful as she imagined Palio was want that wretched woman as his wife?

Chatham didn't know if she should feel depressed, angry, or disgusted. Whatever mix of emotions she was feeling, she knew she had to put him out of her mind. Now she knew where she belonged. She belonged with Trip; she always had. He was there for her; he loved her, and most importantly, he wasn't complicated. Today she would tell him. She only hoped that he would show up to the boat race and forgive her after her very obvious rebuke.

Chatham shook herself off and fluffed up her billowy white gown. She held her head high and gingerly walked across the deep plush carpet toward the receptionist. Her biggest account awaited. Harlan awaited. She shook her head, trying to focus and forget about what the beautiful woman behind her had said in the elevator.

What would she do with all this information?

CHAPTER XLI – *LOST & FOUND*

≈

"Good morning, Miss Ross," The receptionist greeted officiously.

Chatham smiled. "How did you know?"

"I'm paid to know," she said in a "better than thou" manner.

Chatham's phone began to vibrate.

"Shall I announce your arrival then? They have been waiting, and I'm sure you know how Harlan feels about having to wait."

"Yes, I know. I am so very sorry. Could you please excuse me for a moment?"

"Miss Ross..." The receptionist was clearly not happy.

"Yes, I know, I'm late. I'm so sorry. I'll just be right back."

Chatham stepped over to the chairs in the receptionist area to answer her phone. "Hello?" she whispered into the mouthpiece.

"Well, I never!," came the tart voice at the other end of the line.

"Hello?" Chatham repeated.

"How could you have forgotten my innocent young children? I mean, really Chatham, how could you? Was it something I said? Have I ever been a bad neighbor to you – ever?"

Chatham had no idea what her neighbor was talking about. "Excuse me?"

"No, there is no excuse this time. How could you

leave my children on your porch this morning and simply not take them to soccer practice? Do you hate them? Or maybe it's me you hate. I am simply appalled! Do you know that Herby called me on his cell phone, interrupted my tennis match no less, and said that he and Sarah were left... stranded? I never even got to play. I've been banging on your front door for a full half hour, and no one is answering! How can you cower behind closed doors like that and shut away the world? I demand an explanation!"

"Seriously, I have no idea. I am not even there; I'm in New York City."

"New York City. Well you must have taken your children with you then."

"Actually, no. I have friends staying at my house. I didn't get your message until this morning, and I did call home to leave a message, even though it was an obvious inconvenience to have you back out at the last minute."

"It wasn't the last minute. It was the night before."

"Most people don't leave voicemails at midnight the night before and not follow up the next morning, Annette."

"Well, I didn't want to wake your children; I was being considerate."

Chatham was trying not to lose it. She was really more concerned about no one being home. "You say you knocked on the door?"

"Knocked? I banged, thumped, and kicked is more like it. I may have dented it just a touch. I thought you were hiding from me. You can surely understand my protective motherly instincts coming out."

"And no one was home?" Chatham could feel her

breath getting shallow.

"Didn't I say that already? Well, never mind, it all worked out and I'm sure you're sorry. You can just drive for me next week to make up for it."

Chatham was beginning to panic. How could no one be home? She responded absently. "Fine. Bye."

Chatham flipped the phone closed, which buzzed on cue. It can't be another call she thought as she smiled weakly at the heated receptionist. This better be Tom or Theo, she thought.

"Hello?"

"Now don't panic, I'm sure there's a logical explanation. You did say that Tom and Theo are gay, right? They wouldn't be faking it or anything and be child kidnappers or something, would they?" Henrietta tried to be as gentle as possible with her probe.

"What? What are you talking about?"

"Well... you know how I'm on your kids soccer emergency form and all?"

"Yes," Chatham answered cautiously. "Henrietta, are my kids OK?"

"Well, I was hoping you could answer that. See, they called to tell me that no one could be reached at your house and..."

"Out with it, Hen."

"Well, Maddy and PJ didn't show up to soccer practice today. I know you took Camp with you, but I thought that maybe last minute, you took all three."

Panic gripped her. "No, I didn't take them. Tom and Theo are staying over. I have been trying to reach them. My neighbor just called and said that she's been knocking and no one is responding. Listen, I think I have to call the police."

"Wait, look. Don't over react," Henrietta said soothingly. "I'll go in the house and see what's up, OK? If something is deathly wrong... I mean, sorry Chat. I didn't mean to say that word. If something is up, I'll call the cops and, either way, I'll call you right away. I'm getting into my car now, OK?"

Chatham thought about the situation and decided that there had to be an explanation. But she didn't have much of a choice. She silently prayed Henrietta would figure this mess out quickly. "OK, just call me right away! Even if I'm in the middle of the presentation."

"Isn't that over by now?"

"Probably. Call me, OK?" Chatham hung up and cowered over to the annoyed lady behind the desk. "I am so, so sorry. I will just be one more minute if that's OK. Alright then, I'll be... I'll be right back."

Chatham ran to the elevators as fast as her spiked heels could make it through the thick, sinking carpet. She couldn't very well give a presentation, in character, when all she could think about was her kids. She had to find her dad and Camp and Trip and head back home, where she belonged.

Trembling, Chatham pressed the down button and waited. Her shoes were killing her so she slipped them off of her feet and held them in one hand while the elevator took forever to reach her. Chatham could feel the burning eyes of Harlan's watchdog and secretly prayed that she wouldn't be given away. But it didn't matter. Nothing did. She just had to find her kids.

The door opened after what felt like an eternity. Chatham was about to step in when the Italian lady and Lizard stormed out. Not having time to worry about them, she climbed in the elevator.

The ride to the lobby seemed like an eternity. She was trying to figure out what the best plan of action was, when the doors finally opened. As soon as she stepped off, she saw a girl running toward the elevator. It was Maddy! Following Maddy was PJ and then Theo and finally, Tom.

"Mommy, you're here!" PJ ran toward Chatham and threw his entire 89-pound body up into her arms, which caused her to stumble back.

"PJ! Maddy!" she exclaimed. "Thank god you're safe." She squeezed her children as tightly as she could. A sense of relief washed over her.

"Hi, Mom," Maddy followed.

"Chatham, oh thank god! Here you are." Tom raised his arms in the air for the drama of it all.

"Hi Chatham," Theo echoed. "You look great."

"What are you doing here!" Chatham demanded in a syncopated tone. "Why didn't you call?" She couldn't believe her partner was just going to stand there complimenting her stupid outfit instead of explaining what in the world he was doing in New York with her children.

Tom looked at Theo and back to Chatham. "Well, it's a long story. We should probably sit down somewhere …"

"Mom, we went to your gym!" PJ suddenly chimed in, derailing the conversation.

"My what?" Chatham asked, confused.

"Your health club, E. Anytime?" Tom said.

Chatham finally let go of her children and stood up. "How did you know about that?"

"Long story."

Chatham was coming to her senses. She was relieved to see everyone, but she still had no idea what was going on. Too much had happened in this short morning. She was having a hard time keeping up with it all. "What are you all doing here? You had me worried half to death. Henrietta is looking for you and my wacko neighbor probably knocked my front door down. I was just leaving to find Trip and Dad and Camp to come home, where I belong."

Chatham encircled Maddy and PJ with both arms once again. She nodded her head to signal for Tom and Theo to join in.

"Nice dress, Mom, can I borrow it sometime?" Maddy asked. Everyone laughed along as the group broke their embrace.

"You still haven't told me why you all flew clear across the country to find me. My god, who bought the tickets? I can't afford that."

"Actually you can," Tom replied in a sing-song manner as he reached into his coat to withdraw the weathered papers. He handed them to Chatham. "You might want to sit down for this."

"OK?" Chatham said, moving toward the lobby's leather chairs.

"Say hello to never working again, my dear."

Chatham just held the packet in her hand. "I don't get it."

"Open it," Theo encouraged.

"Yeah, Mom. Open it," Maddy added.

"I want to help," PJ insisted. He helped Chatham untie the knotted leather tie that surrounded the thick folded document.

Chatham opened it gingerly.

"I want to read it," PJ demanded.

"OK, PJ, you read it."

"Three million dollars. I did it!" he exclaimed. "I read three million dollars." PJ skipped off with Theo to look out of the big picture windows that held a view all the way down Park Avenue.

"What is this?" she asked, turning to Tom.

"We're rich!" Maddy exclaimed. "Can we please go shopping at Bergdorf's Mom, can we? And Barney's and Saks and... wow! Three million dollars is a lot, huh Mom?"

Chatham was dumbfounded. "I don't understand."

"Do I need to explain everything to you?" Tom reprimanded gently. "Well, Theo was cleaning up the ants yesterday from the bottom shelf of your food cabinet. By the way, that jar of marshmallow puff was half open, and it was really disgusting."

Chatham looked over at Maddy. They'd have to talk about this hormonal sugar thing. "Go on..."

"So, after he cleaned up, I swear to goodness, one million tiny little creatures right, Maddy?"

"At least."

"Yeah, at least." Tom gave Chatham a tsk-tsk shake of his finger. "So, Theo, being the hero that he is, wanted to find the nest." Tom and Theo exchanged a lover's glance. "You know, so we could completely eradicate the problem.

Maddy was very helpful by getting him a flashlight."

"That's right, Mom. I was helping to clean it all up," she said enthusiastically.

"So he climbed back into the bowels of the shelf and shined the light all around to look for the mother ship, you know, the nest. And he found this shoved into a secret compartment thing that looked like an oversized peg hole." Tom looked so proud as he tapped the document in Chatham's hands with a perfectly manicured forefinger.

"So what is this? Why was it in my house?" Chatham asked, holding out the foreign papers.

"Your retirement, honey," Tom answered with a cha cha of his hips.

"My retirement? It looks like a policy of some sort."

Tom put his hands on his hips, bent over at the waist, and leaned toward Chatham for emphasis. "Exactly."

"Exactly, exactly what? I don't have any policies, remember?"

"You don't, but he did."

"He who?"

"He Peter."

"My Peter?" Chatham was beginning to understand. She scanned the document more closely.

"He took out a three million dollar insurance policy a year before his death, and he didn't tell me about it? But why?"

"Look at the back of the envelope," Tom instructed. "Read it."

Dear Chatham,
Surprise. I have purchased this policy for our

379

retirement. I know you always thought I had tons of money. Truth is, I didn't. My parents have always lived on 100-percent credit. They don't even own their house on Belvedere; they rent it. I only make enough to pay for the mortgage and the kids' schools, but I know that I'll make more when I become partner. Just in case, I wanted to buy this for you because I love you and I wanted to make sure we have all that we need as we grow old together.

Merry Christmas!

The note was dated right before Peter left on his overseas trip. He was planning to give it to her for Christmas.

Chatham didn't know what to say. Tears welled in her eyes. "Is this… is this real?"

Tom knelt beside the chair. He held her hand in his. "It is. It really is," Tom said. "I took the liberty to check to see if this seven-year policy, bought a year before Peter's death and not discovered until well after, was still valid for claim. I explained to the insurance company that I'm your very close family, partner, uncle kind of thing. I think they bought it. Anyway, good news. It's yours. All of it." Tom smiled.

"So this is why you flew across the country? To give me this?"

"Well I couldn't simply call you on the phone, you'd have a heart attack and I am not going to be responsible. Oh, and there's one catch."

"What?"

"You have to sign the papers today and get them to the lawyers' offices here in New York. This is the last day of the extension period and if you don't make it, you don't make it – any of it."

All of this was so much. Chatham couldn't think fast enough to process it all. "Sign? Now? Where do I bring them?"

Tom fished out a scrap of napkin with an address scribbled on it. "Take me to 59th and 5th please. The law offices are next to The Plaza Hotel."

Chatham quickly signed the papers. "Does anyone have a Kleenex?" she asked. "This has been... this has been quite the morning."

Theo handed her his handkerchief.

Maddy hugged her tightly. "I love you, Mom."

"Oh, sweetheart. I love you, too."

"Me too?" PJ asked.

"Of course, PJ," Chatham said, wiping her nose. Her heart ached for Peter to be with them. This life-insurance policy was just another reminder that he was no longer with her. But she was grateful. Even beyond the grave, he was taking care of his family.

Chatham stared at the policy and attempted to collect herself. She gripped Maddy's hand and slowly stood up from the chair. It was strange how the last five minutes had completely altered her life.

"So, did we get the business?" Tom asked. "I mean... just because you're rich, doesn't mean you're going to quit on me, does it?"

Chatham had completely forgotten about the meeting. "Oh my god!" she exclaimed. "I came down here, because I couldn't get a hold of any of you. I was planning on blowing off the presentation."

"I suppose that's fair," Tom said.

Theo placed his large hand on her shoulder. "You can't let that outfit go to waste though, Chatham," he said.

"He's right, Mom," Maddy agreed.

Chatham looked at her watch. "I'm already an hour late. I doubt Harlan is even there."

Tom smiled. "Well, you might as well go up there and see."

"How long do we have to file those papers?"

"Six o'clock."

"Do I have to be there, in person?"

"Well, your signature does. I'm not sure about you. I think it's OK if I take them. I just knew if I over-nighted them, they could miss you. Really, I was being thoughtful."

Chatham hugged Tom. "Tom, you're the best. OK, why don't you take everyone to file the papers and then meet me at the little boat race in Central Park, OK? That's where Camp and Dad will be. I think that will give me enough time in here and, hopefully, we'll have two things to celebrate." Chatham was determined to nail this audition, despite her extreme tardiness. She kissed Maddy and PJ and turned to go.

"Love you guys."

"I love you, sweet dreams," PJ replied, reciting the evening ritual.

Chatham was about to walk up to the elevator when she remembered. "Oh, Tom, do me a favor?"

"Another favor?" Tom answered playfully.

"Can you call Henrietta and tell her all is well? The place is probably swarming with police by now."

"Consider it done," Theo said, as he put his arm

around Tom.

When Chatham arrived at the penthouse once again, she walked proudly in her bare feet up to the tightly wound woman behind the desk.

"You can show me in now." Chatham was ready for anything.

CHAPTER XLII –*PROGRESS*

≈

Gino rolled over and draped his arm over Maria's small frame, which was thinly covered in the black satin sheets of his king-sized waterbed. They laughed as any movement caused them both to sink into the middle, their bodies touching. They couldn't help themselves as they kissed, caressed, and consumed each other. They were making up for lost time.

"Don't you think we should get going?" Maria asked dreamily.

"Why? It's not noon yet. The race starts at noon. We have time."

"But what do we do until then?"

Gino kissed her shoulder, her neck, and her skin below the satin.

"Gino, stop it. You're distracting me."

"Isn't that the idea?"

Maria sat up in bed, not caring that the satin layer had fallen away.

"Gino? What are we going to tell them?"

He continued kissing her far below the sheets. "Who?" he murmured.

"You know who."

"Oh, yeah, my best friend."

Maria ran her fingers through her long hair. "You're right, your best friend. And my employer, once removed, who probably thinks I want to marry him, which I don't..." Anymore, she thought. How quickly Gino had stolen her heart.

Maria nuzzled against Gino's dark black hairy chest. "I've had my man right here all along, I've just been too preoccupied to notice."

"If you think I'm lettin' any more time go by without you in my life, you're fuckin' crazy," Gino said. He kissed her neck softly. "I still can't believe we haven't seen each other what with our family ties and all."

"Uncanny, isn't it? But we're here now, and that's all that matters." She kissed him with the passion of their night flaring up once more. The thought of losing site of him made Maria's adrenaline soar. They were sure to be late to the big event.

≈

The cab driver pulled up in front of a discreet building that didn't look like much more than an extension of the public library.

"Are you sure this is it, pal?" Trip asked the driver as the car slowed to a stop.

"You said the writer's hotel, right? Everybody who's in the know knows this place, pal. So are you getting out or what?"

Chloe watched Trip fold back the black-out curtain so that his new creature could have a look.

"What do you say, Spitfire? Ready to take a look?"

"Spitfire," Chloe asked. "Who named him that?"

"I did," Trip replied. "I always name my pets. Actually I try out many names and when they react to one, that's their name."

"Hey, pal. You gunna pay or what?" the driver quipped.

Trip looked at the meter and handed the driver a

ten-dollar bill.

"Keep the change?" the driver inquired, expecting nothing short of a yes.

Trip nodded. He reached over Chloe to unlatch the door so that she could exit first.

"Well, here it is," Trip said. "Shall we go in?"

Chloe was so excited. She didn't really care where they were, as long as they were together. "Sure," she responded as casually as possible. Could he hear how loud and fast her heart was beating? How long had she dreamed of going on a date with Trip? Years? Technically, it wasn't a date... but she allowed herself to fantasize. She simply couldn't believe that she was in the middle of New York City with the man she had always loved, secretly. Her brother's best friend, who was, unfortunately, in love with Chatham. Chloe didn't want to do anything to ruin her relationship with Chatham, so she determined to proceed cautiously.

Chloe did have feelings for Harlan, yes, but he was really more of an adventure. She had been seeking adventures ever since her brother died. In fact, Chloe had never really mourned the loss of her brother, and, consequently, the loss of contact with Trip. But here she was, alone, with Trip in this very romantic setting. She could barely contain herself.

≈

They entered the quaint building. Sure enough the main room was crammed with a sea of books. They were everywhere, floor to ceiling. Old-bound books, new books, books about history, travel, love, cooking, drama. Anything the mind could imagine was in a book form somewhere in that room. The two friends just stood there in awe of the history that surrounded them.

"I still can't believe I ran into you," Trip said a few minutes later. He was suddenly amazed that he was following the taxi driver's advice with someone other than Chatham. He couldn't help it. He had to follow his heart, which was practically jumping out of his skin at the sight of Chloe. Could this be the same Chloe who he dreamed about throughout high school and college? After Peter's death, she just disappeared to New York, and he hadn't seen her in years. Wow. Trip still had feelings for Chatham, deep feelings. But, he had to confess, they couldn't hold a candle to the torch walking next to him.

"Funny, huh?" Chloe replied. She winked flirtatiously. "Destiny, I guess."

"So, this is supposed to be a cool hotel... well library/hotel place," Trip said. He didn't want her to think he brought her there for a reason other than books, even though he had. The wrong impression would spell disaster.

"Oh, a book barn," Chloe quickly replied.

"Book barn?"

"Yeah, they have tons of them in upstate New York and Connecticut. They've been around for centuries. In fact some of the guest books from different ones have ended up in the Smithsonian. Lots of famous writers and politicians go to them to hide out, sign their names, and sometimes, leave original writings or lines from upcoming speeches and stuff."

He nodded. Great, Trip thought. I'll have to personally thank that Texas/New York taxi driver for his *original* idea.

"They call them book barns because, in the old days, after meals and reading in the main house, everyone would retire to the barn to sleep. They're much nicer now." Chloe was busy talking and rummaging through the shelves.

"What are you looking for?" Trip asked, slightly deflated.

"There's usually a guest book somewhere that everyone signs and leaves little messages in."

Trip spotted the black leather-bound book on a side table next to the fireplace. "This, maybe?"

Chloe beamed. "That's it!"

Chloe and Trip sat next to each other on the extra large leather chair positioned right next to the roaring fire. Trip could feel his heart skip a beat as Chloe bumped her elbow into his side with each turn of the page.

"Oh my gosh!" Chloe exclaimed. "Look, here. See this scribble?" Trip leaned forward, their two heads almost touching as they strained to read the inscription.

"My favorite clothing designer of all time was here." Trip had always wondered where Chloe's unique dressing style emanated from. "And look! She even sketched one of her upcoming designs." Chloe scrunched up her nose to read the fine print. "This was only last week!" Chloe looked down at her own outfit. "Wow, she basically drew what I have on!"

Trip grinned. She was adorable and sexy at the same time. Watching her get excited sent adrenaline up and down his spine.

Chloe exhaled in awe as she turned to face Trip.

Their mouths were inches apart.

Trip didn't know what came over him. He looked deep into Chloe's sable brown eyes, leaned forward, and met her lips with his own. What began as a soft meeting of highly sensitive skin, quickly turned into a fervent exploration of the hidden depths of the other's inner most being. Their hearts beat as one while the fire roared brighter and the guest book fell to the floor without so much as a glance.

When they finally came up for air, the two newly discovered lovers stood up slowly. Without a word, they walked to the counter and checked in. As they climbed the winding marble stairs to the only suite in the hotel, Trip swept Chloe up into his arms and carried her. Chloe held Spitfire in one hand and buried her head in Trip's warm, strong neck, where it belonged.

≈

Chatham opened the floor to ceiling doors that led into the mahogany covered board room of one of New York City's largest companies. Models of yachts were strewn across the back credenzas with hanging glossies above them of Harlan shaking hands with the Who's Who of the entire country.

Her heart was in her throat. She was extremely late. Life-insurance policy or not, this account was very important to her. She tried to clear all thoughts of Peter, her electric kiss with Palio, her renewed commitment to Trip, her newfound wealth, and her questions of Harlan's possible involvement in a very bad scheme out of her busy mind. She was here to win the business, bare foot and all.

Harlan sat on his throne at the opposite end of the

room. Chatham wished she could have done this presentation over the video conferencing system. At least looking at Harlan's larger-than-life nose and lips would have made her laugh. Now, she was terrified.

"How nice of you to *finally* make it, Chatham my dear." Harlan looked directly at the clock. She was almost one hour late. "You are very lucky I am still here."

Time to dance. Chatham saw the Georgina and Lizard duo seated next to him at the large conference table. Her nervousness skyrocketed. "Yes, thank you Harlan. Actually, you can imagine how it is to get a cab ride in this city. Why, I had to walk here in the end, and well, you know those grates that pop up unannounced on the sidewalk? Well, I got my heel stuck in more than one... so, it's lucky I got here in one piece, wouldn't you agree, Harlan?" Chatham was babbling. Shut up, she told herself.

"Why don't we just get to the point?" Georgina's icy voice insisted.

Chatham turned to see Georgina staring at her with eyes like daggers. Did she recognize me from Monte's last night? Or was she just livid she had spilled her entire life plan to me in the elevator? she wondered.

Harlan was clearly annoyed with the interruption. "Be quiet," he said abruptly.

A pointy-nosed, pip-squeak of a man sat to the right of Harlan, the position saved for second in command. Chatham had been in enough board meetings to know. Harlan leaned over to whisper something to the squirrelly character, who subsequently got up and left the room.

Georgina watched the man skitter out a secret side door of the conference room. He looked back at her and smiled just as the door closed behind him. The exchange was not missed by Chatham.

"Chatham, my dear. Please proceed."

Georgina scribbled a note and handed it to Lizard, who abruptly left the room as well. The Italian beauty coyly smiled at the bald boss at the head of the table.

Witnessing this terse flurry of activity made Chatham feel uneasy. What was Harlan's relationship with Palio's girlfriend, and how did the amphibian from E. Anytime fit in with this odd couple?

Harlan impatiently strummed his fingers on the oak table. "Is something wrong, my dear?"

Chatham took a deep breath to gather herself. "No, Harlan. Nothing's wrong." Chatham looked around at the rest of the board members. There were four of them in pinstriped suits. MBA corporate types who spent most of their time crunching numbers in tiny cubicles, seeking ways to expand the company empire.

Chatham was about to begin her presentation when a cell phone rang somewhere under the table. Harlan reached under and withdrew a secret phone.

"What? No. NO! Fine." Harlan hung up the phone. "I must go."

"Go?" Chatham knew she couldn't let this moment go by. "But Harlan, the presentation, the board approval. We need that today if we're going to get the campaign done in time and launched by the fourth of July."

"I have to go. If you had been on time maybe you'd already have the board's approval," he said condescendingly. "You'll have to come back next weekend."

Chatham moved to desperation mode. There was no way she could arrange another last-minute trip to New York over a weekend. Not after everything that had happened with this disaster of a trip.

Chatham climbed up onto the table and belted out her presentation in her best Marilyn Monroe impersonation. She got through the entire song. Harlan stood by the door and watched her, as though he was caught in a trance.

As a finale, she twirled in her white dress.

Harlan looked around at the other board members who nodded their head in unison.

"You've got the account," Harlan barked as he turned to leave the room. Just as the door was about to close behind him, he caught it with his foot.

"And Chatham, my dear?" Chatham was still in shock.

"Yes?"

"You're the talent in the spot. Just don't wear that red thong for the shoot." And he was gone.

Oh my god! Chatham realized what had happened. She must have overdone it on the twirling. She could feel her face flush red.

Board members chuckled and began to leave the room. As Chatham gathered herself and prepared to exit, the same telephone from underneath the table rang. Mr. Squirrel entered the room just in time to answer it.

"Yes, of course," was all he said. He turned to Chatham. "Harlan would like for you to be at the boat race this afternoon."

"Oh yes, I was planning on it. Thank you." After that, the room began to clear.

Georgina stood up and walked up to Chatham, her nose inches from Chatham's face.

"Don't even think about getting near my fiancé," she warned, thrusting her ring in Chatham's face. "He's mine." And with that she spun around and left the room.

CHAPTER XLIII – *ON THE WAY*

≈

Tom, Theo, and the kids headed to the lawyer's offices by The Plaza Hotel to deliver the signed papers.

"Not to worry," Tom said to the group. "We have plenty of time. Besides, I'm starving. Let's stop to eat in the dining room."

"Are you sure, Tommy?" Theo asked. "Shouldn't we turn the papers in first?"

"Oh, would you relax!" Tom scolded. For once Tom wasn't being neurotic. "We have plenty of time. Lawyers don't even get in until eleven anyway. We can drop off the papers and be at the race by noon. Piece of cake." Tom watched as a waiter passed by with a platter of eggs benedict, croissants, and fresh berries.

"Speaking of cake." Tom followed his nose into the main dining room as his brood scurried to keep up with him.

≈

Palio was having his usual, scrambled eggs, bacon, and coffee. After being felt up by several men in blue earlier that morning, he felt that he deserved a good breakfast. Apparently that elevator boy hadn't liked him too much. It took a lot of effort to convince the policemen that he wasn't a gigolo trying to hook up with multiple women in the hotel. Just one, he thought. The passionate kiss with Chatham was unlike anything he had ever experienced in his life. Just the idea of it sent his spirits soaring. Palio desperately hoped she would be at the little boat race. He recalled how Georgina had scooted out of the hotel a little too quickly, yet Palio was actually glad to have some more time to think before he had to serve as her escort to the main event. He was still confused as to how she persuaded him to buy her the Tiffany ring in exchange for the painting. Just then, Palio's phone rang.

"Hello?" he answered.

"How's my favorite son?"

"Your only son. Well, sort of. How are you, Pop?"

"...So?"

"So? So what?" Palio knew what was coming.

"So, you know what. How did it go last night?"

"Go?"

"Come on, my boy I've been dying to call you all morning."

Palio gripped his coffee mug. "Pop, you're a worse gossip than most old ladies." He heard a chuckle on the other end of the line.

"Give an old man a thrill. What happened with my friend Georgina?"

"Nothing, Pop, really."

"Nothing? She sure seemed interested in you."

"It's business Pop, just business," Palio said, although he wasn't sure if she would agree with him. He looked at the clock. He had a little while before he had to pick her up for the boat race. If only his father knew.

"I think there might be someone else who is interested in you too, eh?" "Pop..."

"Someone from a place where it's warm?"

Chatham jumped to the forefront of Palio's mind as it had every minute since their kiss. He was amazed by his father's attention to detail. "What are you talking about,

Pop?"

"Monte saw it, too. Trust me, we know about these things."

Palio could almost see his father grinning. "Pop, come on."

"I think a little lady whose Pop makes tiny little carvings has more than just a passing interest in you. She couldn't keep her eyes off of you all night."

"Pop, for god's sake. She's taken." Palio felt the pain of defeat all over again. He remembered how upset Trip had been.

"Taken, shmaken. I liked her papa and her son, so I'm sure I'd like her. I just have a feeling."

"I thought you wanted me with Georgina," Palio inquired.

"I just want you to be happy."

"And Maria?"

"Ahhh, Maria. Now that's a girl worth talking about, but I'm afraid there's more to that than either of us know."

Palio had no idea what his father was talking about. "What do you mean 'more than we know'?"

"Listen, I've got to go get ready for the race. I'll see you there, eh?"

"Wouldn't miss it for the world, Pop." They said their goodbyes and Palio hung up the phone. Was he missing something with Maria? Why was he always the last to know?

Palio grabbed his blazer and set out to walk the short distance back to The Pierre.

≈

Palio sat in the lobby of The Pierre waiting for Georgina, but his mind was on Chatham. He desperately hoped she would attend the little boat race. He needed a chance to explain himself and the kiss from that morning. Did he dare hope that they had any kind of future together? The look on Trip's face in the stairwell had haunted Palio that morning. The man was clearly in love with her, not that Palio could blame him. But the questioning plaguing his mind was: Was it reciprocated? The way she had responded so passionately to his kiss left Palio hopeful. He just needed the chance to talk to her, without interruptions or distractions.

"Earth to Palio?" Georgina flashed him a beautiful smile. "Your mind somewhere else?"

Palio shook his head. "Yes, it was. Sorry about that." He rose from his chair. "No problem at all." She smoothed her black miniskirt with her freshly manicured hand.

The diamond was still on her ring finger, Palio noticed. He tried to shake off the discomfort he was feeling around this very gorgeous, but very strange woman. Hopefully their business transaction would be complete after the race today, he thought, and they could go their separate way..

"Shall we?" he asked, gesturing toward the large double doors.

"Oh no!" Georgina suddenly exclaimed. "I've forgotten your father's present in my room."

"No problem. I'll just wait for –"

"Actually would you mind terribly if you came with me? It's rather large, and I'm not entirely sure I can carry it by myself."

Palio shrugged. Might as well, he thought. He didn't want to be late to his father's race; they were behind as it was.

≈

Chatham didn't know what to be more excited about: Harlan's approval of her Marilyn pitch, the discovery of Peter's life-insurance policy, or the fact that her entire family was all together in New York. As she made her way to the elevators at The Pierre, she was nothing but smiles. She couldn't remember the time she had felt this good, this alive.

I think I'll take the stairs, she thought. After all, the stairwell had been a very interesting spot earlier that morning. She wouldn't mind revisiting it, not that she hadn't already replayed the tender embrace in her mind several times.

She glanced at her watch. Half an hour till the race started. She needed to be quick in her transformation from Marilyn back to Chatham.

"Happy birthday, Mr. President," she sang to herself as she walked the final steps leading up to her floor. She made her way past the spot where Palio had kissed her more passionately than she had ever been kissed before. Her heart raced just recalling the special moment. What would Georgina think of her soon-to-be husband kissing another woman, she wondered. Did Palio plan to call off his engagement? Did she dare hope? "Stop it," she commanded. "You are committed to Trip now. That is how it should be and will be and you will tell him today," she reminded herself firmly. Chatham stood up straight and pushed the fantasy from her mind.

As she walked down the green-carpeted hallway to her room, Chatham caught a glimpse of a couple walking closely together up head. The woman's legs were long and thin under her tiny black skirt. Her long curls fell beautifully across her back. Her hand was placed in the crook of the gentleman's arm, and her head was nuzzled up close to his shoulder as they walked.

That's sweet, Chatham thought. She wished she had someone to walk with like that everywhere she went. An image of Trip's face suddenly came to her mind. Chatham knew that she and Trip were the logical and correct match and she owed it to Trip to explain herself.

From down the hall, Chatham heard the woman giggle. It was a forced, high-pitched squeal that she instantly recognized. Chatham froze. She glanced ahead to see the couple stop at a door. The woman slowly pulled out a key card from her purse. "Oh Palio, you're too much," she cooed.

Chatham watched as the man who had kissed her just hours ago, the man whom she had been willing to love again for, followed the Italian temptress into her hotel room.

≈

"Are we ready to go?" Maddy complained.

Tom signed the check. "You, my dear, are not very patient. Don't you know it's a virtue?"

"What's virtue?" PJ asked.

"Something you should have," Tom quickly replied.

"I know it's been a long day, children. But we needed to eat in order to preserve our strength and the lawyer's offices are just around the corner. I think one landmark meal in exchange for an entirely new life isn't asking too much, now is it?"

Maddy shook her head. "I guess not."

"Row, row, row your boat gently down the stream," PJ sang.

Theo gently patted PJ's knee. "That's right, buddy. We're going to the boat race right after this, OK?"

"OK, Theo. We will go to the race."

Ten minutes later, the crew walked up to the lawyers' office around the corner from The Plaza. Tom quickly hopped ahead of the group. "Wait here, everyone," he instructed.

"Tom?" Theo asked.

"What!" Tom practically shouted. "Can this not wait five minutes?"

"You might want this," he said, handing him the policy.

Tom grinned. "What would I do without you, Theo dear?"

"Well, remember. Patience is a virtue."

Tom scowled and quickly turned on his heel. As he ventured up the main steps of the brownstone, he was quickly disappointed. Affixed to the mahogany door was a green piece of paper. Be back in the afternoon, the note said. Although Tom thought this was highly unprofessional, he simply shook his head and flipped his scarf around his neck. They'd all go to the boat race and come back later, that's all, he decided. He glanced at his watch. There was no need to worry, they still had plenty of time.

≈

"So, what's our game plan?" Maria asked Gino. She let go of his hand as they walked toward the race.

He winked at her and took her hand once more. "What's da matter? You got somethin' to hide?"

"Well, no. I just… They're your family, Gino. Shouldn't we wait to tell them about us?"

"Far as I'm concerned, I've been waitin' too long as it is. I don't wanna wait anymore."

She was hoping he'd say that. She kissed him on the cheek. It had only been two days with her Italian stallion, but she couldn't imagine life without him. Have I really been pining for the wrong Capriatti all these years? All this time, the answer to her heart was right before her eyes.

"Maria!" Gino whispered harshly. "Look!"

She followed his gaze to a nearby bench, right beside the water. Despite the flurry of activity, Maria saw exactly who her lover was pointing to. "Oh my god! What are Bambini and his goons doing here?"

"Hell, if I know. It can't be anythin' good."

They quickened their pace toward a small cluster of trees.

"The mafia is at the little boat race. It doesn't make any sense," Maria said, thinking out loud.

Gino rested his hand on the bark of the tall oak tree. "Maybe it really is just to watch the race?"

"I remember Mr. Capriatti saying Bambini had a lot of money riding on The Lucia."

"Who wouldn't? He's gonna win, no question 'bout it."

Maria wasn't sure it was that simple. "I think we should keep an eye out for Palio and Mr. Capriatti. Just in case. Maybe the mob's here for nothing other than shits and kicks, but I'd rather be safe than sorry."

"Shits and kicks?" Gino chuckled. "You really are the gal for me," he responded, as he pulled her tightly and kissed her fully on the mouth.

≈

Palio didn't know if he was nervous for his father, eager for the possibility of seeing Chatham again, or fed up with the ever-seducing Georgina. It was probably a little of all, he reasoned.

"Thanks for helping me with the sign," Georgina said quietly.

"No problem," he replied. Those were their first words since Palio had rejected her sexual advances in the hotel. He should have known better than to go up to her room. The "large" present for his father was nothing but an oversized poster-board sign that she had made for The Lucia. "If you're not rootin' for The Lucia, you're a loozzah!" the colorful banner read. She could have easily carried it down herself.

Palio had cringed when he read it, although he hadn't had time to fully dwell on the horrendous ditty before he was affronted with a full-blown sexual attack by the olive princess. Somehow he was able to weasel his way out of it. He only hoped he hadn't grossly offended her, because he still desperately wanted to secure the painting for his father. But enough was enough. The sooner this race was over, the sooner he could end all contact with this insane woman. And hopefully, he could then spend more time with his Marilyn Monroe.

When the cab dropped them off, Palio walked with Georgina toward the buzzing activity. Colorful flags waved in the breeze. Pockets of people surrounded the excitement. Some had planned ahead with lawn chairs and binoculars. Others stood in groups around the water and observed the competing drivers as they made last-minute adjustments to their small one of a kind boats.

Palio quickly spotted his father among the crowd. Next to him stood Mr. Ross and Camp.

"Gentlemen!" Palio exclaimed as he approached. "How are the champions today?"

Mr. Capriatti grinned. "Not yet, my boy! But very soon!"

"Hi, Palio," Camp said. "I brought my Game Boy!"

Palio tussled the boy's thick hair. "Awesome. We will definitely have to play that today. No way are you going to beat me again!"

"Don't bet on it," Mr. Ross said. "His thumbs are glued to that crazy device."

Palio shook his hand. "You're telling me. Is it just you two today?" He hoped his intentions weren't too obvious.

"Chatham and the rest of the family will be here soon, I believe," Mr. Ross said.

Palio nodded. He wondered if that included Trip.

"Palio, you're being awfully rude," his father said sternly. "Aren't you going to introduce your… friend?"

Georgina stepped forward, extending her free hand. "Mr. Ross, I believe we met briefly at dinner the other night. I'm Georgina."

Palio had practically forgotten all about the olive princess. He wasn't accustomed to her silence.

"I'm so excited to be here, Mr. Capriatti," she continued. "Look! I even made you a sign."

"A loozzah?" Palio's father chuckled. "I like it. Well done, my dear!"

"Pop, where's your boat? Shouldn't it be on the water by now?"

Mr. Capriatti nodded toward the bench directly behind them. His precious box was atop of it, still under lock and key. "They let groups of five warm up on the water at a time," he said. "I think we're in the next few batches. Besides, I don't want to bust my Lucia out just yet. Don't want to give these cheaters a sneak peak of what my boat can do."

"Yeah! They're all gonna eat your dust... err, water?" Camp questioned.

They all laughed.

Just then, Palio saw the great Bambini and his mob of meatheads. What were they doing there? he wondered.

"I think I'm going to take a seat, if you don't mind?" Georgina asked Palio, pointing to the bench right behind them with The Lucia atop of it.

He shrugged his answer. When had she ever asked permission for anything?

She sat down and placed her large sign over her lap. Palio thought she looked incredibly somber, but she gave him a sly smile.

A loud foghorn pierced the blue sky.

Camp gave a loud holler. "Wahoo! Two more groups and then you're up, Mr. C!"

He grinned at the boy. "So, Mr. Ross, we're running out of time. You were just telling me how you think my boat is flawed?"

"Flawed?" Palio chimed in. "How so?"

Mr. Ross held up a miniature replica of The Lucia. "I was working on this late last night, and it suddenly occurred to me. Your rudder is too wide. She won't be able to angle her way through the pack."

Mr. Capriatti shook his head. "With all due respect, that simply isn't true. I've looked into every detail myself. I'm fully confident in my vessel. She's as fine as she'll ever be."

"I'm sure your boat sails wonderfully, Mr. C. I'm just tellin' ya that you're not going to win with that rudder. My guess is that you have hardly tested her turn radius?" Mr. Ross questioned.

"I have seen to it that she is fully capable in every capacity to win this race."

"I thought you wanted my help."

Mr. Capriatti put his hand in the air in protest. "Now please don't misunderstand me, friend. I do want you help. I value your opinion."

Mr. Ross stared at the replica in his hand. "Clearly."

"Even if you are right, Mr. Ross, what good will it do my father now?" Palio asked.

"Aha!" Mr. Ross exclaimed. "I just so happened to have crafted the perfect rudder for The Lucia last night." He reached into his pocket and revealed his handiwork.

"This baby will make her glide through the water like a goddess of the sea."

Mr. Capriatti stared at the polished wood shaped like a dorsal fin. He extended his hand. "May I?"

"Be my guest."

He fiddled with the small, essential piece for a few moments. "Do you really think this will work?"

"I'd stake my life on it," Mr. Ross said proudly. "My replicas never lie."

Palio looked at his papa. "What do you say, Pop?"

"Well, I know I didn't come here to lose. So, what the hell? Your guess is better than mine."

Mr. Ross beamed. "We haven't much time, sir. We need to quick if we are going to attach my rudder in time for your warm-up."

"No! WAIT!" Camp suddenly screamed.

Palio jerked around just in time to see Camp take off down the stretch. His short legs were pumping incredibly fast. Up ahead, Palio saw a little red-headed boy sprinting along the water's edge.

"My boat! My Lucia!" Mr. Capriatti exclaimed.

Palio turned toward the bench, only inches away from where they all stood. His father's precious box and Georgina were gone.

≈

"I don't know if I've ever seen a real boat race before," Trip said. "I gotta say, I'm pretty excited about it." He squeezed Chloe's hand tightly as they sat in the back of the cab.

She grinned, the dimples perfectly accentuating her

406

great smile. "I've done a lot of things today that I've never done before," she said.

Trip raised his eyebrows. "Is that so?" This girl consistently surprised him. How could she be everything and more? How could she be irresistibly cute and incredibly sexy at the same time? How did she make him completely forget everyone and everything else? She had him captivated, utterly and entirely.

"For instance...I've never pet a numbat before," she said, stroking Spitfire's fur. "I've never been in New York with you."

"Both true."

"And I've never kissed you in the back of a taxi cab. . . ." her voice trailed off.

Trip stared into her almond eyes. He gently stroked her face. Tilting her beautiful face toward his, he planted a sweet kiss on her supple lips. "I love kissing you," he whispered. "I can't believe we haven't been doing this for years."

"It just feels so..."

"Right?"

"Perfect." She kissed him once more.

"Sorry to break it up back there, but we're here," the taxi driver said.

Chloe practically leapt from her seat. "Off to the races!" she exclaimed with girlish joy.

"Let's go, Spitfire," Trip said to the animal in his hand. He paid the driver and slipped out of the taxi.

As they walked up to the busy New York street, Trip grew nervous. Obviously, Chatham was going to be there. But how could he face her? Hadn't he come on this trip to confess his love for her? Just last night he was thinking of proposing for Christ's sake! And now? Now he was holding hands with the woman who had swept him away years ago, and then again today. Just one morning of passion with Chloe had awakened his senses. He deserved to be loved as Chloe loved him. He was tired of waiting for Chatham to offer him the remaining pieces of her broken heart. It wasn't him she loved, and it never had been. With Chloe on his arm, Trip was finally seeing things clearly.

"Oh no," Chloe muttered. She quickly jerked her head down, as if she was hiding from someone.

"Chlo? What's up?" Trip looked up the street to see if he saw anything alarming. A large crowd had gathered to watch the boat race. He had difficulty deciphering faces.

"You like me, right?" she asked as they continued to walk.

Trip grinned. "You could say that."

She returned his smiles, clearly pleased with his answer. "That's good, because I'm about to tell you some news that you might not particularly enjoy."

Trip slowed his pace and turned toward her. "OK..."

"See that short, bald guy up ahead? He's wearing a khaki suit and a green tie. Up there by the light pole."

He nodded, not sure where this was going.

"Well, I've kinda been seeing him the past few weeks.."

"I see…"

They had finished crossing the street. The new couple was now surrounded by the gathering of boating fans.

"I decided before you even stepped into the picture that I was going to end things with him." She squeezed his hand as if to reassure him.

"You're sure?"

"More than ever. In fact," she said, "hang on one second."

In a flash, Trip saw her bound up to the unattractive man several yards off. "Gabrielle!" she yelled.

Trip hoped she'd return soon.

≈

"Who is that?" Georgina asked Harlan as she watched the little brunette skip away.

The bald-headed man sighed heavily. "Well, she was my lady friend, but I guess she's decided to end things." He turned toward her.

"Can't win 'em all, Harlan, especially when you're nothing but a fat fuck."

"Maybe not in love anyway, my dear," he said. "But in business…"

Georgina smirked. She liked this philosophy. "With me, you'll always win despite that unfortunate face of yours."

Harlan turned toward the race. "Walk with me. Tell me where things stand with the Capriattis. Is Palio groveling out of your hand yet?"

"Things are running a little slower on that front than I would like," she admitted. She felt her cheeks flush as she recalled the events from just a short while ago. Never in her life had a man resisted her sexual advances. She had literally thrown herself at him and nothing.

"I see you have the diamond," Harlan probed.

"But not the proposal," she admitted again.

"Well you better figure something out then. I'm sure I don't have to tell you that our futures depend on it."

Georgina jerked her head toward him. "I'm well aware of what's at stake here, Harlan. But remember, you are nothing without me. Nothing."

He chuckled. "Little testy today, are we?"

"Actually, I came all the way over here to give you a present."

"Oh?"

"Your grandson is in the boat race, isn't he?"

Harlan nodded his head. "The information you possess truly astounds me."

A loud foghorn blared. The New York crowd cheered with great enthusiasm.

"Guess it's about to start, eh?" Harlan mumbled to himself.

"Then I suppose you may want this," Georgina said. From her large black bag, she revealed a little boat. "I give you The Lucia," she presented it to him.

"Capriatti's boat?" Harlan said in disbelief. "How did you… Why did you?"

Georgina shrugged. "Just consider this a reminder that we have each other's best interests at heart. Good luck to your grandson. I'm sure he'll take the prize easily now."

"Yes, yes I'm sure he will," Harlan said simply. Disbelief etched across his face.

≈

"Goin' somewhere?" a large man blocked the

pathway of the little red-headed thief.

"Move over, pal," the boy snapped. He held a black box close to his chest.

"Not so fast, you little twerp," another man said, grabbing the kid's. "I could snap you like a toothpick."

"Go ahead and try," the boy yelled.

The man noticed several heads in the crowd turn to see what the fuss was about. He grinned to them, as if to say, "Everything's just fine." He knew most people would recognize him. He was, after all, the Mafia Boss. No one had the balls to confront the great Bambini, except apparently this snot-nosed kid.

"Let me go!" the boy struggled.

Bambini tightened his grip. "Not before I take what you've stolen from me."

"It's not yours!"

"Ah, see that's where you're wrong. I have a lot of money on the boat you're clutching to your chest, so you see… in a sense, that boat is mine. And I want it back." With one quick motion, he snatched the black box from the boy.

"Hey!" the little boy squealed. "Give that back!"

"I will. I'm sure Mr. Capriatti will be glad to see his boat again, you little thief."

"Well if that isn't the pot callin' the kettle black," a deep voice came from behind Bambini.

He turned to see who had the audacity to talk to him like that. A fat, bald man stood before him. "Harlan?" Bambini asked.

"Grandpa!" the little boy ran over to his side.

"Son, you better run to your station. The race is

going to start any time now."

With a quick scowl toward Bambini, the redheaded boy darted off.

"So you have to resort to stealin' from small children now, Bambini? I didn't realize times had gotten that bad."

Bambini thrust out his chin in objection. "That kid is a menace. He stole Capriatti's boat." He held the box up in the air as if to prove his point.

Harlan took a few steps closer toward his old comrade from long ago. "Actually, he didn't."

Just then, Bambini noticed the small boat Harlan held behind his back. "You didn't!"

Harlan smirked. "Anything for my family, huh?"

"You bastard."

"I'll take it you've got a lot of money ridin' on this little race?"

Bambini clenched his fists. He had half a mind to send one of his goons over to rip the bloated buffoon to shreds. It was entirely too crowded, however.

"Business must be bad if you've got to resort to gambling for income."

Bambini shrugged. It was no secret. With his recent arrest, his drug business was more difficult than ever. He needed something fresh, a new approach to trafficking. Something no one had thought of before. "It's been better, not that's it any of your fuckin' business."

"I'd like to make it my business." He gestured toward Bambini. "You and I, we're reasonable men. I think we can help each other out?"

Bambini's interest was piqued, but how could he

know this bald little shit wasn't screwin' with him? "Oh yeah? And how exactly are we gonna do that?"

"Easy. You've the goods, and I've got the means… if you know what I'm sayin'."

Bambini raised his eyebrows. Was Harlan really suggesting goin' into business together?

"Listen, let's not go into the full details of it here. But just so you know I ain't fuckin' with you, here." He handed him Capriatti's little boat. "Meet me at the Laundromat in ten minutes. You can have one of your goons tell you who wins."

Bambini nodded as he watched Harlan walk away. Out of the corner of his eye, he saw a familiar face. It was the kid who had been with Capriatti earlier that day.

"Lookin' for this?" he asked the kid.

"That's Mr. Capriatti's boat," the kid said meekly.

"Well shit, kid, I know that. Here, it's up to you to get it to him in time for the race to start." He handed The Lucia to him. "Better run fast."

For the first time that day, Bambini's mind was no longer on the race.

"You," he barked at the goon standing beside him. "Stay here and watch. Report back immediately after it's over, got it?"

"Whatever you say, boss."

≈

OK, Chatham, you really *really* need to get up now, she told herself. For the past twenty minutes, she had been lying on her bed in the fetal position. Tears streamed down

413

her face. Emotions were running wild within her, and she had no time to decipher all of them.

Seeing Palio with Georgina had dealt her a harsh cup of reality, and she hadn't been prepared for it. With all the emotional trauma her heart had endured so far today, she had felt the only appropriate response was to wallow.

Though she felt no better, she gathered quickly gathered herself. Stripping out of her Marilyn dress, a cruel reminder of this morning's passionate embrace, Chatham hopped into the shower. The warm water awakened her senses and left her feeling somewhat refreshed.

After changing into a comfy pair of jeans and a light blue t-shirt, she had just a few minutes to get to the race. Suddenly, she had a stroke of brilliance. She grabbed her purse and rummaged through the crevices until she had what she was searching for. She pulled out her cell phone and punched in the number from the card.

"Billy Bill?" she asked. "This is Chatham Ross."

"Yes ma'am? What can I do for ya?" his Texan drawl was even thicker over the phone.

"I'm in a pickle. Any way you can be at The Pierre to get me in like… well nowish?"

"It's your lucky day. I'm only two minutes out."

"Great! Meet ya out front."

She tossed her wet hair in a haphazard ponytail, dabbed on some foundation and rouge, and was out the door. Willing herself not to look down the hallway where Palio and his Italian goddess undoubtedly were, she hurried to the elevator.

Just then, her phone buzzed.

"Hey Tom," she answered.

"Chatham, sorry we're running late to the race. We'll be there in just a few minutes though so don't worry about us."

"Don't worry about it. I'm not there yet either."

Tom sighed a girly breath of air. "Phew then! Well we will see you in a few then sweetie."

Chatham hung up, smiling. She could hear PJ singing "Row your Boat" in the background.

"Well hey there, Miss Ross," Billy Bill said as she climbed into the back of the cab.

"Hi Billy Bill. I'm tryin' to get to the little boat race. Think we can make it in time?"

"Only one way to find out, ma'am," and they were off.

≈

"Carefully now, I'm just going to take this rudder off gently," Mr. Ross said, narrating his every movement. Camp had just sprinted toward them, Lucia in hand. He was completely out of breath, and they were nearly out of time. The story of how he got it back would have to wait.

"Quickly," Palio said. "We have four minutes."

Mr. Ross's skillful hands quickly attached his secret weapon, the crowning glory for the boat.

Palio gripped his father's shoulder as they both watched him work. He could tell Pop was a bundle of nerves and excitement.

"Racers please take your spot at the start line," the announcer boomed over the intercom.

"Almost there…" Mr. Ross muttered.

Palio looked at Camp, who was completely slumped

over in the bench. "How ya feeling there, bud?"

"I'm… just…really…tired."

"Camp, tired?" a sweet voice asked.

Palio saw the pretty brunette walk over to the bench and wrap her arms around the tuckered-out kid.

"Hi Aunt Chloe!" Camp exclaimed.

"Hi sweetheart! Where is everyone?"

"Yeah. You here just with Grandpa?" Trip asked.

Palio wished this guy would stop showing up to things. At least this time he was with another girl. And were they holding hands?

"Hiya, Trip," Camp said. "I don't know where everyone is, but the race is about to start and Mr. C has to fix his rubber."

"His what?"

"Rudder," Palio corrected.

"Finissimo!" Mr. Ross suddenly exclaimed. "Now go get this beauty on the water!"

Mr. Capriatti didn't have to be told twice. He took his prized possession and walk toward the starting position.

"Good luck, pop!" Palio called out.

Camp handed something to Palio. It was the miniature horse drawn carriage that Palio had given Camp.

"Don't you want it?" Palio asked.

"I already have one, remember? Camp replied. "You get one too, for good luck." Palio tussled Camp's hair and the two of them began cheering for *The Lucia*.

≈

Chatham arrived just in time to hear the gun sound. Geez how many people go to this thing? she thought as she wandered aimlessly through the crowd.

"Chatham, over here!" she heard Tom's voice.

"Mommy!" PJ came barreling toward her. "Look! Boats! Like row, row, row your boat –"

"Good job, sweetie," she said, giving him a tight squeeze.

"How are you, Chat?" Theo asked. "Holdin' up?"

For some reason the question brought tears to her eyes. She held onto PJ, who was still singing, and nodded her head.

"Chatham, I'm so sorry but the lawyers weren't at their damn offices! I mean, what is that about? Does everyone in New York think they're entitled to a 3-hour lunch?" Tom was practically yelling to be heard over the boisterous crowd.

"That's OK. We'll just go after the race, alrighty?" She forced a smile. "How are you, Maddy?"

Her daughter nodded her head, but her eyes were on the race. "Let's move closer, Mom!"

The motley crew edged closer to get a better look.

"Trip!" PJ suddenly exclaimed.

Chatham followed her son's gaze until she saw him, Chloe, Camp, and her father. And Palio all huddled together a few yards away, their eyes all on the water. She tried to breathe, to focus on anything but the blinding attraction she felt to the handsome Italian.

"Well, c'mon everyone! Let's go join the posse," Tom yelled. "Maybe someone can tell me what damn boat we're supposed to be cheering for."

As they approached them, Chatham noticed Trip was standing awfully close to Chloe. Was his arm around her? she wondered. She couldn't tell from this angle. Too many bodies. Too much shouting. It was all a little much for her in her emotionally fragile state.

"Which one is ours?" Maddy shouted as loud as she could.

Trip saw and made eye contact with Chatham, and instantly jumped six inches to the right. There was now a large gap between him and Chloe. Something was definitely going on between them.

This is so awkward, Chatham thought. Has Trip's feelings for her been in her head this whole time? Did Chloe think she was a complete idiot?

Her sister-in-law smiled enthusiastically and waved.

"We're the navy blue one with the orange sails," Trip shouted to everyone.

Just then Palio took his eyes off the water and his father's boat for the first time since the race began. Chatham saw his dark eyes lock onto hers. Her heart froze. She tried to remind herself what he had been doing just minutes ago and with who, but she couldn't concentrate. Despite the cheers from the crowd, despite the commotion around her, everything seemed to stand still as she stared at him.

"Can we talk?" he mouthed.

Before she had a chance to answer, she was reminded why her answer should have been no. The Italian goddess swooped around the other side of Palio. She put her arm low around his waist and kissed him on the cheek.

Palio tried to move away from her, but Chatham knew it was just part of the show for him. He clearly hadn't wanted to get away from her thirty minutes ago in the hotel room…

Chatham looked away, pretending to be interested in the race that looked like it was almost over. The blue ship with orange sails was the clear frontrunner. None of the other miniature boats were even close. Just once, she wished she knew what it felt like to come out on top.

≈

"Did I tell you or did I tell you?" Chatham's father beamed, as Mr. Cariatti brought over his first place ribbon.

"That was incredible! My Lucia was soaring across the waters like a dream."

"Congratulations, Pop!" Palio said, patting his father on the back.

"Excellent race, sir," Theo chimed in.

"Great job, Grandpa!" Camp said, obviously confusing the real victor of the race. "I totally want to enter this next year!"

"I bet your grandpa can make that happen, son," Mr. Cariatti said. "That is, if he'll come work for me."

Chatham watched her father's face flush with color. "Who me?" he asked.

"If it wasn't for you, Mr. Ross, we would have never made it. My boats need your insight. Please? Come work for me."

"Do it! Do it! Do it!" Camp clapped in a syncopated rhythm.

"Do it! Do it! Do it   !" PJ joined in as the two Ross boys began dancing around in celebration.

"Why not, Dad?" Chatham offered over her two sons boisterous cheers. She pretended not to notice Palio studying her.

"It'd be fabulous to decorate the little boogers," Tom chimed in.

"Grandpa, will you name one of your boats The Maddy?" Maddy squealed.

"PJ! PJ is a good name. Grandpa, PJ should be the name."

Mr. Cariatti beamed. "See? The whole family is already on board. What do you say?"

"What the hell?" Chatham's father said. "Count me in!"

Despite her feelings, Chatham couldn't help but smile at her little family. Maybe they'd be OK after all.

"Now everyone, we are off to Monte's to celebrate! My treat!" The boisterous cheers continued. "Now has anybody seen Gino?"

≈

"I knew something was up!" Maria exclaimed. She and Gino were staked outside the Laundromat, using her special gear to listen in on Harlan and Bambini's conversation. "They both left the race all of the sudden after we saw them talking."

"You've got great instincts, baby," Gino said. "Although I gotta admit that these two are a lot dumber than I thought comin' back to the Laundromat. How stupid is they?"

"Don't you see? It's the perfect place to come back to. It's been a few weeks since Bambini was busted here, and no way would the cops think he'd ever be that stupid to come back here."

Just then they heard Bambini's voice over the signal. "So you're tellin' me that you want to traffic my goods in your boats?"

"Are you recording this?" Gino whispered.

Maria nodded. What kind of security agent did he think she was?

"That's exactly what I'm sayin', Boss. Once that olive princess marries the Capriatti boy, I'll practically have a monopoly on little boat manufacturing. With my yachts, it's too hard to avoid searches as cross the border. I'm tellin' you. These little boats are gonna make us rich. This could be a very real and very lucrative business venture for the both of us."

Bambini was silent for a moment. He would deal with the double dipping issue later, now that he had Georgina's little plan figured out. She was trying to take both of them to the cleaners, but they beat her to it. Bambini let the thought turn up the sides of his mouth. "How many shipments do you think we can do?"

"A month?" Harlan asked.

"Nah, a week. I've sources all over, so getting the coke won't be a problem."

Maria raised her eyebrows and looked at Gino.

"I don't think the boats will be a problem either, but I won't really know till I have a look at the numbers. I'm waiting on that dumb bitch to do her half of the bargain and then we're in."

"How long do you think?"

"A week? Maybe two?"

"I'm sittin' on so much right now, my friend. Ever since my recent bail-out, I've had to be incredibly careful.

Haven't been able to get a load out in a few days."

"Oh my god!" Maria exclaimed. "Do you think it's in the Laundromat? Should I call the cops?"

"Shhh!" Gino said, trying to turn up the volume on the signal.

"…sometimes the best places are the most obvious," Bambini said. "It's right under their noses, no pun intended." He cackled at his own joke.

Gino nodded his head to Maria. "It's in there. It's gotta be. We gotta call this in, baby. This could be huge."

"We got the Mafia Boss for drug possession and Harlan for conspiring to traffic drugs." She hit the tape recorder.

"Baby, this is big! This is real big. Call it in, hurry. Before they leave."

Maria picked up her cell phone and dialed the cops while Gino peeled outta the parking lot.

≈

Palio got out of the cab in front of Monte's. Georgina had tagged along with him. She was like a bad habit he couldn't get rid of. Outside the restaurant, Palio spotted Mr. Ross and Chatham talking quietly. Were those tears in her eyes?

He escorted Georgina into the restaurant. Palio had to figure out when he was going to talk to Chatham. He had to explain himself. This whole Georgina thing had spiraled out of control. He owed it to Chatham and to himself to set the record straight. Tonight, he would talk to her. Tonight, he would tell her how he really felt.

≈

"Go, sweetie. The kids can stay with me for a few days. You need some R&R time, just to yourself."

Chatham knew it was incredibly sweet of her dad to offer, but being along sounded horrible. Wasn't she always alone? Wasn't she always busy, filling her days with mindless activities? Sure, she could catch up on some sleep, but would that really fix the problem? She was still alone, single, and depressed. This trip had made that abundantly clear.

So a man had kissed her on the stairwell? So what? He clearly had lots of women to mess around with, so what was some sloppy single mother who lived across the country to him?

"Chatham?"

She shook her head, willing herself to not become a prisoner to her own mind. "I'm sorry, daddy. I'm ruining your celebratory dinner."

"No, of course you're not." He put his arms around her. "Tom and Theo and I have the kids, OK? We will take care of them for a few days while you go home and take care of yourself. Why don't you take the red eye tonight? Sleep on the plane, huh? Does that sound good?"

"I just want to be in my own bed in my own house."

"Then go do it."

"Are you sure, Dad?"

He grinned. "Are you kidding me? Those kids and I are going to have so much fun we aren't gonna know what to do with ourselves!"

Maybe this would be OK, Chatham thought. She could use a break.

"Now you go on to the hotel and pack your bag. I'll tell everyone you said goodbye."

She wanted to argue, but she couldn't bear seeing Palio's face one more time. She needed to get out of New York and out of his life. For good.

"Thanks daddy. I think I'll walk to the hotel. It's just a few blocks."

"Be careful, baby girl." He kissed her on the cheek and returned to his celebration.

≈

Palio immediately noticed that Mr. Ross came back alone. Chatham was no longer with him. Panic set in. Was she leaving? Was she back at her hotel? He needed to ditch this dinner and find her.

He put his napkin on his plate and walked over to Mr. Ross who had just sat at the head of the long table. He was talking to Monte.

"Excuse me, Mr. Ross? Where is Chatham?" Palio inwardly winced at the sound of his own voice. He sounded like a lovesick puppy.

"She's headed back to her hotel, son. She's gonna take the red eye home tonight."

"What no! She can't... Excuse me, sir." Palio rushed to the door to follow after the woman he was sure would be his wife one day.

"Palio?" an annoying voice confronted him.

He whipped around sharply. "Yes, Georgina? I'm about to leave."

She sultrily walked to the front door. "I don't think so," she said.

"Excuse me?"

"You're not going anywhere."

He lifted her hand off the door handle. "I'm tired of your manipulation. Goodnight, Georgina. I hope I never see you again."

He was halfway out the door when she said, "That's a real shame. I hope you're father doesn't die of heartbreak when you have to tell him why you didn't get the only thing he ever asked of you. The only thing he ever wanted to remember his long dead wife."

Palio's heart seemed to sink to his knees. "What are you going to do with that painting, Georgina? I thought we had a deal!"

"We do." She licked her lips and smirked. "Here's the deal. You stay here with me tonight, and I'll give you the painting in the morning."

Palio saw his father, proudly donning his blue ribbon, laughing with Mr. Ross and Monte. Palio's father had done so much for him. All he had ever asked for was this painting. Could he wait one more night to find Chatham?

Though his heart felt like it would burst, Palio weakly nodded his head at the woman in front of him. "Deal," he said. The Italian beauty had never looked uglier to him.

≈

Gino and Maria stormed into the restaurant, holding hands and full of smiles.

"Everybody!" Gino shouted. "Listen up! We have some pretty incredible news."

"Gino, my boy, is everything OK?" Mr. Capriatti asked.

"It's better than OK, Pop. Tonight Maria and I busted the Mafia Boss, Bambini for drug possession. He was sitting on ten kilos of coke!"

The restaurant was eerily quiet. Everyone seemed interested to hear what had happened.

"And! And Harlan, the evil yacht owner and candy man, was there, too! Now they're both in jail!"

The room erupted into applause and cheers. Tom leaned over to Theo. "I'll have to tell Chatham that we need to get a new account."

"It was incredible!" Gino said. He turned toward Maria. "This woman is absolutely incredible," he said, almost to himself. He put his hands on her face and gently pulled her to him. The restaurant exploded with whistles and applause.

Gino quickly got on a knee. He stared up into the eyes he loved more than anything and asked, "Maria, will you marry me?"

Maria melted in his arms, her answer plain for the entire restaurant to see... even a very confused Palio.

CHAPTER XLIV – *HOPE*

≈

Chatham gazed absently out of the kitchen window. She didn't even notice the chipped coffee cup edge greeting her lips and passing the steaming liquid into her mouth. Peter had given her that cup, a memento from one of their first dates in college to a local coffee shop. He had discretely bought the same cup she drank out of that night and handed it to her when he said goodnight. Peter was always doing little things, thoughtful things, to let her know he cared.

A loud bang on the kitchen window caused Chatham to swallow too big of a gulp.

"Ow, oh my god!" Chatham screeched as she jumped up to prevent the spewing coffee from landing on her worn robe, another gift from Peter a Christmas eons ago.

The face of her best friend Henrietta popped up to join the knuckled fist.

"Do you think you could possibly hear when someone rings the doorbell ten times?" her friend's muffled voice fired through the glass.

Chatham ran over and opened the window to hear her friend more clearly.

"What, do you think I'm going to climb through? The door would work much better." Henrietta was always tossing out snarky comments, never intending real harm.

"Oh, Hen, I'm sorry. I must have been daydreaming. Come on around, I'll open the door. Yes, of course I will," she muttered. Chatham headed over to the kitchen/family room door that led to the backyard, holding it open for her friend.

"Well that was a great way to start my day," Henrietta said, brushing off the twigs and leaves she had collected while shimmying into the thick hedge below the windowsill.

"Want some coffee?" Chatham asked absently. "You might want to leave a dime on the counter now that I lost any chance of collecting the money Peter left for me. I fucking hate deadlines." Chatham set about to pour Henrietta a cup.

"Listen Chat, look on the bright side; you never had it anyway."

"It seems like nothing works out for me, Henrietta. I'm just one big failure. I can't keep my husband alive; I can't keep my family together; I can't seem to make any relationship work; I can't even fulfill my volunteer commitments. I couldn't even remember to turn in the damn life-insurance policy on time! I'm worthless." She sat down and put her head in her hand.

Henrietta gently stroked Chatham's shoulder. "Hey, just because it didn't work out with Trip or the sexy Italian guy, doesn't mean it can't work out for you ever."

"I'm just dreaming, Hen," Chatham replied sadly. "Trip has always been there for me, ever since Peter died and what do I do? I dump him, just like that, without as much as a thank you for being my friend – right after we slept together, no less. And now he's off with Chloe like nothing ever mattered."

Chatham reflected on what could have been. But did she really want it? She wasn't sure of anything any more.

Henrietta leaned forward to emphasize her interest. "I thought you said nothing happened."

Chatham set her friend's cup of coffee on the kitchen table. "Come on, Hen. I was in my underwear in the morning. You're the one who told me that was a huge red flag."

Hen waved her hands in the air. "Still, he never said you did."

Chatham went on. "Yeah so after I dump the man I probably should have stayed with, I decide to give it a go and let Palio know that I am, in fact, interested." Chatham turned and looked at Henrietta dead on. "More than interested."

Henrietta nodded.

"But that Italian ice princess got to him before me. He's engaged to be married, and he didn't even tell me when he decided to kiss me in the stairwell. And let me tell you, it was some kiss!" Chatham's emotions were beginning to fly. She felt her world was spinning out of control.

"You are totally confused, girl."

Chatham's voice drifted off. "You can say that again."

"And?" Henrietta probed.

Chatham braced her hands on the kitchen sink for support. "And what? It's over. Nothing even happened, and it's already over. Seriously, how do I compete with that?" She looked down at her pathetic threadbare robe, which could no longer be determined if the original color had been light blue or drab gray. Her feet were calloused from neglect and the chipped toenail polish, well, that hadn't changed either.

"Chat, can I be perfectly honest with you?"

"Why not," Chatham responded. "You can't make it any worse."

"Don't take this wrong. I mean, you know I'm your best friend and I only want to help, right?"

Chatham wasn't sure she wanted to hear more. "Uh, I guess so. What are you getting at?"

"Well, truth is, you're a mess."

"Great." Now it was Chatham's turn to throw her hands into the air.

"I mean, come on girl. You haven't had a haircut in how long? A year? And your toes? If you don't get some nail polish remover and get rid of last year's red blots, I'm going to chisel that crap off."

Chatham laughed softly, before turning solemn once again. "When do I have time? I have no time for anything other than kids and work. You know that better than anyone, Hen."

"No time?" Henrietta answered, staring at her friend with false shock and a twinkle in her eye. "Well then, I would say it's time you adopted Henrietta's standard chronometer reference."

"Your what?"

"It's my own internal alarm clock that rings with vengeance when I'm in desperate need of a makeover." She pointed at Chatham's robe. "Honey, yours starts right now with the trashing of that very ancient, piece of shit blanket you're wearing." Henrietta jetted out her hip and held her hand, palm side up, for the deposit.

"What? Are you kidding? Peter gave this fluffy robe to me. It has sentimental value." Chatham gathered the worn threads close around her neck for protection against this sudden crazy woman who was supposed to be her friend.

"Sentimentally speaking? It's crap and it belongs in the garbage with your wallowing self pity, OK?" Henrietta helped her friend relinquish the tattered wrap.

"And?" Her hand remained extended.

"And what? You've already taken my warm and fuzzy comfort zone."

"The cup."

"No!"

"Yes. Hand it over."

"No, it was one of our first dates."

"Do you think Mr. Armani wants to see you drinking out of some college memoire? At least invest in a Villeroy and Boche pattern for goodness sake. It's Italian."

"Really?" Chatham grudgingly loosened her grasp on the cup, watching with horror as her best friend, or was it her enemy, launched it into the garbage can.

"Come on, Chat. It's been years now. Have you even emptied his clothes out of your closet?"

Chatham attempted a confident pose. "Yes, I did." She hoped she sounded convincing.

"When? Last week?"

"Before I left for New York, actually. I just had a feeling, that's all, that I was…you know, ready. Sort of. I think…"

Henrietta put her hands on Chatham's shoulders. "And where did you stash the wardrobe? Because I know you didn't throw it away."

Chatham's knees folded into each other as her shoulders hunched and the edge of her nail made its way between her teeth.

"Well…"

"Yeah, I thought so."

Henrietta must have been psychic because she headed right to the guest-room closet and threw open the door.

"Aha! Expecting a guest to move in, are we?" Henrietta turned to see the tears coming down Chatham's face.

"Chat, it's time."

"Time?" Chatham could barely see her friend between the streams pouring down her face.

"Time." Henrietta took the edge of the tattered robe that was still in her hand and wiped away Chatham's tears.

"Look, get dressed. We're going to go get a little pour moi time. Because honey, you definitely need it." Henrietta turned back to scoop up the Peter pile. "Throw on something. Not sweats. Jeans. Those cute ones I got you for Christmas three years ago. The pair that must still have the tag on them because I've never seen you wear them."

Chatham felt guilty as she lifted the brand new jeans out of her bottom drawer, tag and all. She quickly ripped the marker off and slipped into them. They still fit. The pleasant surprise lifted Chatham's mood just a little.

She reached for a box she hadn't opened in forever, which she thought contained a pair of ankle high black Ellen Tracy boots that zipped up the side. Instead, she found a note inside. As the crisp piece of paper unfolded she instantly recognized the writing. It was from Peter.

Dear Chat.

I know if you find this, it means that I am no longer around. I've always had this weird feeling that I would go before you. Why the shoebox? Because I know you. You wouldn't wear these shoes until you were ready to dress up again and consider dating. I bet it's been at least four years.

So I threw them away and left this note in their place. The fact that you're even considering wearing them must be that you are ready to try again, to open the door to new possibilities that may be knocking. I love you and I always will. I want you to move on Chat. To live your life again, have a husband you can love and give the kids a dad. You deserve it and so do they. I'm going to sign off now. Remember that love can knock twice for you.

Your loving husband, Peter.

Oh, and PS. Don't try to be super woman, and, yeah, throw my stuff away. I know you...

Chatham collapsed in the middle of her closet. She silently folded the piece of paper and put it back in the shoebox, placing the parcel back right where it would stay, at the far back corner of the top shelf.

Tears trickled down her face. She missed him so much. Something told her, after reading that note, that Peter had done the ultimate thing. He had given his life so that she and the kids would be taken care of, forever. At least that was how Chatham saw it. The note was so sure of itself, so final.

There had always been unanswered questions lingering in her mind about the ice castle accident in

Sweden. The police report had said that the other car was only going five miles an hour and Peter was going 90, headed right for an ice bank. Does slipping on the ice cause a car to jolt into high speed? Secretly, Chatham thought that Peter might have been driving that fast, on purpose. She would never know.

Regardless of the circumstances, and the fact that she didn't end up getting the money he left for her, she somehow knew that she and the kids would be OK. She'd never be fully recovered from losing him, the love of her life, but she knew it was time for her to put away her past life and move on. It was time for a fresh start.

Chatham slowly picked herself off the floor and walked to her bed to retrieve the picture of Peter that she kept on her nightstand. It was so worn around the silver frame from so much handling. Chatham kissed it one more time and put it in the same shoebox with the secret letter and closed the closet door.

Peter would always hold a precious place in her heart, but her heart was thawing now from a multi-year freeze. This crazy weekend, if nothing else, had shown Chatham that she was ready to love again.

She smiled faintly. How did he know that she was ready to move on, yet she just needed the permission? Chatham lifted her teary eyes just in time to see a bright orange monarch butterfly break free from its chrysalis and land on a small branch near the window pane.

"To live my life," she said to herself. "A new life."

"Hello? Is anyone home?" Henrietta burst into the bedroom. "Are you ready or are you day dreaming again?"

"No, I'm fine. I'm ready, let's go." Chatham closed

the door behind her with a new sense of hope.

≈

The two friends made their way down the hall, across the kitchen, and were about to exit into the garage when the phone rang.

"Let it go," Henrietta insisted, "or we'll never get there for god's sake."

As Chatham shut the door she heard what sounded like Trip's voice.

"Look Chat. I don't know if you're there, but hey, if you are and you're not picking up…Look, I don't want this to get in the way of us . . ."

Chatham and Henrietta stopped short in their tracks.

"Yeah, so, I think we need to talk. I'm coming over after work, like usual, for Sunday dinner…OK? I'll bring KFC. OK then. See you at five."

The call ended and the red message light blinked silently. Chatham looked at Henrietta with wide blue eyes.

"I don't want to hear it," Henrietta cut her off before she could speak. "Pour moi, remember?"

Chatham was about to climb into her Sequoia, an auto pilot routine, when Henrietta grabbed her hand.

"Today, we're taking a walk on the wild side," Hen said with a slight raise of her eyebrows as she guided her to the two-seated black jaguar parked in front of Chatham's house; an exact reflection of Henrietta's personality.

Chatham acquiesced, actually happy to have someone else take the lead for once. She realized that she was just plain tired of having to be everything to all people. Mother *and* father, successful businesswoman, perfect private school patron. When did she have time for *moi*?

"What time do frick and frack and the kids get home?" Henrietta asked as they settled in to their respective places in the luxury mobile.

"Six, I think."

"That leaves you a full hour with the Tripster." Henrietta looked at her steering wheel. "Start," she said with deep authority. The car's engine purred into active mode. "Cool, huh?"

"It's voice activated?"

"Only to mine. Listen to this." Henrietta assumed a more sultry position, gently tilting her right shoulder. "Fuck me."

"You bet, baby," the sexy male voice responded.

Chatham's seat began to warm.

"Feel that?" Henrietta winked.

"Yeah, but how did you get that voice?"

"Aw, they give you a bunch of choices depending on your mood. I usually default to *Mr. Sex* as I call him. Makes me feel good, if you know what I mean."

Henrietta pulled away from the curb and headed toward the swankiest salon in Marin County.

"You are too much, Hen," Chatham laughed. The laugh felt good.

CHAPTER XLV – *EXPOSED*

≈

Gino and Maria kept at a safe three-car distance. They wanted to make sure that the olive ice queen left the United States once and for all. The limo's blinker signaled right at 59th and Park and swung in front of The Plaza. Gino swerved to the right and created his own lane in order to grab the only yellow curb spot across the street.

"You are so perceptive," Maria complimented, for she had eyed the spot just a split second before. And in New York, finding a parking spot was basically impossible.

"Yeah, I know this city alright. And I'm looking forward to getting to know it even betta." He leaned over to plant a big wet kiss on his new love who gladly reciprocated. When the two finally unlocked lips, Maria shrieked.

"Oh my god, look!" Gino followed her terrorized gaze.

Down the steps came Georgina with none other than the bald-headed boat guy on her arm. They stepped into a very long stretch limousine, which was not in a hurry to go anywhere.

"Friggin' conniving bitch," Gino said without thinking.

"Exactly what I was thinking," Maria said, binoculars in hand. "She's got a ten carat Harry Winston on her finger for sure."

Gino grabbed the binoculars. "Lemme see. Oh yeah. At least ten," he said as he watched Georgina lean into her escort.

"That's the guy I saw at the docks," Maria added.

"Yeah, that's when I saw you," Gino added. Maria blushed.

They faced each other at the same instant. "And the little boat show," They said in unison.

"Something's not right," Gino said. "What's this chick up to anyway? Come to papa baby and tell me a story."

"She gets too close to you, and she'll be yesterday's news if I've got anything to do with it," Maria blurted without thinking.

Gino laughed. "You think I waited this long to dump you for some freeze-dried number? I've only been waiting for you my entire life."

Maria and Gino gazed into each other's eyes. Love could be so grand.

"But something's not right, like I said."

"Well, if in doubt, open ears wide," Maria smiled as she placed her ultra-powered listening device on the dashboard and aimed the satellite dish toward the stretch limo.

"You are somethin', you know that?"

"A girl does what she can," Maria replied coyly. "Now, wasn't it a story you wanted?"

You could hear dust drop inside Gino's car as Maria turned the signal knob until it tracked the conversation.

"That wasn't our agreement," the female voice said with ice cold clarity.

"It is now," the burly voice retorted.

"Listen, you fat fuck. You're working for me now. I am marrying Palio and that means, I own it all. If you want the little boat company to traffic your fucking coke, then you go through me and me alone, got it?"

Maria and Gino could practically see steam rising out of the limo.

"Get out," the man replied with force.

"I will not. We had a deal."

"Let's just say, I found other sources."

Gino and Maria watched as the back door opened and Georgina came tumbling out, landing in a puddle that lined the side of the drive. The limo peeled away without so much as a brake light. They watched as the Italian ball buster stood up, dusted herself off, and stared after the limo; a vengeance in her eyes that could kill the toughest criminal.

"Now what?" Maria asked.

"I don't know."

Georgina reached into her purse and retrieved her cell phone. She punched in the numbers with pointed force, her entire body getting into the act. It was obvious that she was more than put out.

Maria and Gino leaned forward so as not to miss a word.

"Hi," Georgina said, her body language softening instantly with the delivery. She'd clearly played this game before.

"Georgina?" came the surprised voice at the other end.

"I'm so sorry to call. I know what you must think, but I just can't stop thinking about you." She fiddled with the heel of her stiletto, which had lost the rubber base during her fall. "Fuck."

"What? Are you OK?"

"Oh, sorry. Listen, I want to talk. Can you come pick me up and maybe we can go somewhere quiet and cozy and maybe talk?"

"She looks bored," Maria blurted as she watched Georgina stick out her hip, cross her arms and look up to the sky.

"There's nothing to talk about, Georgina," the voice replied.

"Palio," Maria said, recognizing his voice.

Gino nodded.

"What do you mean? I thought we had something – something special," Georgina said, practically whining.

""If he buys that shit, I swear I claim the right to shoot him," Maria said.

Gino laughed at his hot-blooded girlfriend. One of the many qualities he found irresistible.

"Georgina, I can't pick you up even if I wanted to, which I don't."

"You can't? You don't?" She looked slightly dejected. "You mean you won't."

"That too. Look, I'm not even in New York. I'm back in San Francisco."

"Where that pretty housewife lives?" Georgina looked annoyed.

"Where my club is, remember?"

"Oh, that. Well, how about if I get on the next flight and come out to see you? Maybe we can seal our deal in proper fashion?"

"Look, Georgina, I just don't know."

"But I thought we had something. Something

special. You gave me this ring."

Maria could tell Georgina was putting on her best sexy voice.

"It was for the painting, Georgina. Remember? For my father?"

"I think… I think I love you," she quickly whispered.

"This girl has issues," Gino said bluntly. He leaned over to Maria and kissed her cheek.

"Surely you didn't think that was a proposal?" Palio continued. "Look, Georgina. I need to call you back."

"Fine," she snapped and hung up.

Maria and Gino watched Georgina sulk over to a nearby coffee shop, her broken stiletto in hand.

"Looks like Palio has some sense after all," Gino said.

Maria grinned. "Thank god."

≈

Palio hung up with Georgina. Whoa, she could turn the faucet on and off in an instant. She was clearly delusional.

"Sir?" a voice asked from his office door.

"Hi, Lizard. What is it?" Palio wasn't in the mood for company. He had to figure this whole thing out.

"I'm really sorry, Palio. I screwed everything up," Lizard confessed.

Palio had no idea what he was talking about. "Screwed up what?"

"The whole health club expansion thing. It was me who slid the fake research report into your files that made you want to expand your clubs to the crappy parts of New

York. I was sort of blackmailed to do it, if you know what I'm saying. I got so used to the strip mall and the cute little bakery, and I started getting into the whole workout thing, as you can see by my very stylish ensemble. . ."

All Palio heard was babble. "Lizard, slow down. What are you talking about? You're not making any sense at all."

Lizard put both of his scaly clad hands on Palio's desk and leaned forward. "Look, if I hadn't planted the fake report, you would never have bought the shitty club, got it?"

Palio reached into a drawer and retrieved the falsified document. "You mean this?"

The site of the report made Lizard visibly cringe. "Oh, man, I'm really sorry. I was just fucking greedy.

Things were starting to make sense.

"Who, exactly, put you up to this?" Palio asked.

"It was her and him."

"Lizard, get a hold of yourself. Who is her and who is him?"

Lizard bit his lower lip. "Georgina and Harlan. They were in it together. Well, and Bambini too, I mean for the health club part of it. And something with the olives, too."

Palio looked sternly at Lizard. "You're losing me."

"OK, it goes like this. Georgina is the daughter of some olive picker in Italy."

Palio raised his eyebrows in disbelief.

"Yeah, you heard me right," Lizard continued. "Olive picker. Dirty nails and all. And I'm not sayin' olive owner. Well, Georgina sees her dad crying one day, talking to his wife, because the family is going to be kicked off the land. He wasn't pickin' enough bushels of olives to earn his keep, if you know what I'm sayin'. So Georgina, being the oldest, and not far from marrying age, gets all pissed off and decides that she is going to represent herself in the next city, Florence, as the daughter of the owner of all the olive vineyards across Timbuktu. She says to herself, if they are gonna make my family break our back to put expensive food on their tables and fancy cars in their garage, then they can pay us for it."

Lizard had Palio's undivided attention. "So she isn't rich after all."

"Not a red cent."

"But how did she get the painting to sell to my father?"

"It was all part of the plan." Lizard made quotation marks in the air for emphasis.

"Please, go on," Palio encouraged. He wanted to hear all there was to hear.

"She convinced this guy in Florence to sell her the famous painting on an IOU, as in fuck you, because I'm not going to make good on none of it."

"The family was that well known?"

"Like the Pope."

"But why did they believe she was the daughter?"

"Remember, the family lived on the land and so she had plenty of time to listen to how they talked and see how they walked and what they ate and shit like that. She just said she was the daughter who always studied. Studied, my ass. Studied everything there was to know about the family; that's what."

"And they bought it?"

"Georgina can be pretty convincing when she wants to be."

Palio nodded, remembering how she had convinced him to buy her a five-carat diamond. "OK, so he sells her the painting. Continue, please." Palio leaned forward in his chair.

"Yeah, that's right. Well, she isn't a dumb broad as you can probably tell, she'd been *studying* for a long time. She decides to hit a triple. She researches rich Italian transplants in the United States who might be interested in art and who would have something to give her in return. What does she find?"

"What?" Palio was totally drawn in.

"Your pop."

"But how?"

"Wasn't he in the market for some holy painting for your mother or something?"

"Actually, yes, but he only told close friends in New York, I believe."

"Well, you know that commercial. You tell two friends and they tell two friends?"

"The shampoo commercial?"

"Yeah, that one. So, eventually word got to Bambini who was also in the market to bring in some good Italian products where he could take a big slice. His drug business was slumping due to transport problems. And he wasn't doing as much killing either, unless somebody crossed him, like the old mafia boss. Bambini blew him away because Frankie wanted his son to date Bambini's daughter and Bambini said no. Frankie told his son to do it anyway.

"Wow," was all Palio could manage. "I thought it always related to drugs or money laundering or something like that."

"What, are you crazy? It's love that drives all of us. Hasn't your mother taught you nuthin'?"

Palio sat back. This story was simply unreal.

"So, where was I?"

"The part about Frankie being knocked off."

"No, before that." Lizard was trying to remember.

"You said something about a shampoo commercial."

"Yeah, the tell two friends thing. OK, so word gets to Bambini that your pop wants a cool painting such as the one Miss Olive Bullshit has to offer. Bambini is still in touch with family from the old country, so word gets to him. He also hears that she's the daughter of the richest olive guy in the world, so he thinks. Hey, I can arrange a meeting between Roberto Capriatti and this olive painting heiress. I get a big fat piece of the Capriatti empire if she marries Capriatti Junior and I guarantee her 100-percent domination in the importation of olive oil and associated asundries on the Eastern seaboard of America in exchange."

Palio ran his fingers absently over the miniature carving of the horse drawn carriage that Chatham's father had made. "And?"

"And nuthin'. Works like a charm. You were the added bonus in it all. And your boat company. The exercise joint thing came later when she found out that Bambini had some shitty workout outlets in the meat-packing district. She figured that if I doctored up some fake ass document and slipped it into your files, you'd be convinced to pay top dollar for the shit, then she'd convince you that you didn't really want it anyway and you'd sell back to Bambini for a nice chunk of change. She'd make money on both sides, basically."

Palio stroked his chin, deep in thought. "And my pop's mini boat company?"

"Yeah, that one sort of came in to play, too. It was a bonus package according to Georgina."

"…A bonus."

"Yeah, I think she called you the crown jewel of it all."

Palio smirked. Well, at least her attraction may have been authentic.

"Until she said she'd get rid of you after a few roles in the hay, if you know what I'm sayin'."

Palio looked alarmed. "Thank goodness I never went there. I might find a pitch fork."

They both chuckled.

"So she sees that your Pop has this mini boat deal, and it's big, so she meets some dude through her contacts who makes really big boats; we're talking hundred footers for the whose who of fabulously wealthy. Remember, she studies a lot before she moves."

Palio couldn't believe the planning and foresight that went into this woman's determination. "OK, so she studies a lot."

"Yeah, that's the understatement of the year. You following me so far?"

"I'm tailing you."

"Yeah, good. OK. So, she has her people."

"She has people now?"

"That's sort of where I come in."

"Now we're getting to your valuable contribution."

Lizard assumed the shameful stance once again. "Like I said, I was greedy."

"How did you two meet?"

Lizard shook his head. "I kind of... worked for Bambini for a while." He threw his arms up and began to pace around the room in his green skin-tight body suit.

Palio remained calm. "I see."

"See nothing, is what I say. I used to work down at the Fulton fish market, scaling fish for five bucks an hour when Bambini comes in one day. He says, 'You, Lizard! You're pretty fast with the knife.' 'Scales 'em as I sees 'em sir,' I said."

"So that's how you got your nickname," Palio mumbled.

Lizard nodded. "Bambini said to me, 'How about you come work for me doing some scaling?' I asked how much. I had no idea who this guy was. 'Enough to make it worth your while. How does five grand a week sound?' he asked me." Lizard started pacing again. "Well, I just about peed my pants. I was in. I mean, you'd be in for that kind of money, right?"

Palio wanted to hear where this was going. "So you went to work for Bambini."

"Yeah, but I never did nothing bad. You know what my job was?"

"I can only guess."

"I was the fuckin' fish scaler. I did it every day, for ten hours a day, at whatever restaurant he ate at. I scaled the slimy bastards. Everyone called me Lizard. I got used to it."

Palio looked at his very vibrant outfit. "Looks like you've adopted it as your own."

"Well, yeah, you could say that. What the hell, if you can't beat 'em."

"So?"

"So, Bambini tells me that this Italian chick is coming to visit and I need to do what she says. I had a new job."

"And how was that for you?"

"Better than scaling fish, I can tell you. Well, at least at first. Fish don't abuse you verbally, you know what I'm sayin'?"

Palio wondered if Georgina could be extra tough when she wanted something. He knew there was something about her that leaned toward dangerous.

"So, she tells me that because she's here for the olive deal with Bambini and the painting deal with your pop, she needs to find a third party in the mix. Remember I told you about the triple?"

"Go on."

"She tells me she's looking for someone to sell your pop's very successful mini boat company and candy empire to. Well, I've spent a lot of time around the docks, you know, scaling fish and all, and I happen to see all the big, fancy yachts that pull into port day after day. On my breaks, I used to talk with all the first mates and shit. I find out that this bald-headed guy named Harlan is the richest one yet. But I find out something else, too." Lizard looked around to make sure none of the buffed-out patrons were listening at the door.

"What did you find out?" Palio wanted to shout, but restrained himself.

Lizard just smiled with a sly, slimy grin. "I find out that the Harlan dude runs coke from Panama by way of his big fat, rich guy boats. But word has it that he was getting nervous because the international water patrol cops were getting suspicious of all the vacation trips that he was going on. He was looking for a more efficient way to traffic and for a more reliable supply source because his Panama connection kept getting their labs blown up..."

Palio sits back in his chair, aghast. "A perfect match," he ponders under his breath.

"There's more. He also has a big investment in lemon drops and wants to expand. Who has the largest jellybean operation in the world?" Lizard looks over at the jellybean contest jar sitting on the E. Anytime counter.

Suddenly, it all made sense. Without thinking Palio stood up and lunged toward Lizard, holding him in a choking grip.

"You told him to make a deal with my Pop?"

Lizard shoved Palio's hands away and stood back, gasping for air. "Hell no. Remember Miss Studious? She makes sure to meet Harlan at some Italian boat show she knew he'd be at, fills him with her lies and plans and he buys it hook, line and sinker. A sexy woman can be very convincing," Lizard added with a sickly lick of his lips.

Palio was furious. How could he have been so blind? "Sorry about that, man."

Lizard put his hand on his neck. "Man, it's OK. I understand. I'd hate me, too. Yeah, so she's been working it from all sides ever since." Palio sat back in his chair, practically exhausted from the intricacies of her plan. He had learned in five short minutes that Georgina was a poor Italian girl from an olive field that wanted revenge on behalf of her family. I can't really blame her for that, he thought. She poses as the daughter of the wealthiest olive grower in Italy and starts looking for ways to carry her influence across the big blue ocean to America. Palio's pop just happened to fall for stage one of her get rich quick scheme; and he had more to offer, which caused her to develop her plans even further.

Palio sat there in silence for what seemed to be an eternity. He barely noticed Lizard, who seemed to get more nervous by the minute.

"Palio, for god's sake, will you say something? Yell at me! Tell me never to come back again. Something."

Palio was developing his own plan, and Lizard might just be able to help him out. "You say you own the strip mall with that little bakery down the street?"

"As far as I know, unless I've pissed her off so much that I don't anymore."

"And you're still under the employment of Miss Georgina and Mr. Bambini or Harlan – or both really?"

"Far as I know. What did you have in mind?"

"Well, if she has other plans that include me, let's help her fulfill her plan."

Lizard threw his hands in the air. "You crazy? You can't marry that whack job. She'll just bump you off and take everything you've got."

"Just leave it to me. I've got an idea, and I'm going to need your help."

Lizard pulled a chair up close to Palio's desk as the two huddled in hush whispers. After about twenty minutes Lizard jumped up and shook Palio's hand.

"Thank you, very much. For you to trust me like this, it means the world to me. Consider it done."

Palio returned the embrace and smiled. "OK, but you owe me coffee and donuts when this is all over from that little pastry shop of yours."

"Only the best for you my friend," Lizard agreed, and he was gone.

Palio spent the next hour on the phone putting the pieces in motion.

≈

Georgina began to panic. Her plan wasn't working. Palio had to marry her, that's all there was to it. But now he was three-thousand miles away, and she couldn't do anything about it. Georgina had to think. She turned abruptly and made her way back into The Pierre Hotel. She walked the long lush carpeted hallway to Sirio, the hotel's bar and restaurant, for a much needed cocktail. She had to calm her mind. Georgina took a seat at the bar and ordered, absently.

"Scotch on the rocks." She fiddled with the giant diamond on her wedding finger and reached into her purse for the simple gold wedding band that rested in the zipper compartment. This was her actual wedding band.

Only a few people knew this secret, including her real husband, of course. It was a stupid wedding really. Not even a real wedding. She had always secretly loved the son of the olive plantation owner, ever since she was six, and right before she put her plan into action, she told him. He told her that he had always loved her too and gave her the simple gold wedding band to wear in private. They went through a secret marriage ceremony in the olive fields before the foreman, who Georgina didn't know was also a pastor in a local community church. They even consummated their love, her first. Georgina always thought the ceremony was only symbolic because no one could know that the union existed. It was unheard of for the heir of an olive empire to marry beneath him.

Georgina reminisced painfully how she had thought that at least, in secret, they were promised to each other. One week later, she had learned that her love was engaged to the daughter of the owner of the largest candy factory in all of Italy. It was an arranged marriage by his family. Georgina was devastated, which was the impetus for her plan.

For the next hour or so, while drinking another scotch or three, Georgina ran through the plan, step by step, every detail. Where had she gone wrong? She had put every ounce of her being into this plan. She sold the painting to Mr. Capriatti, through Palio, in exchange for the diamond, which would provide enough money for her family to live on for the rest of their lives. But she wanted more. She wanted it all. She would also be the only importer of olive oil on the Eastern seaboard, thanks to her deal with Bambini. But still, it wasn't enough. The health club expansion would just be cold cash in her pocket and the miniature boat company would be sold to Harlan, after she married Palio - even though Harlan disgusted her. And the candy company? She initially planned to take that one for herself and move it to Italy so that her parents had a new place to work. She would expand the candy company to be so big that it would put her lover's wife's family out of business. He would marry beneath him after all and wish that Georgina was still his bride when all of this was said and done. It would be her revenge.

The plan to sell all of the Capriatti businesses to Bambini *and* Harlan was a last minute adjustment. She decided to forget about the candy vengeance plan and just take the money. Bambini and Harlan hated each other from the old days and, as Georgina saw it, they could figure out the double dip long after she was gone.

Georgina was determined to marry Palio, solidify all the transactions, and then return to her family and live out her life in luxury. The one glitch? She never expected to have feelings for Palio. Now her groom was on the other side of the country, and she couldn't do anything about it. Georgina wiped a tear away that had suddenly appeared at the corner of her eye. Crying for her double loss was not part of the plan.

"Hey lady," came a voice out of the dark crevices of the oak-paneled room. "Need a ride?"

Georgina turned to see the woman she despised lean her un-groomed head of curls out of the shadows.

"It's Georgina. You know that, Maria." She quickly wiped away her tears, wanting to appear strong.

"Looks like you might need a friend," Maria offered.

"No, thank you," Georgina snapped and spun around to nurse her cocktail.

"I hear there's a deal to be made," Maria offered.

Georgina's curiosity was piqued, and she looked

back over her shoulder.

"What are you talking about?" she asked in as much of an "I could care less" tone as she could muster.

"Look," Maria shot back quickly. "I know you don't like me."

"Is it that obvious?"

"You're not exactly my type either, but listen, I want to help."

"Why would you want to help me? I haven't ever done anything for you."

"Other than make my life miserable?" Maria paused for a moment. "No, seriously, I want to help. I know you're here to make a deal or two, and I think I can help. Well, we can help."

"What do you know?" Georgina asked, curious as to whether or not her plan was public knowledge.

"Let's just say, we have sources," Gino replied, suddenly approaching the two women.

"This had better be worth my time," Georgina warned.

"Well, if you could just trust someone for once in your life, maybe you'll actually get what you want," Maria reprimanded with a light smile.

Georgina couldn't believe that anyone would want to help her. She had been betrayed so many times that she had no one left to rely on but herself. Should she take a chance, just this once?"

"Well, what do you say?" Gino asked. "We don't have much time," he pressed.

"What if I trust you, and it doesn't work out?"

"Then have us whacked," Maria smiled.

"I don't associate with those kind of people," Georgina defended.

"Really? My very advanced surveillance sources would beg to differ. Especially those that troll Little Italy?"

Georgina knew they were on to her. "All right, fine. I'll go along with you. But if you fuck me…"

"Not interested," Gino quickly replied. "Come on, we gotta go."

"I didn't mean literally," Georgina snapped, grabbing her purse and sliding off her leather stool. "You are paying, aren't you?" she said to Gino, batting her eyes at him mockingly. Stay sharp, Georgina told herself as she strained to focus. The three scotches had taken effect.

"Now I know you aren't moving in on my territory, are you darlin'?" Maria said, mocking Georgina's accent.

"Please," Georgina replied curtly. "I'm a princess, remember?" If they knew everything, then they might as well call her by her proper title.

"Your majesty," Gino offered, bowing as he opened the hotel door to the darkened town car awaiting them.

CHAPTER XLVI – *RESOLUTION*

≈

Palio was exhausted. He was glad that Lizard had confessed and that the plan had been put in motion. But something was nagging at him. Palio simply couldn't accept the realization that Chatham was spoken for. It was more than his heart could handle. Trip had won, and Palio had lost her. Maybe that was how life was supposed to turn out. Guy next door gets girl. What right did he have to think that he, some Italian loser transplant who spent the majority of his time on the other side of the country, would ever be chosen over a husband's perfect replacement? What was he thinking?

He placed the delicate carving on the desk, pulled out his wallet, and withdrew a worn, lavender colored piece of paper with a handwritten note on it. The stationary had a picture of a blue jellybean at the top; his mother's stationary.

Dear Palio,

I am so sorry that I have to leave you. I know I don't have much time. You must marry and have a family. It may not be the same family as your Papa and me; it might be a more modern family. But you are made to share your love with another who is your match. You will know it when you meet her. Trust your heart, it will never deceive you.

I love you, my Palio.
-Mama

He replaced the note and slid the wallet into his back pocket. Just then Palio looked up as the gym door opened, and Trip walked in.

≈

Chatham couldn't believe how nervous she was. It was 4:45 p.m. Fifteen minutes until Trip would show. What would he say? What would she say? It was all so confusing. Was their relationship about to change forever? Did she want this? Trip was family, yet, so much more. But how much more? Wasn't that the question?

A glimpse of herself as she passed by the mirror hanging in the hallway made Chatham stop in her tracks. Wow, she really had transformed. Her mousy blond locks were cut in a tapered, Jennifer Aniston style with gentle highlights throughout. Shadowed tones of brown and sage made her eyes look like a lush forest with a deep blue sea in the center. Her lips were coral like a reef with the setting sun shimmering on them. The trip to the salon had done wonders. Henrietta had even convinced Chatham to wear the pair of Seven jeans she had given her and a silk black turtle neck to complete the casual, yet sophisticated look. Chatham glanced down at the strappy black shoes that peeked out from under the flared bottom of her pant legs. A new coat of nail polish, deep pink. What a difference, Chatham thought, remembering the chipped toenails and dowdy windbreaker. It seemed so long ago.

Chatham was deep in thought when the phone rang. It was only by the fourth ring that Chatham was able to make it to the receiver. Too late. Voicemail had already kicked in.

"Chatham? Yoo-hoo. I thought I'd at least catch

you home right before Sunday dinner hour. We're on our way out to La Folie in the city, so I'll make this short. Oh, it's Victoria in case you haven't guessed. So, I just wanted to remind you that you have an auction meeting tomorrow morning. If you could make sure to stop by Il Fornaio to pick up the good kind of coffee; their house blend is superb, and.."

Chatham picked up the telephone in one swift jerk.

"Vicky?"

"It's Victoria."

"Yeah, whatever. So, Vicky, I didn't volunteer to run the auction, I just agreed to come up with the theme. However, now that you've roped me into the lead role and I wouldn't want to disappoint everyone you lied to, I guess I'll take it and run with it." A surprising silence filled the air. "Now, I hope you remember how to get to Il Fornaio because I need for you to be in charge of hospitality for all the meetings. Make sure you leave plenty of time to stop by the gourmet bakery for the good croissants too, OK? And, Vicky?"

A whimper responded.

"We probably need enough for forty very hungry and thirsty women. Thank you so much for your kind and generous donation. We wouldn't want any turned in receipts now would we?"

Chatham could almost see Victoria shaking her head no. "Good. We must keep the bottom line as low as possible. After all, this is a fundraiser. Alrighty then, have a nice day and I'll see you tomorrow." She hung up the telephone and fell into a heap on a kitchen chair.

"I can't believe I did that," she said to the empty air.

"Very impressive," came a voice from inside the front door.

Chatham looked up at the man standing before her. She was at a total and complete loss for words.

"What are you doing here?" was all that she could manage to spit out.

"I heard you like Kentucky Fried Chicken. In fact, wasn't it you who came up with that slogan? Finger lickin' good?" Chatham stared and answered from somewhere deep in her brain.

"Actually, I was the Shake and Bake chicken. I lost the KFC account to some huge agency from New York."

The tall, dark, handsome man moved a few steps closer. "New York, you say? I hear it's a fantastic place to visit. Especially before Labor Day when white is in fashion."

"White, yes," Chatham answered, still in shock at what was happening.

"And isn't it New York where they have fancy hotels with names like Palace and Plaza and Pierre?" Chatham took the first breath since he had walked in.

"Yes, actually. The Pierre is very nice."

"Especially the stairwell at The Pierre, if I recall." He came closer.

Chatham's heart was in her throat. "The stairs you say? I rather enjoyed the very snug elevator experience, myself." A tingling sensation started in her toes and made its way to her heart. He was standing directly in front of her.

"How snug was that?" he asked, moving close enough to almost touch.

"A little snugger," Chatham found herself saying. It took all of her will power to not wrap her arms around him completely.

"Really?" He moved so that their toes were touching. "This snug?"

"Snugger, I think."

Palio leaned in and gently took Chatham's chin in his hand. He let his lips brush against hers with barely a whisper.

"Like this?"

Chatham couldn't stand it any longer. "Exactly." She wrapped her arms around Palio's neck and got lost in the most passionate kiss she had ever known. Their mouths yearned to explore and drink up the other's soul. Their breath became as one. The only thought that went through Chatham's mind was that she loved this man, fully and completely, and she was not going to let anyone or anything stop her from finally having what she long deserved.

The phone rang somewhere in the back of Chatham's mind, a voice that seemed to linger in a foggy dream.

"Chatham, are you back yet? You do know that you are driving carpool for me this week. After all, you owe me."

Palio reached around Chatham's waist, picked up the receiver and hung it up again. Nothing was going to interrupt the kiss that he had been dreaming of for far too long. She was his perfect match.

THE END

EPILOGUE

≈

The school gym was a flurry of activity. Decorations were being put up and volunteers were enjoying the special coffee and pastries from a certain pastry shop in the strip mall nearby. There was excitement in the air.

Since Chatham was in charge, she put Henrietta as her Co-Chair in charge of assigning the heads of the committees. Henrietta chose Tricky Vicky to head up solicitations, and made sure that she worked hard to pay back every volunteer hour that she had sucked out of Chatham and Henrietta combined.

"That's great, Vicky, but could you maybe switch it around and put the white cases of wine on top instead? People tend to prefer white with salad and red with meat. Well, of course you knew that."

Chatham's neighbor, Annette, was making sure that the Silent Auction table featuring the Tennis Round Robin, her donation, of course, was appropriately appointed with pink and grey racquets, balls and nets, to keep with the auction themes colors.

Chatham glanced at the twelve-foot movie clapboard hanging from the ceiling. There was Theo lifting Lizard onto his shoulders to write the theme words in chalk on the giant prop. She clicked a picture of the two for her scrapbook, and one of Tom below who was, as usual, telling Theo to stop flirting with every male species that came into his presence, even if it wasn't exactly human.

Maddy, PJ, and Maddy's new boyfriend, Dane,

were sucking the helium from the helium balloon tank, when they were supposed to be filling balloons to place at the gym entrance. Chatham found herself laughing as their voices squeaked away at ten octaves higher than normal, while singing a Barney the Dinosaur song that PJ launched into: "I love you, you love me, we're a happy family..."

Camp sat at a small drafting table with grandpa, chiseling a perfect replica of Fred Astaire from a photograph. Chatham had a feeling that the family tradition was being passed on right before her eyes.

Her attention was drawn to the door as Gino, and Maria entered carrying the largest display of virgin olive oil she had ever seen. Exactly at the same time, the two of them looked over at Chatham and lifted their chins in a "Hey, how you doin'?" kind of greeting. Did someone choreograph that dance?

Right behind them came Mr. Capriatti with three of the newest miniature boat models that were planned for mass release next month, minus the drugs.

Trip and Chloe were busy chasing one of Trip's bizarre bird donations around the gym.

"Don't worry, Chat," Trip yelled as he dashed by. "This one doesn't go to the bathroom, it reabsorbs." Chatham couldn't help but laugh at their playfulness. They were meant for each other.

On stage was Billy Bill, Chatham's choice for Auctioneer, busy practicing his lines.

"Heck, y'all, just like I say as the new spokesperson for The Idle Spur Restaurant, this here auction item is all beef and no bull, and worth every penny." Chatham thought he looked pretty slick in a tux, ten-gallon hat and cowboy boots.

Georgina had gone back to Italy to face charges of impersonating a prominent community figure. She was looking at ten years. But leave it to Georgina, her supposed marriage to the olive empire's eldest son, was, in fact, legitimate. In fact, he had been searching high and low for her in the hopes that she would still take him as her husband. He never did marry the arranged marriage choice. Rumor had it that all charges were being dropped and she would be left sitting right where she wanted to be all along, queen of her own empire. Funny how things work out.

Chatham's eyes filled with tears as she thought of how far she had come. Her life was filled with several interesting characters who had all become extensions of family. Her kids were happy, and she had found a new strength somewhere deep within. She knew everything was going to be just fine.

Chatham felt a strong arm sweep around her waste and pull her tight, like a caveman taking control.

"Have I ever told you how sexy it is when a girl cries?"

Chatham laughed with abandon.

"What are you a Neanderthal or something? Taking advantage of a poor girl's emotional weakness like that, and with my mascara running and everything."

Palio took her face in both his hands and kissed each black streak as it ran down her rosy cheeks.

"I'll take you any way I can get you," he said and planted the most romantic kiss on her the entire auction crew had ever seen.

ABOUT THE AUTHOR

J.B. Miller is a published author of fiction, non-fiction, award-winning poetry, music, and numerous articles and blogs. *No Time For Love* is her first novel. She resides in the San Francisco Bay Area with her husband and three children.

Praise for *No Time For Love*

"JB Miller makes the Chick Lit genre real"- TMG Books

No Time For Love speaks to the hearts of women everywhere who dream of their prince charming, yet have no time to find him. Ride along with champion Chatham Ross as she takes you on an adventure that is sure to make you cheer for love at all costs.

www.ingramcontent.com/pod-product-compliance
Lightning Source LLC
Chambersburg PA
CBHW070306040726
47501CB00018B/201